# THE ISLES

## SARA FRANCIS

## Book 1 of *The Terra Testimonies*

Third paperback edition © 2019

Cover design by Sara Francis © 2019
Cover image from Stefan Kunze - www.unsplash.com
Logo artwork © Sara Francis
Author photo © Carlise Azmitia

PUBLISHING

A special thanks to my family who supported and helped me from the start. I wouldn't have made it all the way without them.

I dedicate this book to Samantha.
Thanks to her imagination and friendship, the spark of The Isles was fanned into the roaring fire it is today.

Seek Truth!

# Is it all a lie?

# CHAPTER 1

## Alison: I

I don't think life was like this before the Accident. I remember hearing stories about the world becoming somewhat like this one, but I never thought it would really happen.

Oh, sorry; I should probably back it up a little. As of this morning, the Headmaster of the Isles has ordered all of us to keep a record log about ourselves, our pasts, how we're feeling, what we ate for breakfast, and weird things like that. So, basically, we're supposed to keep a diary; a very descriptive one. He said that these will be the only personal items we're allowed to keep other than our toothbrushes and clothing.

Huh. There's really no point to this; they'll just take my diary away too, sooner or later.

Anyways, hello: I'm Alison, from the Isle of Biomechatronics Testing, and this is my "record log." I am eighteen years old, and I was the first successful test subject of the science of biomechatronic implantation.

Eight years ago, a terrorist group we call the Invaders raided my hometown. That tragic day is forever burned into my memory. They set houses on fire, stole goods, blew up whole blocks, and murdered almost everyone they saw. I was lucky enough to survive, but not without consequences. I lost my entire family that day.

We were running for our lives down a narrow street. The buildings were ablaze, bleeding bodies lay everywhere, and the beautiful autumn sky was hidden by thick black smoke. Screams and gunshots were the only things to reach our ringing ears. My father led us through the destruction. He was as frightened as everyone else, but he kept his wits about him for our sake. He confidently gripped his pistol and fended off anyone who came near. Unfortunately, we weren't even halfway out of the city when he ran out of bullets. He resorted to his knife. When they attacked, he slashed and knocked them down. With no time to finish them off, he left them lying in the burning streets, covered in cuts and cursing him.

Following close behind, my mother carried my youngest sibling in her arms. I can't remember if it was a boy or a girl. I pulled the twins along and did my best to comfort them. Trudging through ashes, we were on our way to an old farm, a safe house, but our enemy beat us to it. Just when we thought we were in the clear, a bomb exploded in our refuge. Any object within a twenty-yard radius was scorched with fire. We were on the outskirts of the blast, but if only we had been delayed for a few more seconds…

In that moment, time seemed to slow down. I watched as my father ran towards my mother and shielded her and my siblings. Wrapping his arms around them, he prepared to take the heat of the fire.

I fell behind and desperately tried to catch up to them. My eyes met theirs for the last time. I saw the fear and desperation in their faces as they shouted at me to stay put. I ignored their pleas and kept going. Suddenly, the blast consumed my loved ones and blew me across the field. Pain like I had never felt before surged through my body, and I passed out.

When I woke up, I was covered in a teal gown, lying on a strange table. The light was dim—one lonely lamp hung above me. People in masks were leaning over me and doing something to my body. The tools they were using were not those of a doctor. Their instruments whirred and beeped as they operated. Regaining my senses a bit, I began to feel the pain. Severe agony was shooting up and down the right side of me, where I was injured the most. I glanced over and was so horrified at what I saw that I began to scream.

From my shoulder to my feet, charred skin was sloughing off my body, and blood was trickling through cracks in the black crust from my neck on down. Worst of all, my right arm and half my right leg were gone. The "doctors" immediately injected me with an anesthetic that caused me to lose feeling and consciousness in less than a second.

The second time, I woke in a comfortable bed, wearing the softest white T-shirt and bottoms I've ever felt. Looking around, however, I wondered if I were in a prison cell. Each wall was a uniform dull shade of gray, and one naked light bulb dangled from the ceiling. Across from the bed was a large metallic sliding door with not a window in sight. At the foot of the bed was a small, lonely bookshelf that longed to be filled. A room about the size of a broom closet was located next to the bookshelf. It held only a sink and toilet.

Finding strength, I sat up and began to stretch. As I moved, something felt a little different than normal. Out of the corner of my eye I saw a faint gleam; I looked down at my right side and saw metal. The arm I'd lost had been resurrected as a machine. Tossing off the covers, I took another look at myself. I lifted up my shirt and pulled down my pants to see that the entire right side of my torso and right leg had suffered in the same fate. It felt like my heart stopped. I sat there dumbfounded, not knowing whether to scream or cry.

Finally, I came to my senses and struggled out of bed. My body reacted exactly the same way it did before the Accident, as if nothing were wrong; the metal parts of me still felt like me, and they obviously had something like nerve endings, because they weren't numb or anything. I could feel the soft cloth on my mechanical parts as well as on the original me. I walked into the bathroom, looked in the mirror, and was—well, shocked isn't a strong enough word for it.

My skin was pale, and there were staples running all the way across my forehead where an incision had been closed. My hair was no longer long and chocolate-colored; it had been chopped off even with my ears and had turned as white as an old woman's. The brown eyes that matched my mother's had become a depressing shade of gray, and four thin, dark lines formed crosshairs in both my irises with my pupils at their center. Not only that, but there was a faint line that looked like a chain extending from my pupils to the right corner of each iris.

Not wanting to believe what I was seeing, I stood there staring and pondering for a good long while. I wanted to cry, but no tears would fall. What is this? I wondered, distressed. Couldn't I even cry anymore?

My thoughts were interrupted by the sound of the metal doors bursting open, revealing a man standing on the other side. He was tall and lanky with a full head of unkempt red hair. He had light skin and a crooked nose and wore a green collared shirt tucked into black dress pants. "Ah, you're awake now," he greeted, smiling. His English had an accent different than my own, but it sounded kind. Holding out his hand and looking at me with warm blue eyes, he said, "I know you're scared, but don't be afraid. Things are changing for the better."

He led me out of my room, down a corridor lined with doors exactly like mine on both sides. At the end of the hall was an elevator. The man bent and stared at the panel next to it. When it finished scanning his retinas, there was a faint ding of a bell and the elevator doors opened. Once inside, he pushed a small silver button with the letter L on it.

"What does the L stand for?" I asked him, speaking aloud for the first time. My voice sounded normal, thankfully.

Looking at me with a smile, he replied, "'Lobby'. Haven't you ever been in an elevator before?"

"I don't know," I said automatically. Then I thought about it. "Maybe, but I wasn't expecting a lobby in a building like this."

He nodded. "I can see that you're confused. Don't worry, you'll get used to things." After a moment of silence, he slapped his palm against his forehead and apologized, "Oh, where are my manners? My name is Cameron Allaway, but you must refer to me as Mr. Allaway. You see, formalities are very important here. When you meet anyone, you must refer to them as Mister or Missus unless told otherwise.

# ALISON: 1

There's more to go over, but they'll explain it to you later, Alison."

I almost started to panic. I was about to ask him how he knew my name when there was another *ding* and the doors slid open.

It didn't look like a lobby to me. The ceiling was about thirty feet high and had one enormous circular skylight in the center that displayed the starry heavens. It was clearly late at night, but the lights reflected off the snowy white walls, making it as bright as day inside. On the other side of the ginormous room there were three large sets of tinted glass doors.

Staring at the doors, I wondered, *Are they unlocked?* After considering a few pathetic escape plans, I shook off the desire to run away and went back to looking around.

To my left and right were dozens of rows of desks covered in office supplies, some with computers. Tall bookshelves served as dividers between every three rows or so. On the walls were more doors. There were doors everywhere.

*One of them has to be unlocked,* I told myself, rethinking my plans.

Unfortunately, any hopes of escaping were crushed when Mr. Allaway pushed me along to a high counter that made a complete circle in the center of the lobby. In the middle of it was a tall pole with a spinning silver sphere at its peak that had "Help Desk" printed on it. Two men were conversing behind the counter. They stopped when one of them looked up and noticed us approaching. "Ah, Mr. Allaway, welcome back. I see you have brought our guest," said the first man, a grin on his face.

His voice was also accented, but his accent was harsh, unlike Mr. Allaway's. He was a tallish fellow wearing a white collared shirt adorned with a lime-green tie and gray buttons. He had short black hair, a wide face, and a bushy moustache. His eyes were dark and seemed very intimidating, as did his strong build and the ugly stitch scars that scrawled across his neck.

Addressing me, he said, "My dear, I apologize for all the confusion. Allow me to introduce myself. My name is Nikita Patya, but you must call me Mr. Nik." Leaning over the counter, he reached for a handshake. With my normal left hand, I timidly shook his.

The man grinned and continued, "I am the Headmaster of every facility here on the Isles. You have already met our Scottish friend, Mr. Cameron Allaway. He runs this particular facility, where he works with biomechatronics. I hope he has treated you well."

Standing there terrified, I nodded automatically.

"Splendid. Now, I would like you to meet my companion, Mr. Walter Jarvis," the Headmaster said, turning to his friend. "He oversees another facility not too far from here."

Mr. Jarvis was a shorter fellow with a clean-shaven face and dark blond hair shaved in military fashion. He wore an unbuttoned leather jacket that showed a stained white T-shirt underneath that hung down to his denim pants' waistline. Looking at me with pale gray eyes through round glasses, he said, "You may call me Wally if you vish." He had an accent as well. It was harsh, like Mr. Nik's, but sometimes his W's sounded like Vs. Despite their accents, the two of them spoke English quite clearly.

After a good, long pause, I stuttered my reply: "P-p-pleased to meet you both."

"All right, now that we all know each other, let us get down to business," Mr. Nik replied, smiling. It was one of those smiles that don't reach the eyes. I never saw him smile any other way. "First off, my deepest sympathies for you, Miss Alison; I know how you must feel after the experience you have just endured. The people who took your loved ones from you are a terrorist group we call the Invaders." The mustached man took a deep breath through his nose and shook his head. "They are still out there in their destructive rave," he said solemnly. Changing his tone, he continued, "Nonetheless, here you will be safe and you will learn to protect yourself and others. We can also teach you more about your new biomechatronic implants and what advantages they give you, other than keeping you alive and mobile, of course. You should feel proud that you are the first human being to survive these upgrades."

This was all very difficult for a petrified ten-year-old girl to take in. Not knowing what else to say, I just agreed. I would do anything to keep others safe, but who would I be protecting?

"I am glad to hear it," Mr. Nik replied. "Now you must go back to your sleeping quarters and rest there for the night. It has been over a week since your surgery, and you still need time to recover. You will be moving around a little more tomorrow, and we will explain more about what goes on here."

Wally then chimed in, "Don't vorry about it. You vill love it here in no time! We vill see you tomorrow, sunshine. Sweet dreams."

After all that, I followed Mr. Allaway back to my lifeless room. Walking in, I noticed a big tray beside my bed, holding a bowl of steaming hot soup, a few slices of warm bread, and a glass of water. Not having eaten in a week, I ran to the table and began to scarf it down. "Slow down there! I don't want you to choke," Mr. Allaway warned.

Taking his advice, I plopped myself on my bed and chewed slowly.

"That's better. Oh, before I forget, here are some new clothes for you." He handed me a few pairs of baggy jeans, six gray T-shirts, and another set of fluffy pajamas.

"Thank you, sir."

"Don't mention it, lass."

There was an awkward silence between us. I stared at him in quiet as I ate my bread. He looked back with his kind eyes and seemed lost in thought. After a few moments, he shook his head and came back to his senses. "Well, I had better be going; lots of jobs to take care of," he said finally. "I bid you farewell." Finishing his goodbye, he flashed a toothy smile and exited my room, with the doors shutting automatically behind him.

When I checked, the doors were locked. That worried me, as did the fact that all my "rescuers" had odd accents. At one time, I would have been able to recognize them; but most of my memories seemed to be locked behind a veil of some kind. I had the impression, for some reason, that only Mr. Allaway had English as his mother tongue.

Once my meal was finished, I prepared for bed. I lay under the covers for a good long while, going over all that had happened that day. Finally, fatigue took over me, and I was fast asleep.

Oh my goodness, the battery on my recorder is dying! I must have "written" a lot. I'm glad the machine uses voice recognition to type what I'm saying; otherwise this would be even more tiring. It does have a "pen and paper" option, though. I guess that comes in handy when you're in places where you can't speak.

Duh, I didn't even say what we did today! That was the whole point of this. Oh well, today was boring anyway; just more training. Our annual Isles Meeting is coming up soon. It should be slightly more interesting, but that's about it.

Anyway, I will continue my tragic story tomorrow night. I thought this whole "log" thing would be pointless, but I feel better having gotten all of this off my chest. It's like my own personal psychiatrist. It's nice to feel like I have someone to talk to about personal matters like these. If I've learned anything within my eight years here, it is this: *Never trust anyone.*

# Chapter 2

## Sami: I

Okay, so let's see. Hi, my name is Sami, and I am currently a
test subject and resident of Isle VI. I am female, 5'6" tall, and fifteen
years old. My physical features are: straight jet black hair (on my body
as well as my head), green luminous eyes, pale skin, sharp nails, and
pointy teeth. Some skills I possess are: keen eyesight, the ability to
jump six times my height, excellent hearing, being fast on my feet,
and a great sense of smell. (Sometimes I wish I didn't have that last
ability.) I was thinking of recording my weaknesses, but if anyone
finds this, they might use it against me, and that would not end well.

Oh, I should probably mention that Isle VI is where they attempt
to create new species by splicing one creature's genetic makeup with
another. So, basically, they turn any living thing into a mutant monster.
I have the DNA of *Felis catus* Spliced into mine, affecting some of my
appearance and all my abilities. Believe it or not, I am very thankful to
be a mutant-cat-human-thing. I don't look *exactly* like a feline. I still
resemble a human, except for the few properties I mentioned before.
A girl I know had rhinoceros DNA Spliced into hers, which had not-
so-nice results. I feel so sorry for her, even though she is the biggest,
strongest person I know.

Anyway, so this is my record log.

I think I will begin by explaining how I came to be a Mutant. I do not remember everything, but I will do the best I can. The day I can most clearly recall is when it was my turn for experimentation. I was about ten years old, the usual age for a child to begin to fulfil their duties as a test subject. Before that day, I had to take constant tests, train for hours on end, and learn all the rules of our Isle. There are many. It was painful, but almost everyone pulls through.

I was awakened the morning of my experimentation the same as always. The man in charge of our facility gave instructions over the intercom system and explained to us where we needed to be for the day. "Good morning, everyone, this is Carl Mallory with our special morning announcements. Once you are packed and prepared for the day, proceed to the cafeteria as usual to receive your morning nutrients. Afterwards, test subjects of Ranks One and Two will head to the training grounds. Ranks Five and Six will meet in the village. Rank Four will head to the rooftops. Rank Three will get together in the Laboratory. That is all for now. *Carpe diem!*"

Once his message was finished, I got ready to "seize the day," as he had said—and always said at the end of each announcement. I put my then-toffee blonde hair up into a ponytail and dressed myself in our casual uniform: ratted jeans, a T-shirt black as coal, and muddy combat boots. I don't know who picks these things. After I was all set, I left my cell and went to the elevator.

As I waited to reach the cafeteria floor, I began to be overcome by a mixture of emotions. At first I was ecstatic. I thought that I wouldn't have to continue training after my experiment, but I was dead wrong. In fact, it became ten times more difficult. I was also nervous, but who wouldn't be? My life was about to change, and I was not sure what to expect.

My thoughts were interrupted by the elevator *ding*, and the doors opened. Entering the cafeteria, I realized I was late. Everyone else was already eating breakfast.

There were six rows of long tables for the six ranks, each rank consisting of almost one hundred members. The test subjects sat in

Rank order, starting with Rank One on the far left and going up to Six. Looking over to the counter to the left of the tables, I didn't see anyone in line. *The food might be all gone*, I thought, worried. I rushed over and was just in time to receive my breakfast.

I went over to my table, Rank Three, and was delighted to see that my two closest friends had saved a place for me. As I sat down, one asked, "What took you so long? You don't know how hard it was for us to save you this seat!"

"Sorry, Becca," I apologized. "I guess I lost track of time."

Becca gave me a look of understanding. I could tell she was nervous, too. Sweat dripped down her nut-brown face. Usually, her hair was in perfect braids; but today it was all frizzed up in a bushy ponytail. Even the way she ate her breakfast sandwich told me she was scared.

Then Lucas, my other best friend, chimed in, "Geez, Sami. We're ten years old now, practically grown-ups. You gotta take your responsibilities seriously."

*He* was one of those things no one could take seriously. His short, messy, sandy-blond hair hung over soft, sea-blue eyes. His stature was not very impressive; he seemed like a wimp to everyone. His accent, which we learned later was Australian, didn't help him sound intimidating.

Becca and Lucas had been my best friends since Rank One. The three of us were almost inseparable. "Okay, okay. I'll try harder next time," I promised.

Smiling, he replied, "Good. Oh, did you hear that Mr. Mallory is coming to escort all of Rank Three to our experiments personally? Isn't that exciting?"

"Are you serious? That's amazing!" I replied ecstatically. Honestly, it was thrilling. No one in Rank Three or lower had actually seen Mr. Mallory in person, so this was a big deal.

Becca nodded and said excitedly, "You're actually just in time. We're about to do the *thing*. After the *thing*, he's going to come out and give a speech."

The *thing* was a simple, stupid chant that everyone clapped along to. Rank Six led it every morning to get us pumped. We were never sure what they called it, so being ten-year-olds, we just called it the *thing*.

I had finished scarfing down my breakfast when Rank Six's table stood up and began the chant. It started with the countdown of each rank and then was a call and response:

*Six. Five. Four. Three. Two. One.*
*The day has now begun;*
*the day has now begun.*
*No task is big or small;*
*no task is big or small.*
*For good we do it all;*
*for good we do it all.*

We ended with a loud cheer and banged on the tables.

Once we were finished, a woman gave us instructions over the loudspeaker. "Very good, everyone! Now settle down. Our speaker will be entering any moment now. Sit up straight, make yourselves presentable, and give Mr. Carl Mallory a big hand!"

Everyone applauded when Mr. Mallory entered. He made his way to the tall podium on the farthest side of the room, closest to Rank Six's table. Our table was right in the center. Thankfully, I was seated at the left side, so I didn't have to turn around to see him. He was directly across from me.

I was shocked at his appearance. I was expecting a strong, intimidating man, but Mr. Mallory was far from that. Standing there at the podium was a scrawny, sickly-looking guy with long, dirty-blond hair that seemed as if it hadn't been brushed that morning. He scanned the room with his mysterious green eyes. He made eye contact with me; and when he did, I felt my heart stop. *Why am I so scared?* I wondered, as I stared back at him for that split second.

Mr. Mallory smiled at me, looked away, and began his speech. "Good morning, everyone, it is a pleasure to see all your friendly faces again!"

"Good morning, Mr. Mallory," everyone replied.

Adjusting the microphone, he continued, "I would first like to say how honored I am to have such fine folk living under my care here at Isle VI. It is truly a blessing. Next, I want to personally thank each and every one of you for your contributions towards science and the common good of humankind. The world owes you a great debt."

He sounded sincere, and we all seemed to buy it.

Continuing, he said, "Today is an exciting day for us all. This is the day when our Rank Three members receive the next stripes on their brands. It is also the day when they take part in their first experiments. Stand up, Rank Three."

As soon as we stood up, the room was filled with acclaims. For once in my life, and I think I can say the same for my entire rank, we felt important, valuable, and loved. It made us excited for our experiment and especially our next stripe. Every member on all six islands had brand numbers burned and inked into the backs of their necks, but it was exclusively at Isle VI that you received another stripe each time you moved up a rank.

Unfortunately, that feeling of importance was over in an instant. Mr. Mallory motioned with his arms to quiet the crowd, and we all sat down again.

Once we were quiet, Mr. Mallory went on, this time in a sterner tone. "I know this is an exciting day for everyone, but I need to explain something. Our members of Ranks Four through Six also underwent experimentation. However, theirs was a little different. The experiments we will be performing today have been altered to make them more affective." Looking around at the crowd, he noticed that the faces of Rank Three had become worried. He did his best to reassure us; "Do not fret; it is perfectly safe. Remember, the purpose of this is to evolve ourselves into the greatest beings we can become so that we can change the world. Thank you all, and keep up the good work. *Carpe diem!*"

He exited the cafeteria to the sound of applause.

"Did you *hear* that? We'll become something greater!" one Rank Three member said.

Another agreed, "Finally, we'll be the best of the best!"

Feeling perplexed, Becca asked, "Evolving into something

greater? What does that even mean? Aren't we already at the top of the food chain? Why do they want us to go higher? It doesn't feel right."

Lucas nodded in agreement. "Yeah, this doesn't seem… natural. I don't know anything about my past or how anything originated, but one thing is for sure: humans are humans. We shouldn't tinker with that."

I had the same thoughts myself, but we may have been the only ones who did. The rest of our rank seemed completely fine with it and kept talking about the experimentation excitedly. It's not like we could have done anything. If we had tried to run away, who knows what they would have done to us?

Finally, the woman on the loudspeaker returned and told us to leave the dining area and proceed to our designated meeting places. Those of us in Rank Three headed down to the Laboratory.

Every time I went in the Laboratory, I was always amazed by its enormous size. You could fit all six ranks inside. Rows and rows of lab counters, seated for four, were located on either side of the room, with a wide aisle between. An endless supply of any science-related thing you could think of was collected in one area. Each wall had glass windows all across it, showing other experimentation rooms.

Becca, Lucas, and I went to the nearest lab table and sat down. Once everyone was seated, we waited for instructions.

After a few suspenseful moments, the announcer lady finally spoke: "Time to begin the testing. We will proceed in alphabetical order. Once you are called, go straight ahead through the closed doors that are labeled 'G-E-H-T-A'." Turned out this was short for Genetically Enhanced Human Testing Area. She continued, "Subject One: Alex. Brand number: 632652."

Alex rose and began walking towards the lab. I was in a row so far back that I could barely see him exit the room through the ceiling-high doors. Once Alex left, the room was filled with the murmurs of concerned students.

"Does anyone know what they are experimenting on us with?" I whispered to my friends. "The Isle is named after the experiments they run, but we do not even know what those are, exactly. I have always been too scared to ask the higher ranks."

"Yeah, it's kind of upsetting," Becca responded, her voice faltering. She was scared more than Lucas and me. After all, her name started with *B*.

A few other *A* names went in before it was Becca's turn. Terrified, she stood up shakily when her name and brand were finally called. I grabbed her hand and said, "Don't worry, we will see you later. I promise."

She did her best to smile through her fear and went on her way. The doors closed behind her, and Lucas and I sat in silence.

We waited for what seemed like forever before they reached the end of the *L* names. "Lucas. Brand number: 622789."

"Well. This is it; the end of my normal self," he said, standing up. Taking a deep breath, he looked at me with his pretty blue eyes, his face sad, and said, "I'll see you later, Sami." He looked like he wanted to say something else, but he stopped himself and rushed to the doors. He was the first of us to actually move faster than a turtle for their turn. Knowing him, he wanted to get it over with.

As for me, I didn't want my name to be called. I sat at the table and fiddled with some of the equipment to keep myself distracted.

Finally, I was called. "Sami. Brand number: 605287."

The sound of my own name startled me. I dreaded it, but it was finally said after hours of waiting. I tried to look confident but ended up crying as I made my way towards the doors. When I reached them, I stood there staring for a good long while. Finally, I mustered up enough courage enter.

Just being inside gave me the jitters. An operating table was in the center of the room, with masked doctors and scientists huddled around it. Glancing up, I saw Mr. Mallory and a few other men watching me intently from behind glass windows. I realized that Mr. Mallory was encouraging me over the loudspeaker. He sounded enthusiastic, which scared me. "Congratulations, Sami! You have finally won the privilege to contribute yourself entirely to science and the better of humankind!"

*Contributing myself entirely to science and humankind?* I

thought. That made me feel more discouraged than encouraged.

He went on, "Once you are seated, you will be injected with a strong anesthetic, and we will do the rest." Flipping through pages in his hand, he at last said, "You will be experimented upon with the genetics of *Felis catus*, the common housecat. There is a 51.3% chance of success, so not to worry! Just enjoy your nap."

After saying this, the doctors strapped my legs, feet, and head to the table and injected me with very strong "sleepy juice" as Lucas called it. I wondered what his "chance of success" was as the world went away.

Well, I think that is all I am going to tell you for today. Sorry to leave you hanging, little record log, but I am beat. Training was grueling today, and I need my sleep. Recently, I've been sleeping in and ending up being late to breakfast. I think they are going to hang me for it one day.

Oh, I forgot to tell you. I had cereal with meat for breakfast. It sounds gross, but it isn't. You see, cats must eat meat or they will die. The scientists call cats "obligate carnivores." I think that is something we are supposed to write in here… or was it just an example? To be honest, I don't know what the purpose of this record is. I don't mind it too much, though; it helps me clear my conscience. Anyway, I will keep going with this later.

Good night.

# CHAPTER 3

## Aaron: I

Hey-oh, the name's Aaron. I'm one of the head geeks here at Isle III, Research and Development. However, that island name is too lengthy and boring, so we usually just call it Isle III. My friends and I wish we could change the Isle's name to "the Nerve Center," but our founders took that name for their "office." It's ridiculous. Our island is the biggest, most important, and hosts the annual "Isle Meetings"—and yet it has the most boring name.

Anyway, I shouldn't complain. I'm lucky enough to have the privilege of meeting people from the different islands on a regular basis. I've also gotten to know our Isle Keepers: the guys in charge. They come to us for advice, equipment, upgrades, and a multitude of other things. It's good and bad. When you're in charge of a lot that goes on, things can get pretty complicated.

Before I continue, I'll spew out a few facts about myself. I figure one of the reasons for these record log things is just in case our minds get wiped from the "Memory Be Gone" ray we're working on. There have been some mishaps. I guess that's what happens when you put a bunch of teenagers in charge of expensive things. So, I'm going to play it safe.

# THE ISLES

Okay, so I already said my name. I'm a teenager at present; not sure how old exactly. I do know that I am way too young for the responsibilities that I have. 327983 is my brand number. I have short, naturally spiky blond hair, and I wear black-rimmed rectangular glasses. My eyes are a gorgeous shade of sapphire; well, that's what all the ladies say behind my back when they think I can't hear them. The girls talk about me all the time.

I'm kidding. No one says that.

My height is exactly 6'1.27". Tall for my age… whatever it is. I guess you could say I have a muscular build, but I'm definitely not as buff as the guys from Seers, who are our "military" you might say. One thing for sure is that they're big kids with bad attitudes. There are always a few graduated Seers members hanging around here, stopping trouble before it even happens, as if they're psychic or something.

And lastly, because our Isle's color is royal blue, we all wear collared tops in that color, along with jeans or nice black bottoms for more formal occasions. When we reach a certain Stratum, our term for level or grade, we receive a white lab coat to wear.

Next, I think it's time for a little bit of background. It would be awful to forget the little I remember of the past, especially the day I got promoted to Overlord. That's what our Isle Keeper, Mr. Brian Bamber, calls the lucky few who become his assistants. He's an older fellow, so perhaps Overlord was a thing back in his day… not totally sure. Anyways, I'm blessed to be one of them.

It all started when I was still in Apprenticeship. The name of our training program always made us feel like we would be people of greater value once we graduated, but it wasn't that simple. To be "someone" after graduation, we had to pass numerous tests and prove our potential. These tests were given once every six months. If you failed you had to review everything you had already learned and then retake the test. And by "everything," I mean *everything*. We had to know science, mechanics, engineering, and every other impossible subject. By doing this, our superiors could determine whether someone had what it took to do the impossible, and apparently, I do.

I was really nervous the morning of my first Commencement

# AARON: 1

Test. I was deadly afraid I would have an "accident" during it. Since I was still little then, it wasn't uncommon. I was always an anxious kid who could never stay dry. Mr. Bamber thought it had something to do with the trauma I suffered during the Accident, but that's all a blank to me, just like all my life before here. Thankfully, something told me to pack all the underpants I owned before I went to the cafeteria for breakfast.

Our cafeteria is different than every other Isle's, because it's more of a library lounge. Hundreds of thousands of books occupy enormous bookshelves all around the room. Computers sit on tables of all shapes and sizes, locked down so no one can take them to their rooms (it used to happen a lot). In the center of the gray tile floor is a large cobalt-colored circle with a silver "3" inside it. On the left and right are beautifully carved, rounded-off wooden stair cases leading to an open second floor. A mezzanine, I think they call it. I never was interested in architecture.

When I entered the cafeteria, I didn't make eye contact with anyone. I made a hard right and went straight to the food counter, which was just an open window in the beige wall. After getting breakfast, I walked to one of the nearest shelves, grabbed a book on mechanics, and sat down. Glancing around, I noticed that none of the other students in my Stratum seemed to be having a good morning either, which sort of made me feel better. One of my friends had tremors up and down his body as he attempted to read the twelve books that lay open in front of him. A girl I knew had the worst hair day ever and looked like she hadn't slept in years.

While I was finishing up, a short, plump, white-haired old man in a wheelchair rolled out of the elevator to the center of the room and began to speak. If he hadn't had a microphone clipped to his obnoxious yellow tie no one would have heard him. "Good morning everyone," he said in a soft, nasal voice.

"Good morning, Mr. Bamber," we replied in unison.

"It is that time of the year again—Commencement Testing," he told us with a smile. "If you pass, you will graduate from Apprenticeship, no matter your Stratum, and move up to something greater. Throughout all the years we have had these tests, only seven people have passed with a score of one hundred percent."

I almost choked on my toast. *Only seven?* I thought, trying to wrap my mind around it.

Behind me, I heard one of the girls began to cry. Embarrassed, the Keeper shook his head and begged, "Please, don't worry! If you fail, you may retake the test as many times as needed until you succeed. However, you will have to wait six months until the next is offered to try again; but the test is different each time."

The girl calmed down. *There's still hope for future us*, I thought.

With a grin on his face, he ended his speech. "So, strive to do your best, everyone! When you are all finished with your meal, head straight to your classrooms. Your professors will explain what to do next." He was about to wheel himself out of the room when he remembered something. "Oh, and best of luck to our newbies in Stratum Eight who are testing for their first time!"

That was the first time I wet my pants. I couldn't handle the pressure. While the room echoed with the clapping of unenthusiastic students, I quickly grabbed my backpack and rushed to the nearest boys' room. Once I was clean, I headed straight to my classroom.

My room was on the second floor, and all the way towards the end of the long hallway. The hall's coloring was blinding white, and it was wide enough for five people to stand shoulder to shoulder. Wanting to be early, I ran through the crowd, past the lockers, and motivational posters. Occasionally, I glanced into the glass windows next to the classroom doors to see if the teachers were there yet. Looking in, I saw no adults. It always amazed me how no two classrooms were alike. Some had desks lined up neatly, others had experimenting tables, and some were just filled with computers; each was unique.

Finally, I reached my classroom, #20. I'd always hated it. Not only was it far away and too small for my class, the huge framed portrait of Mr. Nik on the back wall was scary in a way that was hard to define. There was no motivating caption to it or anything: just his face. I heard some of the older students call it "Big Bro." At the time

I didn't understand, but finally, I was told that it was a reference from one of Mr. Bamber's favorite books. It was one of those stories that seemed to predict the future, even though it was written long ago.

I stood outside the door in front of the painting, trying to catch my breath. Rather than have to stare into Mr. Nik's terrifying eyes, I went inside.

My teacher wasn't there yet, but once again, it was a struggle to find a seat. I thought I had arrived early enough to get a spot, but I was wrong. Almost everyone else was accounted for. I went to the back and stood up against the closets. There were about thirty of us, and maybe fifteen desks. No tables, no extra chairs, just the lonely fifteen desks. They were all taken. One of the teachers believed that this was good discipline and that no extra seats should be added. Our homeroom teacher disagreed, but she couldn't do anything to fix our problem.

Trying to ignore the doorknob poking me in the back, I looked around at the stuff in our room. Ahead of me was an electronic whiteboard the size of the wall itself. In front of that was the professor's chrome desk, with a lovely, comfortable swivel chair to go with it. We were always jealous of that chair. Standing in the back for hours, trying to take notes, is torture. To my left was the glass window looking into the hallway. To the right were bookshelves recessed into the pale blue wall. Bookshelves are everywhere on Isle III.

About five minutes before the bell rang, the rest of the students piled in and lined up next to me. Finally, the irritating electronic bell went off and our teacher entered the room. "Good morning, everyone," she said. Only a few kids replied. We were all too nervous to speak.

Mrs. Yuki Pieper wasn't so bad. She was a sweet, middle-aged lady in charge of Stratum Eight. She had slick, dark hair that was pulled back into a low ponytail. She wore a white lab coat over her ankle-length black dress. Her almond eyes were dark but beautiful and soft. More than one of us guys had a crush on her. Putting her papers down, she went on. "As you know, today is the day of your first Commencement Test. Now, you know that we have done practice tests throughout the last month, but," she sighed and looked kindly at us, "I am afraid this test might be too hard for many of you."

The way she said it made me *very* uncomfortable and caused me to pee my pants… again. Sorry, I was still little, and I had a bad habit of doing that. The medics called it enuresis to be nice. My younger years were the hardest for me. I raised my hand and asked to be excused. With a look of understanding, she let me leave, but I had to come back quickly. After changing once again, I speed-walked straight back. When I returned, I was shocked to see everyone gone. I was afraid I had missed it.

Thankfully, Mrs. Pieper was still in there, grading papers at her desk. "Don't worry, Aaron, they just left," she reassured me without looking up. "I wanted to give you an explanation of the testing before you headed in. You missed that when you were in the lavatory."

I must have been blushing, because she giggled when she looked up at me. "Don't worry; you aren't the only one that happened to today."

I let out a sigh of relief, and she smiled once again. That smile faded, and she continued in a more disappointed tone. "I'm worried, Aaron. I feel like these tests are quite unfair to you children. After all my years of teaching here, I have noticed that many of you lose heart after a while. Your self-esteem is lowered in so many ways."

Concerned, I quietly asked, "What do you mean by that, Mrs. Pieper?"

"I know most of the older students, and I have watched them grow from your age on up," she began to explain. "Some have become lazy, thinking that what they're doing here is pointless. Others have grown so fervent that it has become their top priority to be the best of the best. It isn't bad to do your best, but they're always filled with anxiety and anguish. It isn't right for children to have so many worries. They forget that these tests don't mean anything about their future life here on Isle III."

I understood what she meant, even at that age. I saw it in some of the kids from the higher Strata. A few of them were still normal, but others seemed to focus totally on their education. Some just didn't care anymore. I made a vow to myself that day that, when I got older, I would make it so that other kids wouldn't have to work so hard to feel good… and that everyone got a place to sit in their classrooms.

That was a big promise, and one I intend to keep. I know it sounds ridiculous, but I'm glad I made that promise.

"Forgive me for telling you all that," she said abruptly. "Now, let me explain to you how the test works." She stood up and turned on her whiteboard. Six icons popped up, each one outlined in a different color. She tapped the one surrounded by Isle III's signature blue. "First, you are going to take a written test," she began. "On it are all the things you have learned since you arrived. Believe it or not, this is the easiest part." She pointed to a chart of subject categories on the document. "Here are some sample questions for each section. I can only ask you one of some of the categories. Otherwise you will be late getting started with your test." She tapped the first one: Astronomy.

*This is an easy subject*, I thought, as I pushed my glasses up the bridge of my nose.

She asked the first question. "'Give the name of the large, spectacular arch-like eruptions seen on the sun's limb.'"

I didn't have to think about that one. "Prominences," I replied instantly, pointing my finger into the air.

Quite surprised, Mrs. Pieper said, "That's correct." She continued to ask me about five more questions, each time seeming surprised and happy at my answers, before a timer on her watch went off. "Oh my goodness! You are going to be very late, so let's hurry to the testing area!"

I wanted to ask her about the other tests that I needed to take, but I didn't want to push it. We had to race to get to the top floor. I had never been that high up before; and, man, was it incredible. We came out of the elevator to find ourselves in a long, narrow hallway made entirely of glass. One hundred stories up, I looked out and saw the entire island… and it's a big island. To the left, the beautiful morning sun reflected off the water. To the right, you could see our enormous training fields. Beyond its electric fences were markets, storehouses, airports, shelters, and a few large mountains. Our Isle was big enough to house the occupants of any three other islands. About 26 miles, or 41.8429 kilometers away, you could sort of see Isle IV: Assets.

Assets is in charge of life's necessities; they are our farmers and merchants. Unfortunately, their crops are regulated to "protect" the island and its atmosphere, and each Isle only gets so much. That's their excuse, anyway, and, the more I have researched it, the more I think it's nonsense. Most of the food goes to the facilities to feed the children, and the villages and cities get what little is left. I always felt sorry for them.

After a few seconds of gawking at the sight, my teacher nudged me along. At the end of the hall were long glass doors, and behind them a large, cozy waiting room. It had wall-to-wall gray carpeting with hundreds of comfortable chairs. Large flat-screen televisions were installed on each of the off-white walls, except the one to the far left, which was made of glass, overlooking the water.

Wanting to gawk some more and maybe sit in one of the cozy chairs, I began to wander off, but Mrs. Pieper grabbed my backpack, which jerked me to a stop. "No time for sightseeing," she reminded. "We have to get moving." She hurried her steps, and I followed.

We went to the end of the room, which had a high, long, lonely desk with no one sitting at it. At that age, I had to stand on my tiptoes just to try and peek over it. To the left was a door that blended in with the walls. The brass doorknob was the only thing that gave away its hiding spot. Going inside was a little awkward; the door opened on an enormous, theater-like auditorium with four levels. It had wooden walls, red carpeting, bright lighting, and desks everywhere.

Almost every Stratum was there: Eight to Twenty. Each section was separated from lowest to highest, so we were down at the front row before of the platform. We were seated in alphabetical order; and since no one had last names anymore, the first empty seat was mine. Everyone was already busy writing when I came in. Due to the acoustics, the entire room was filled with the echoes of our footsteps, causing most of the students to look up from their desks to watch us.

After I sat down, the intimidating eyes left me and went back to their tests.

Before Mrs. Pieper went out, she whispered into my ear. "You'll do great—don't be afraid. Relax. Tension is the worst thing, so don't forget to breathe." Then she rubbed my spiky hair and exited the room through a door to the left of the stage stairs.

Letting out three deep breaths, I looked down at my desk and prepared for the test.

All right, I think it's time for me to hit the hay. It is one o'clock in the morning. I have a lot of Overlord business to take care of tomorrow, so I need my beauty sleep. Honestly, this is fun! I've never told anyone any of this before, even if I am just talking to myself. Maybe I'll install a vocal circuit into the dictation machine so it can talk back to me. I mean, it is an electronic device, after all. But I will continue my riveting story tomorrow night; so, in the famous words of Shakespeare, "Take pains, be perfect, *adieu*."

Man, I'm such a nerd.

# THE ISLES

# CHAPTER 4

## Alison: II

Ugh, what a long day. An alarm went off around five o'clock this morning, which caused a panic throughout the entire facility. We all went into "stealth assassin mode," as we call it, and patrolled until the evening... only to find out it was only a drill. Jerks. I absolutely *despise* surprise drills. We didn't get to eat at all until after the last part, which consists of a painful critique. They only point out our flaws and how we could correct our skills; they never tell us what we did right so we can do it again. I think that's a strategic error. *That* took until twenty minutes ago, and now, it's after ten. Thankfully, they're allowing us to eat in our rooms, so I'm eating as I'm ranting. I know you aren't supposed to talk with your mouth full, but I don't think this counts. And my recorder has no problem understanding me.

Okay: so, where did I leave off? Oh, that's right. I'd just finished telling you about my terrible first day here, or at least the first day I remember. Now, on to the second.

I was awakened the next morning by Mr. Allaway's voice coming through a speaker in the corner of my room. "Good morning, Alison. I hope you slept well, because you have a big day ahead of you. First on our day's agenda: Breakfast! Once you're ready, head to the elevator and go to the second floor. We will be waiting."

Fearing I would get in trouble for being late, I quickly got dressed in the jeans and gray T-shirt I'd been given and rushed to the elevator. That ride felt like it took hundreds of years. I wondered what was going to happen? I had so many questions, but I was afraid that they wouldn't let me speak.

Finally, the bell went off and the doors opened. The cafeteria was relatively small—compared to the Lobby, of course. There were round tables set up everywhere, with beautiful flower centerpieces on each. Buffet tables were arrayed against the back wall, displaying many types of foods and beverages. The floors were covered in red carpeting that went nicely with the gray walls and scenic paintings. The lighting gave the cafeteria a comfortable feeling.

Sitting at the largest table in the center of the room were seven men, including Mr. Allaway, Mr. Nik, and Wally. At the tables beside it, workers peacefully enjoyed their food and each other's company. Mr. Allaway called to me from his table. "Come in, Alison. You must be hungry; please, make yourself a plate."

After I got my food, Mr. Allaway motioned for me to sit next to him. Obeying, I walked over and plopped down in the seat. It was terrifying for a young girl to sit at a table with seven grown men. "Wow, she *is* a pretty one!" exclaimed an older, properly dressed fellow with crazy white hair and a soft, nasal voice. He looked at my arm, and his eyes widened in wonder. "May I see your prosthetic? I have never seen a Bionic up close before."

Nervously, I raised my right arm, which left him staring in awe.

"Incredible," he gawked. "You have perfectly fit my neuron-response technology into a human being! I'm happy it was successful, Cameron. I wouldn't want any of my work to have been in vain."

Mr. Allaway smiled and told me to put my arm down. He was afraid the old man would get too obsessed with it. "Of course it worked out, Brian. Your technology is truly breathtaking. You'd win a Know Bell for sure if the world wasn't in ruin. The equipment and parts you gave me worked like a charm. Now, let the poor girl eat."

I didn't know what a Know Bell was, but maybe I just didn't

understand what Mr. Allaway said. Sometimes his accent was kind of thick.

Brian apologized, "Ah yes, I am sure you are hungry, Miss Alison. Forgive me."

I smiled and began eating. Honestly, that was the first time I was ever grateful for being left-hand dominant. I was afraid what would happen if I got food on my new robotic prosthetic.

After the men and I finished, Mr. Nik, who was sitting straight across from me, spoke up. "Now that we are all done, I think it is time to begin the introductions. Of course, you know a few of us, but I will tell you all the names in order of seating. To your right is the keeper of Isle I, Cameron Allaway, a Scottish inventor."

Mr. Allaway gave me a comforting smile.

"Next to him is keeper of Isle II," Mr. Nik continued, "Doctor Damian Agro. Isle II, called Saviors, is where we train people in the field of medicine. It is also where we take the injured or sick who need medical attention."

Dr. Agro reached his hand out to shake mine. He was a very muscular man with smooth, black skin. He wore a doctor's coat with a blood-red button-up shirt underneath, and a stethoscope hung around his thick neck. His dark eyes stared at me with the utmost concern as we shook hands. "I hope you are feeling better," he said in a strong Nigerian accent. "Those burns of yours were very bad. I treated them as best as I could."

I didn't notice my burns until he mentioned them. "I forgot I even had them, thank you," I said.

He rubbed his bald head, grinned, and replied, "Always happy to help. It's what we Saviors do."

*Saviors? Who names themselves or an island that?* I thought after hearing it the second time. It seemed a bit self-righteous.

Mr. Nik then went on. "This older fellow to Dr. Agro's right is Mr. Brian Bamber of Isle III which is the Isle of Research and Development."

"How do you do?" said Mr. Bamber, bowing his head slightly.

Rubbing his mustache, Mr. Nik said, "Next, is me. I know

I introduced myself to you yesterday, but I will do it again for consistency. I am Mr. Nikita Patya. I am the Headmaster of all the Isles, which means I oversee everything and help whoever needs it. However, I reside at Isle III. It's nothing like my homeland, Russia, but it will do until the world is at peace again.

"To my right is Mr. Calvin Agro, younger brother to Dr. Agro. He oversees Assets: Isle IV. He overlooks farming and keeps in check all our supplies: food, clothing, toiletries, you name it, he's got it."

Mr. Agro, um, Mr. Calvin Agro, looked like his brother. However, he was shorter, rounder, and wore grass-stained overalls over his asparagus green T-shirt. He seemed jolly. Another difference was that he had dark brown hair...well, a wig.

*He's a farmer; wouldn't that just get dirty and in the way?* I thought as I peered at the uneven toupee on his head.

The Assets keeper interrupted my staring. "You may call me Mr. Calvin. It gets confusing calling us both by our surnames."

"Nah, just call him Shorty McBaldo," Wally interrupted.

Mr. Calvin's facial expression was less-than-jolly now. "Ha ha," he retorted, "as if I haven't heard *that* one before. It isn't even clever. A child could come up with a better insult than that."

Wally began biting on a plastic straw with a smug look on his face. After a moment he replied, with the straw sticking out of his mouth like a cigarette, "I do have plenty of other names, but in the company of a young lady they are not appropriate." He winked at me. "Anyhow: to move it along, you know me, but I did not give you my background. Prior to working here, I vas a general in the German military and a good friend of Nikita. He figured this place needed defenses, so I volunteered to help. I oversee Isle V, Seers, vhich is where I train young men and women in the art of combat and defense."

He didn't need to tell me he was a general. His haircut and even the shape of his face gave it away. The tiny glasses almost threw me off, though. Also, his uniform was military-styled with a camouflage pattern, but it was not the usual army green. It was navy blue.

Before Wally could say anything more, Mr. Nik finished up the introductions. "Last, but certainly not least, that gentleman to your left is Mr. Carl Mallory, head of Isle VI. He and Mr. Bamber knew each other back in America. He does research and experiments with genetics. He believes that after the fall of Adam, humans lost part of their divine nature. Because of this, he is of the opinion that by combining humans with the best qualities of animals, the creatures that never fell away from God, we can evolve into what we are actually meant to be."

*That's weird*, I thought. Trying not to dwell on it, I smiled at the scientist.

Compared to everyone else, even Mr. Bamber, Mr. Mallory was out of shape and sickly. He had long, unkempt hair that sometimes got in the way of his bright green eyes. He wore ripped jeans and a black shirt under a lab coat. Worst of all, he had an unpleasant aroma. I wished I wasn't sitting so close. "Great to meet you," he said with a grin.

Once the introductions were complete, Mr. Nik became serious. "All right, now that we are all acquainted, it is time to explain what is going on."

"Might vanna get comfortable, Sunshine," Wally warned me. "It might take a vhile."

After I shifted a little in my seat, Mr. Nik went on. "As you can tell, we are from all over the globe, which means the Invaders have spread rapidly. We have named this invasion the Accident, because most of the world kept denying what was happening. Unfortunately, it is very real and only the beginning of what is sure to come.

"About 35 years ago, the Invaders began taking over in small, visible ways. Recently, this became global. Wally has had a hunch for many years now that something like this would happen, so we reached out to others interested in helping us with our plan to stop the Invaders. When these fine gentlemen joined us, we began building these facilities in case things fell out as Wally saw it. That's one of the reasons why he named his Isle 'Seers'."

*How did he know?* I thought. I peered at the Seers Keeper, trying to figure it out.

Mr. Nik noticed my doubts and reassured me. "He recognized

the signs first and did something about it. Trust us, he is loyal, and he will do anything to stop the Invaders. The truth is, everyone knew this would happen sooner or later. After all, history repeats itself."

*Which part of history? And how did they all think the same thing?* I wondered.

"And so the Invaders bombed, destroyed, and took over most of the world," Mr. Nik continued. "They are the cruelest of villains, torturing their prisoners, abusing women and children in the most disgusting ways imaginable and—" he paused for a moment. His eyes couldn't meet mine. He took a deep breath and said, "I won't tell you anything else. There are many more horrific things, but you don't need to know about them."

Hearing all this, I took a moment to choke back tears. My family had died at their merciless hands. To think that others were suffering much worse just about broke my heart. Mr. Allaway rubbed my back, trying to console me.

"I am so sorry, my dear. We know how you feel," Mr. Bamber said comfortingly. "I watched as they beheaded my children and grandchildren, right in front of me." His eyes became watery as he spoke. "One of them was only a year old. They then left me to die." He took a shaky breath and calmed down. "Thankfully, Carl was visiting me that week. He saved my life."

"As you can see, Alison, we all know how you feel. But you have nothing to fear; you are safe here now," Mr. Nik reassured in a soft tone, "These islands are heavily guarded, using the most advanced technology we have. The Invaders have no idea we are here. As far as they know, their atomic bombs destroyed these Islands. Let us keep it that way".

I nodded and asked, "Where is everyone else? You must have saved other people besides me."

"Good question. At the moment, most of them are recovering back at Isle II," he answered. "Unfortunately, not all were as lucky as you. We tried to save some by doing the same surgery we performed on you, but you were the first to survive. Now that we know what works, we are hoping we can save more."

# ALISON: II

Standing up, Mr. Nik addressed everyone in the cafeteria. "Okay, enough talk. It is time for training to begin; everyone back to your posts."

After the workers left, Mr. Nik told me what I would be doing for the rest of the day. "Alison, Mr. Allaway is going to teach you how to use your new technology. I am hoping to meet with you all again soon."

With that, everyone cleared out. Only Mr. Allaway, a few workers, and I remained. The entire meeting took about two hours, so it was about nine in the morning when it ended. Standing up, Mr. Allaway stretched and asked, "So, are you ready to see what you can do?"

He led me outside, where I was greeted by the crisp autumn wind. The facility was dead-smack in the middle of the island. The scenic training fields were out behind it. It was bordered with high mesh fencing that went all the way to the beach at the edge of the island. The view of the water was spectacular. The sun danced on the waves as they smacked against the beach. I took a deep breath and let the ocean air fill my nostrils.

"Ah, I see you like the view," Mr. Allaway noticed. "It's grand, is it not?" Pointing at two islands in the distance, he said, "Those two Isles out there are Assets and the Genetic Testing facility." Then he stretched a bit and held his arms out. The salty wind whipped against him, blowing his untucked gray dress shirt back and forth.

I copied him and, to my surprise, I could feel the breeze through my robotic implants, as if nothing changed. "Why can I feel the wind?" I asked, amazed. "I mean through the metal."

Smiling, Mr. Allaway replied, "It responds normally, just as if it were your flesh, correct? It moves when your brain tells it to. Therefore, you can feel what it experiences. However, you won't be able to sense any discomfort; there is a feedback function preventing that. If you stub your metallic toes or hold your right arm over a fire, nothing will happen. You can feel good, but not bad."

I was ecstatic. It would be rather depressing not to be able to feel sensations such as this with your entire being. Letting out a deep breath, I asked, "Okay, so what am I supposed to do?"

Still standing with arms outstretched, the Isle Keeper replied, "First, I want you to go over to those American football sled things and push one all the way to the white line and back to me."

Out of the five sleds, I chose the one in the center. They were shaped like men and had crude faces drawn on them, like a little kid got into some markers and went crazy. I gulped when I saw that the white line was 120 yards away, the exact length of an American football field. *That explains the equipment*, I thought.

Being that I was left handed, I pressed my left shoulder up against it and tried to push. It didn't budge. I stopped when I became sore.

"Switch shoulders!" Mr. Allaway called.

I did as he said and tried again; this time with my robotic shoulder. The dummy felt weightless. It was incredible! I pushed it to the far end of the field, then turned it around and brought it back to Mr. Allaway in no time at all. Kneeling on the ground and panting, I asked, "How did I do?"

"Better than I expected for your first time!" he exclaimed, helping me up. "Now, I want to see you cut that time in half. Do it again, with your right shoulder still."

I took a deep breath and rammed into the sled like a real football player. I made it there and back in no time; pretty good for a ten-year-old. I was more confused than proud, though.

Clapping, Mr. Allaway chuckled and effused, "Amazing—it really works! You did it! Oh, this is spectacular!" He rubbed his fingers through his messy red hair and attempted to contain his excitement. "I would *love* to see you push it to the limit, but not right now. Once you get your armor, *then* we will push you more. Let's see how much you can lift."

He brought me to a stacked pyramid of six wooden barrels and explained, "I want you to push them over and then throw each one as far as you can with your right hand."

A pretty ridiculous request, but I obeyed. I knocked over the empty barrels, no problem. They had no lids, so I was able to grab the rims. Lifting the first with ease, I threw it overhand. It came crashing to the ground five feet in front of me.

"Oops… sorry," I apologized.

"No, no, don't be," he told me, "Barrels are difficult to grasp. Also, usually people cannot lift them with one hand. Try again, but this time, throw it discus style. Do you know how to do that?"

I shook my head.

"That's all right. I will show you." He went over to a bin on the sidelines and grabbed a small metal disc. "You might want to step back a bit," he warned.

He held the disc out, rapidly spun around, and threw it. It went surprisingly far. "Sort of like that, you see? Now, try again."

I picked up the second barrel and gave it another go. This time it worked; the barrel went almost as far as Mr. Allaway's disc.

"Nice! Now do it again," he instructed, "and keep doing it until you get it about five feet from the end of the first field, where you had to run to."

I had to go get all six barrels twice before I succeeded, apparently in less time than Mr. Allaway had anticipated. We continued similar training exercises like that until late in the evening, when I could barely move.

I lay in the grass looking up at the starry night sky after a long run. Mr. Allaway lay down next to me. "You did an impressive job today," he complimented, scratching the side of his crooked nose. "I hope you are getting used to it a wee bit."

"Thank you," I replied. "I kind of am, but it's tiring."

Understanding, he said, "Yes, I agree. Unfortunately, this was the easiest training you will endure. It is going to get much harder. Be prepared."

I was disappointed but didn't want to say it. I did, however, ask him a question that had been troubling me: "Will there be other kids like me?"

Mr. Allaway sat up and looked at me caringly. "Yes, my dear. Not many, but there will be more. What we did to you was not merely a science experiment." He looked at me and said seriously, "You were dying. We did it to save you and to give you a new potential. We want to do that with others." He looked out at the ocean and became lost in thought for a few moments. Finally, he said, "There is a boy, about your age, who lost both his legs to the Invaders. We rescued him from Argentina along with a few of our new staff members. My scientists are working on him as we speak; in fact, it's about time I go check up on them. You, however, have to get some rest." With that, he rose, helped me up, and led me back inside to the elevator.

Before I went up, I thanked him for everything and asked him what we would be doing tomorrow. "Hopefully, our patient will wake up and you can meet him," he told me. "If he needs more time, then you will train some more alone. Don't think about it, though; you need rest."

After he said good night, I headed up to my room.

That's it for today. I'm going to sleep now. Hopefully, we won't have any more surprise drills. If we do, I refuse to get out of bed.

# CHAPTER 5

## Sami: II

I am back! Did you miss me? Okay, so: continuing.

When I woke up after entering the lab, I felt weird and my head, hands, and feet were strapped to a table. When I tried to look around, a small electrical surge went through my body. Any sort of movement sent shocks, signals to warn me to stay still. The only thing I could see were dim lights on a metal ceiling. Thinking a little more, I realized I was back in the Laboratory.

Wanting to be set loose, I began yelling. "Hello? Anybody? Where am I?"

"Be quiet! You are disturbing the other test subjects," a man's voice said loudly from behind me.

Timidly, I begged, "Will you please let me go? Where are my friends? What happened to me? Why do I feel different?"

"Hush!" the man snapped, "You are giving me a headache." I heard his footsteps coming closer, until he was leaning right over me. It was Mr. Mallory.

"Oh, I am sorry, Mr. Mallory," I quickly apologized. "I didn't know it was you."

He showed me his crooked smile and replied softly, "It's cool.

But I would just like to say that you are as healthy as ever. You'll get used to your new genes. I personally choose genomes for each child, so I know what you can handle and what you cannot."

"Wh-what do you mean?" I asked nervously.

He glanced down at the black electronic clipboard he was holding and began to tap some numbers into it. My straps came undone, and I weakly sat up. Looking down at my hands, I began to scream. Mr. Mallory tried to shut me up, but I couldn't stop. So, he clasped his hand over my mouth and carried me out of the Laboratory. It was very unprofessional, but he had no other choice. We rushed past dozens of other tables holding my changed Rank members. The horrifying sights were too much for ten-year-old me, and I passed out in the Keeper's arms.

The second time I woke I was sitting upright, gagged, and strapped to a chair. Looking around, I felt like I was in some kind of pre-school confinement room. Simple motivational posters hung on the walls, and there were a few bookshelves filled with children's reading books. There were toys in bins up against the soft yellow walls. Right ahead of me were two wooden doors. On either side of me sat a few of my friends.

Sitting in alphabetical order, to my right was my friend Russell, whose appearance had altered dramatically. He'd grown a tail; a *tail*. A long, fluffy, red-orange striped tail hung off the back of his seat. His adorable face was covered in red fur with white around his nose, mouth, and eyes. Long claws took the place of his fingernails, and his arm fur was dark brown. His now-red hair was cut a little below his furry ears, which remained in the same place. The most disturbing difference was his eyes. They became almost all pupil; you could barely see the white. I learned later that he had been Spliced with the DNA of *Ailurus fulgens*: a Red Panda.

That's what they call it: Splicing.

When his eyes met mine, I was frozen in fear. I must have not looked any better, because he reacted the same way. We stared at each other for a few moments until we finally looked away. I turned to my left and saw another friend of mine, Shawn, a few seats down. Another cute boy had been transformed into a hideous Mutant.

For some reason, he had received the genes of *Erinaceinae*: a hedgehog. Brown and cream quills covered his back and a few shot out of his head, and he was soaked in blood because of them. His arms and face were covered in white fur. He grunted as he clenched and opened his fists, scratching himself accidentally with his claws. He kept his eyes shut tightly, but I already knew they looked like Russell's. Blood trickled down from his mouth because of fangs that had grown in. His ear-length brown hair was now sharp and caked in blood.

I was not sure he was still sane.

I couldn't see anyone else, but I could hear whimpers, grunts, cries, and peculiar animal noises. Thankfully, Russell and I seemed fairly content.

Looking down at myself, I saw that my hands and arms were covered in black fur, but not too much. Guess I was no longer a blonde. I looked like a very hairy man with long sharp nails. Because we were all wearing long hospital gowns, I could see my furry feet with their piercing claws, but that was about it. I was dreading seeing what the rest of me looked like.

Despite all that, I felt somewhat normal. One thing that was different was that I smelled a mixture of many different aromas quite clearly and could distinguish each one from the others. Also, my hearing had improved. I could hear Alex, the first of us who had gone into the GEHTA, grumbling all the way on the other side of the room. I heard him as clearly as if he were sitting next to me, shouting in my ear.

The noises that filled the room were so overwhelming, in fact, that I began to get a splitting headache. *I hope I get used to these ears*, I thought.

As time went on, technicians carried in more of my companions. I must have emptied my tear ducts eight times watching them come in. I couldn't handle how much they had changed, and the obvious pain they were going through.

Pulling it together, I tried conversing with the girl they put next to me, Santuzza, but it was hard with the gags in our mouths. Besides,

I wasn't sure what I could do. When the scientists plopped her in the chair, she began to cry. Then suddenly, her tears stopped, and she became full of rage. She began to thrash about, uttering muffled curse words in her native language. Thankfully, I didn't speak Italian.

Santuzza was the one who was Spliced with rhinoceros, like I wrote down yesterday. Her skin had changed entirely; its color turned gray and became thick. Her hands were bulkier; her fingers flat and like little hooves at the tips. Her sparse hair was gray and had a boy's cut now. Her eyes were spread out further than before and were all black. She was huge. Her poor nose had become a large horn with nostrils right underneath it. Her top jaw protruded further over her bottom one, and her lips were pointed like, well, a rhino's. The only thing that didn't change was her ear placement. That was a plus.

About two hours went by until everyone, supposedly, was inside. Finally, Mr. Mallory entered the room with a male doctor to his right and a female scientist in a lab coat to his left. "Hello, everyone," he began, "I hope you are all awake and recovered. It has been almost three weeks since we first experimented on you all."

*Three weeks?* I thought. *That's how long it took to change?*

"I have some splendid news," he continued, interrupting me. "Everyone survived!"

A dead silence fell over the room. We weren't sure whether to be happy, perplexed, or upset because some of us *could* have died.

Ignoring our stunned silence, our Keeper continued, "I know you're wondering as to why there are a few empty seats. Well, the reason is that some of your friends need special living conditions. Don't worry; they will be back soon. Now, we are going to set you free. However, you must stay put; don't try to run away."

*What are we, animals?* I thought—and then stopped myself.

The woman scientist tapped a few buttons on her clipboard and the locks opened.

Immediately, I took off the gag. While doing so, I brushed my finger up against a tooth by mistake; my tooth cut me. I felt my face and realized that two of my teeth were sharp and hanging out of my mouth even though it was closed. My cheeks had three long things sticking out on either side of my button nose. I pulled a piece of hair in front of my face; it had become the same color as my fur. I slowly stood, but something got caught on the chair.

It turned out to be my long tail. It felt so natural that I didn't notice it until then.

*I wish I had a mirror*, I thought as I turned in circles, trying to see it.

"I know you're all probably upset, but trust me," Mr. Mallory went on, "you are all still the same beautiful young ladies and handsome young gentlemen as before. You were all so cooperative; I am very impressed." He went over to one of the toy bins, picked up a ball, and tossed it to one of the girls in the front of the line, who was incessantly whining.

She grabbed it and began chewing on it.

Mr. Mallory laughed. "Right on. Your canine teeth will grow in soon, if they haven't already. Use that to soothe the pain." Turning to the rest of us, he went on, "Now, it's time for dinner. Feel free to eat as many helpings as you need. Some of your appetites have changed, so take note of that! The other Ranks have already started eating, and I explained to them that you all will come back looking different. But be prepared; they may stare."

We all lined up single file and alphabetically. The walk from the "confinement" room to the cafeteria was awkward. I kept stepping on Russell's tail, and Santuzza, behind me, was getting whacked with mine. Not to mention the dozens of faculty members staring at us as we walked past. Finally, we entered the cafeteria. As soon as Alex walked in, it fell silent, and all heads turned. The younger kids in Ranks One and Two were the most confused. Even after we all got our food and sat down, the little kids kept staring, while the older ones began whispering amongst themselves.

I sat down in my usual spot, hoping Lucas and Becca would find me. After a few minutes, Becca found me first. "Oh my goodness, Sami, there you are," she greeted. "It's so hard to tell people apart now." She looked at me for a second, smiled, and gave me a compliment. "Domestic cat looks good on you. Honestly, they chose some odd animals." Looking down at herself, she rubbed her arm fur and said, "I don't mind mine too much. We look similar, which is pretty cool. I mean, we're both cats. If you couldn't tell already, I am now Cheetah. *Acinonyx jubatus*." She struggled to pronounce the scientific name.

I looked at my reflection in my soup spoon and saw how distinct my cat features really were. My face was hairy, but pale skin showed through it. My nose was black. My eyes had definitely changed: Luminous green cat eyes had replaced my light brown human ones.

Becca was right, though. We did look almost the same, except her fur coloring was that of a cheetah, and her eyes were golden. The light fur color complimented her darker skin tone nicely, and her hair remained the same color and texture as before. Instead of a ponytail, she let it hang free over her shoulders. Her smile was just as bright as before but her teeth were sharp and deadly.

"Where is Lucas?" I asked.

With a disappointed look, she replied, "Honestly, I don't know. I hope he finds us."

Just then, a boy wearing ginormous round goggles and a long black cloak tapped Becca's shoulder. Quickly turning around, she gasped, "Lucas?"

"Yeah, it's me," he replied softly.

"Where have you been? Come and sit down," she told him, patting the seat next to her.

Lucas struggled to sit, as if he didn't want to sit on something behind him. I thought he might have had a tail too, but nothing else really looked different about him. His hair and skin color was the same. His voice hadn't changed either. The only noticeable things were the little hairs that stood up all over his arms.

"Wow, you guys look awesome," our friend complimented. "Well, you were awesome before, but being how everyone changed, I think some of the other girls are going to be jealous." He took a shaky breath. "Sorry it took me so long. I was looking around at our other Rank members. Our lives are now a lot… weirder."

Becca agreed. "Yeah. I already feel really different. Sami, can you hear things better now?"

"Yeah, it's annoying," I complained. Suddenly, I yawned and felt my eyelids get heavy. "Whoa, this is weird. Why am I tired?"

Seeing me yawn made Becca yawn. "You *are* a house cat," she said, with her hand over her mouth.

"Well, I hope I'm not this tired *all* the time." Taking a deep breath, I got a whiff of all the delicious food that was out. "I can also smell and see some things better too. How about you?"

She nodded.

"I bet I see better than both of you," Lucas murmured to himself.

"We heard that, Lucas," I taunted. "What's different with you, anyway? How come you get cool goggles and a cape?"

He became tense and grumbled, "It doesn't matter. You guys are lucky, you got the cool genes." He hung his head down and whispered, "Mine are just creepy, and I hate myself now."

That was unexpected coming from him—entirely out of character. Usually, he would say something slightly egotistical, and he would never put himself, or others, down. Thankfully, Becca did something first. She stood up, grabbed his arm, and dragged him towards the bathrooms, with me following close behind. She was strong and fast. Then again, Lucas doesn't have much meat on his bones. We went inside the larger handicapped bathroom. "All right, Lucas," she began. "What happened? I thought I would *never* hear you say you hated yourself."

Lucas paused for minute, sniffled, and then took his goggles off. Involuntarily, Becca and I backed away.

His eyes were about half the size of his head now and multicolored, with tiny circles inside—like a creepy bug's. Then, ever so slowly, he untied his cloak, and two pairs of long, transparent, membranous wings come out of hiding. Lifting his arms and shaking his hands, he said, "Ta-da! Lucas the freak is here, crossed over with *Anisoptera*. I'm part *dragonfly* now." He spit out *dragonfly* like it was a kind of curse word. He crossed his arms and complained, "Everyone else was crossed with mammals—why not me? I'm scarier than a bunyip! It ain't fair. Everyone's eyes are still somewhat normal. I have compound eyes. I see everything, and it is overwhelming. I can't stop eating, I always need to eat, constantly. I am scared, a-a-and—," he spluttered. This went on for a few minutes until finally he calmed down.

Honestly, they should have saved those kinds of experiments for the older kids. It was too much to handle at ten.

Becca put her hand on his shoulder, looked him straight into his big bug eyes, and said, "These changes are hard on everyone. But this is us now. And just remember, the normal, awesome, funny Lucas did not change. How Lucas appears on the outside is the only thing that *has* changed."

He blushed and put his goggles back on.

Hoping to encourage him, I chimed in, "Hey, you have wings. I think that's pretty cool. And don't you know dragonflies can hover like helicopters and fly upside down?"

Lucas managed a smile and flung his cloak over his wings. "Thanks, girls. I think we should head back now; I need more food."

We raced back to the cafeteria. Becca beat us by a long shot, which was a surprise. Because of her asthma, she had always been the slowest; Lucas usually was the fastest. I guess asthma didn't affect her anymore.

Lucas went straight for the food counter, while Becca and I sat back down. He returned with a tray stacked full of bread, cookies, milk cartons, and whatever else he could grab before they closed for the night. We thought he'd eaten a lot more than a normal ten-year-old boy before, but this was insane.

Finally, the woman came over the loudspeaker to give us all our night instructions. "Good evening, everyone—and welcome back, Rank Three. As we all know, next month is Rank Promotion. Everyone who has done well this year will be promoted to the next rank and select members of Rank Six will be graduating. Now, your activities: Ranks One and Two, head to the Laboratory for science class, Ranks Four, Five, and Six head to the rooftops for stealth training. Rank Three, head to your sleeping quarters. Have a good evening, everyone."

# SAMI: II

After that, we all got up and headed to our rooms. Trying to sleep was hard. I couldn't get comfortable with my tail. I had to lie on my stomach, making it hard to breathe. After the first hour of fidgeting, I gave up and fell into a deep sleep.

Speaking of sleep, I am done for now. I realized a little later that house cats usually sleep a lot. That explains why I'm tired most of the time. That is not always the best thing, especially if we are in the middle of combat practice. I am getting a grip on it, though.

# THE ISLES

# Chapter 6

## Aaron: II

Ah, finally back in my room. This is my favorite time of day. Sadly, it's over way too fast. Okay! Time to go on with my riveting tale.

I sat there staring at the electronic desk that displayed the test for a good ten minutes. A blue button that said "*Ready?*" flashed on the black screen. Taking a deep breath, I picked up the stylus attached to the side and began testing.

I had no idea what I was so worried about in the beginning. The first sections were easy, but then they became a little confusing—but only because the solutions seemed way too simple. So, I went with my gut answers. *I don't need to get every single question correct, right?* I thought to myself after answering another easy question.

A few hours later, the bell rang for the students to put down their pens and await the results. I wasn't able to answer the last five questions. My test disappeared when the clock reached zero and was immediately graded, but it didn't tell me my score.

I waited in agony for five minutes until Mr. Bamber wheeled out of the door to my left and onto the stage in front of us. His facial expression gave no clues as to what the results were like.

He read his clipboard for a few minutes before addressing us. Clearing his throat, he began, "Boys and girls, I am happy to say that this is the greatest turnout of Commencement Testing we have ever had. Almost 75 of you have passed this first part of the exams."

While whispers filled the room, I just sat there, with my heart sunken down to my shoes. *I failed*, I thought in despair. *Nice going, Aaron, on top of peeing your pants and coming in late.*

"I see that many of you are upset," he continued. "I want to remind you all that these tests are for experience. I know for a fact that not everyone will pass them. So, don't think less of yourselves because of these tests. You will still graduate at the end of it all, receive a job when you leave here, and live like any normal Isle member would. Think of these as just promotions for a select few people."

*Well then, why bother giving these tests?* I thought rudely. I saw what Mrs. Pieper was talking about. He meant well, but it wasn't working.

"Okay, now, on to the next part," he continued, tapping some things on his clipboard. "Look at your desks. They will give you your next instructions. Be sure to follow them. I will see a few of you in the next room; if I do not see you, enjoy the rest of your day." After he finished, he wheeled back out the way he came.

I stared intently at my desk. Nothing came up. Many of the students had gotten up and left already before anything happened. Finally, blue words came up on the screen: *Follow Mr. Bamber.* Confused, I grabbed my backpack, got up, and went through the door he had exited through, with about seventy others following behind.

The room was pitch black when we entered. The only things to be seen were small lights outlining a narrow path. I turned around and noticed that the door I had entered through was gone. Without hesitation, I followed the trail. I kept walking and walking, but still nothing. I heard footsteps behind me… or was it in front of me? Both? I heard the voices of other kids getting frustrated, wondering when it would end.

After going a little farther, I decided that something must be wrong. I looked around, but I could still see nothing. The only instructions were to follow Mr. Bamber. Nothing else.

*Maybe that's it*, I thought. *There are no rules*. So, I put my hands out in front of me, to act as feelers, and ventured off the lit path.

As I walked, I listened intently to try and hear the noise of a wheelchair. We went in not too long after Mr. Bamber. If it really was a long hallway, then we could probably still hear him. I was too busy thinking about what it all meant when I hit a wall. I groped along it for a bit until I realized that it wasn't flat. It was bellowed out, as if we were in a dome. *Duh*, I realized. *We're walking in circles*. Wanting to help the others out, I shouted to them. "Guys, we've been walking in circles!"

I heard some students yelling back but couldn't understand what they were saying. I continued to call for them, hoping they would follow my voice. The sound of footsteps became louder and louder, until we were all shoulder to shoulder, holding onto a railing attached to the wall. An older boy's voice behind me stated, "Good call, kiddo. I think we should follow this railing around and see if we can find an opening."

"Good idea," I replied, "But how will we know when we get back to the place we started?"

"I'll wait here," he told me. "You lead everyone around, and if you come back to me, then we have to think of something else. Shout if you find anything."

It was a good plan, so I began walking. I went about one hundred feet until I stubbed my foot on something and yelped. A girl behind me asked if I was all right. Trying to act all manly, even though it really hurt, I told her I was fine. I reached down and felt what I'd hit. It was a panel. I opened it and randomly pushed the buttons inside. A trap door opened on the floor in front of me, light flooding out, revealing a steep staircase with a door at the bottom. I yelled to the boy who had stayed put to catch up with us.

Once he caught up, we all went downstairs. Behind the door was a long, poorly-lit corridor that smelled like a horse's, uh, bodily wastes. The sound of splashing water echoed throughout. We were in a sewer.

"No wonder everyone else failed. These tests don't make any sense," a boy complained. I agreed with him. We were prepped to pass a difficult written exam, not to walk around in circles and then find ourselves underground. After a few minutes of standing there and listening to everyone complain, the boy who had stayed behind earlier stepped out and addressed everyone.

"Listen, I know this is really agitating and confusing, but we have to keep going," he said. "We'll all do it together. This should be the first time that more than one person has passed with one hundred percent. And once we've all succeeded, we can complain and say how ridiculous and stupid these tests are."

Everyone agreed and tried to stay positive, but most of them were still aggravated.

"Thank you all. Now, let's continue. Oh, I'm Mark from Stratum Fifteen, by the way." He was a pale, tall, fit fellow with bright blue eyes and full dark hair. The ladies didn't mind having him sort of lead us, and I overheard some of them start obsessing over his looks. The reason *I* didn't mind was that I admired him for bravely stepping up. No one else would have done that.

"All right, let's get down to business," Mark said, clapping his hands together and ignoring a few compliments from the girls. "I believe it's a good idea to start walking and see where this will lead us. Sound like a plan?" After the crowd agreed, he went on, "Okay, good. We have to watch our step, though, it's very slippery. Be careful of the contaminated water down here." The girls were grossed out and started complaining even more. Nonetheless, we began walking. We didn't train for missions much; we were a group of geeks who spent all our time in labs and workshops. So that was new.

After about a kilometer, we reached other pathways. People rejoiced when we hit the first fork, hoping that there would be cleaner paths on the other side. The worst part was having no place to rest without getting dirty. Just by walking, the older members' white lab coats were covered in disgusting slime. "Okay, anyone have an idea?" Mark questioned as he tried to wipe grime off his coat.

A few people suggested checking the walls for markings or

perhaps a map. Others said that the best-lit path had to be the correct way, or that we should look on the ceiling for an opening. We couldn't decide. While they were bickering over which way was the most logical and scientific, I realized something. Going over to it, I found that the darker, spookier-looking path to our right had a stench less foul than the other. The air was cleaner. I learned that trick from an old book about a wizard, a little person, and a ring. See, you *can* learn something from books!

"We should go this way, Mark!" I yelled. "The air is more tolerable."

Mark went to the tunnel and took a deep breath through his nose. "Well, what do you know? Nice job, squirt," he said, rubbing my head, accidentally making my glasses crooked.

"Thanks," I replied, fixing them. "My name is Aaron, by the way."

Smiling, he said, "Nice job, Aaron."

We walked along the nicer-smelling path for a while. There was less nasty water and other… remnants down it. That made me happy.

Finally, we reached a tall ladder leading to a circular opening at the top. Everyone raced up it, and again we were filled with disappointment. Thankfully, it smelled much better there, but it was an empty room colored pure white, with electronic pens in a metal bucket on the floor in the center. Each wall had its own question written in big red letters. The question on the front wall was, "*What is the center of gravity?*"; to our left read, "*How many seconds are in a year?*"; the right, "*How many letters are in the alphabet?*"; and behind us was, "*What is a word made up of 4 letters, yet is also made up of 3. Sometimes is written with 9 letters, and then with 4. Rarely consists of 6, and never is written with 5.*"

Now, surely the greatest student minds in all the Isles could easily pass four simple questions. Psych! Apparently not. Answers were written all over the walls in approximately twenty different colors. There were many similar answers, but there were some so different they made no sense.

Only seven passed, huh? I wondered, looking around.

Going over to the bucket, I grabbed an electronic pen. When I clicked it, it made an odd noise. On the side of it, a message popped up: "*Write down your own answers.*"

*We can't help each other?* I thought nervously.

The others must have taken it like that, because an uncomfortable silence filled the room. Even Mark was quiet and seemed to be thinking hard. He stood staring at the question on the back wall.

I started with the one in the front: "*What is the center of gravity?*" That seemed too easy. Most of the old answers on the wall were lengthy, scientific explanations, but I felt like that could not be correct. *Can a simple question be graced with a simple answer?* I thought. With nothing to lose, I went for it and wrote my solution on the wall in a new purple hue, setting the answer apart from the previous ones.

After I finished answering the last question, my pen made a noise and displayed another message: "*Hold on to me. If you have passed, I will be your ticket out.*"

I chuckled. *A pen with personality. What will they think of next?*

Looking around, I saw a few others had finished, and now stared at their pens, dumbfounded. When everyone was done, all the pens made a noise simultaneously. Suddenly, all the kids ran to the front of the room and lined up. Two doors appeared, and a small panel opened in the wall with a slot in it.

I was confused until I read the message: "*Congratulations! The tests are over. Line up single file, place your pen into the slot, and exit through the door that opens for you. Results will be posted later.*"

*That was anticlimactic*, I thought, disappointed.

I lined up second to last. Mark let everyone rush ahead of him, so he was behind me. I watched as the students ahead of me went out either through the right or the left opening in the wall. Finally, it was my turn. Shaking, I tried to put my pen in the slot. Mark put his hand on my shoulder and reassured me. Once I put it in, my pen was sucked into the wall. After a few seconds of nothing happening, it got spat back out.

My heart felt like it went to my shoes. I looked at the side of it, hoping for a message. But there was none. I began to cry… a little; just a little, but enough for Mark to pity me.

"Don't worry, I'm sure it's just broken! So many people went before us. Watch—it will do the same thing for me." He put his pen in and, believe it or not, it did the exact same thing.

"See? Told ya. Defective," he tapped it with the side of his pen. "We should probably fix that for them, don't you think?"

I wiped away my tears—there were only a few—and smiled.

Suddenly, we heard a *whoosh* behind us. We turned and found that a small door had opened to a reveal a new hallway—more like a tunnel. Our pens didn't tell us what to do, so we went in.

I didn't have to duck going through, but Mark did, which must have been uncomfortable. At least it wasn't too far of a walk, although I was sick of moving by then. I was ready to just sit down and do nothing.

Finally, we reached the end.

I was ecstatic to find chairs on the other side. I have never been so happy to see a wooden chair in my entire life. There were two of them set up in front of a mahogany desk, with a number 3 beautifully carved in the front. We were in an impressive office. Behind the desk was a large landscape painting of the seven Isle Keepers, standing in order, with the Headmaster in the center. The interior was designed exactly like the cafeteria: wooden walls lined with bookshelves and a gray tile floor.

Immediately, I went to a chair, sat down, and let out a sigh of relief. "I will never be unappreciative of chairs ever again," I confessed.

Sitting down, Mark laughed and agreed. His eyes looked up, and he did a double take. His smile faded, and he quickly stood up.

Confused, I turned around to see Mr. Bamber wheeling into the room from a door hidden inside one of the shelves—which was awesome. As soon as I saw him, I followed Mark's example. Mr. Bamber grinned and motioned us to sit. He wheeled over and stopped behind his desk. Once he was settled, he made eye contact with us both, which made me queasy. With a big smile on his face he said,

# THE ISLES

"Congratulations, you both have passed the Commencement Tests with a 100% score!"

That was the third time I peed my pants.

And I will stop there. I don't feel like talking about my embarrassing moment right now. Tomorrow I will, though—maybe. I mean, it's not like anyone is going to read this, it's just for me. I hope.

# Chapter 7

## Alison: III

Back to my flashbacks.

Mr. Allaway wasn't kidding when he said training was going to get harder. It was only the second day, and I woke to the sound of a blaring alarm at six in the morning, which was agitating. After the alarm stopped, an electronic voice told me to head down to the cafeteria ASAP. I was still exhausted from the day before. As you can see, getting up early has upset me since I was ten. I sluggishly got dressed, freshened up, and headed towards the cafeteria. I sat at the middle table again to eat, but this time only Mr. Allaway was sitting with me. The other staff members were still at their seats from yesterday, but there were fewer of them.

After a few minutes of awkward silence, Mr. Allaway casually said, "So, the boy we did surgery on survived, and he's awake and recovered now. He will be joining you today."

My jaw dropped. I couldn't believe it. A million questions swirled in my head, but I couldn't speak. My mouth hung open for so long that Mr. Allaway pushed it closed nonchalantly and continued eating his pancakes. Unsure of what to say, I just continued eating as well, but in a much better mood than when I had woken up.

# THE ISLES

Finally, Mr. Allaway smiled and gave me more information. "His name is Axel, which is an interesting name for an Argentinian. It is of German origin, I believe. I find it fascinating." He became lost in thought, again, pondering the boy's name. He shook his head after a moment and explained, "Anyway, you must help him get used to things. He is struggling to walk on his new legs."

Instantly, I replied, "I promise I will."

"Splendid," he said. Finishing up his breakfast, he pushed his sticky plate away and told me, "I will bring him to the training fields. Can you head there on your own? Or have you forgotten the way?"

Assuring him I could find it, we both got up and headed out. When I got there, I sat in the grass and stared at the scenery. I waited for what felt like forever, until I heard my name being called. Quickly, I jumped up and went to Mr. Allaway, who was helping a boy walk to the field. He had a pale skin tone, but still tanner than mine, and cuts and bruises covered his arms. The bangs of his curly white hair covered the staples that ran across his forehead. Both of his legs were robotic, and he seemed to be really struggling.

So I ran to help. Because I reached him so fast, his dark gray eyes looked at me, horrified. I apologized and offered to assist him. He slowly nodded, as if he was processing what I was saying. I put his arm around my shoulder and helped him along. At the time, I was the same height as him; but as we got older, he soon grew past me.

Once we reached the field, Mr. Allaway walked Axel through a few tests, just like what I had to do the day before. However, instead of throwing barrels, he practiced kicking them with both legs. It took him almost the whole day to get used to his prosthetics and complete the tests.

I didn't mind; I took a nice long nap.

I awoke to Axel tugging on my hair. I opened my eyes and was startled to see him staring me dead in the face. He pointed to Mr. Allaway, who was calling my name. I sat up so quickly that we bashed heads. I yelped and Axel yelled something in Spanish. *No wonder he couldn't understand me*, I assumed. "Sorry," I slowly apologized in English. I was going to attempt some Spanish, but I didn't want to make a complete fool of myself.

Surprisingly, he replied, "It's all right, it was my fault."

Puzzled, I asked, "Wait, you can understand me?"

With a funny look, he replied, "Yeah. My mother was from England, but my father was from Argentina. After they were married, she stayed in his country. I know both languages."

I was relieved I could understand him. His accent wasn't too thick; he spoke English quite clearly.

"Are you two all right?" Mr. Allaway called.

"Fine," we responded simultaneously.

"Good, now come over here," he yelled. Once we were next to him, he told us, "You're going to have a race. First one to the end of the fence and back wins."

I didn't think it was fair, since Axel had two robotic legs when I only had one. He could run freely, while I was sort of hopping along. Clearly, he beat me.

"Exactly as I predicted, which is good," Mr. Allaway concluded as he entered the data onto his clipboard. "Now, we won't have a barrel throwing contest, because obviously, Alison would win. Sorry, Axel."

He blew a raspberry at me. I shrugged.

"Which is fine," Mr. Allaway reassured. "In time, you will each be given body armor to assist your organic limbs."

Confused, Axel asked what he meant.

"It will take quite a while, so don't worry yet," Mr. Allaway explained. "To put it in simpler terms, the armor is something to help your human parts work as if they were robotic. So, Axel, you will be able to throw barrels too."

Axel gave a little cheer.

I was more skeptical than excited. *Just how are they going to do that without replacing our body parts?* It seemed impossible. And yet, seeing how they had rescued us from our deaths, I sort of trusted them.

However, my level of trust changed over time.

After a long day of training, we headed inside for dinner. Axel sat with Mr. Allaway and me at the middle table. The first thing Mr.

Allaway asked was about his name. The Keeper was obsessed with it for some reason. The boy explained that he was named Axel after his grandfather on his mother's side, who was German. He definitely had a confusing lineage.

I asked him more reasonable things, like what he remembered about life before. He said he wasn't sure, that it was all bits and pieces, but he had watched his family die as well. His parents, grandmother, and older sister were beaten to death by the Invaders. He choked back tears many times while telling his story. Unfortunately, we had a lot in common.

After his story, the three of us ate in silence for a while. Finally, Axel spoke up. "Mr. Allaway, I have a question," he said, while poking at his beans.

"Yes?" the Keeper replied, not looking up from his electronic clipboard, which he always read while eating.

"Why can't Alison and I remember anything? And why do we have these ugly staples in our foreheads?" He poked his wound and quietly yelped.

Mr. Allaway put down his clipboard. Looking at Axel caringly, he explained, "It's for the best. Here we are, starting over. We're going to fix things. Memories of the past and nostalgia are just heartbreaking. Almost everything is lost. I give you both my greatest sympathies and condolences."

Axel and I sat in silence and pondered this for the rest of the night.

In fact, I still think about it and wonder if they can be trusted when they took away who we were.

Anyway, right before curfew, Mr. Allaway brought two doctors to the cafeteria. Both were holding strange needles in their hands. He told us that we were going to get "branded." Before we could ask questions, we were strapped to chairs and given small towels to bite down on, which I took to mean it was supposed to hurt.

It did. Without warning, they began stabbing the needles into our necks. First, they burned the brands into us, then they inked over them. Thrashing and yelling made it worse, so we soon learned to sit there and take the pain. We ended up with a permanent marking which was to be sort of like our student identification. Whoever saw the markings would know who we were and which Isle we belonged to. My number is 100000, and Axel's is 100001. Once they were finished, they fastened a cold pack to each of our necks and sent us on our way.

Axel and I rode in the elevator together up to our bedroom floor. Exiting, we headed to our rooms. Mine was right up against the back wall, whereas Axel's was to the left before mine. Peeking in his room, I noticed it was no different from my own.

Axel looked around and wondered, "Maybe they will let us redecorate...?"

I shrugged. "Not so sure. They aren't very clear on what we can and can't do just yet." With that, I bid him good night.

Okay, so now I am going to skip to about two years later, when we were twelve.

We hadn't changed much. We got taller and older looking, sort of. Our hair never grew, which was disappointing. I missed my long hair. Anyway, we gained three more "Bionic Buddies" in those few years. Since Axel and I were the "veterans," we always stuck together.

We weren't allowed to see Mr. Allaway as much, since he became quite busy. Luckily, Axel and I were granted the privilege of occasionally having him as our personal coach instead of a team of men from Seers, like the others. He always was happy to see us, and treated us better than the other Bionics.

The body armor he often spoke of took longer to create than anticipated. That was actually better for Axel and me. We had time to grow in strength, speed, and other qualities. Mr. Allaway was almost convinced that we might not even need the armor. Nonetheless, we received it as planned. When it was completed, we were given our suits at the training fields. Only Axel and I received them that day, because we were the readiest. The other Bionics still had a long, hard way to go.

The armor was designed specially for each individual. Since both his legs were bionic, Axel only needed to wear metal armor for his top half. He looked like he was wearing a heavy, metallic, turtleneck long-sleeved shirt with connected gloves. When he put it on, he groaned as if it hurt. The armor shone bright blue where the metal overlapped, but that slowly faded. The one thing that remained lit was a white circle of light over his heart and a line from that circle going down his left arm and around his ring finger.

Jokingly, Axel said, "I guess I'm married to this armor now." They never explained why that was there, so we never thought much about it.

"How does it feel?" I asked.

Looking down at himself, he replied, "Tight and cold. But I definitely feel stronger." After a moment he asked, "Does this armor make me look fat?"

I punched his arm with my organic fist, which was a mistake. "That is *strong*," I muttered as I shook off the pain.

"It *is* armor," he said rotating his arms. "You think I can turn the blue lights back on?"

Before I could say anything, I was given my armor. Axel just had to put his on like a sweatshirt, but mine was much more complicated. Since half of me was already bionic, I only got half of a connected top and bottom. I stepped into it, and suddenly metal straps clasped around my torso, clamping it in place. Then, I realized why Axel had groaned: it felt like a bunch of needles were being pressed into my entire left side, especially around my heart. After the pain faded, the blue lights came on and off, and the white circle and line appeared, just like Axel's.

I began clenching and unclenching my fists, comparing the two. My left felt as strong as my right. The armor moved with me, no problem. It sort of looked funny, because we put it on over our clothes.

For future reference, the workers told Axel he only needed to wear shorts, and his armor would cover his top. I would need a black tank top and leggings; that way, it would look like I was *sort of* wearing a full suit. However, they had to be made with a special fabric, because the armor punched holes into the clothing. It would still look odd, though.

Mr. Allaway then came to the fields, saw us in our armor, and gasped. "Oh my, you two look incredible! How does it feel?"

We gave him positive feedback. He squealed with joy, then immediately explained an interesting fact about our armor. "You see how the metal overlaps? That is because not only is it made of different pieces joined together, which makes movement easier, but it can also grow with you! I know that you have a few years left to develop.... well, Alison, you may not get much taller than that."

"We'll see," I said confidently. I was a little shorter than average height at the time, and I've only grown about an inch since then. It wasn't much, but I still grew.

"All righty," Mr. Allaway continued, "Let's go for a *literal* test run, shall we? Alison, I want you to catch up to Axel, even though he will be getting a five-second head start. You shall be running around the entire island."

"The entire island?!" I asked frantically. "We've never been passed the fences! How will we know the way?"

He smiled, tapped a few things on his clipboard, and said, "Close your eyes. Both of you."

So, we did. Instead of darkness, I saw a screen. *How long have they been able to do that?* I thought, terrified.

"Open your eyes now," the Keeper instructed.

Obeying, we opened. My sight remained the same, but I saw a few words flash in the upper corners of my peripheral vision. They disappeared quickly and were replaced with the distance between Axel and me. Suddenly, a red dotted line appeared on the ground, heading toward the heart of the island. Wherever I turned my head, it always seemed to lead to the same location. If I turned around, the line made a hard right until it was out of my sight, so I had to face the correct way to see it again.

"Personal Global Positioning System, or PGPS for short," Mr. Allaway explained excitedly. "I just punch in a location that I want you to get to, and your eyes will show you where to go. That's why your eye color changed when you were operated on two years ago."

*So they replaced our eyes completely?* The thought made me shudder.

# THE ISLES

"Okay, time to race!" Mr. Allaway exclaimed. We stood behind the starting line, and Mr. Allaway yelled for my friend to go. After Axel got his five-second head start, I darted after him. I ran at a speed that was almost overwhelming for me. I felt as if I were going faster than a race car. The wind blew through my hair, and it was amazing. I soon got the hang of the speed and was enjoying it.

I followed the line down and ran straight towards the electric fence, as if Mr. Allaway wanted me to ram right into it. Words popped up in the corner and counted down to when I needed to jump. I obeyed—and leaped right over it. It was about twenty feet high! Landing with ease, I kept running.

I had never been outside the facility before. I wished I had time to sight-see. I was led through a bog, passed a small town filled with simple deserted shops, and headed right towards the mountain. Approaching it, I realized it wasn't a mountain at all. It was a volcano. I was so baffled and distracted that I almost tripped on a boulder. Then little words popped up in the corner reminding me to focus and catch Axel, so I picked up the pace.

I could see him sooner than I thought; he was about halfway up the volcano's slope. He was so used to running that he just dashed right up the side of it. I was accustomed to jumping, so I leaped up. I could go higher than before. It was tough to get used to, but I did my best. As Axel reached the top, I came within twenty feet of him.

Then, he jumped in.

Panicking, I hopped up as fast as I could. I couldn't see any lava. My PGPS instructions reminded me to follow him, so I did. I stretched out my arms and let myself fall.

I felt like I was dropping forever, until my eye instructions told me to prepare to land on my feet and then take off once I was grounded. Clenching my fists, I prepared for impact. When I hit the ground, I didn't feel any pain, but I was off balance. Collecting myself, I kept going. Inside the volcano, it was incredible yet terrifying. There were natural rocky paths with rivers of lava flowing to either side, lighting the place with an eerie red glow.

Thankfully, I was running at such incredible speeds that I didn't have time to think of the possibilities of what could happen if I was trapped inside a volcano. I twisted down some tunnels, climbed some more, slid down planes, and eventually caught up with Axel.

"Hey!" he shouted, running backwards. "Why are you so close?"

"I won't be for long!" I yelled back and dashed ahead of him. I made it out of the volcano first, but he was close behind. I had to lose him somehow. I was set on winning that race, and nothing else seemed to matter. *Wonder if there's a detour?* As soon as I thought that, I began to see a blue solid line. *Maybe a short-cut?* I left the red path and followed the blue one.

What blue *really* meant was "a million times more difficult."

It had me leap over broken-down warehouses and climb over tall, skyscraper-like ruins. I had seen them from the fields many times, but I'd hoped that there were still some people living there. There weren't. It depressed me.

*Maybe this was the first place the Invaders hit,* I thought, as I ran across a broken rooftop. *Maybe that's why everything is gone.* But that led me to wonder: how were the facilities built? As soon as I noticed that Axel had also taken the "detour" and was gaining ground, I stopped questioning and kept running.

I was almost at the end when Axel decided to put on a burst of energy and run right next to me. I did not let him pass me. I tripped him instead. Not a smart move! Tripping him tripped me. We fell so hard that we skipped across the field and left craters where we hit the ground. We came to a stop about fifty feet before the white line.

I was going to get up and make a run for it but couldn't move. Axel felt the same, and we both stayed put.

Mr. Allaway then came, leaned over us to make sure we were okay, and tapped a few buttons on his clipboard. The lines and words disappeared before my eyes. Putting the clipboard under his arm, Mr. Allaway began clapping. "I am *very* impressed. I didn't actually expect either of you to make it this far. The tech is working nicely, and you both are adapting quickly. Now, I think you two deserve the remainder of the day to rest. Let's take off your armor and get cleaned up."

Axel let out a weak *whoop* and tried to stand up. So did I, but my whole body felt like gelatin. Finally, we managed to stand upright. "Yeah, I believe you both need to rest," Mr. Allaway repeated.

After we took off our armor, we headed to the lounge room, a small library with gray carpeting, couches and a television. As soon as Axel and I sat down, we fell right asleep.

That's basically what has happened up until now. After that day, we continued to train until we got better and more comfortable with our armor. Now our training days are more intense. We have to practice using our weapon upgrades, which is interesting. We now have missiles, rocket thrusters, and other stuff.

Okay, so tomorrow is our annual Isles Meeting. We get separated into different groups and speak with members of other Isles. It's nice to see other people, but I hope I don't get into a fight like last year. That was awful.

# CHAPTER 8

## Sami: III

The day after our transformations was painful to get through, but we all managed. That morning at breakfast, which I was late for again, the kids from the other Ranks continued to stare, whisper, and laugh. It was aggravating. Ranks Four, Five, and Six should have felt our pain at least a little.

*They were experimented on too, but with what? They look completely normal,* I thought, annoyed. Becca could tell I was getting upset and did her best to calm me down, but it was no use. Lucas, on the other hand, brushed it off and continued to eat his skyscraper stack of waffles. "Eh, ignore the blokes," he said after a while, with the fork hanging out of his mouth. "Besides, you two look awesome. They're probably jealous."

Grumbling, I continued to eat my plate of sausage. I was never a huge meat person, but I had a ravenous hunger for it now. Finally, breakfast was over, and we did the *thing*. Then, the woman over the loudspeaker gave us our morning instructions. Rank Three was to head to the training grounds this time. Hoping that we would learn more about our new selves, we lined up single file, alphabetically as always, and headed out.

# THE ISLES

Our facility and training grounds are different compared to the other Isles, or so I've been told. Our main facility is large and from an aerial viewpoint, it resembles a six…or a nine, depending on the angle. Instead of using the vast fields behind the facility, our training ground is enclosed in the hole of the six. Why? I don't know. Mr. Mallory likes "safe spaces", apparently. Thankfully, there is an electric shield protecting the sides of the building; otherwise the Ranks would have broken many windows during training.

Once we were outside, we halted and awaited further instructions. Mr. Mallory then came out alone, carrying a megaphone and his clipboard. We did an about-turn to face in his direction.

"Good morning, Rank Three," he called.

"Good morning, Mr. Mallory," we replied.

Smiling, he put his megaphone and clipboard on the ground and motioned us to take a seat on the grass. Once we were settled, he straightened his lab coat and black T-shirt, stepped forward, and explained what was going to happen. "I know I have said similar things before, but I will say them again. I know it's hard, and you all are wondering, 'Why me?' But believe me, you are all the breakthrough of the millennium. This is who you are now."

At the sound of that, the crowd filled with murmurs and whispered complaints. *We didn't ask for this*, I thought. *No one wanted this.*

Ignoring the mumbling, the Keeper went on. "Okay, now, let us begin! Alex, you are up first! Come here and stand by me."

Alex slowly got up and went next to Mr. Mallory.

"How do you feel today, Alex?" the Keeper asked, as if he were a television show host.

Awkwardly, the boy replied, "Um... okay, I suppose?"

He definitely didn't look okay. He looked like someone had woken him from a nice, long nap. His eyes had become rounder and were now a disturbing bright green; his tan face was covered in soft salt-and-pepper fur. The fuzz on his arms was black, matching the color of his new tail. His teeth were small and sharp, and his ears were darker. His hands had changed almost entirely. They were more delicate, and his fingers had sharp nails that grew unnaturally long, especially his middle one.

"Do *not* stare at Alex like he is some sort of freak," Mr. Mallory scolded harshly after a few kids whispered among themselves. "He has been Spliced with the DNA of *Daubentonia madagascariensis*; the aye-aye, in common terms. It is a primate native to Madagascar." Grabbing Alex's hand, he held it up to the crowd. "You see how his middle nail is longer than the others?" A few kids giggled. Rebuking them, the Keeper said, "Don't be immature. This nail is special because it can make holes in trees like a woodpecker, helping the aye-aye get to its natural food, grubs and beetles. Isn't that incredible?"

Everyone just sort of sat there staring, without saying anything. Finally, Santuzza, my rhino friend, spoke up. "And just why is he an aye-aye? Why were we all changed? What's the point of all this?"

Sympathetically, Mr. Mallory replied, "I personally chose a creature for each of you, based on your personalities and how much you can handle, Santuzza. This is the one I chose for Alex. He will be an excellent lock picker during field work because of these nails. You, on the other hand, will be great at busting through walls or enemies in combat."

He looked around at us all. "I know you don't understand now, but you will soon enough," Mr. Mallory continued.

*Field work? Combat?* I wondered. *Did they just experiment on us to use us for fighting?*

When Santuzza relaxed a bit and backed off, Mr. Mallory went on. "All right, Alex. You are going to show everyone what you can do. I know you're tired, because you are nocturnal now; but I would like you to go over to that very tall oak tree, climb to the top, and poke your head out so we can all see. Do it as fast as you can; I will time you."

The oak tree was the pride and joy of our training grounds. It was beautiful and much taller than the average oak. The older kids liked to hide in it and claim it as their own. The Ranks were always having disputes about who "owned" the tree. Taking a deep breath, Alex went to the base of the tree. He was never good at the rope courses we trained on, and I wondered if he would be able to manage this task. What didn't help was that Ranks Five and Six were training on the rooftops nearby. A few of them had their eyes locked on my friend. After some mental preparation, he gave Mr. Mallory a thumbs-up.

"Okay!" Mr. Mallory yelled. "On your mark, get set, go!"

Alex swarmed up the tree as animal instinct took over. He moved unnaturally fast and had no problems at all. In about thirty seconds flat, we saw his head at the top of the tree, and he waved at us. Filled with bewilderment and excitement, we cheered as loud as possible.

Mr. Mallory clicked his stopwatch and wrote down the results. Picking up his megaphone, he shouted to Alex to return and sit back down in line. As Alex was walking back, we all applauded, and a few of us made odd animal noises.

Mr. Mallory continued to introduce and test everyone in some way. I won't tell you about all of them, but I *will* talk about Becca's, and especially Lucas's.

First was Becca. He called her up, told us that she had been Spliced with a cheetah, and explained her test: She was to sprint around the entire field within two minutes, which seemed impossible. It was about a mile around, and the shortest time any human had ever run it was around four minutes. Nonetheless, she confidently took up the challenge and prepared herself at the starting cones. Just before Mr. Mallory started the countdown, he said to Becca, "You might want to try running on all fours. You've noticed your arms are longer, I'm sure, and you'll find them almost as strong as your legs now."

Taking his advice, she got down and prepared. He counted down, clicked his stopwatch, and Becca darted.

We were all blown away, almost literally. As she zipped past, some of the training equipment was knocked flat by a gust of wind. Before we knew it, she was back to where she had started, and Mr. Mallory clicked the timer. "Forty-five seconds!" he shouted. "That was absolutely incredible!" He ran up to Becca, grabbed her, and swung her around in a circle. We couldn't help but laugh at this amusing sight. After that, she seemed dizzier than she'd been from running around the field. Once she collected herself, she went back and sat down.

When Lucas's turn came, he obviously did not want to get up there. Mr. Mallory had to grab his prickly arms and pull him up to the front. Once Lucas was on his feet, Mr. Mallory started his explanation. "As you may notice, you have all been Spliced with the genes of Class Mammalia only. However, two students have been chosen for Splicing with selected DNA of classes different than your own." Putting his hand on Lucas' shoulder, he complimented, "Lucas here is an incredible student, and I am personally very proud of him. He always does what is right and makes others happy. He does not realize how special he is, which is why I decided to honor him."

Some of the students began to get jealous that he and some other kid were chosen instead of them. Personally, I was kind of happy for Lucas. I always knew he was a great kid. I was glad someone else saw it too. Turning to my friend, the Keeper smiled and said, "Lucas, remove your goggles and cape please."

Hesitantly, the boy obeyed. All of Rank Three gasped when Lucas revealed his bug eyes and transparent wings.

"As you can see," Mr. Mallory went on, "Lucas has been crossed with the genus *Anisoptera* from Class Insecta. He is Dragonfly."

The kids sat and stared with their mouths open. Not knowing what else to do, Lucas uncomfortably waved at the crowd of gawking ten-year-olds.

Interrupting the awkward silence, Mr. Mallory told Lucas what he had to do: "I want you to practice flying. Dragonflies can fly forward, backward, upside-down, and more. Can you do that for me?"

"I'll try," Lucas said, standing upright. "I haven't flown yet." He stepped back a few feet and began to flutter his wings. It took him a few minutes, but he eventually got himself airborne; obviously, the Splicing had made him much lighter than before. Once he was in the air, his face lit up like the sun. He flew around us for a bit to get used to it, and it appeared to be like second nature to him. Getting cocky, Lucas decided to do some backflips.

Seeing the older Rank members on the rooftops watching the air show, Lucas went higher and higher, until he was eye-level with them.

We watched as he flew towards and around them. He scared one of them so badly that she almost fell off the roof.

After a while, Mr. Mallory called Lucas back to take his place. The boy landed dramatically and held his hands up for applause. As we clapped, he put back on his goggles, grabbed his cloak, and went back to his spot. "Not gonna put this on yet," Lucas said as he wrapped the cloak around his waist. He wanted to show off his wings some more.

Mr. Mallory continued going through the names. It took a little while, and my cat instincts decided to take over. I accidentally fell asleep. When I was called, Russell had to poke me to wake me up. Startled, I jumped to my feet and screeched. My Rank laughed; I was so embarrassed.

"Enjoy your catnap?" Mr. Mallory teased as I went over to him. I hung my head, but he brushed the hair out of my eyes and told me to chin up. Then, he explained to everyone what I was: *Felis catus*, a domestic housecat. Personally, I did not think of them as very useful creatures. I thought they just ate, pooped, and slept. I wanted to be helpful, not a nuisance.

Thankfully, the Keeper made me feel better about that. "These creatures are among my favorites. They have excellent reflexes, incredible hearing, and sensitive touch. Not only that, but a cat's brain closely resembles that of a human. Groovy, right?"

Everyone began chuckling.

*Groovy? Who says that anymore?* I wondered, looking up at him. The era he grew up in must have been a weird one. A few words like that slipped out from time to time, but usually his vocabulary was modern.

Obviously embarrassed, Mr. Mallory cleared his throat and continued, this time trying to sound more intelligent. "But that is beside the point. Her new agilities will make her a great fighter; and even better, cats are not easy to kill. I have a feeling Sami here will be going on many dangerous missions in the future."

I was afraid of that.

My test was a tricky one: I had to use my sense of hearing to dodge incoming tennis balls that were being shot at me from all directions. I was blindfolded, and everyone was to make a lot of commotion around me, attempting to throw off my senses. Mr. Mallory stood behind one of the automatic tennis ball shooters and watched me as I mercilessly got pegged.

I was about to give up hope until I heard Becca and Lucas shouting advice and words of encouragement through the noise. Becca yelled at me to calm down and focus on the task at hand. Okay, she may not have said it as intelligently as that, but that was her main point. Lucas, on the other hand, told me not to die. Becca's advice was better, so I took a deep breath and tried to listen.

The unnecessary noise faded out, and I could hear the clicks of the machines. I could connect the sounds to their devices and knew where they were coming from. After a few minutes, I got the hang of it and was able to avoid the tennis balls with ease. I even deflected a few with my hands.

Running out of ammo, the machines stopped, and Mr. Mallory removed my blindfold. I believed he was impressed. He mouthed a few more positive "hippie" phrases, as he called them, and told me to take a seat. After I went back, he continued to call up the rest of the Rank. It was interesting to see what everyone had changed into, and what they could do. From mice to lions, we had an army of ten-year-old Mutants.

Finally, we approached the end. To everyone's surprise, Xavier was the last person to be called up, and we were quite confused. The only Z kid, Zeke, wasn't there. Indistinct babbling began amongst the Rank members. Some thought he might have died or was still sick from the transformation. Others suggested that maybe he was the other "chosen" one, like Lucas.

However, everyone forgot about poor Zeke when food was mentioned. We had rarely any breaks throughout the day, so no one could think of anything else. Before Mr. Mallory dismissed us for supper, he pulled Lucas aside and quietly conversed with him. I tried not to eavesdrop, but when I heard my name, it automatically caught my attention. The only thing I could catch was Mr. Mallory saying, "Of course. Tell them over supper."

Lucas then jumped back in line, and we headed for the cafeteria.

"So, what was Mr. Mallory talking to you about, Lucas?" Becca asked after we were settled.

From behind his mountain of macaroni and cheese, Lucas explained, "Mr. Mallory wants me and Zeke, the other kid who was experimented on differently, to get 'acquainted,' as he put it. I never really knew Zeke, so I guess he wants us to become friends or something… but I was kind of nervous, so I asked if you two could tag along. He said it wasn't a problem, as long as we don't say anything to the others."

Becca said exactly what I was thinking: "Oh, okay, I thought it was something serious. When are we going to see him?"

Through a mouthful of food, he replied, "When we're done eating, but before bedtime." After a few more helpings, Lucas finally finished, and we left to go visit Zeke.

Mr. Mallory met us in the elevator. "Hello Lucas, Becca, and Sami. Ready to go visit your Rankmate?" We admitted we were, so he opened a hidden panel on the wall and scanned his thumbprint. Symbols representing a smiling face popped up above the door, and when the doors opened, we entered an elevator car.

As we descended, Lucas asked innocently, "There's a smiley-face floor?"

Before Mr. Mallory could answer, the doors opened. Exiting the elevator, we heard rock music playing over a loudspeaker. The place we found ourselves in was dark; the only light was a blue glow emanating from a large aquarium in the center of the room. As we went in further, we saw a few powered-down computers lined up against the walls.

Inside the aquarium was something quite shocking: Zeke. He was curled up in the left corner at the bottom. Moving closer, we got a better look at our sleeping friend.

He had grown a royal-blue fin on each of his calves and forearms, and two fins on his back above his rear end. He was only wearing black trunks, so we could see that his torso was covered in small scratches, and there were three larger slits on each side that fluttered open and closed: gills. His tan skin had transformed to a pale blue hue, but his hair remained a sandy blond.

Several minutes of staring passed before Mr. Mallory said, "As you can see, Lucas, you and Zeke were the only ones I believed could handle the privilege of being Spliced with different classes: for you, Class *Insecta*; and for Zeke, Class *Chondrichthyes*. Everyone else has always been tested with organisms from Class Mammalia, even before I started working here."

"Wait—if Ranks Four, Five, and Six went through this, then why do they look the same?" Lucas asked.

The man sighed. "Before I worked with Mr. Nik, I tried these experiments on my own. The first round of subjects changed as much as you have, but they had other… side effects than changes in appearance. When I got here, I started small and gave the older ranks a small dosage, slightly altering their abilities. For example, a subject who can run the hundred-yard dash in fifteen seconds was able to run it in only eleven seconds when given Cheetah DNA. Now we know what works and have built up to where we are today. We believe that crossing animals and humans can help us reach our true potential and become the best of the best."

Lucas nodded slightly and went back to watching Zeke sleep.

Out of curiosity, I was brave enough to ask Mr. Mallory a question. "Why is there weird rock music playing? And since it's so loud, how is Zeke sleeping?"

Mr. Mallory laughed and answered, "Excellent question. I was never fond of this music, since it came out later than my youth. I much prefer 60's and 70's music over 80's. But I find the origin of this band's name interesting. Apparently, it was taken from initials seen on a sewing machine." He chuckled and shook his head. "Anyway, there were multiple tests done on this species back before the Accident that proved that songs from a certain heavy metal band from Australia, where Lucas was born, seems to calm down sharks. That's why we have one of their more popular songs on loop: to help Zeke relax. He has been quite violent and restless, sadly, which has driven the other scientists crazy. Once Zeke finally fell asleep, they shut everything down, packed up, and left for the night."

So that was how we found out Lucas was Australian and learned an interesting piece of information about sharks and music. I had that song stuck in my head for days; I never knew the words, though. I only knew the title was something like *Black Win Black* or *Back on Jack*. It was very confusing.

Our conversation about Lucas's homeland and music was interrupted by a loud *BAM*! as Zeke woke up and slammed against the glass. Lucas screamed like a little girl. Once Zeke saw us, he slumped back and sat down. He seemed like he was happy to see us, because he smiled a big, sharp-toothed smile. His eyes, which were all black, danced excitedly. "Hi, Zeke, how are you?" Lucas called.

Zeke began to respond, but we couldn't hear him.

"Oh, I almost forgot!" Mr. Mallory exclaimed. "One moment." He dashed over to one of the computers, turned it on, and began pressing some buttons. "Okay, speak again, Zeke."

"Hello? Can you hear me?" Zeke asked. Thrilled, we all let him know we could, even though he sounded a little warbly. "Oh good, I'm glad you guys are here. I've been so lonely," he replied thankfully.

We sat down and conversed with him for hours. We told each other stories of our experiences with our changes, our feelings about it, and jokes, lots of jokes, and made puns... especially ocean puns. Finally, Mr. Mallory had us bid Zeke goodbye and escorted us to our rooms.

After that, we visited Zeke as many times as possible, and the four of us became close. We all grew older, stronger, and wiser... well, sort of. Zeke was eventually let off the "smiley face" floor, as we all called it. He just had to be in a mobile tank that he controlled from inside.

Mealtimes were fun, because to feed him, we would toss his food inside the tank and watch him gobble it up. A few times, the stronger Rank members got peanut butter-and-jelly sandwiches stuck to the cafeteria ceiling somehow when trying to do it. The adults never noticed until one of them fell on our lunch lady a few weeks later. Our entire Rank had to scrub every toilet in the facility as punishment. That was brutal.

It is amazing and upsetting to realize how time has flown. Those years are gone. Today we are all Rank Six, have all our stripes, and will soon graduate.

Tomorrow, we have our annual Isles Meeting, which I think is boring and fun at the same time, if that's even possible. The past couple of years we just stayed within our Ranks and did dumb demonstrations. Our Isle had some complications with another, so that's not always the best. It will be interesting this time nonetheless, because they said they will be changing it up a bit.

# THE ISLES

# CHAPTER 9

## Aaron: III

All right, time to talk about my incident of wetting my pants in front of our Isle Keeper. I am so happy I grew out of that habit.

I could hardly believe what I was hearing. *I passed with a perfect score?* It made me nervous enough to have an accident. It was so embarrassing.

Thankfully, Mr. Bamber was an understanding fellow. He just laughed and directed me to a small single bathroom located in his office. Facing the front of the desk, the bathroom was on my left, hiding behind another bookcase. To reveal the restroom door, Mr. Bamber took a book called *Toilets of the World* off a shelf.

While I was in there cleaning up, I heard Mark and Mr. Bamber discussing something outside. Quickly, I changed into my last pair of spare underpants and went back out. I sat down and apologized once again to Mr. Bamber. "Don't worry about it," he replied with a smile. "You aren't the first person that has happened to when I gave them the good news. Besides, I'm getting old; happens to me too, sometimes."

*Too much information*, I thought.

"Okay, now back to business," Mr. Bamber continued, fiddling with his ugly yellow tie. "As I was just explaining to Mark, you two seem to be the only ones intelligent enough out of this bunch to personally help me."

That was a shock. *What do we have that no one else does? I wondered.*

"Now, I know you are probably thinking I am a mean, nasty old man for 'picking favorites,' as people would say," he went on to explain, "but I need problem-solvers. Not just for algebra equations, but for real-life situations. So, I thought, 'stick children in a box with minimal direction and see how they escape!' And you two succeeded. I mean, sure, the others got out, but it was thanks to you two that they did. This is the first time more than one person has passed."

What Mark had said earlier in the sewer had become a reality. The look on his face, however, showed he had hoped *everyone* would pass.

Reading his expression, the old man said, "Mark, don't look so down. I know you were hoping for more, but that is what I like about you! You are not a man of self. You are a man for others, and at only seventeen years old!"

Mark got red in the face and thanked Mr. Bamber for his compliment.

"Now you, Aaron," Mr. Bamber continued, "you are the youngest person to ever pass and with such flying colors! You should feel honored. Usually, I get older people who graduate too soon, but you will be with me for a long time. You will have many responsibilities as you get older."

Stunned, I just sat there, unsure of what to say. *Responsibilities?* little me thought. *What kind of responsibilities is he talking about?*

"Okay, now, I bet you're both wondering what those tests had to do with any of this, am I right?" After we nodded, he explained, "I told you that I need children who can solve real-life problems. In simpler terms, I need people who have common sense. Common sense is like a rare superpower here, you see. All that you are taught in Apprenticeship are facts and numbers. If I could change the curriculum, I would. But you have to 'dance with the one that brung ya'," he said, chuckling hard. Mark grinned, and I laughed quietly, just to make the Keeper feel good.

Wiping tears from his eyes, the Keeper got back on track, turned to me, and asked, "Now tell me, Aaron, why did you stray off the path? Do you have a good explanation or theory? You could have been killed. It might have been a trap."

After thinking for a few minutes, I responded, "I didn't really think of the outcome, to be honest. I just knew something wasn't right."

"*Mhm*," he said, putting his elbows on the desk and tapping his forefingers together. "And Mark? Why did you decide to step up in front of all those kids? You were always quiet in class and never spoke to anyone. You never asked why you had to do things, you simply did them. So why question it all now?"

Mark turned red, again. Letting out a deep breath, he said, "To be honest, I was never really a people person. But I could *not* take their complaining anymore. Someone needed to take charge. Also, something about this whole thing never seemed right. Just because I don't question anything doesn't mean I am not skeptical about it."

The Keeper let out a belly laugh. "Honestly, I'm on your side. I was watching you all the entire time, and I know how you felt back there." Wagging his finger at Mark, he told him, "Never be afraid to question things. That's the way to get answers." He leaned closer to us. "It isn't really encouraged to ask questions but, between you and me, I would keep on asking," he whispered.

The redness in Mark's face receded, and he smiled.

Speaking of questions, I began to think about the ones in the last room. I wondered if we had actually answered them correctly. Timidly, I asked, "Mr. Bamber? What were the correct answers to those odd questions in the white room?"

"I was waiting for you to ask that," he replied grinning. "Those were something called 'riddles'. Have you ever heard of them?"

I shook my head. To be honest, I thought they were mathematical equations at first. Mark said he was confused as well, but he might've told me that to make me feel better. I was never sure.

"Riddles aren't entirely important in life, but at the same time they are," Mr. Bamber said. "You answered them correctly."

"How?" I asked, shocked. "The answers were so simple and different than everyone else's that it seemed ridiculous!"

Smiling, our Isle Keeper replied, "Why so surprised? That's what a riddle is. Think about it. 'What is the center of gravity?' You both wrote down '$V$'. Now, why? Because it is; no further explanation needed. For the long one on the back wall you both wrote down 'Correct', because that riddle was not a question. It was simply stating how many letters were in each word. And there are only 7 letters in *ALPHABET*, which you also answered correctly. Finally, there are only twelve *Seconds* in a year: January 2nd, February 2nd, and etcetera."

Finished with his explanation, Mr. Bamber rolled out from behind the desk and bid us to follow him out through the bookshelf he had come through. On the other side was the top floor of the Library. To think that we had passed the door of his office so many times and didn't even know it! I glanced over my shoulder to see that the shelf closed behind us. Ironically, the first book that caught my eye was a travel guide for wheelchair users.

The Library was empty, but the aroma of tomato soup and grilled cheese lingered in the air. We had missed dinner. My stomach began to growl at the scent of it. Mark was hungry, too; he hugged his belly tightly. Noticing our hunger pains, Mr. Bamber reassured us. "You may have missed dinner with the other Strata, but there will be food for you. Your new colleagues from Stratum Zero are waiting for you."

That sounded so cool. It reminded me of a secret agency that no one new about. And technically, it was, until a little while after we joined.

We headed down to the first floor via elevator, and Mr. Bamber led us to the far back of the Library. No one ever went to those shelves. He took out a few books that I had no idea existed: riddle books. *Okay, Mr. Bamber must choose the books for the secret doors on purpose,* I decided. After pulling out three, he pressed his hand up against the back of the shelf. There was a ding, and the shelf moved aside. It revealed dual metal sliding doors that opened noiselessly. Inside the room beyond were seven other guys, all young enough to be students in the Strata. They wore the uniforms, and I recognized one or two from meal time. Mark knew a few already; he walked right up to the older boys, shook their hands, and began conversing with them.

A younger fellow, seemingly about a year or two older than I was—however old I was— walked up to me and introduced himself. "Hello! My name is Cecil." He looked at me with kind, bright emerald eyes, and gave me a smile. His honey-colored hair was cut slightly below his ears, and he had short bangs. He was an inch or so taller than I was, but I surpassed his height as we got older.

"Hi," I replied shyly. "I'm Aaron."

Shaking my hand gently he replied, "Nice to meet you, Aaron. Welcome to Stratum Zero: Mr. Bamber's special Stratum of talented students. I used to be the youngest member, but now I think you've earned that title."

After talking with Cecil for a bit about random stuff, Mr. Bamber told us all to sit down. The room seemed like an ordinary laboratory. It had four lab counters in the center, shelves around the perimeter filled with equipment, a few computers, and frosted windows on the wall parallel to the library entrance. The only special thing about it was that it was a secret.

I sat with Cecil, Mark, and another member at the front right table. Mr. Bamber wheeled in front of the whiteboard and addressed us. "Hello, my little Overlords! Thank you for all being here this evening, I know how hard it is for you all to sneak out of class and training to be here."

*Overlords? Sneaking out?* So many questions began to fill my head. Not wanting to interrupt, I kept quiet.

"Now, as you know, we had our Commencement Testing today," he said, "and as you can see, we have two new faces with us now. I would like each of our veteran members to come up in order and introduce themselves. Tell them your name, number, where you come from, and the Stratum everyone thinks you're in."

The first boy stood up and went to the front of the room. "Hello, I am Darrell, Overlord Number One. Supposedly, I'm from Brooklyn, New York, in the United States of America. When I'm not here with

Stratum Zero, I am with Stratum Sixteen."

Hearing where he was from, Mark chuckled to himself. *Does he remember where he is from, too?* I thought, looking at my new friend.

Everyone clapped for Darrell and then the next one came up. "Leo, Overlord Two, and I am from Sweden. Stratum Thirteen."

He sat down and everyone applauded again. That continued until they all introduced themselves. The third was Takuma from Japan, also in Stratum Thirteen, but he passed the following year. Dayo from Africa was fourth; he said that all the students in Stratum Twelve, where he's from, sing the Banana Boat song whenever they see him. He warned us not to sing it, otherwise bad things would happen. At the time, I wasn't sure what that song was, but after hearing it, I understood. Winfrid from Germany was fifth; he and Nilam, from India, were both from Stratum Ten, but also passed at different times. Last was Cecil, who was in Stratum Nine and from the United States. Once their introductions were over, Mr. Bamber introduced the two of us. "Everyone this is Mark, from Stratum Fifteen. He will now be Overlord Eight. And this young fellow is Aaron, from Stratum Eight; he will be Overlord Nine. They are both most likely from America."

*America*? I wondered. To be honest, I never gave much thought as to where I came from. I was always at Isle III. Pushing it into the back of my mind, I waved to the welcoming boys.

Mr. Bamber smiled and beckoned us to go back to our seats. "Okay, so now that we are all here, let's get started," our Keeper continued. "We will explain what the duty of an Overlord is. Oh, and 'Overlord' is just a fancy word for someone who has great power or authority, which is your new privilege. It's a powerful term; I enjoy it very much."

Mr. Bamber began to "show us the ropes," as he put it. He pulled up different slideshow presentations on the electronic whiteboard. It was a lot of information to take in, so I won't explain it all; but basically our job was to keep all the Strata in check, oversee the major projects that get shipped to other Isles, and other important leader-like duties. After going through the slides, Mr. Bamber made one last point before we ate dinner: "Oh, and most importantly: someone who has not graduated yet will be my successor when I die."

That was so unexpected that it hit me like a train. I sat there for a few minutes with a shocked expression on my face. *One of us, or someone to come after us?* The thought that a student would oversee the entire Isle scared me the most, but I was sure he would choose an older student who knew what he or she was doing. Right? Now that I think about it, that was a selfish thought. I didn't take into consideration that he said *"when I die"*.

My thoughts about that comment were interrupted when food arrived. I was so caught up in the moment I'd totally forgotten about my growling stomach, even though it kept screaming for help in the middle of our Isle Keeper's presentations. Mouthwatering dishes were brought out: sandwiches, burgers, fries, and many other delicious foods that were high in carbohydrates and had barely any nutritional value whatsoever.

After a few hours of socialization and stuffing our faces, we headed to our rooms for the night and rested for the next day—my first day with duties from Stratum Zero. Before heading to my room, I took a quick detour to find Mrs. Pieper. When I found her and told her the good news, she began to cry tears of joy and gave me such a tight hug I felt my bones cracking. She was happy for me, but sad to see me go. I promised to visit her when I could, and I did. I often went to see her to tell her how I was doing, and when I needed advice on anything.

Throughout the years, I fulfilled my duties as best as I could, but it was a lot of work. Building machinery, inventing useful items, putting teams together to work on projects—and we even had to train for combat more than anyone else, which was painful. We continued to try and keep Stratum Zero a secret.

As of last year, there were fourteen Overlords, and we gained our first girl, Marci. Mr. Bamber had been waiting years for a girl to pass, and now his waiting was over. Not too long after Marci got in, Darrell graduated, and the new Overlord One needed to be named. We all voted for the new Number One, and Mark was chosen. He was the obvious choice, even if he didn't think so. Everyone will be devastated when he graduates next year. As Overlord One, Mark made some good changes to our Stratum. He convinced Mr. Bamber that the students had a right to know who groups the teams, assigns the projects, and gets all the heavy lifting done.

He agreed, and we stepped into the light. We let everyone know. Not only did this earn us more respect, but it made the students follow our example. They looked to us for advice and even asked for words of encouragement, which was something.

So that's basically it in a nutshell. I mean, I could tell a lot more stories, but Mark told us all to be well rested for the Isles Meeting tomorrow. The fourteen of us are the main helpers of Isle III, so we have to behave and look our best. I wonder what we're going to be doing and/or discussing this time…

# Chapter 10

## Alison: IV

So, today's meeting was interesting…. Axel and I were the Isle representatives, again, so we got to see everything up close. Apparently, this year's meeting is spreading across a span of three days, so I wonder what the next two days will be like.

Waking up was quite difficult for everyone this morning. Mr. Allaway wanted us all to be the best of the best at the meeting, so he worked us double time, which fried our circuits… literally. My armor had to be repaired twice before we left for the meeting. At least it's more waterproof now. Anyway, despite our exhaustion, each Bionic managed to be packed, presentable, and at breakfast on time. After we ate, we headed on our way.

Mr. Allaway and other staff members travelled to Isle III, Research and Development, by speedboat. And when I say speedboat, I mean *speed*boat. Isle III's not just across the stream; it's quite a distance away. While they took a boat, Mr. Allaway thought it would be more entertaining, and showy, if we all flew in. They had added a rocket feature to our robotic feet just for that. It's pretty cool, but I hate showing off.

Looking down, we saw that ferries from every island were

heading into port, each carrying the student inhabitants of their Isle's facility. Since I was one of the Bionics' representatives, I suggested that we circle and scan the island. We did and were able to get a feel of its terrain and where everything was. It seemed to change every year, as if the Research and Development Island could never make up its mind.

Once we knew Mr. Allaway and the staff were ashore, we flew down to the docks and asked for further instructions. "Just line up and follow me," he said, then began leading us to our destination. "I am honestly not sure what's next. It's as much a surprise to us Keepers as it is to you all."

He brought us to Isle III's training grounds, which were about ten times larger than ours. What was impossible to comprehend was how they had managed to create such a wide variety of different terrains. The section we all met on was a large grassy field. Not too far away, a thin white line separated it from a dense forest. No one could see what was beyond that.

Looking around at the crowd, I saw trainees of all six Isles attempting to remain as cool and collected as possible. Most of them were nervous wrecks, naturally. We had been given a briefing before leaving that this year's meeting was going to be new and difficult. No other information was given, so what was to come was a complete mystery.

After people-watching for a bit, we Bionics were led to our seating area. We were sitting straight across from Assets, and they didn't look happy to be there. It was as if they had been pulled unexpectedly out of the farming fields. Their uniforms were dirty, their hair was matted, and a few still had their agricultural equipment in hand.

My staring was interrupted by the sound of someone tapping a microphone, immediately drawing my attention to the stage in the center of the bleachers. The stage was made up of seven round metal platforms: one in the center, and six in a circle around it. Mr. Nik stood on the center one with his microphone. "Welcome, everyone!" Mr. Nik began. "As you know, this year's Isle Meeting is going to be a little different than normal. Usually, we only talk about current issues and discuss future plans, and mingle with one another. However, we have other things in mind this year. First, we'll begin with our usual introductions, performed by our island representatives."

Finishing his speech, Mr. Nik received loud applause and backed away from the microphone. Once he sat down with the other Keepers, the representatives went to the surrounding platforms, each with their Isle's Roman numeral on it.

When Axel and I reached our spot, we went over what we were going to say again. It was amazing to think that eight years ago, he and I were small, confused children. Now we are young adults, just as confused but more confident. I hadn't changed much; I was only slightly taller and more mature looking. Axel, however, had changed a lot. He had become stronger, taller, and more self-reliant than the scared kid I met all those years back.

After we finished planning, Mr. Nik introduced us first, since we were from Isle I. As the platform rose, Mr. Allaway gave us a wink; he wanted us to show off some more. We took off from the platform and flew over the audience, did a few tricks, and then cruised back to the center. The younger kids gasped and were blown away; the older ones weren't as amused. It wasn't the first time they'd seen flying Bionics.

Clutching the wireless microphones, we began to introduce ourselves. "Hello, fellow Islanders," I began. "I'm Alison, and this is Axel. We're from the Isle of Biomechatronics Testing, where we experiment on bionic implants with the help of the disabled survivors of the Invaders, such as ourselves. Our job is to make sure the equipment is safe to use on the common folk in dire times of need."

Axel then took over. "Without us few test subjects, the equipment given to us by Isle III might never be safe to use on the Mainland. Our job is to perfect their equipment, and even modify it to create the ultimate robotic prosthetics. We're looking forward to meeting you all."

Everyone cheered as we descended back to the platform.

Next was Isle II. Their representatives were a teenage boy and girl wearing buttoned up, knee-length lab coats over black jeans and blood red T-shirts, with stethoscopes hung around their necks. "Good morning, everyone," the young man said. "My name is Ethan, and this is Zita. We are from Isle II, Saviors."

Ethan was a shorter fellow with an olive skin tone and dark hair. His serious brown eyes scanned the crowd, as if trying to seek someone out. His partner, Zita, had light green eyes that were friendlier. Her frizzy ginger hair complimented her pasty skin tone. She was about as tall as Ethan. Picking up where Ethan left off, Zita began to explain what their Isle was about. "Our job is to attend to the sick, wounded, and dying. We care for mothers who are about to give birth to their beautiful babies, and make sure that their children are sent to their destined Isle so they may grow up for a purpose. We mix medicines, and our graduated members are posted at stations on each island. At our own Isle, we are a home to survivors, and house patients in our facility."

And so ended the Saviors' introduction. Something about their purpose didn't sit right with me, but I didn't dwell on it.

Next was the Isle of Research and Development. Their representatives were fellows named Mark and Leo. They were dressed almost exactly like the members of Saviors, except the shirts they wore underneath their unbuttoned lab coats were blue instead of red, and they lacked the stethoscopes. Mark explained that their job was basically to keep the Isles functioning, and to develop new equipment. "Without us," he said, "the other facilities would not have such incredible technology. We invent the basic tech; you modify it to your liking." Going on, he quickly mentioned their island itself played an important role as well: Besides hosting the Isle Meetings, it was also the home of Mr. Nik and Mr. Bamber, as well as the Keeper's office, the Nerve Center.

After them was Assets. Two not-very-cheerful representatives by the names of Nate and Paulina told us that their jobs were to provide necessary resources to the rest of us. They wore ripped, stained overalls over asparagus-green T-shirts, and their movements were sluggish. Paulina actually started nodding off after their introduction! Still, honestly, without them I think the Isles would most definitely fall apart. I'm always appreciative of the poor Assets teens. Working around the clock, they farm the crops, raise the animals, sew the clothing, package the supplies, and basically provide the things we need for survival.

The fifth was Seers, our protection program. They were in charge of making sure that mischief never happened within the Isles, and that no one got in or out. They knew what was happening, when it was happening, and who was doing it. No one wanted to mess with them. Their male representative was Yared, a darker-toned fellow with a strong stature. The female was Ursula, a coltish, solid young lady who seemed like she meant business. Her flaxen hair fell loose over her shoulders, and her dark eyes watched everyone like a vulture waiting to snatch its prey. They wore dark cargo pants, combat boots, and navy-blue tank tops that seemed comfortable, but Yared and Ursula looked as stiff as rocks.

Last but not least was the Isle of Genetic Testing. Their representatives sure gave us a show. There was only one person on the platform, and he wore large round goggles and a black cape. Next to him was a large, veiled box. Confused murmurs could be heard throughout the crowd as the platform rose.

"G'day, ladies and gentlemen: Humans, Bionics, and Mutants!" the caped boy began. Without giving the crowd time to understand, he removed his cape and goggles—revealing two pairs of wings and rounded insect eyes.

A few children began to scream as he started flying low to the ground. The ones sitting in front attempted to back away, but he wasn't offended. In fact, he laughed. "I get that reaction all the time. Sorry for my appearance, but this is what happens when you get chosen for Isle VI." He hovered over the box and removed the covering to reveal an enormous fish tank with a boy inside…well, what used to be a boy. He looked like a human-shark baby now.

The dragonfly boy put the microphone in a stand and placed it next to a speaker on the outside of the tank. Shark Boy began to introduce himself and his partner. "Hello. My name is Zeke, and this is Lucas. We are from the Isle of Genetic Testing, and, as you can see, we mean business. Our job is to see if it is scientifically possible to distribute animal abilities to humans. So far, we have been working with many species, and it is going well.

"Our job is a long process that requires much work, but it's for the greater good. Our Keeper, Mr. Mallory, believes that humans can evolve into so much more that what we are now with just a small push from science, and that's what we're trying to do. Once we're evolved, we can truly survive and never live another day in fear. As we say, '*Carpe Diem!*' That's Latin for 'Seize the Day'!" Their performance ended with a standing ovation, but their words also didn't sit right in my stomach. Besides, they were our rivals. They think that their "natural creature" abilities will prove that the use of prosthetics and implants will no longer be necessary. Still, I kept quiet and gave them respect.

Finally, all the introductions were done, and it was time to separate into groups of at *least* six, containing at least one person from each Isle. The groups of only six were for the older members. Since I was the oldest in Isle I, most of the members of my group were more mature… in age at least. On my team were Ethan, the representative of Saviors; Mark, the representative of Research and Development; Marlene of Assets; ten-year-old Jeremy of Seers; and a cat-lady from the Isle of Genetic Testing named Sami.

We met at a clearing in the woods. After brief introductions, we sort of stood there in a circle for a good long while, staring awkwardly at each other. Sami and I exchanged unfriendly glances. I was hoping another fight wouldn't break out between our islands; that did *not* end well last year.

Thankfully, Mark interrupted our glaring. "Well, now that we're here and introduced, why don't we see what we're supposed to do, huh?"

It was sort of the obvious thing, but no one else suggested it. We Bionics were the ones who received the messages, since we could see them right before our eyes. "Nothing is coming in yet," I told them. "Is that normal?"

Ethan shrugged, fiddled with his stethoscope, and said, "Maybe the others haven't finished introducing each other as fast as we have. We are the smallest group. I'm just hoping that we don't have to do any training drills." Looking down at his uniform, which was too long for his short size, he confessed, "I don't think I'm dressed in the proper attire."

"Neither am I," Mark replied, plucking at his own white lab coat. "I wish they'd told us to bring our navy combat uniforms, like the Seers members have. *That* would've been nice."

Marlene tugged on her light brown hair and complained, "Why are they taking so long? I just want to take a nap… and maybe eat something. I haven't eaten since four this morning."

*No wonder she looks as dead as a doornail,* I thought.

Suddenly, a small voice suggested, "Take a nap on the ground. You're probably used to it. We can wake you up when we get a message." The kid, Jeremy, seemed way too young to belong to Seers. He didn't look very strong and was too cute. I don't think many people took him seriously. His large blue eyes looked at Marlene with compassion, and he gave her a warm smile—something you don't expect from a Seer.

She smiled, rubbed his blond, crew-cut hair, lay down, and started snoring almost instantly. After a few minutes of discussing how someone could fall asleep so fast, a message came in. It was very anticlimactic, but no one complained. In fact, we rejoiced at the simple three words: *"Time for lunch."* Immediately, we woke Marlene and planned to race back to the cafeteria, but Mark suggested that we jog back as a team. Listening to Mr. Goody-Two-Shoes, we headed back… together.

Since Isle III's cafeteria couldn't fit everyone, half of the groups had to eat outside in the fields. We arrived just in time to get a table inside. We were happy we were assigned the second terrain; I felt bad for the kids who met miles away. Going inside, we found a table in the corner, against some bookshelves on the second floor of their beautiful library.

While we were eating, we started opening up a little more to each other. It was a chance to see how everyone else thought about how the Isles were run. It made me feel good to realize that most of us had similar thoughts. If I ever brought up my worries with some of my Bionic friends, they would attack me and shut me out. Unfortunately, Jeremy was like that too. All of us but him were suspicious about Mr. Nik's actions, of whether what we were doing was worth it. Jeremy just rejected any thought of suspicion and adored Mr. Nik and his way of things.

"Aren't you even a little curious about why he does things the way he does?" Marlene questioned. "For instance: why are we only allowed to meet with each other once a year? I mean, sure, we each have duties to attend to. But I heard that, back then, people used to be able to rest on the last two days of the week. We don't even get that."

Jeremy stared down at his grilled cheese sandwich and replied, "It's for the best. He makes sure that we can handle these things. If we take time to have too many social gatherings, we might get wrapped up in all that."

Looking puzzled, Ethan stated, "Well, sometimes the folks who *can't* handle these things need support from those around them. Relationships can save lives, especially in young teens. Trust me, I know. I read that in the olden days, some young adults felt so alone that they did terrible things to others and themselves. If they were just acknowledged, maybe those things wouldn't have happened."

Jeremy sat in silence for a few minutes, until he finally thought of a good argument. "Well, sometimes those relationships are the *cause* of the disasters around us. If we get too wrapped up in caring for others, our duties may be ignored because of it. If we can avoid relationships altogether, then maybe problems can be avoided."

*Who spoon-fed you your information, kid?* I wondered but didn't say it out loud.

We sat there awkwardly until Mark spoke up. "You know, Jeremy, you and Ethan are both correct." Looking at him, seeming perplexed, Jeremy asked how.

Mark smiled and explained. "It's true that sometimes we can get so wrapped up in other people that we forget about where our place is and what our jobs are. But no matter what, there is always someone who depends on us. I remember my life quite clearly before the Invaders, and it was the love I had for my siblings and friends that drove me to continue doing my duties. If you only live for yourself and don't care for the people around you, you can get lonely and upset, hence Ethan's point. Do you understand?"

Jeremy sat there looking down for a few minutes. I'm pretty sure Mark had hit the nail on the head. What I was more interested in, though, was that he said he remembered his past *clearly*. No one that I've met had ever admitted to that before.

For the first time, Sami spoke up. "I agree with you, Mark," she said, timidly. "I think I can say the same for the rest of us. My question is: what are Mr. Nik's *true* intentions for keeping us apart from each other? I mean, sure, some of the Isle members quarrel with each other from time to time, but that happens *inside* the facilities as well."

Mark sat back in his chair and started twirling his soup spoon between his fingers. "Here's what I've learned from my time being here. Everyone has secrets, good or bad. Mr. Nik is obviously hiding something from us all, as are our Isle Keepers. It could be something good that he doesn't want us to know yet, or he could be an evil psychotic maniac set on using us to defeat the Invaders just so he can take over."

*That's a harsh and very specific assumption*, I thought. *He obviously thinks things through.*

He continued to explain the latter half of Sami's question. "Another thing: people are people. It doesn't matter whether we're black or white, fat or slim, smart or dumb, Mutant or non-Mutant; we're all the same. It doesn't matter what you look like, or where you come from, or what you believe in; there are always people who are good, and people who are bad. That's something that Mr. Nik does understand, which I'm grateful for. He never underestimates someone just by looking at their outside. As for fighting with each other: everyone quarrels. That's nothing new. My guess is two things: First, he wants to minimize the quarrelling between rival Isles. Second, he knows that if we spend too much time together, we can grow stronger and maybe even overthrow him and the other Keepers if we get any ideas. Think about it."

Sami nodded, and we all understood what he meant. Before Jeremy could retaliate, I received a message telling us to regroup outside. Immediately after, another message in all capital letters told us to use the bathrooms before we headed out. That meant we were going to be out there a while. So we headed to the restrooms, then outside. Can I just complain and say how long the ladies' bathroom line is compared to the guys'? It's not fair.

Anyway, once we were outside, we saw Mr. Nik standing at the center stage with a microphone. He tapped it three times and gained everyone's attention. "Welcome back. I hope you are all well-acquainted within your groups, because you are going to be training together for the rest of the day. I want you all to get used to working as teams, because… well, in the end, we will tell you why. Your designated message-receiver will soon get the next set of instructions. Best of luck to you all!"

Mark chuckled and said, "See? Secrets."

As soon as I received the message, I passed it on to everyone: We were supposed to go back to our first meeting spot. Before doing so, however, we were to gather a few things— without the other groups seeing. "How many things do they expect us to get?" Marlene complained. "Our meeting place is over in the next terrain. It's not like we have an enormous amount of land to search for stuff."

Sami reassured her, saying, "I'm sure they're not the kinds of things that you're thinking of, Marlene." Yawning, she added, "I hope it doesn't take too long."

After reading the list aloud, I didn't think a single item on it was anything anyone was thinking of, and it was going to take longer than Sami would've liked. I originally thought maybe some sticks or a fancy rock, but no, it had to be things that were impossible to find in a meadow terrain. Ethan became agitated. "How are we supposed to find metal scraps, cable, durable wheels, a strong metal bowl, and a bunch of other ridiculous stuff? Do they want us to raid the stage?"

That idea was a bust. We looked over, and saw that other groups were already fighting over pieces of the platforms. Before anyone could complain, I suggested something. "Well, they said *on the way,* but we *could* always take the long way around. Maybe... through the facility itself and back around?"

Looking horrified, Marlene said, "You want us to steal from *inside* Isle III? Are you insane? We could get in so much trouble!"

Sami supported my idea. "I think it's a good plan. They didn't give us any rules; they just told us what to do."

"Bingo!" Mark exclaimed, pointing towards the cat-girl. "If anything happens and we weren't supposed to do it, I'll take the blame. I live here, after all. So, why don't we work on getting the metal bowl first, huh?"

First, we hit the kitchen and snuck around. It was dark and vacant, which was great. Sami found the largest bowl in no time. Leaving the empty room, we went on to the rest of the things we needed: we stole from classrooms, took machinery apart, and even raided the warehouse. It didn't seem right that we were sneaking around and stealing equipment, but we figured it was our only option. It was difficult carrying everything at once, so I flew the heavier items to our meeting spot, zipped back, and grabbed some more. When we were finally with all the pieces in the woods, I received another message. It read: "*Good work. You are the first team to complete the scavenger hunt. We will work with these pieces tomorrow; as for now, head to your sleeping quarters.*"

Now I was ready to complain. "Seriously? They make us steal all this stuff, and now they won't even tell us what for?"

Jeremy, who looked like a zombie by then, just asked, "Where are our sleeping quarters? I don't mind if we wait until tomorrow."

"Yeah," Sami agreed, her green eyes beginning to close. "I think Jeremy, Marlene, and I need to go to bed."

Marlene nodded. "Sleep sounds good."

They were right; and it was getting late. Our hunt had started late in the afternoon, and it took us about four hours to collect everything. The sun was gone, and the moon had already come out. "Don't worry," Mark said, "I know where our designated cabin is. Since we're a team now, we'll have to share. It's not too far from our meeting place."

Apparently, it was too far for Jeremy; he passed out from exhaustion on the way. We took turns carrying him until we finally reached a log cabin. "Wow, when you said cabin, you weren't kidding," Ethan said.

Mark snickered and headed inside.

It was small, and all it had inside were three sets of bunk beds. Nothing else—not even a bathroom. That was outside. What it did have was a wrapped sandwich on each bed. I chose the bottom bunk against the right wall, and Sami chose the one above me. Ethan carefully placed Jeremy on the bottom bunk against the back wall, and he chose the top one. Mark and Marlene chose the bunks to the left. "Well, this is awkward," Marlene was the first to say, while sitting on her top bunk. "I've never had to share a room with anyone before, let alone five others, three being guys."

"Just be thankful there are only six of us and not thirty, like some of the other teams," Mark reminded her, looking up at her from his bunk.

After we took turns using the outhouse and unpacked our backpacks, we settled into bed. It took me longer, because I had to take my armor off. "Whoa, whoa, wait," Sami blurted as I stepped out of my half-suit. "You aren't *all* robot?"

"No, just my right side," I answered.

Lying down, Mark propped his head up on his elbow and asked, "How did that happen, if you don't mind me asking? I'm sure I'm not the only one curious about that."

After they pressed me a little bit, I told them the story. Interested and amazed, they all listened intently. Marlene and Sami stayed awake throughout the whole thing, despite how tired they were. "That's amazing," Marlene marveled. "I'm sorry about your family."

I thanked her and wiped away my tears.

Changing the subject, Ethan said, "All right, it's almost time for bed." He reached into his knapsack and pulled out a book. "I'm not sure about any of you, but I think it's time to write in our record log thingies."

"Oh yeah, I almost forgot about those," Marlene confessed. "I don't see the point, but I guess it will be interesting—in time."

"I'm sure it will be," Ethan responded. "Oh, I brought some pens, because I don't think the speech recognition can understand us all talking into our microphones at once. I'm still amazed how it recognizes our voices and writes what we say onto actual paper." He threw us all pens. *I guess he has a point*, I thought chuckling to myself. Get it? *Point*? Okay, I was never a good jokester. Well anyway, it was interesting, but I'm sure Mark and the other Isle III members knew how it worked.

So that was all today, and now my hand is cramping really *really* badly. I'm surprised Mark and Sami are still writing. She said she was tired… Marlene passed out within the first ten minutes, and I think it's my turn now.

# THE ISLES

# CHAPTER 11

## Sami: IV

Okay, so today was Day Two of the Isle Meeting Challenge, as was revealed this morning. I am *so* tired; I hope it won't take as long as yesterday to write down what happened.

It was a rush to get ready this morning. There was a line for the bathroom and changing into clean clothes in that little outhouse thingy was hard. Thankfully, Mark suggested that he and the boys wait outside the cabin until the girls were ready. I appreciated that.

I was very curious about Alison's armor. When she put on her robotic suit, she would grit her teeth and inhale sharply. It was like something was shooting into her, connecting her nerves with the technology. I wanted to ask her if my hunch was correct, but I kept my mouth shut. *Can't get too friendly with a Bionic*, I told myself.

When it was the boys' turn to get ready, Alison, Marlene, and I waited outside and wondered what we were going to do that day. "Any messages yet, Alison?" Marlene asked.

"Nothing yet," she replied. "Maybe once everyone is ready, I'll get something." But even after the guys came outside, there was still nothing. Mark suggested we head back to our meeting spot. It was sunrise when we got there, and Alison suddenly exclaimed, "Oh, I got something!"

It was funny watching her read the messages. She had a blank expression on her face and would dramatically stare off into the distance as she read. Despite our rivalry, Alison had started growing on me, especially after hearing her story last night. Sometimes I'm happy I don't remember my past. I wouldn't want the burden of knowing that I lived and my family didn't. Then again, it would've been nice to know I was happy before this.

"It says that they're sorry for the delay," she read, "and we should head to the cafeteria to grab some food and head right back here ASAP."

Jeremy's stomach growled. He had fallen asleep last night before eating the sandwich left for him. "Sounds like a good idea to me," he mumbled. Looking at him sympathetically, Mark asked if maybe some of us could go grab the food and rush back so Jeremy didn't have to walk all the way there and back. "No, no, I am fine," Jeremy said, yawning.

I yawned after him. "Man, now I'm getting sleepy again," I muttered. Wanting to stay awake and keep myself busy, I offered, "I can go get some things, Mark."

"I can go with her; we can be back in no time," Alison added.

Mark agreed and told us to be back soon. Marlene stopped us before we left; she was determined to make it a race. She counted down, and then we dashed off. I was running on all fours, but Alison was still able to keep up with me two-legged. Things like this sparked our island rivalry. We made it back to the grassy field in less than ten minutes. Only a few Mutants and Bionics were there. *They had the same idea*, I thought as I spotted several of my fellow Mutants. Alison waved to a friend of hers, whom I recognized as the other representative: The boy with the curly, white hair.

There were paper bags lined up on the ground; we grabbed six and raced back. When we returned, Marlene decided our race had ended in a tie, because she wasn't paying attention. (I clearly won by a nose.) We handed out the bags and opened them up. Each contained three sandwiches and three large bottles of water.

Jeremy scarfed down his first sandwich and drank the entire water bottle that went with it. He wanted to eat the other ones, too, but Mark took the bag away from him and put it in the boy's backpack for later. While the rest of us were eating, Alison informed us of another incoming message: "They want us to build something out of the items we collected yesterday."

"Like what?" Ethan demanded with a mouthful of turkey sandwich.

"Doesn't say anything about *what* we have to make, just to make something," she admitted. "Wait…" she stared off again, "okay, something useful. That's all it says."

Ethan groaned and finished his food with a distressed look on his face.

"I am sure we'll think of something," I encouraged. "I mean, it doesn't have to be *that* intricate if they didn't tell us what to make."

Wiping her mouth with her forearm, Marlene put in, "Yeah. We can just throw it all over and say we made a junkyard."

Mark chuckled. "We could most definitely do that, but that's not useful."

"Sure it's useful!" Marlene argued. "It's art."

"Art is useful, but I have a better idea," he smirked.

"Of course. The geek has all the answers," Marlene teased.

Grinning, he said, "Fine, I won't tell you. Tell me something that you would make with these pieces, and then I will tell you *my* idea."

That was hard. What *I* would build with metal scraps, cords, and metal bowls is a tall mobile metal slide. We could use the heat from Alison's rockets to weld the metal together and use the bowls as the sleds. The cords and gears I would use to make a pulley to pull myself up and down. What we would use it for I had no idea.

I suggested my plan, and Mark laughed, making me feel a little foolish. What he said made me feel better, though. "That is an *incredible* idea," he said, smiling. "I don't think that's what they have in mind, but you're actually very close. I didn't think of using Alison's technology to weld it together. Now my idea can actually work!"

"So, what is your idea?" Ethan questioned. "All I can think of is using the metal scraps as stretchers and using the cords and gears to make a conveyer belt to send items back and forth."

Mark didn't dismiss his idea, either. No one else could think of anything, so we just stood there awkwardly. Breaking the silence, Marlene asked once more: "All right, smart guy, what is your idea?"

"Well… How about a catapult?" he said finally.

"A catapult? Seriously?!" Jeremy whined. "How were we supposed to think of that, and what is it for, anyhow?"

"That's just it—they didn't *expect* us to think of it," Mark concluded.

Frustrated, Jeremy started banging pieces of metal together out of protest. Marlene snatched them away, telling him his rhythm was horrible. When they had finished quarrelling, we got to work. Ethan worked with the gears and cords. Marlene and Jeremy were on wheels. Mark and I held the metal in place while Alison welded it. I'm surprised we didn't get burned, but she was very precise.

"Sami, good job on getting the largest bowls," Mark complimented.

"Yeah, you can personally fit in these bowls, they're so large. Now we can really call it a *cat*-apult," Marlene joked.

Finally, we finished and with only minor injuries. Ethan was happy to attend to them. "Now we just have to figure out what to do with it," I said.

"I have an idea," Jeremy suggested, grinning evilly.

*Bad idea, bad idea*, I thought throughout all of it. Never take advice from an immature ten-year-old boy. They had me sit in the bowl and do a test launch! We aimed it so I would land in the ocean if Alison couldn't catch me.

"Ready, Sami?" Mark didn't wait for an answer; he just started a countdown. "Three, two, one, go!"

That was the most terrifying experience of my life. As soon as he said go, he hit a lever and I was launched into the air. I wonder what that must have sounded and looked like to the teams below: a mutant cat girl letting out a horrid feline screech while being launched across the entire island! I thought I was going to hit the water until Alison flew in and grabbed me. I clutched her so tightly I am surprised she could not feel my nails through the metal. I did not want to let go.

Once we got back, I wobbled over to the nearest tree and threw up behind it. It was embarrassing, but I was so sick I couldn't help it.

"Okay, maybe next time we won't use a human test subject," Mark noted, grinning. Everyone agreed and tried to contain their laughter, except Jeremy. He rolled on the ground laughing and pointing at me. I wanted to test the catapult with him next.

Thankfully, Ethan had some medicine to give me to calm my stomach. I sat down for a little bit until the next message came in. "Uh oh!" Alison gasped. "Duck!" We all dropped as she shot into the air up and grabbed a boulder that was headed straight for us. With both hands, she stopped it from hitting our contraption.

*Wow, is she strong,* I marveled as she put the rock down. Shaking, Jeremy stood up. "Maybe someone thought our test shot was an attack or hopefully a misfire!" he cried. Then another boulder came for us. Marlene pulled him out of the way, while it smashed the tree behind them.

"But why are they continually firing at us if it's a misfire?!" Marlene exploded when the attacks kept coming. "And how come they also thought of making a catapult?"

"Down, everyone!" Ethan yelled as he tackled her to the ground before she was hit head-on by a scrap cannonball.

"What's going on?!" I shouted.

"I don't know!" Alison cried. "The message just said to duck!"

"We're under attack. Everyone stand back-to-back and face opposite directions," Jeremy commanded. "Don't kill, only stun." In this, the little guy definitely knew what he was doing.

We sent back the lovely presents our rival catapult-makers sent us. Alison grabbed the cannonballs in midair and quickly returned them; we used our catapult for the rest. After a while, Jeremy suggested we split up, and we headed forward in an attempt to stop the attack at the source. Thankfully, before leaving our islands we had all been required to place at least one weapon in our backpacks for defense purposes. Jeremy and Ethan had pistols, but Mark had tranquilizers to use instead. Marlene had sheep shears and Alison was already a walking (and flying) weapon. I wasn't used to artillery, so I relied on my own strength.

Everyone headed out except for Alison and me; we stayed back and kept using the catapult. It took about fifteen minutes of defending before there was a ceasefire.

"What's going on?" Alison wondered as she looked around.

"Not sure," I responded, panting. I began shouting the names of our teammates, hoping they were all right. We heard Jeremy yell something back but couldn't make out what it was. Out of concern for him, I asked Alison if I could see if he and the others were all right. She agreed, and I bolted in Jeremy's direction while she stayed by our contraption.

When I caught up, I was confused by what I saw. The four of them were standing in what looked like a metal scrap heap. Some parts were on fire; others had already disintegrated into ash. Its creators, however, were nowhere in sight. Marlene saw me coming and started to explain. "We kind of destroyed their robotic artillery… but it was out of self-defense, so don't start pointing fingers."

"That doesn't matter," Mark chided. "The real question is, why were they shooting at us?"

I saw Ethan crouching next to Jeremy, who was sitting on a big pile of metal with tears in his eyes, holding his arm. "Where does it hurt?" Ethan questioned.

Humiliated, Jeremy answered, "Nowhere. I am *fine*." Looking frustrated, Ethan decided to bandage his entire arm. Jeremy wasn't pleased, but he didn't object.

I circled the heap of metal, hoping to find an answer. Technology was *not* my specialty, so I couldn't come up with anything. Carefully standing up, Jeremy quietly suggested that we head back. Returning to the clearing, we noticed Alison was nowhere in sight. I called her name a few times before I got a response.

She was sitting at the top of one of the trees, hoping to get a better view. Once she was down, she told us she had received another message. "It said a lot, so here it is in brief: 'Sorry about the attack. We wanted to see how you all responded under pressure. That's what will happen when the Challenge finally begins…'"

"*Challenge?*" Marlene interrupted. "I thought we just were supposed to get acquainted with each other, not fight battles!"

"Well, it doesn't necessarily mean 'fighting'," Alison argued.

"Anyways," Mark chimed in, "What else did it say?"

"All it said was to keep an eye out for the next challenge," she went on. "That was the second one out of who-knows-how-many. They gave us a map, though. I was trying to follow it from a bird's eye view while I waited for you guys."

Confused, I asked, "Wait. Did they give you a physical map or a map that flashes across your eyes for a few seconds?"

Alison let out a sarcastic laugh. "No, I can still see the full map if I choose to, but right now all I see is a red line on the ground urging me to follow it."

"That's sick," Mark complimented.

"That sounds like our best option, but who's going to stay with the catapult?" Ethan demanded.

"No one will have to. I have an idea," Marlene announced.

She had interesting ideas. We were going to disguise the catapult with leaves, dirt, and sticks, but we had to put it in a hole first. Alison and I worked together on the digging. Thankfully, it didn't take long and it wasn't too deep, but we were able to hide the bottom half of it. Carefully, we pulled the arm back and lowered our masterpiece into the dirt safe house.

After we finished "cleverly" disguising our contraption, we followed Alison, who was following the "map." We had to go through almost every terrain, find landmarks, and dumb little objects on the way. "This is stupid," Jeremy grumbled after we found another piece of garbage. "I hate this. There's no point…," he rambled like this until Marlene slapped him in the back of the head. That girl did *not* care that he was only ten. The boy learned his lesson after the third slap.

Wanting to get it over with quickly, we jogged the whole way. Ethan and Mark weren't used to the exercise, which was quite comical. Every ten minutes one of them would almost pass out. "Running is my brother's thing. Not mine," Mark panted, putting his hands on his knees.

"What were your siblings like?" I curiously inquired when we stopped.

"They were amazing, but unfortunately I didn't know them for that long," he replied, sitting down. "My brother was the fastest guy you could ever have met. He was a junior Olympian, hoping to go onto the real Olympics. He could run miles and not even break a sweat. My sister was an expert piano player and seamstress." He smiled as he remembered his family. "That's only a few facts about them. There is… so much more."

I wanted to ask more questions about what a normal life was like, and what he meant by not knowing his siblings for long, but we had reached our destination. "This is it?!" Ethan hollered, throwing his short arms into the air. He grabbed his dark hair like he was going to start pulling out of his head. We were on the edge of the island. We stood on an empty beach, with rushing waters not far away. The view of the sun setting on the water was beautiful, but we weren't interested in sight-seeing at the time.

"No, it isn't," Alison admitted. "It says to go into the water." Shading the sun out of her eyes with one hand, she said, "Wait. I see something."

"What is it?" Marlene asked eagerly.

Looking a little harder, Alison shouted, "It's a person floating in the water, and they look unconscious!"

Forgetting his complaints, Ethan bolted for the ocean. When it came to people's lives, Ethan didn't mess around. Rushing into the water with no concern for himself, he took on the heavy waves and swam all the way out to where a child was floating. Without thinking, Alison flew out and pulled them both back to shore.

It was a little girl. She wasn't breathing. Quickly, Ethan begin to administer *CPR*.

The girl coughed and opened her eyes. Ethan asked her if she was all right. Jumping up, she said she was fine, handed him a wet letter, and ran away. Confused, Ethan wondered if she was actually human or not.

"Words cannot express how much I hate these so called 'challenges'," Marlene moaned.

Everyone agreed with her statement and pressed Ethan to read the letter. "All it says is: *'Congratulations. You have passed the next challenge. If you have any complaints, you may deliver them at the end of the week'.*"

"There's another week of this random mumbo jumbo?!" Marlene croaked.

Mark reassured her, "No, just one more day, but you guys stay here for the entire week. Well, that's what I heard, anyway."

"Since we're here," Jeremy interjected, "Can we just relax on the beach until we get some new instructions? The other teams are doing it." He pointed toward some other groups who were located a little ways away from us. Some were relaxing; others were rushing into the water. I noticed that there were more floating children amongst the waves. I guess the challenge was same for everyone. *Hopefully those kids are just a kind of machine*, I thought.

We deserved a few calming minutes watching the sun set, even though I hated beaches. The sand always got in my fur, and I disliked water now. Despite all that, I had a good time with everyone. We made sandcastles, dug moats that were dangerously deep, and covered Marlene half in sand after she fell asleep. She must have been used to that, working in the fields every day, because when she woke up she wasn't fazed. Finally, the sun set and we decided to head back to our cabin.

Jeremy didn't fall asleep this time, even though he rode on Alison's back the whole way. All he wanted her to do was fly really fast. They compromised, and she sort of floated her way back so they didn't get too far ahead of the rest of us. I was happy the little boy was opening up to us now. He kept asking Alison a lot of questions: how her armor worked, why she was the first Bionics test subject, if she remembered her family, and things like that. Alison wasn't afraid to answer; she had told us her story last night while he was sleeping. Her armor she had a hard time explaining, but she told everyone that she had siblings like Mark did. She said she had a pair of twin siblings and a baby sibling; a brother, she thought.

"What were their names?" Jeremy asked innocently.

Looking distraught, Alison confessed, "I don't know. For some reason, when I woke up after the surgery, I couldn't remember."

Mark seemed especially confused by this. "That's weird. They were probably just hidden in your brain after it went into shock. After all, your family must have been the last thing you were thinking of when you were hit by the blast. Is there something that might trigger you to remember?"

Thinking for a second, Alison replied that she was unsure. "Maybe if I saw a picture of them or even a name, that might help. Isn't it odd that we don't know our last names?"

"I have a few theories about why we don't," Mark told us, "but those are stories for another day." He sure did have a lot of theories.

We reached the cabin and got ready for the night. We ate our lame sandwiches and took turns freshening up in the stream out back. That was really 'roughing it,' as people say, but at least we smelled a little better. After we were all finished, we tucked ourselves in and started writing in our logs as we were told to.

And now here I am. I actually don't mind my teammates so much. They are all cool people, and I am beginning to feel comfortable around them. I am going to be depressed when we won't be able to see each other again for another year. Maybe I can ask Mr. Mallory, or ask Alison if she can talk to Mr. Nik since she knows him, if we can regroup maybe once more before the next meeting. That would be enough for now.

# Chapter 12

## Aaron: IV

I hate hate *hate* this ridiculous Challenge! The first two days were bad enough, and today my group had to fight one of the strongest teams of all. Am I happy we made it to the finals? Yes! Am I disappointed we lost when we had fifteen teammates and they were only a team of six? *Maybe!*

After the crazy challenges from days one and two, we thought we were ready for anything. I mean, come on, we made an army of tiny blasting robots out of scraps! We thought that was pretty good. I mean, sure, they went crazy and fired on a nearby team, who destroyed them mercilessly. But other than that, totally fine! We felt less embarrassed when we heard that other teams fired on each other as well. Maybe that was part of the Isle Keepers' plans. They were watching from somewhere.

Anyway, this is how the third day went down.

Thankfully, we had Yared, the representative of Seers, on our team. He was the self-proclaimed leader. No one minded. He had experience. However, a huge surprise was that he wasn't very strict, like the other Seers members. He asked everyone's opinion on the challenges, and we all worked together, but he made sure we all stayed in a group and cooperated.

"All right everyone, Bionic Bob just received another message!" Yared called the third morning.

Bionic Bob was the nickname of Robert, one of the younger Isle I members. We weren't sure if he liked being called that, but we did it anyway. All the Bionics wore complicated armor to try and match their no-longer-organic body parts. He had lost both of his arms due to a form of torture he underwent when he was taken by the Invaders. That happened five years ago, when he was eight; thankfully, he was found and brought here.

I shuddered at the thought. *What a tragic experience that was.*

"Ready for the message? It's a long one," Bionic Bob started. Once everyone was quiet, he cleared his throat and read what it said: "'*Good morning, everyone, and welcome to Day Three of the Isle Challenge! Surprise! You have been tested ever since you sat down for introductions. Now, the next phase is the most difficult of all. This evening, after you get some practice in, we are going to see how well you can work together as a team in a life-or-death scenario. After that... well, we will discuss what happens once we determine the winners. Good luck!*'"

"Well, things just got worse," I mumbled.

Apparently Bug Boy, that kid Lucas, heard that, because he rebuked me. "Hey, four-eyes, don't worry. I'm sure things will be fine. I mean, it's not like we'll be facing off against our mates purposely this time, so no sweat."

Okay, first problem with his statement: He calls me "four-eyes" when he technically has one hundred eyes in each of his giant eyeballs. I'm sorry, but he was frightening to look at. When he got comfortable around us, he kept his goggles off and let them hang loose around his neck. Anyway, the second problem with his statement: man, was he dead wrong.

After Bionic Bob finished relaying the message, Yared had us train for this surprise "life-or-death" scenario challenge, which was a real hoot. The Seers had us running laps around our meeting spot and practicing basic fighting skills.

# AARON: IV

Our group met on the awful desert terrain. We always had to find streams to gather fresh water, because we weren't allowed to head back to the cafeteria until we were told to. I really felt like we were surviving on our own in the wild, even though we were technically in Isle III's backyard. Finally, our ridiculous training ended and lunchtime came around. Packed lunches were waiting at the cafeteria for about an hour before we got to them. It took us a while, because a few of the younger members passed out on the way there.

We were expecting the disappointment of a lonely sandwich and a mini water bottle when we peeked inside our paper bags. To our surprise, we were given an enormous apple, almost the size of Bug Boy's eyes, and a candy bar along with the sandwich and a tall bottle of water. "Save the apple and half of your water for later," Yared suggested. "You never know what kind of situation we'll be getting ourselves into."

Complaints were heard from a few of the younger kids, but they did as they were told. We sat down in the grass, ate, and rested. About an hour after we finished, Bionic Bob received another message: It was time for our final challenge to begin. Our only directions were to head to the shoreline and await further instructions.

Arriving, we noticed that another team was waiting at our meeting spot, claiming it was theirs. Yared started conversing with their designated representative, who happened to be Winfrid, one of the Overlords. A quarrel began to break out. Naturally, the two most hard-headed teenagers out there decided to try and negotiate. I didn't see what the problem was, but apparently, the shore wasn't big enough for both teams. As if feeding off the negative emotions, the younger members of both sides started to bicker for no reason.

After the arguments began to intensify, the members in charge of messages from both teams received identical instructions. The squabbling was put on pause to discuss the commands. "*Match 1. Fight until there is a victor. One rule: no killing.*"

Mixed emotions flowed through the participants on both sides; rage, confusion, and fright predominated. I felt more concerned than anything else. *Why would anyone listen to such a terrifying order?*

I wondered. I didn't think anyone in their right mind would begin to hurt one another for no apparent reason. Sure, we were bickering, but that didn't mean anything. But apparently, I was the only logical one on both teams, because they *all* began to fight. I was unsure of what to do, so I stood there awkwardly while the rest of my team rushed into action.

Yared barked orders like a king leading his army in battle. He had a good strategy, but Winfrid's members were stronger than ours. Team Winfrid had twelve Islanders while Team Yared had fifteen, but Winfrid's were older. Our youngest was about ten or so, poor kid. I saw one of their Mutant members, who was Spliced with the genes of a Ram, chasing after our little Asset.

Acting on instinct, I pulled the boy out of the way and let "Ram-Man" slide across the sand, causing a collision with some of his own teammates.

The three Mutants on our team fought empty-handed, while the others used whatever weapons or tools they could find or had brought with them. The Saviors used their medical utensils. Yared and the other Seers used pistols and gave the extras they had to me and the two others from Isle III. Our three farmers from Assets used anything from hedge scissors to shovels.

Yared was a raging tornado and did not stop until the battle was won. Bionic Bob threw Team Winfred members into the ocean. If his aim was off, Bug Boy was flying nearby to fix that. It was interesting to see Bionic Bob go one-on-one with Ram-Man. *I'm really coming up with awesome nicknames for people today,* I thought, as I mentally tagged my friends and opponents.

The fight went on for about twenty minutes. Unfortunately, blood was shed and people were seriously injured; pistols will do that. A few of the members lay unconscious on the ground; the rest kept fighting. Whenever I fired a shot, it was always to the legs. I was blessed with having good aim; a slip like that could have led to disaster. I stuck with the kid from Assets that I saved from the Ram-Man. We hid behind bushes that lined the far edge of the beach. Thankfully, we had a few moments to catch our breath now and then.

# AARON: IV

The boy sat with his back to the leaves, while I carefully watched the inhumane commotion. Clutching a large shovel to his chest, he looked up at me with gray eyes and thanked me. "Gee, I really appreciate what y'all did for me back there."

Without looking down, I replied, "It was no big deal."

Sitting up straight, he responded, "No big deal? Shoot, you saved my life. I'm Donald, but people call me Donnie." He held out his dirty, callused hand for a handshake.

Hesitantly, I shook it and introduced myself. "Aaron. Pleased to meet you, Donnie."

After our short rest, Donnie began to prepare to jump back in the fight. He straightened his ripped denim overalls, tied his bootlaces, and held his weapon tightly. "Oh, I almost forgot!" he exclaimed a little too loudly. He reached into his knapsack, which was about as large as he was, pulled out a small wooden bucket, and put it on his head, covering his short, dirty-blond hair. He most definitely was a farm boy.

I smiled and knocked on the bucket. "So, are you ready?" Donnie asked.

"I guess so, but I don't like this," I confessed, adjusting my glasses.

Agreeing, he replied, "Me neither, but that's what the instructions told us to do. So, we should do it."

*Geez, that's his mentality?* I judged. I hoped the others had better reasons for following the order.

Counting down from three, we jumped out from behind the bush and ran into the fight, but we were a bit too late. Team Winfrid had already surrendered. All their members were on the ground, coloring the sand and ocean with their blood. Every one of their kids was covered in bruises, cuts, gashes, and there were a few with broken bones, teeth marks, bullet holes, and… unimaginable things. I saw people I knew writhing on the ground in pain. Winfrid looked the worst; you could actually see his skull through a dent in the back of his head, and his right arm seemed to be almost detached. Yared and his army must have been beating on his right side pretty badly.

Suddenly, there was a whirring in the distance. Looking over,

I saw five sand buggies carrying three adult staff members to the scene. Without saying a word, they stopped before us, retrieved all the members of Team Winfrid, and prepared to leave. We shouted to them, asking for answers. A few of our team members even got in their faces and screamed. We received no response; they ignored us. They said nothing, made no eye contact, and drove away, leaving us and *our* wounded behind.

"Well, this is just great!" Lucas complained as he frantically flew in circles. "First, they tell us to beat up our mates, and then they come and take them all away without saying anything! Some of 'em are probably dead, and we didn't bloody know when to stop!" Directing the blame to Yared, he began ranting and raving. "Yared! Why did we even listen to the message in the first place? There was no purpose in all that! We should not be out for blood, especially when it's blokes we know! What's the gain?"

As Lucas was yelling, I felt my own blood boiling in agreement. However, I kept quiet, determined to listen to both sides of the story.

Calm and collected, Yared breathed hard through his nostrils. "Because it had to be done," he chided. "I have a good idea why they want us to do this, and I have a feeling it won't end well if we don't respond to the maximum each time."

Finally, I exploded. "Well, what do they want us to do?! I am sick of their secrets! Don't any of you find any of this suspicious? You *do* know we don't have to listen to them!"

"Yes, we do!" Yared bellowed back. "Don't you understand? *They are in charge of us.* They basically have control over us. Yes, I find it suspicious. No, I don't agree with their ways. But if we don't do what they say, we won't be here to find out the truth." Coming over, he stood in front of me and stared me in the face. Even though I was several inches taller than him, he still intimidated me. Jabbing his strong, dark finger into my chest, Yared gritted his teeth and whispered, "I know some of you 'smarter' fellows think that the Seers are all brawn and no brain, huh? Well, I may not remember my life before this, but I know when *something* is wrong. But we always have to stay on our toes and follow orders." He let out a deep breath, backed away, and concluded, "Now, let's move on."

To be entirely honest, I wasn't expecting that from him at all. I'd always felt like all the Seers were brainwashed into thinking what the Keepers wanted them to. Probably for two reasons: One, we provided some funky technology for them that I have never seen before and that seemed dangerous to humans. Two, the younger members seemed to be quick to defend everything the Keepers say and do.

So after that, we did what the instructions told us to, with no complaints.

We had about five more fights that day. Luckily, they were shorter, because each team we went against had fewer members than normal due to injuries. I thought we would have more fights than we did to reach the "final match," but some of the teams still in the running collapsed of pure exhaustion before even reaching the battlefield.

It was dusk when we finished the second-to-last fight. The final one was scheduled to begin at dark, back at the first field behind the facility. We waited in agony for the sun to go down and the moon to come out.

Finally, the time came for the last match.

When we arrived, the field was lit with stadium lights, and not a soul was to be seen. Taking advantage of the opportunity, Yared went over the battle plan with us. I still thought what we were doing was ridiculous, but we had no choice except to continue.

The plan was to do a tag team battle. Seven people would fight first. If they got tired, they would swap out with the other eight. At the end, when the opposing team was weakened, we would all charge at once. Yared predicted that there had to be about eighteen members on the team we would be fighting. How else would they have gotten so far?

Suddenly, without warning, we were being shot at. Thankfully, no one was hit. Either they were warning shots, or someone had terrible aim. Scrambling about, our team took whatever cover we could find. "Stay calm. Stick to the plan!" Yared yelled frantically. *He* didn't look calm. After the shooting stopped and we judged it was safe, we stepped out in the open to once again see no one.

"Where are they?!" Lucas yelled as he flew around scanning the area. "I can't see them! That's a problem." He was right. If a bug with much more peripheral vision than a human couldn't see the enemies, then we were in trouble.

Grabbing my pistol tightly, I aimed it at anything that began to move.

"Come on out, you cowards!" one of the girls yelled. She tried to sound confident, but her voice cracked mid-sentence.

"You want us to come out?" a grisly girl's voice said, echoing off the facility's walls.

Suddenly, the outside lights began to flash on and off like a scary horror movie. A high- pitched screech pierced our ears over the loud speakers. A few of the younger members began to scream, and some started to cry. Yared began to scold them, but he cut off mid-yell. We all called for him, but there was no answer. When the lights flashed back on for a second, we saw his pistol and knife lying where he had been standing.

Then, the lights stopped flashing and remained off, giving us only moonlight to see by.

Without warning, our team members began to disappear one by one. It started with the ones in hiding, and then those standing in the field. Even Bug Boy went missing after a few minutes. I wasn't going to go without a fight, though, and neither were my three teammates that were left. Donnie was still there, so he ran up and stood back-to-back with me. "Don't worry, Aaron, ain't no way they'll use trickery to get us."

"I appreciate your bravery, Donnie, but I think they have us out-numbered," I told him, looking around. "There's no other way they could kidnap all our friends that fast."

I felt Donnie's body shaking, and I heard his head clanging against his wooden bucket helmet.

"Surrender yet?" the girl's ghastly voice called out, breaking the silence.

"Never!" I bellowed without hesitation. "It's time you show

yourselves and fight us face-to-face!" My remaining teammates shouted in agreement.

The voice chuckled unnervingly. "Sure about that? That wouldn't be fair... to you."

Surprisingly, Donnie challenged them. "Enough! I'll take y'all on by myself; do yer worst!"

The voice seemed as amazed as I was. "Oh? All right, then, have it your way. We'll send out our fighters, but one at a time. Here comes the first."

I heard a low growling to my left. Looking over, we saw a mysterious black figure emerge from the shadows and open its piercing, luminous eyes. Immediately, Donnie ran to the center of the field to face it. Grasping his shovel, he dropped into a low stance as he approached the creature. "Gimme all ya got!"

His opponent stared; then the white glow of an eerie smile shone in the dark. Donnie began to sweat and shake.

Then, the creature charged.

My young friend froze where he stood. Intending to protect him, I tackled the black figure before it got close. Believe it or not, I actually did that! It must have been the adrenaline rush. We rolled a few feet before the Mutant got up. Shocked, it stood there staring at me awkwardly for a few seconds. "I don't think you were the one who challenged me," a female voice said.

*It's a girl*, I thought, embarrassed. *This is awkward.*

"Uhm... I'm sorry, but I couldn't let you do that to him," I apologized. "He's just a kid. I challenge you now: hand-to-hand combat."

I could see her toothy smile again. "Fine, but let's make this quick. We're running out of time." She punched my gut without warning, and the pounding pain went from my stomach all the way to my head. I was so taken aback that I fell over, gasping for air. My glasses had flown off. For a few seconds, I groped around the ground looking for them. Finding them, I wiped the dirt off and put them back on. "Huh...I guess I won," she mocked, and prepared to charge at another member of my team.

Despite the pain, I pounced on her and pulled her to the ground. I sat atop of her and began throwing punches at her face. At the time, I didn't care she was a "she," but now I kind of feel like a jerk. Thankfully, she blocked most of my attacks and threw me off. Jumping to her feet, she charged, and we sparred. We had a straight two minutes of punching, kicking, scratching, and even biting. The scratching and biting was all her, by the way.

While this was going on, I didn't realize that my three other team members had been taken. I did notice when the lights flashed back on, but when they did, neither I nor Cat-Woman expected it. We both covered our eyes, but she hissed. Recovering quicker than she did, I side-kicked her in the stomach, and she went flying.

It was a pretty cool move, actually, but I feel bad about it now.

"Oh…Aaron, is it?" the creepy voice said.

At the sound of my name, I frantically turned 360 degrees. "Who said that?! Where are you?! Where is everyone?!" I hollered desperately.

"Don't worry, they're up here!" she called.

Looking up, I saw on the roof of the facility what looked like a fishnet filled with tied and gagged people. They'd captured all my teammates.

"Let them go!" I pleaded.

"Not until you surrender," the girl said again, but this time she seemed to be closer. In fact, she stood behind me, helping her cat friend up, I discovered as I turned around. When I looked at her, I got this weird feeling. She was an older Bionic girl with a strong build. She wore armor; I couldn't tell which parts of her weren't flesh. She had short white hair and piercing gray eyes that looked at me with an odd mixed impression of compassion and intimidation.

Finally, the rest of their team came out and stood by the two girls. I thought thirty or more were going to come out, but there were only four other people.

My heart stopped when I saw their tallest member. "M-Mark?" I stuttered.

He gave me a kind smile and said, "Hey, kiddo. I don't want you to get hurt any worse, so just surrender, okay?"

Still in shock, I took the gun out of my holster, threw it to the right of me, and put my hands behind my head. "Good," he said, sounding relieved. "Now, let's get your friends down and get back to our cabins."

"Wait, that's it?!" I bellowed, "Just like that? No more instructions, just 'Head back to the cabins'?"

The other older boy, that Saviors' representative, answered before Mark. "We already received orders, and so did your team. Alison, can you recall for Aaron what the message was?"

*Alison*, I thought over and over in my head. Why she struck me so much more than the others, I had no idea... Well, except the crazy cat-lady who struck me physically.

"The summary of the message was that we had to end it quickly," she explained, "because they already knew you would lose. Then, we were to head back to the cabins, rest, and heal. Tomorrow, both of our teams are going to meet with all seven Isle Keepers to discuss what this whole thing was about."

I didn't want to leave without answers, but we had to.

The girl Alison and the two other girls, Cat-Woman Sami and Farmer Marlene, freed my comrades from the net. The Saviors' representative asked his fellow Isle Members if they needed help with the wounds of their team; no one had any except me, so no help was needed. Yared wasn't very pleased that he never got to fight, but he kept quiet and led us back to the cabin. The opposing team remained in the middle of the field discussing something before they left.

Now, here I am here in bed, all bandaged up and more confused than ever. Why did they fight so humanely? How did they do that? Also, I'm upset that Mark was on the other team. I am just so angry with him. I'm glad I didn't have to fight Cecil. If I feel like this with Mark, I wonder how I would feel having fought Cecil too.

Another thing was crazy cat-lady, Sami. Sami seemed to give me such dirty looks after I surrendered; I get the feeling she doesn't like me very much. I can't blame her. I did kick her in the stomach pretty hard. She was super-cool about it, though.

Lucas seemed to have some connection with her. Once he was freed, he flew to her and started arguing. Lucas seemed more upset than the rest of us, not at all understanding. Maybe how he feels about Sami is how I feel about Mark right now. He was just able to express it in words to Sami's face.

Alison, on the other hand… something about her just gave me a weird feeling. Not sure what it is; I never felt like this with anyone else. Ugh, this is going to annoy me forever. It's definitely not love, I can tell you that. Maybe I'll get some answers tomorrow.

# CHAPTER 13

## Alison: V

So, last night's "Final Challenge" was successful, even though that one was mostly improvisation. The other battles stuck to the plans step-by-step, but that kid Aaron messed up the last one. Nonetheless, no one got seriously hurt, and we won. So, mission success.

Today's meeting with the other team and the Isle Keepers was a different story.

Waking up this morning, we were happy that the challenges were done. The last few days of our week here are dedicated to associating with everyone and discussing other matters. As for how we were physically feeling, we were okay—except for Sami, who was still recovering from last night's fight. All she did that morning was complain about that Aaron kid. She wouldn't talk about anything or anyone else. I tried to ask her what her friend Lucas was babbling about to her last night, but she just kept talking about Aaron. If I didn't know better, I'd think she was becoming obsessed with that spiky-haired geek. But I kept quiet and didn't say anything.

We headed to the facility to pick up our food bags. There weren't many, and we got there within twenty minutes of receiving our instructions. *Maybe the other teams got different directions,* I thought.

Finally, the team we beat last night showed up. Their leader, Yared, walked up and immediately started yelling at me. Why me, I'm not sure. We didn't have a leader, and if we did, it would be Mark.

"You and your team are complete cowards!" he sneered. "You think that was *fighting* last night? If our weakest member hadn't surrendered, you all would be so full of holes you wouldn't know what to do with yourselves."

Hearing this, Aaron kept his head down.

"You're the weak ones, not my team!" Yared shrilled. "You don't deserve to call yourselves victors." He gritted his teeth and threw a punch at me.

Unfazed, I nonchalantly grabbed his fist and began to squeeze until he squealed. "We were doing what we were supposed to, with minimal bloodshed. They said no killing, so we took that as our top priority. Injuring one another falls in that category. If you don't like it, I can give you something reasonable to yell at me about." I threw his arm to the ground and his body followed.

"That was a nice comeback, my dear Alison," Mr. Allaway's voice rang out from the loudspeaker. I smiled. Mr. Allaway always had my back. "Grab your food bags," my Keeper instructed, "and come into the cafeteria."

We were told to sit on the stairs leading up to the second floor. Our team sat to the Keepers' left. I felt like we were in a time out.

Mr. Nik had the floor first and began by congratulating us. "Words cannot express how pleased I am with these results!" he said happily. "Before I explain why you're all here together, I would like the winning team to explain to us what their battle strategy was for last night! It was incredibly unique and unbelievably effective."

Unanimously, we all decided that Mark should be the one to explain it. He headed down the stairs and received the microphone from Mr. Nik. Before giving it to him, though, Mr. Nik looked surprised to see him. Then, he shook off whatever he was thinking and gave the microphone to our friend. The Keeper of Isle VI, Mr. Mallory, gave Mark a wink. From behind Mr. Nik, Wally scrutinized Mark's every move.

# ALISON: V

*What's that all about?* I wondered, noticing the subtle reactions.

Ignoring them, Mark began, "Hello, everyone, I'm Mark if you don't already know that. So here is what my team and I had in mind last night for, um… well, beating you. Every time, we based our fighting strategies on one thing: no one gets hurt. The easiest way to achieve this was to kidnap you all and force you to surrender. Our advantage last night: the dark. However, we had some doubts about the plan. For example, your advantage: number of members. Thankfully, you solved that problem for us by using the 'tag-team' tactic.

"Here are the steps of our plan, in brief. Step one: kill the lights to provide an eerie, ghostly effect. Alison did a terrific job with that. Step two: capture opponents. The more we minimized your numbers, the more confused you would become, and the easier it would be to win. Step three: maintain captives. That was the hardest part; some of you really did give us a fight, especially Yared, Lucas, and even Donnie; I still have a bite mark in my arm from that little guy.

"Anyway, Marlene created what seemed like a large fishing net out of some leftover chains and ropes from the catapult we made the first day. Ethan was in charge of taking out the members with a non-toxic sleeping gas. Then he would gag them and place them carefully in the net. If they gave us trouble, Jeremy clonked 'em on the head. For anyone that happened to, I'm truly sorry. Step four: force remaining members into surrender, which in the end was just Aaron. I have to hand it to him: he held off for a long time.

"That sums up our plan. You guys were awesome opponents and definitely put up a fight. Thank you."

We were the only ones who genuinely applauded; most of the other team just sat there, a bit dumbfounded. After returning the microphone, Mark ran back and sat down with us.

"I hate to be so redundant," Mr. Nik started, "but wow, you guys are quite intelligent! You are going to be helpful in the near future. Now, do any of the members of Yared's team have any questions that were not answered?"

No one, not even Yared, raised their hand.

"No? Okay, that's fine! It just saves time," he said with a grin.

"Now you may eat your breakfast while intermingling with each other. The food counter is open for dessert. I believe both sides have earned it. In a little while, the rest of the teams will be joining you for a few days of relaxation, so enjoy!"

Then, he and the other Isle Keepers, who were just awkwardly standing there, exited the cafeteria. It was a weird silence at first, but then people began to open up.

Lucas and Sami were talking again. It was a real shock to see Lucas properly introducing Aaron to Sami. I was so proud. I hoped she would forgive him. He seemed to be apologizing an awful lot. I know it wasn't my place, but I went over and butted in anyhow.

"Hey, uhm, sorry about last night, I was just doing my job," I overheard Aaron say.

Sami didn't even look up from the cup of tea she cradled in her hands… err, paws… hand-paws… Anyway, she didn't even look up when she told him it was fine.

"Are you sure? Because I feel like kind of a jerk," Aaron asked, his face as red as beets.

"I said don't worry about it!" she snapped. That wasn't really like her. She was always kind and a little timid. Something about Aaron brought out a different side of her.

Feeling like Sami was being rude, I put my hand on her shoulder and whispered, "Sami, he is genuinely sorry. I think he deserves to feel forgiven by you saying it nicer." Surprisingly, it felt sort of normal to boss her around like that. After opening up to all of them about my past, I felt my teammates were like my siblings.

"Okay," she sighed. "I forgive you, Aaron. It really wasn't a big deal. I did the same to you."

He let out a deep breath. "Thank you," he said, relieved, fiddling with his glasses.

"Yay, we're all friends again!" Lucas exclaimed with a smile. "Now, why don't we sit down and wait until the rest of our mates get back?"

I sat at their table until the others returned. At first, I felt a bit awkward, being three years older than them, but I kind of got used to it. We talked about our lives on the Isles and about our particular jobs or responsibilities, if we had them. Aaron's life was interesting but sounded stressful. He and the other "Overlords", whatever those were, were the ones working behind the scenes.

After we chatted for a little while, Mark came over and sat by Aaron who suddenly became quiet and refused to look in his direction. Apparently, the two of them had grown close since they passed the Commencement Tests together. Mark told us later that he always saw Aaron as a younger brother; maybe that's why Aaron felt betrayed. Before Mark could even say something, however, an announcement came over the loudspeaker. "Would the six victors from last night and Aaron of Isle III please head to the homeroom of Stratum Zero? That is all, thank you."

We were all so confused. I was glad Aaron and Mark knew where they were going; the facility was so big. The rest of us would lose our way just looking for the bathroom. Quietly, Mark told us that we needed to use the second entrance. Most of the kids were crowded into the cafeteria, where the first entrance was; that would cause a scene, no doubt.

Walking down a long hallway past a dozen empty classrooms on the second floor, we finally reached the door. It was hidden behind a large, vain painting of Mr. Nik. The painting scared me. Whenever I saw it, I wanted to set it on fire or shoot it with a missile. His dark, menacing eyes seemed to pierce my very soul.

Sorry, that was a bit extreme, but that's how I feel about that portrait.

Mark tapped a few parts of the wall next to the painting. It made a *ding*, and a retinal scanner emerged from the wall. Once it finished scanning his blue eyes, the painting slid into the wall and opened a door behind it.

All seven Keepers had been waiting for us. Mr. Nik himself was standing in front of an electronic whiteboard, while the others sat at the counters towards the back of the room. Mr. Nik greeted us and beckoned us to be seated. Sami, Mark, Aaron, and I sat at one lab counter, while Jeremy, Marlene, and Ethan sat at the other.

# THE ISLES

"Hello again. Let me start by apologizing for the confusion you've encountered these past few days. All will be explained right now." He pulled up a presentation on the board. It displayed images of a map of the Mainland before the Invaders came.

"Before I explain the slides, know this," he said, pointing his remote at us. "Those challenges only served as evaluation tests. We wanted to see how you could respond in different, sometimes peculiar, battle situations. We don't stick kids in a stadium and make them kill each other just to satiate an audience's hunger for death. Unlike the leaders in that age-old story book, we actually value life. We said no killing, and you all listened. Yes, some teams put a few kids in comas, but they are not dead. That is the important part."

Pointing to the first picture, he continued. "This is what life looked like before the Accident."

It was a map of the world, or so I assumed. During all the years I've been here, I had never seen a map of the entire Earth before. It was beautiful. Seven names designated seven landmasses; they were colored green, and the water was blue. There was a lot of water, much more than land. A few black dots peppered certain parts of the map, but they looked insignificant. Then the slide changed, and we gasped. The small black dots spread across almost every square inch of the landmasses on the map. A few places had big red X's on them; others had yellow X's.

"I can guess you understand what this means just by looking at it," he went on, rubbing his bushy mustache. "The red X's are the places that have been completely destroyed using nuclear weapons. The black dots are the Invaders; and, as you can see, the Mainland is overrun. Thankfully, there are a few places remaining that people have fortified as safe havens. Those are the yellow X's. Most of them are large cathedrals that have underground catacombs that the Invaders have not yet discovered. In ancient times, you see, churches, temples, synagogues, and other places of worship were safe, because the enemies had respect for the religion and beliefs of the people. Because of this, many innocent civilians survived back then. But now we are not so lucky. No one cares anymore. The Invaders will do whatever they can to attain power."

The Headmaster stared at the map longingly. Snapping out of it, he continued, "Now: this map is from eight years ago, when we first started taking in survivors. That is where you come in. We need to compile a new map, take in new survivors, and hopefully take back the Mainland. I believe that with a few more months of training, we can cover and reclaim more ground than we ever thought possible. It is time. You passed some major challenges this week, and many others throughout the years you have been here. We believe that you all are worthy of leadership. In fact, we want you to be the leaders of your regiments."

That first part was a lot to take in. Then he just decides to throw in that lovely bit in the end. *Leaders of your regiments,* I wondered, *Is he kidding?*

Jeremy said precisely what we were all thinking: "Wait, what?"

The Keepers all laughed. "I know this is confusing for you," Wally said, adjusting his round glasses, "but you don't have to vorry about it, Jeremy. You vill probably be second-in-command to another member we have in mind. You are still very young. But since you vere part of the winning team, ve thought it only fair to include you in all this."

Mr. Nik agreed. "Yes, definitely second-in-command. For each regiment, there should be a lead command and two under him or her. If you were a little older, Jeremy, you would have been first. As for the rest, you are all qualified for command and to lead your entire Isle into combat. And there is at least one member from each facility here, so that makes choosing much easier!"

I felt my circuits frying. It was too much too handle.

"Relax, everyone, and just breathe. You're all too tense," Mr. Mallory remarked, pushing his long blond hair out of his face. "Breathe with me. Ready? In… and out."

Breathing with him didn't really help. It just made us feel awkward and like we were in therapy.

"Thank you, Carl," Mr. Nik said appreciatively. "Now, before I explain to each of you how this 'leadership' thing works, I am going to call you up one-by-one and give you your position and an item to help you stay in direct communication with all seven of us. You are going to need it when you take your first trip to the Mainland in a few days."

Circuits were still frying and breathing didn't help that. He said all that stuff, and then he just casually mentioned we were returning to the Mainland, where our enemies were running amok. *This guy is crazy,* I thought. *Not even like a little crazy; he's like super crazy.*

Mr. Nik waved to the six other Keepers to come stand at the front of the room. It always amazed me that the order they stood in was always the same—starting with Isle I's keeper, Mr. Allaway, and ending with Mr. Mallory of Isle VI. Mr. Nik stood in the center between Mr. Bamber and Mr. Calvin.

"First, we will call up the seconds-in-command who are present," Mr. Nik announced. "We will do it in order of Isle. First up: Aaron of Isle III. Come up to your Keeper and receive your bracelet."

*Seriously? A bracelet?* I thought, bitterly. *Is it a friendship bracelet? Are we braiding each other's hair now?*

Shakily, Aaron walked up to Mr. Bamber and was given his item: a metal bracelet packed with the technology of a supercomputer. Mr. Bamber whispered something inaudible in the boy's ear. Aaron returned to his seat and started fiddling with his new toy.

"Next up: Jeremy of Isle V."

Happily, the little kid jumped from his seat and went up to Wally. The boy stood at attention and saluted his Keeper. Wally saluted back and handed him the device. Before Jeremy could rush back to sit down, Wally bent down and whispered something in his ear, too.

Now I was starting to get curious, but I figured I'd be next, so I would know in a second. As soon as he was seated, Mr. Nik was ready to call up the first-in-commands, but he decided to do it counting down instead of up. I was disappointed.

"Sami, Isle VI," the Headmaster called. "Congratulations, you are now in command of everyone on your Isle—except your Keeper, of course." Everyone applauded as Sami slowly walked up to Mr. Mallory. He clipped the bracelet onto her furry wrist. Along with that, the Commander received a clipboard and a thick backpack. The clipboards were, are, like the ones the Keepers have. Before sitting down, Sami also had some secret whispered into her ear.

"Next: Marlene of Isle IV, Assets. We are skipping Seers, because we have not officially picked out the first-in-command yet. Sorry!"

Marlene went up to Mr. Calvin, and the exact thing happened to her as had happened to Sami, and the other members who went after. Finally, it was my turn, but Mr. Nik had a few extra things to say first. "I am not sure if all of you know this," he announced, "but Alison has been with us since the very beginning of our success. Throughout these eight years, we have watched her grow and develop in a way that words cannot describe. I believe I can say for all the Keepers what an honor it has been to have you here with us, Alison, and that we could not be prouder that you are the one qualified to lead Isle I."

Walking up to Mr. Allaway after that felt weird. I didn't know that he and the other Keepers were proud of me or anything. I thought I was just another experiment. *Now I'm not sure what to think of them anymore,* I thought.

To my huge surprise, before Mr. Allaway handed me anything, he gave me a big hug. When he pulled away, I noticed he was starting to tear up. *What a softie,* I thought with a grin on my face. He handed me the backpack with the clipboard inside, but no bracelet. He told me that whatever came in through the others' bracelets would come in through my eye-message-receiver-thing. He finally gave it a name, though. Either it took him a few years to think of it, or he just forgot until that moment. He called it the Optic Transmitter.

Anyway, before he dismissed me, he whispered one word into my ear: "*Pancakes.*"

I thought it was so funny; I started giggling uncontrollably as I went back to my seat. I could hear the Scottish Keeper laughing at himself as well. Here we are having this intense moment, and he whispers "pancakes" into my ear!

After I sat down and took out the clipboard, I understood what it was for. The first thing that my clipboard did was ask for a password. I typed in "pancakes." Sure enough, it unlocked. Everything seemed very confusing. The only things I could recognize were the names of all the Bionics. They popped up in order of arrival. I tapped my name, and various files came up. They included information about when I arrived, if anyone came with me, about my surgery, and so on. At the bottom of the screen, there was a button that said *Quick Message*. Just for the heck of it, I selected that, typed "Hi", and clicked send.

That text popped up on my Optic Transmitter milliseconds later. *I can send messages now?* I thought excitedly. I went back to the list, selected Axel's name, and sent him a message: *Hey, it's Alison, do you copy?*

Within seconds I got a response that popped up on my clipboard and my Optic Transmitter. *Alison? What? How do I know this is really you?*

I sent back a message saying that I would explain later.

After about fifteen minutes of us playing around, Mr. Nik brought the meeting to a close. "All right, now that you all have a little familiarity with your new devices, it is time to head back out and see everyone else. Also, commanders: while you are out there, I want you to talk to two of your friends that you believe are a good fit for your second- and third-in-commands, if they are not already chosen. We will be in contact much more than usual, and we will see you all tomorrow to discuss other things."

I knew I was going to pick Axel for my second-in-command and have already told him everything. I'm still deciding on my third-in-command, but I don't think I really need one. There are only fourteen of us Bionics, after all. Eh, I think I need to sleep on it. Today was too crazy and horrifying for me to think about anything else.

# CHAPTER 14

## Sami: V

Well, yesterday was surprising, and today was even more so.

Last night, I talked a little with Becca and Lucas about what had happened. They were stunned. I didn't have time to explain the second- and third-in-command positions, because we had to head back to our cabins with our groups. Today, I talked to them at breakfast about them taking those positions. "What, us? Seriously?" Lucas asked excitedly after I told them.

"Well, of course! You two are my best friends, and I trust you more than anyone else in our facility!" I replied.

Pushing her frizzy brown hair out of her eyes, Becca asked, "Are you sure you don't want some of the older members?"

"No way!" I argued. "Besides, I wouldn't know who else to choose."

"What about Zeke?" Becca suggested.

Turning around in my chair, I saw Zeke swimming around in his tank, flirting with the girls who were watching. They were all giggling and throwing food into his tank as if he were their cute little pet. I turned back around and disagreed—He seemed too obsessed with himself and girls to handle such responsibility. After convincing them to accept, I was called to meet the Isle Keepers in that secret classroom again.

Once we were all present, the Keepers sat with their Isle members and explained our roles and all the information on our clipboards. It felt weird that I had information on everyone who lives and has lived on my Isle.

Mr. Mallory sat next to me at one of the lab counters. Thankfully, he didn't smell as bad as usual; either that or I was used to his unique aroma. Placing his elbows on the table, he rested his chin on one of his fists and pointed to my clipboard with the other. "You see all these names here?" he said. "If you select a name, you'll be able to see almost everything about them. Go ahead, pick one."

I tapped on one of the first ones: Amanda. In her folder were a bunch of different facts about her: her brand number, age, position, health, and more. What really intrigued me was the fact that she wasn't a test subject. "Wait, people live outside the Isle VI facility? I was never sure."

Smiling, Mr. Mallory replied, "Yes, there are many people outside. We saved more than you think. They're usually the elderly folks who are too old for the facilities and couldn't stay at Saviors. Adult brains stop developing in their twenties; that's why we only teach children and teenagers. It's like the saying, 'You can't teach an old dog new tricks.'"

I never thought of the facility as modern day "school" before. *I guess that's why they sometimes call us students*, I realized.

"Oh! and if you tap here, you can see where she is and what she's doing," Mr. Mallory said excitedly.

I did as he said, and a map of Isle VI appeared. There was a red dot revealing Amanda's location, and a small camera button appeared in the corner. Out of curiosity, I selected that, too. Suddenly, the map became smaller and moved to the bottom right. Black and white surveillance footage appeared of an older woman in rags, sitting by a street corner selling flowers.

"Who is she?" I asked.

"Amanda is a nobody," Mr. Mallory replied in a gloomy tone, his green eyes locked on the old woman. "As you may be able to see from her surroundings, she lives in the ruins of one of the old villages that were originally located on Isle VI. Don't worry, not all of them are that shabby-looking. We'll do our best to fix up that town soon."

*I hope so,* I thought as I watched the poor old woman. I felt bad for her and the others living in that town. *But Isle III already has all their villages repaired and up-to-date, so why can't she just move there? Or why doesn't she move to one of the villages on Isle VI that's fixed?*

Even after the Isle Keepers finished teaching us what we needed to know, I kept pondering Amanda's situation. I conjured up an idea that, since I now have permission to basically go wherever I want, I would be able to visit her and take her to a nicer location.

Interrupting my thoughts, Mr. Nik said, "All right, everyone! I hope you all are familiar now with your new responsibilities and how to use your new devices. It is time for you to introduce to us the members you have chosen to be your seconds- and thirds-in-command. At this time, you will go out and prepare them to meet us. However, we won't meet here; we will be meeting outside in the field. See you all in fifteen minutes!"

Once he finished, all the students scurried out of the classroom and went to find their colleagues. Thankfully, Lucas and Becca were always together. They were relaxing at one of the cafeteria tables, playing cards with some other kids. "Hey, there she is," Lucas greeted as he casually stole Becca's poker chips when she wasn't looking.

"Are you two ready?" I asked, ignoring his thievery.

Taking a deep breath, Becca nervously replied, "As ready as we'll ever be."

As I led them outside, I explained that they had nothing to worry about, and that the Keepers were all very nice. "But what if we mess something up? What if we aren't really fit to assist your command?" Lucas questioned frantically as he tugged on his black cape.

"If they think I can lead, then you are definitely qualified to help me," I reassured him.

When we reached the field, we found everyone waiting for us.

Thankfully, they didn't mind us being late. Mr. Nik had us all sit in the grass next to the Keeper of our Isle. "Good choices," Mr. Mallory whispered to me.

Mr. Nik immediately had us begin introducing our second and third seats. Each commander was to stand up and tell everyone about those they picked. Isle I started us off. "Hello, everyone," Alison began, "This is my best friend, Axel." Axel stood next to Alison, rubbed his white curly hair with one hand, and shyly waved with the other.

"The reason I chose him," Alison continued, "was because he's been here as long as I have, and we've been best friends since the beginning. He's the person I trust the most out of the other Bionics." Everyone applauded and they sat down. I wondered why she didn't choose a third-in- command. *Maybe because there aren't as many people on Isle I as there are on the others,* I concluded.

The rest went up one by one and pretty much had the same things to say about the people they chose. It was either best friends, trust, or loyalty. Ethan of Isle II chose Zita, the other representative, as his second, and a fellow named Harold as his third. Harold was several inches taller than his short companions. His skin was tan, and neatly brushed blond hair covered his head.

Mark already had Aaron as his second for Isle III. They both decided to choose Cecil, another "Overlord," as their third-in-command.

Assets' new leader, Marlene, chose that boy Donnie as her second, and a young girl, Ava, as her third. Ava was an adorable child with caramel-colored skin and bushy hair that was tied up into pigtails. They were both around nine or ten years old. I didn't want to question why she chose such young members.

As for Seers, Jeremy was only the second-in-command; so the male representative of Isle V, Yared, was chosen to be first. I was surprised, since he was on the losing team. Apparently, Jeremy felt sorry for him and asked the Keepers if he could be first. Yared looked as excited as ever, though, and thanked Jeremy in his "speech." The female Seers' representative, Ursula, served as the third-in-command, which she did not look happy about. I guess she wasn't thrilled that ten-year-old Jeremy was ranked higher than her.

Last, but not least, it was my turn to stand up and introduce Becca and Lucas. Nervously, I began, "Hello, everyone, I am the new first-in-command of Isle VI, Sami, and these are the members I saw fit to be my second- and third-in-command. The reason I chose them was not only because they are my closest friends but also because of their skill sets." No one else had mentioned that yet. Taking a deep breath, I went for it: "Becca has cheetah blood running through her veins. She can reach speeds so fast that only machines can match her. Also, since she is a feline, like me, her hearing, sense of smell, and sense of touch are the best of the best. Lucas, on the other hand, has sight like none other. He sees everything, and he can fly. Also, dragonflies are known for their ability to take out targets with efficiency and pinpoint accuracy. Of course, Lucas has never tried that on a human before, but I assure you, if there is ever a need, he will not disappoint you."

With that I finished, and we sat down. Mr. Mallory gave me a thumbs-up. The other Isle Keepers also looked impressed. Once everyone was done, we spent a few minutes intermingling. We got along pretty well; the only time there were quarrels was when Yared started complaining to us about failing the final challenge. *Why is he whining?* I thought after he and Ethan had a disagreement. *He's head of Seers now.* One thing's for sure: Ethan knew how to stand his ground and defend his team. The Savior put the Seer in his place, and it was never mentioned again.

After about 45 minutes of chatting, Mr. Nik decided to get serious. "Now it is time to discuss our plans for you all. As the first-in-commands may know–"

"Excuse me sir," Yared interrupted, "can we find a shorter name than 'first-in-command'? I find it annoying."

Not upset, Mr. Nik smiled. "Of course. Let's see. Mr. Bamber?"

Mr. Bamber, who had fallen asleep, sat up abruptly in his wheelchair and yelled, "I am innocent!" Looking around a bit, he apologized, "Oh sorry, Nikita, were you calling me?" We all laughed. Not embarrassed, Mr. Bamber wiped the drool off his tie and wheeled over to Mr. Nik.

"Yes, you are innocent, and yes, I was calling you," was the Headmaster's rejoinder. "The first-in-commands want a new name for their positions. You are good at naming things; what would you suggest?"

Mr. Bamber fiddled with his tie while he was thinking. "Well," he started, "you could always call the second and third, the second and third seat, or just two and three. As for the first, you can simply be called 'commanders.' But that's too boring for you, isn't it?"

Yared was the only one complaining that it should be different.

"All right," the old man said, tapping his forehead, "well, some synonyms of commander are: administrator, director, captain, officer, kingfish, big cheese, head honcho, and top banana. There are more, but I'll be here all day if I go through them all."

"I like top banana!" Jeremy shouted without hesitation.

"I think we need something a little more professional, kiddo," Mark said.

"Why can't it just be commander, second seat, and third seat?" Becca questioned, scratching her hairy ear. "They are short and simple."

"Well, I agree with Jeremy," Marlene argued. "I enjoy bananas very much."

A few minutes went by with members arguing back and forth until Mr. Nik made the decision. "I appreciate your enthusiasm, but I will agree with Mr. Bamber's first idea; the one that Becca favors. Commander, second seat, and third seat are much easier to say and remember. That is what you will be known to us as; however, you may let your regiment call you whatever you wish."

Jeremy and Marlene looked ecstatic and gave each other a high five. "From now on, you can call me Top Banana," she addressed Donnie and Ava. Smiling, the second and third seats saluted their commander. Jeremy looked hopefully at Yared, who just shook his head with displeasure. Heartbroken, the boy slumped over and looked intently at the grass.

"Anyway, as I was explaining," Mr. Nik finally went on, "the first mission you all will be sent on is to the Mainland. It will be a sort of … test run. We need to know what is going on now so that we can be prepared to fight it. We will train you a little this evening, but we will do more tomorrow. When this training is complete, you will spend a minimum of three days on the Mainland."

Wally poked the Headmaster before he continued, offering him his clipboard. Taking it from his German friend, he tapped it a few times, showed us a map outline, and said, "You will only spend time in one area, so don't worry about mapping just yet. We will let you know what you are looking for while you are there. Oh, that reminds me." He waved to Mr. Bamber, who removed a box from a pocket in the side of his wheelchair. It contained more bracelets for the second and third seats. They were ecstatic to receive their new equipment. Axel was the only one who didn't need it, since it was all "in his head" already…literally. I tested Becca's and Lucas's by sending a message from my bracelet to theirs.

When he received it, Lucas exclaimed, "Crikey!" which was something I hadn't heard him say in a while. "This technology is incredible!"

"If you think this is good, you should see my clipboard," I teased. I actually wasn't allowed to show him; apparently, it was for commanders' eyes only. I found it odd, but I guess it was only fair.

After we fiddled with our equipment, Mr. Nik and the Keepers headed back to the Nerve Center where they would be sending us our orders. We waited almost a half an hour before receiving our first messages, sent from the Keepers to the commanders from their own Isles. Mr. Mallory's first message was this: *"Hello? Do you all copy? Reply if you get this message; if you don't then it didn't work."*

We told him everything came in okay, and he responded with a smiley face. Now the instructions came in: *"First: I sent you a location on your map. Get to it as fast as you can, any way that you can. Be stealthy about it as well."*

Stealthy won't be too difficult, I thought, looking up at the setting sun.

"Gah! We missed dinner again!" Lucas suddenly complained,

clutching his stomach.

"Don't be such a wimp. You have to learn to go without a meal or two from here on out," Becca rebuked.

"She's right," I agreed, "but now let's head to this place."

It was dark when we found a huge roadblock: the ocean. Mr. Mallory wanted us to head to a completely different island! Looking around, I noticed a few other groups in the same situation. They were also standing at the docks, confused.

"Which Isle do they want us to go to?" Lucas asked as he played around with his map. Thankfully, the bracelets—Mr. Nik forgot to name these too—were large, so the screens could easily be seen. They were four inches long, and the height covered the entire top of my wrist and was metal all around. It was more convenient than taking my clipboard out every five seconds.

"Assets," I finally answered, after tapping the bracelet a few times. "We're lucky. We got the closest one to here."

"But not close enough," Becca said. "You and I hate water, and Lucas can't fly us both across."

We stood there staring out into the distance before Lucas interrupted the awkward silence. "Why don't we steal a boat?"

Concerned, Becca asked, "Are we allowed to do that?"

Quickly tapping something on his bracelet, he replied, "We'll find out in a moment." It took less than a second to get a response.

"That's a bloody ripper!" Lucas exclaimed. "Mr. Mallory left keys in one of the speed boats for us, along with some supplies! There better be a lot of food!"

*That's a new one,* I thought. *Where are these weird interjections coming from?* Before I could ask him about his new vocabulary, Lucas flew as fast as possible to a worn-down, small speedboat that seemed ancient.

"This is the boat?" I demanded, disappointed.

Lucas didn't seem to care as long as food was there, even though Mr. Mallory sent a message telling him to not eat it just yet. "Found it!" Lucas called from inside. "C'mon, let's get over there! I want to eat!"

# SAMI: V

Becca and I hopped in. After three tries, the motor finally started, and we headed for Assets as fast as we could. The speedboat wasn't as speedy as I'd hoped, but we made do. None of us had ever operated a boat before. We almost capsized a few times before getting the hang of it, but finally, we reached the shore of Isle IV.

Walking inland, we were surprised as to what we found. We first came across a dozen warehouses. I expected more fields and farmlands. Reading my mind, Becca said, "I thought they all lived in little huts and sent things out by carrier pigeon."

Lucas chided her, "Nah, this is the outskirts, where they keep all the stuff they make for *us*. That's what it says on the bracelet-thingamabob. Have some respect for the providers of our food!"

Becca apologized sarcastically and rolled her golden cat eyes. "Okay, but seriously," I interrupted, "now what?"

"Why don't we ask?" Becca suggested while sending a message to Mr. Mallory. His response gave her a confused look. Addressing me, she said, "Um, he says that you're the commander, you think of something."

A cold sweat started to break out on the back of my neck. I felt it dripping down over my brand number and stripes. It was weird. I was part cat; I didn't think they could sweat. Anyway, the point is, I was as nervous as anything. Suddenly, Lucas's stomach made a sound like a dying whale, giving me an idea. "Why don't we find shelter, have dinner, and camp for the night?"

"Brilliant! I'm all knackered anyway," Lucas admitted.

Okay, now I *really* had to ask him where his new vocabulary came from. "Where did you learn all those new words? I mean you used some of them before. Now you're saying things I've never heard of."

He smiled. "Ever since I learned where I came from, I decided to research a little on it. I couldn't do much back at our own Isle, so I took a few books out while we've been at Isle III and started catching up. I found a great book called *What Aussies Say* and I've added a lot to my vocab list."

*Well, at least he's learning something*, I thought, shaking my head. "Just make sure you use those terms correctly," I told him.

"No worries, cobber," he replied. If he could still wink he would've.

We started scoping out the warehouses. There were about fifty of them lined up on the coast behind the docks. We chose one of the middle ones to explore. "It looks like the place where they made us wait to get experimented on all those years back," Becca observed.

She was right. It was built the same as the Laboratory, but had more shelves with boxes and food. Looking around, we didn't see a soul. "I don't think anyone's in here, but we should lay low anyway," I instructed.

"Let's make shelter on the highest shelf," Lucas proposed. "That way they won't be able to find us so easily if there are blokes here."

We all agreed and picked our shelf. Once we decided, Lucas flew up while Becca and I climbed the side. Settled in, I instructed, "We can't eat too much. We need to save some for tomorrow." Disappointed, Lucas grunted, threw the rest of his food in his bag, and covered it with his cape so he wouldn't be tempted. Once we were finished, I decided to take first watch. And by watch, I meant write in my record log while occasionally glancing towards the direction of any noises I heard. So now I'm going to wake up Becca for her turn. I didn't get to take a nap today, so I'm "all knackered" as Lucas would put it. My turn to sleep now.

# Chapter 15

## Aaron: V

Of course, Mr. Bamber told us to go to the island that was the farthest away. It took the entire night to get there. We needed our sleep but didn't get any. The day we'd had was insane and terrifying, and today was no walk in the park, and now I'm even more exhausted than before.

It was daybreak when we arrived on the shores of Isle II. Parking our boat, we ventured inland. We found an old abandoned village not too far from the ocean. The houses and markets of the ruined town had been reduced to ash. *The Invaders probably made this mess*, I thought, walking through. Thankfully, the locals inhabited the center of the island, where the Saviors' facility and main hospitals were located.

"All right, guys, let's see if there's anything left in this forsaken town that we may be able to use," Mark announced. "We're Overlords; we can handle it."

Before doing anything, Cecil asked the obvious question. "Um, what exactly are we supposed to do?"

"I've received instructions from Mr. Bamber. I've got it all figured out; you just follow my lead," Mark reassured us cheerfully.

I was suspicious as to why he wasn't telling us but trusted him anyway. We searched for a little while, but realized it was a waste of time. There was nothing there. Leaving the village, we came across warehouses and parking garages with a forest bordering the area. A paved road separated the trees and led to the facility and city where the modern inhabitants lived.

We snuck behind one of their warehouses and laid low. Mark suggested we climb in through one of the windows.

"Are you crazy?" Cecil demanded. "It's forty feet high!" I agreed with him.

Disappointed, apparently that we were no fun, Mark didn't ask again and led us around the front. Being early in the morning, there were only a handful of people around, but they were soon blocking our path. Seeing them, Mark clicked his tongue. "Dang. Any ideas?"

"We could go around through the forest," I whispered, pointing to the other direction.

Cecil, however, had another brilliant idea.

Mark reminded us to be quiet, but I wasn't so sure stealing one of their ambulances was being quiet. Cecil led us to the nearest vacant vehicle. The back door happened to be unlocked but didn't have keys inside. Mark and Cecil went in first and I followed behind, shutting the door. *Where is the gurney?* I wondered as I sat in the open space of the van, which felt as spacious as my room and had more storage. There were cabinets of medicine, drawers of first aid supplies, extra scrubs, and dangerous instruments… but no gurney.

"Why would they leave it unlocked?" Cecil asked, calling shotgun.

Hopping in the front seat, Mark said, "Ugh, because it was just used."

"How can you be sure?" I asked as I opened the door leading to where they were sitting.

Shifting in the seat, Mark replied with a look of revulsion, "Because this seat cushion is disgustingly warm."

While he hotwired the vehicle, I went through some of the drawers in the back. I found some medical masks, gloves, and red T-shirts. "Should we put these on, in case they make us stop?" I proposed, holding out the treasures I'd found. "There's no gurney back here, so I can't pretend to be injured."

"Good idea," Mark approved, taking the gear. "I was just planning to run 'em over if they tried to stop us." That made me glad I had found that stuff, because I wasn't sure he was kidding. We changed out of our blue shirts and put on the masks. The Keepers hadn't instructed us to change our uniforms to fight, so we were still wearing our "geek" outfits. Thankfully, ours didn't look much different from the Saviors'.

Getting the engine going, Mark began to drive towards the road. The natives looked at us suspiciously, but Mark gave them a friendly wave. They waved back and let us go.

"That was easier than I thought," Cecil said, with his mask still on.

"Yeah, I guess they get this all the time," I replied.

We drove away from the warehouses, through the woods, and finally into the city. Looking around, I saw tall brick buildings lined up on clean paved streets with trees planted in holes in the sidewalks. There were apartments and tiny shops filled with anything the inhabitants might need. No one was outside yet, due to the early hour, and everything seemed nice and peaceful.

"Reminds me of my first home," Mark whispered to himself.

After about twenty minutes of driving, sightseeing, and chatting about regular guy stuff, I decided to bring up the real topic. "Mark, I know that you're Commander and everything but can you just tell us what we're supposed to do? We *are* your second and third seats, after all. I thought there would be more trust."

Mark chuckled. "Man, of course there's trust! I just didn't want to tell you until we were on our way... or almost there."

"And why is that?" Cecil asked nervously.

Grinning, Mark replied excitedly, "Because we have to break into the facility control room."

Cecil seemed ecstatic. "Seriously? That's so cool."

I shouted, "No, that is *not* cool!" I thought about it for a second and said, "Okay, maybe it's a little cool, but it's also ridiculously dangerous! We have no idea what they do to intruders here. Scratch that; it's never *happened* before, so they won't know what to do."

Jokingly, Mark replied, "Yeah, they'll probably inject us with a heavy anesthetic, take out all our organs while we're alive, freeze us, and keep us as experimental cadavers."

Cecil began laughing hysterically, but I didn't find it funny. Seeing my disapproval, Mark rolled his eyes. "Someone's no fun," he muttered.

When Cecil was done with his laughing fit, he wiped tears away from his eyes and asked, "All right, besides the cadavers, what else are we here for?

"Not sure yet; we'll find out when we get there," Mark replied.

*Oh, how wonderful,* I thought. We were breaking into another Isle's control facility, and we didn't even know why.

Before anyone said anything else, we reached the heart of the city. We could see the sun rising above the facility in the distance ahead of us. "Almost there," Cecil said, pointing forward.

Peeking out the window, I looked again at the empty city streets. "Wouldn't you think that Mr. Nik would give the inhabitants vehicles to move around in?" I questioned.

Mark chewed on that thought for a bit, then gave his logical theory. He always had one. "My guess is a few things. Main reason is, they don't want traffic to back up when there's an emergency. Other reasons are because Dr. Agro wants to keep the people that they save healthy, and exercise is the best thing for that." Turning his head, he pointed out the window. "Look, there are people already up and jogging!"

*Quite a few people,* too. I observed as the groups of inhabitants jogged on the sidewalk opposite of us. They were folks of all ages, and most of them ran in military-style groups. I guessed it was probably part of their exercise regimen—if everyone was on the same plan.

Out of the blue, Mark pointed to a shop across the street. "Music store!" he shouted and looked at us excitedly. His blue eyes danced. "Can we stop there afterwards? I bet they have some stellar drum kits."

Shocked and taken aback, Cecil and I sat there and stared at him until he became uncomfortable. Clearing his throat, he apologized and locked his eyes back on the road. "Sorry, time to focus now." After a few minutes of awkward silence and glaring, he said, "Stop staring at me like I have twelve heads! I like music, okay? It's been years since I've played or heard it."

*I don't think I've ever heard it*, I thought, disappointed. Sad to say, but I don't think many people from the Isles were exposed to music. Maybe a song or two behind instructional videos, but that was it. I read in one of our books that music was part of the classical *quadrivium*: an older way of learning. I was never sure why they removed it from our curriculum.

Finally, after another period of uncomfortable quiet, we reached our destination. The Saviors' facility was enormous and closed in by high black fencing, giving it a nice yet creepy touch. The front of the building beyond the gate was domed and made of glass. An awning extended over the main doors with black letters on it reading "*SAVIORS.*"

"Wow, their facility looks just like a giant hospital," Mark observed.

"But shouldn't it be more like a medical school?" Cecil wondered.

"Maybe they believe there's no better way to learn than experience," Mark guessed.

I hoped that wasn't the case. I wouldn't want a bunch of ten-year-old students operating on *my* internal organs.

Slowly, we drove up to the gate. We were almost there when we hit a problem: ambulance drivers had to show their identification before they could pass through. Mark cursed under his breath and made a sharp right turn, going down a side street. I was so nervous I began sweating. "What do we do now?" I whispered.

Mark turned right once more, until we were at a street where the hospital was out of eyesight. He parked the ambulance in front of a doughnut shop, which was utterly inconvenient, because the smell made me hungrier than I already was. Looking at me in his rearview mirror, he said, "We just go in unseen."

He left it at that and climbed over me into the back. "Hey!" I interjected as he kicked the glasses off my face.

Not apologizing, he raided their supplies. He began to pack his backpack with random things: tape, gloves, test tubes, needles, titanium staples, and whatever else he could grab. "Don't mind me," he said, nabbing our backpacks and filling them without permission. *No, fill it with food,* I mentally begged while my stomach growled.

When he finished, he quietly opened the back door and looked around. The coast was clear. He hopped out of it and motioned for us to come with. Once we were on the sidewalk, Mark began to walk towards the hospital. "Wait!" Cecil called.

Mark froze mid-step with one leg in the air and turned around, remaining in that same position. He cocked his head sideways and gave Cecil a look that said, *What?*

Cecil pointed to the doughnut shop, like a little kid who'd found a toy they wanted.

After making a gagging gesture, Mark marched back and whispered to us, "One doughnut for you both, and then we go."

We both gave a quiet cheer and went in behind him. Thankfully, there was no one in there, and the manager didn't question why we'd parked an ambulance in front of his shop. He was just happy to see us. His shop was a little rundown but still functioning. The tables were wobbly, the wallpaper was peeling, and some light bulbs burned out, but he still managed to stock his shelves with delicious goodies.

Approaching the counter, I realized we had a problem. We had never been into the Isle cities! We had no idea what the currency was. "Mark, how will we pay?" I whispered.

Mark thought for a moment and then asked what the manager would like in exchange for two plain doughnuts.

"What do you have to offer?" the man said, putting on his stained apron.

Looking around, Mark noticed that some things in his shop needed fixing. "I have a brand-new screwdriver and about a hundred screws."

The manager's face lit up like a beacon. "I'll take it! But a hundred screws are too much for only two doughnuts!" He went back into the kitchen and came out with our order and a loaf of bread. "Here, take this as well," he said, holding it out. "It's fresh!"

Hungry, Mark gladly accepted it. Handing Cecil our breakfast, Mark reached into his backpack and gave the man the screwdriver and screws. "Thank you, thank you, thank you!" he repeated. As we left, the man bid us farewell and went to work right away with his new tool.

When we were outside, Cecil distributed the food. I was so glad we'd stopped. It was almost noon, and we were starving. Not wanting to waste any more time, we walked as we ate. I didn't think we were in that much of a rush, but we didn't stop. With his mouth full of doughnut, Cecil asked Mark some questions. "Mark, two things. First: Why don't you like doughnuts?"

Wrapping up the other half of the loaf of bread, Mark explained, "Because doughnuts are like sweets, and I don't really like sweets or desserts. If I can avoid eating them, I will. That's just me. What was the other thing?"

Licking his fingers, Cecil asked, "How did you know that you needed to trade instead of using paper money?"

Mark was hesitant to answer. "Well," he started, but didn't finish right away. Then, finally: "Mr. Bamber let me know." I got the feeling he was lying, but before I could pester him about it, we reached the fence of the hospital. "Time to get started," Mark told us as he went through his backpack.

"What are you looking for?" I questioned, wiping my sticky hands on my stolen red T-shirt.

"There are security cameras everywhere," he told me as he pulled out staples and tape from his bag. "We need to get around them." He flung his backpack over his shoulder and began walking. Following, we snuck along the fencing a bit until we came to an electric panel. "I'm pretty sure I can cut the power for a few seconds with this," Mark said, opening it. "This electric box is only for this section, so we have to be quick." Messing with the wires inside, Mark told us to be ready to climb on the count of three.

Cecil and I grabbed the fence and prepared. Once Mark

reached three, the race was on. We reached the top in no time but had a problem. It was spiked. Not worried, Mark chose a spot, laid his backpack across it, and then climbed over without getting hurt. "Smart," Cecil complimented after he and I did the same.

Hopping off the fence, I quickly checked my backpack. *No holes in it and nothing important is broken*, I thought as I took out a few shattered test tubes. As I was littering the ground with broken glass, Mark pulled up a map on his bracelet. When we were ready, he motioned us to follow him. We darted across the lawn up to the side of the building. Taking cover behind bushes, we looked around and saw a few Savior teens at the entrance to our left. They hadn't noticed us. Mark put his finger to his lips and moved forward, crouching. We snuck along the shrubs until we came to a back door.

Mark looked both ways, and we ran for the entrance. "Cover me," Mark whispered as he pulled out the clipboard Mr. Bamber gave him and plugged it into the keypad next to the door.

In no time, the lock clicked and the door opened. "That was fast," I marveled.

Saying nothing, Mark went inside. The wing we entered was still shut down from the night before. No lights were on, and no one was there. "This place scares me," Cecil whispered as we passed empty operating rooms. Paying no mind to him, Mark kept sneaking along. He acted like he'd done it a million times, because he sure knew what he was doing. I couldn't even hear his footsteps. He led us to a staircase and sent us a message on our bracelet-receiver-thingies: *Take out the gun-looking devices in your backpacks.*

*When did he give us weapons?* I wondered as I rummaged through my bag. Finding it, I realized that I had drafted the blueprints for them back at Isle III. They were sedative dart guns, thank goodness. They were as small and as light as a pistol, but held twenty small darts filled with a strong tranquilizing serum. When fired, they made absolutely no noise. I was kind of proud of that.

Before we went down the stairs, Mark mouthed us instructions. He told Cecil to watch from all directions and me to stay behind and defend us from the back. Slowly and carefully, we descended. After five flights, the lights in the wing turned on, and we found people: four guards and two doctors. Mark pointed to them and told us to get the doctors while he took the Seer guards. Before they saw us, we fired. Perfect shots to the arm, and they all went down. Mark ran down, started raiding the guards' pockets, and removed some of their clothing. "We need their uniforms," he quietly explained, "and their IDs in case we come to doors that require identification."

We pulled their pants on over our own, buttoned up their jackets, and wore their hats. We were all tall, but the uniforms were still too big for us. Seers are usually heavily built, I guess you could say. Nonetheless, we were dressed and could *maybe* pass as part of the staff.

"Now that we're properly disguised, we just have to act casual," Mark informed, shoving his lab coat into his backpack. Rolling up his sleeves, he continued down the stairs in a stiffer manner. We copied his example and followed him. Our disguises worked on several Saviors students, but we didn't fool the other Seers. I can't count how many we took out. *There aren't this many Seers at Isle III,* I thought as I kicked over an unconscious teen. *Why are they all here?*

Finally, after many flights of stairs and darts, we reached the underground level where the control room was. We halted in the hallway before the entrance. "Why did we stop?" Cecil whispered.

Mark jerked his head in the hallway's direction and mouthed, *Cameras.*

Unsure of what to do, I suggested, "Can't we shoot them?"

"They'll be able to see us aiming is the problem; otherwise that's brilliant," he replied, not wanting to make me feel stupid. "Besides, we can't destroy everything, as fun as it is." He pointed his thumb behind him to the shelves and desks we'd knocked over and demolished. It was mostly an accident. Mostly.

While Mark and I were discussing everything we'd broken, Cecil went through all the backpacks and started tinkering with a few things. When he was done, he returned our packs and told us to get ready. On the count of three, he threw his invention into the hallway. Hitting the ground, the contraption sputtered and began to emit a thick smoke.

"Rule Number One: When in doubt, throw smoke bombs," I said, smirking.

We covered our mouths and ran down the hall. Cecil and I kept watch while Mark accessed the door. In a flash, the keypad turned green and the door opened. Before the two guys at the desk inside knew what was happening, I tranquilized them. Just in case of more cameras, Cecil threw another smoke bomb. Mark rushed over to the computer and started typing in a bunch of crazy stuff. "Okay, the cameras are off for now," he said aloud.

From what I could see through the smoke, the room was much smaller than I expected. The computer banks covered the entire wall opposite the entrance, and there were file cabinets everywhere, filling most of the available space. *Their ambulances have more room than this place*, I thought as looked at all the drawers. You'd think that for a huge hospital, they would have a more spacious control room.

"Quickly, we don't have much time," Mark said, interrupting my gawking. Pointing, he instructed, "Go through those cabinets, and see if you can find documents with these titles: *Welcome to Saviors, Directory, Blueprints, Doctor's Manual,* and *The Saved.* I'll take what I can get off the computer."

Rushing to the cabinets, we searched frantically for the files we wanted. It was tough to see the tiny labels through the smoke, but we made them out. Each one was categorized by numbers zero through ten and then alphabetical within those groups. "What number is it?!" Cecil panicked.

"There are two numbers," Mark replied, not looking away from the computer. "Zero and one. The numbers stand for stages of development."

Cecil went for number one, and I went for zero. I found the last three things he'd said. They were *heavy*, each as thick as a dictionary. "Got them!" I shouted, almost dropping one.

"Me too!" Cecil yelled, holding up two thin books.

*No fair*, I thought jealous as I shoved the three dictionaries into my backpack. Zipping it up, I was surprised at how sturdy it was. *Please don't rip,* I begged it as I flung it on my back.

# AARON: V

Delayed, Mark finally called, "Cool, almost done here!" He rapidly typed on the keyboard. A few seconds went by before the computer made a beeping noise—and then an alarm went off. "Quick, we gotta get out of here!" Mark cried. Grabbing our things, we dashed out of the room, back out of the hallway, and up the stairs. All around us, red lights flashed and sirens sounded. Abruptly, Mark stopped at the top of one of the staircases.

Cecil ran into him and almost fell backwards, but I caught him. "Really, Mark?" I shouted, pulling my friend back to his feet.

"We should find another way out," Mark advised, ignoring my complaint. "They'll be blocking those doors." He pointed in the direction of the one we'd used to enter the building.

To be honest, I was as scared as anything. We'd broken into another island's facility, disturbed the peace, and taken their stuff. We could've gotten in big trouble. Thankfully, I wasn't the only anxious one. Cecil looked like he was about to cry. Mark, on the other hand, was cool and collected, as if he were used to this. *I just hope I don't pee my pants like I used to,* I prayed.

We waited at the top of that staircase for too long. Shouts from the guards could be heard everywhere. Children were crying; people were screaming. It was an awful feeling, knowing that we were responsible for all that chaos and terror.

"Let's go!" Mark finally yelled. We dashed down one hall, but were cut off by five guards. Each had lethal weapons pointed in our direction. Skidding to a stop, Mark shouted, "Next route!" We turned around and ran back, but they chased us. No matter where we went, we couldn't shake them; and more kept coming. They chased us down a corridor and had us cornered... sort of. We had two options: blow through the buff, graduated Seers or go down a hall filled with patients. Within that split second, Mark decided what we should do. "Stay low. Follow me!" he commanded. Grabbing Cecil's wrist who grabbed mine, he pulled us straight through the hallway filled with the poor sick people. As I was dragged through the hall, I looked around and realized that we were on a floor filled with children.

*Thank goodness,* I thought as we zipped passed a few gawking kids. They were easy to avoid, and if we scared them they would just cry and not die of heart attacks like old people. We passed a little boy on crutches who pointed behind us and yelled, "Hurry, they're coming!" as if he knew what we were up to. Reaching the end of the hall, we overlooked the lobby with the wall of windows at the front of the building. Without hesitation, Mark dragged us down the stairs, weaved through groups of Saviors, and led us out the door, barreling through a few still trying to keep us in. They failed their duties miserably as we tranqed them.

Once we were outside, we let go of each other and ran as if our lives depended on it. Rather than climbing over the fence, we dashed right towards front gate, as it was closing from an incoming ambulance. "We aren't going to make it!" Cecil screamed.

"We'll make it!" I yelled back, trying not to let the books fall out of my backpack. Sprinting like mad at the last second, we barely got through without being crushed. "Thank you, God!" Mark shouted to the sky as we ran right back to the doughnut shop.

We finally reached the store and found our ride was still there. "Oh thank goodness, the ambulance," Cecil said happily as we ran and jumped inside. Mark was sweating buckets as he hotwired it. Cecil yelling at him to hurry up didn't help. Finally, it started. Slamming on the gas, Mark drove off as fast as lightning. Unfortunately, I wasn't buckled in and flew into the back door of the vehicle. I hit my head so hard that I passed out.

When I awoke, we were underground someplace. Sitting up slowly, I looked down and saw that I was lying on a dusty kitchen table. I glanced around and saw cabinets against the grimy wall in front of me, and cartons of water on the floor all around. We sat in candlelight, which made it extra spooky. Cecil was to my left, holding the candle in one hand and his tranquilizer gun in the other. I was about to ask what had happened when he shot me a look and pointed upward. I realized what he meant when I heard footsteps and shouting.

Turning around, I saw Mark watching the ceiling like a hawk, clutching his dart gun so hard his knuckles turned white. I wanted to ask how long the other people had been above us, but I dared not distract my teammates.

After an hour, the others finally left. The footsteps faded, and the room was silent. Mark let out a long sigh of relief, as if he'd held his breath the entire time. He leaned back in his chair and rubbed his fingers through his full, short brown hair. "That was close," he muttered with his hands still on his face. Peeking out through his fingers, he looked at me with concern and asked, "You all right, kiddo?"

"Yeah, I'm good; head hurts, though." I rubbed my face and spiky hair and noticed my glasses were missing. "Whoa, wait, my glasses!" I said frantically, patting my face and the table around me.

"Don't worry, I got your back," Cecil said as he threw me my glasses. They were snapped in half in the middle.

Without warning, Mark threw duct tape at my chest, causing me to exhale sharply. "Now you can look like a real nerd," Mark said, winking.

I rubbed my chest, smiled, and taped my glasses together. After that, we remained in the bunker and relaxed.

Actually, we're still there now. It was evening when they were looking for us, so it must be dark by now. Cecil is asleep, and now Mark is waking up for his night watch. I should rest now. I hope tomorrow is a better day.

# THE ISLES

# CHAPTER 16

## Alison: VI

Well, the past couple days have been "fun." Breaking into Seers, picking fights with the toughest staff members, and then embarrassing them terribly was tons of fun. Now, we're hiding out in ruins on the Mainland; such a ball.

Anyway, quick recap of yesterday; our objective from Mr. Allaway was to break into the Seers headquarters and make sure that they weren't using steroids on some of the trainees. They weren't, thank goodness. We stayed there last night and came back early this morning. We were instructed to meet our Isle Keeper on the rooftops; everyone else had different meeting locations.

"Hey up here!" Mr. Allaway called as we were flying back to see him. Once we landed, he greeted us with a handshake. "So, what is your detailed report, Commander Alison?"

I still felt that title didn't suit me very well. Looking him in the eyes, I told him, "Negative. That is my entire report."

It wasn't very detailed, but he didn't mind. "Excellent," he said, checking something off on his clipboard. "We can safely say that Yared is not on steroids. Honestly, the lad scares me even more now, especially since I know that is naturally him." Mr. Allaway paused for a brief second and then shuddered. "Anyhoo, how did it feel? I know you were unseen for most of it, but you fought your way out nicely."

We thanked him, and Axel gave his input, "It was awesome. I would do it again in a heartbeat."

Smiling, Mr. Allaway said, "Perfect, because you'll do it again tomorrow, but on the Mainland!"

That wasn't what Axel meant. Rather than being thrilled, my friend and I stared at our Keeper. "Oh, don't be so negative!" Mr. Allaway said, smacking Axel's armored chest with the back of his hand. Instantly regretting it, he shook off the pain and went on. "I know you've all wondered what it's like outside. Remember, it's just a test run. You did great in the training, so this will be a walk in the park!"

*A park of wrack and ruin*, I thought bitterly.

After a few minutes of our Keeper trying to convince us that it would be fun, we were called down to where our friends and their Keepers were waiting. Flying down to the field while carrying Mr. Allaway, we saw that the Keepers didn't seem very pleased with what their colleagues had told their students to do.

"Wally, your orders were completely outrageous!" Mr. Mallory scolded. "Yared, Jeremy, and Ursula knocked over some of our finest experimental equipment!"

Wally snickered at the scientist's frustration and insulted him in German. Somehow, Mr. Mallory understood him. Pushing the long hair out of his eyes, it was clear the Isle VI Keeper was about to pick a fistfight with his colleague. The Isle VI members knew it was a bad idea and held their Keeper back.

*This challenge didn't go the way they planned*, I thought, as I watched all the Keepers argue with each other about one thing or another. I won't even begin to tell you what the others were complaining about. However, I *will* mention the person whose anger scared me the most: Dr. Agro of Saviors. It was because he was so quiet. Apparently, Mark and his crew left a trail of destruction. He didn't shout at Mr. Bamber, but spoke in a low, firm tone. "I won't ask you again, Brian. Where are those extra files your boys stole?" the doctor said with his hands folded. His eyes were serious, and his brow furrowed. I watched as sweat dripped down his smooth dark skin. At any moment, he could've blown.

Mr. Bamber shook his head, "I'm not sure what you are talking about! They only *borrowed* the ones I instructed them to. Right, boys?" The three of them nodded simultaneously. However, I saw something in Mark's eyes. I couldn't put my finger on it; maybe that was just the way he looked, but I couldn't be sure.

I watched the two Keepers argue back and forth for a few minutes before I realized the Headmaster wasn't present. "Where's Mr. Nik?" I asked Mr. Allaway.

He looked down at me with his blue eyes, smiled, and said, "A little late is all." Giving me a wink, he walked over to Ethan and thanked him for not causing too much destruction back at Isle I. *I really should appreciate our Isle Keeper more*, I thought, watching him talk to the Savior member. *He really is a calm, kind person.*

Finally, Mr. Nik arrived. Instead of using a vehicle, he ran his way there. Slumped over, with his hands on his knees, he panted, "I am really out of shape. Wally, remind me to have you help me with that."

Patting his friend's back, Wally replied, "I'll make note of it."

Standing upright and shaking his legs out, Mr. Nik addressed the other Keepers. "Have you all made friends again?"

No one gave him a direct answer.

"Remember, men, the children were just doing what they were told," the Headmaster reminded, wiping the sweat from underneath his dark hairline. "Everyone suffered damage, but it was for the best. They needed this training, because they depart *today*."

We Isle members weren't ready to hear that. Everyone wanted to protest, but were too stunned for words—except Lucas, who always had something to say. "Are you bloody crazy?" he interjected. "We barely survived yesterday!"

Agreeing, Zita the red-headed Savior bravely said, "With all due respect, sir, I agree with Lucas. Can we please have a little more time?"

Mr. Nik turned her down. "You're ready and it has to be done today. First reason: the time zone of your assigned location is five hours ahead of us. It may be ten-hundred hours here, but there it is fifteen-hundred hours. Two: The Isle Keepers will be departing with the students soon. That means the seven of us can see you off, but we won't be able to overlook your progress *together*. Your individual Keeper will still instruct you from back home but will be unavailable for a few hours. Do you all understand?"

No one asked any questions, so we were dismissed and decided to head to the cafeteria. Inside, we found only a few people playing board games or reading. The rest were packing their belongings. At the counters, the cooks brought us fresh food and plenty of it. We were told to fill up and enjoy it, because we wouldn't be eating like that again until we came home.

The seventeen of us headed to one of the long tables and sat together. At first, almost everyone was too nervous to eat—well, except Lucas, who always ate, and Donnie and Ava, which was weird. In fact, the two little Assets acted like everything was normal.

Curious, I said, "Donnie, Ava, can I ask you something?"

Ava nodded; her cheeks full of biscuit. Donnie looked up and with a mouthful of veggies said, "Shoot. We're listenin'."

"How are you two not worried?" I asked. "We're about to go to a new land that no one has been to in years!"

Looking at me from underneath his bucket helmet, Donnie smiled. "Because Top Banana says we'll be fine! We did great on the training, so we'll do even better on the field. Ain't that right, Marlene?"

Marlene was zoned out, with a worried expression on her face. Donnie said her name a few times and pulled on her blond ponytail before she snapped back into reality. "What? Yeah, totally," she agreed blindly as she played with her rice pudding.

I looked around at the others and noticed that Mark was blanking out as well. Usually, he's the one to make jokes and calm everyone down—but not today. He seemed quite distressed. His lips narrowed, and his pretty blue eyes glared at the table. He sat back in his chair, twirling his knife between his fingers, not touching the flank steak that was in front of him. Suddenly, his concerned expression changed to a furious one. His eyebrows furrowed, he gritted his teeth, and violently threw the knife into the bookshelf to his left, causing everyone to jump. Before anyone could say anything, he apologized, got up, pulled the knife out, and headed to the men's room.

After he stomped away, Sami asked worriedly, "Aaron, what has gotten *into* him?"

Shaking his head, he replied, "We aren't sure. He was looking through the books that Mr. Bamber told us to take from Isle II. After flipping through them, his attitude… changed." He pushed his taped glasses up the bridge of his nose and sighed. "We aren't sure what he found or what upset him so much. He won't tell us yet. He only grits his teeth and says he'll explain later."

Because it was his Isle his group had been at, Ethan was the most concerned. "What books were you instructed to take?"

Aaron looked at Cecil for answers, but his friend shook his head. "Sorry. To be honest, we can't remember. All the excitement from yesterday changed into anxiety for this evening."

"Well, we can always ask him when he gets back," Marlene proposed.

Aaron and Cecil went stiff and shook their heads. "No, you can't," Cecil warned. His green eyes frantically darted from one end of the room to the other, as if watching for someone. "Not here. Later. When we're off the Isles. I feel like that's what he's waiting for."

When Mark came back, we were all quiet. He seemed to be back to his old self. "Are we playing the quiet game?" he joked as he sat down.

Thankfully, Lucas was able to improvise, "Ha! You lost, cobber!"

Mark chuckled, shrugged his shoulders, and began to eat. I was happy to see him back to normal. Maybe he just needed to freshen up. I mean, we did come directly from our training with no stop. *But there must be more*, I thought as I watched our friend. *What aren't you telling us?*

Thankfully, we were all soon chatting again after that. We did our best to keep our minds off what was to come—that is, until we received a message that we were to pack up and prepare to leave. "Man!" Yared grumbled after Axel and I relayed the instructions, "We come back for two hours, and now we have to leave again?"

"We just have to prepare to leave," Jeremy reassured him as we parted ways.

Back in my room, I carefully packed my knapsack with supplies. We were told to pack our navy combat uniforms, which I didn't have, of course, and hunt for anything we thought we might need. The Keepers didn't tell us anything else, or how long we would be there for. I packed plenty of food and water, medical supplies, my record log, and tools in case our armor or prosthetics began to malfunction. Thanks to my nerves, I was shaking as I was packing.

Seeing how scared I was, Axel came into my room, put his hand on my shoulder, and attempted to encourage me. "Alison, we'll be fine! No Invaders will be there. We're just going to check for survivors, okay?"

I was too scared to respond. The point was that he was my responsibility. If this mission went well, all the Bionics would be my responsibility. Not only that, basically everyone was my responsibility. Mr. Nik had pulled me aside the other day and given me personal instructions to keep an eye on everyone. Apparently, he trusted me the most.

As much as I doubted Mr. Nik and his motives, I respected him, and thanked him for his trust in me.

Since I didn't say anything, Axel sighed and gave me a bear hug from behind. That was the first time he'd hugged me since we'd met. Actually, it was the first time *anyone* had hugged me sincerely in eight years. I felt his warm body against mine, and could hear his heartbeat. Blushing, I leaned back into him and placed my arms on his. When he pulled away, I felt better, surprisingly. But I didn't want him to let go. It was such a weird feeling; I had no idea human affection could affect half-robot people like me.

"Better?" he asked, smiling.

I nodded and thanked him. My face was still bright red. He

chuckled and left me to finish packing.

Since they'd given us only an hour to get ready, I was rushed as I checked over my armor for damage and see if the power levels were steady. *So far so good*, I thought, inspecting it. The power levels were fine, because none of the technology needed to be charged… exactly. The robotic implants gained energy from sleep, like a normal body. Our armor, on the other hand, fed off our body's energy and stored solar power. It charged with the stored energy while we slept. Finding that my armor was in tip-top shape, I put it back on and headed out.

It was one o'clock in the afternoon, or thirteen-hundred hours, when it was time to leave. Going back out to the field, we couldn't find the Keepers anywhere. "Where is everyone?" Ursula asked angrily, as she pulled her light hair into a ponytail. She was never the patient type.

Thankfully, I received a message from Mr. Nik: "*Alison, it is your Headmaster. You will be traveling by jet plane. Isle III members know where we are.*"

"Guys, we're traveling by jet," I announced. "He said Isle III students can lead us there."

The Research and Development members nodded and lead the way. "It's not far," Cecil reassured.

He lied. We had to borrow two trucks to get there. Mark drove one and Aaron the other. I was happy Axel and I could fly, because the two of them decided to race. They sped down the roads, raced over the grass, and tried to bump each other. The only enjoyable thing about that was hearing the boys in the bed of the truck scream like little girls. Cecil especially had an ear-piercing screech.

We finally arrived in one piece. Shaking, the other members got out of the backs of the trucks. "If you ever do that again," Ethan scolded, his hands on his knees, "I will amputate your legs so you can't reach the pedals."

"Nah, man!" Yared disagreed, his hands on his dark crew-cut hair. "That was awesome!"

Before anyone could further debate the boys' horrid driving, the pilots came out and brought us to the jet that was set to leave. We hurried in and sat down. Before taking off, everyone was given parachutes and helmets except Axel and I. Mr. Allaway was convinced we wouldn't need them. *I sure hope he's right*, I worried as I clutched my safety bars. We were warned that this was one of the fastest planes that had ever been built, and could reach a speed of Mach 3. At the speed of 2,275 miles per hour, it would still take at least an hour to get there. Crashing at that speed would be fatal, and parachutes would be pointless.

I was already getting sick, and we hadn't even started moving yet. Noticing my worry, the co-pilot said, "You'll be okay! When it's time to jump, we'll slow up."

"Whoa, wait no one said anything about jumping!" Cecil yelled as the co-pilot walked away.

"We might get sucked up in the turbine," Ursula muttered.

Anxiety filled the jet's cabin. No one dared speak. A few days ago, we were getting together for a meeting. Now the Keepers were shoving us all on a plane to send us out to who-knew-where. I felt bad for the second and third seats; everything was pushed on them all at once. *But why? What's so important that it all has to be done so soon?* I wondered.

Before I knew it, it was time. The door closed, and they announced that we were taking off. Within seconds, the jet was airborne and slowly getting up to speed. Faster and higher it went, until our ears popped and our hearts were in our shoes. That had to be the longest hour I've ever spent. I kept my eyes shut the entire time and barely breathed. Flying at Mach 3 is not fun.

Finally, they decreased speed, and we were over our destination. "Time to jump, kids!" the pilot yelled to us from the cockpit as he released our safety bars and opened the back. "Best of luck!"

*That's a long way down,* I thought, worried, as I looked at the tiny landscape below. Why parachutes? The others hadn't trained for this. I looked at my friends, who looked back at me. Lucas flicked the back of his hand towards me, telling me to go first. I was closest anyway. *Thanks, Lucas,* I thought. Clutching my fists, I ran to the exit hatch in the back and leapt out.

Skydiving was more fun than I realized. The wind rushed against my body as I fell; the view was amazing and the experience even more so. I stretched out my arms and slowed down. Looking back, I saw everyone was out, and the jet took off for the Isles. Cecil was screaming like a little girl again as we all plummeted toward the Earth. As we got closer to the ground, the parachutes released, and patches of white silk bloomed around us as they were jerked upward. Axel and I turned on our rockets and began to slow our descent.

I figured it would be wise if we scanned the area we were supposed to explore while we were up there. Mr. Allaway sent us a map through our Optic Transmitters; blinking twice, I could see a red outline of the location he'd chosen for us. What broke my heart was that it was once a city filled with innocent people. Now, it was burnt buildings and vacant streets. The gray, dreary sky gave it a depressing effect.

Landing was a problem for the team members with parachutes. Since the only thing underneath us was rubble, Axel and I had to make sure they all landed safely. Jeremy got caught on the ruins of a tall apartment building, but I got him down no problem. He gave me a big hug to say thanks and ran to Yared.

"What is this place?" Becca asked, as she brushed the dirt out of her golden fur.

"Not is, Becca, *was*," Sami answered.

She was right. Nothing was left. We stood in an empty street gazing at rubble piled upon rubble. It was an eerie ghost city, filled with nothing but terrible memories.

Unexpectedly, Yared looked to me for answers. "So, Alison, what do your elf eyes see? What was this place, and what are we doing here? The only message I got from Wally was that you have all the details."

Everyone turned and stared at me, making me uncomfortable. I closed my eyes for a few minutes before I responded. Collecting my thoughts, I finally answered them. "We're in what was once known as Guadalajara, Mexico, in North America. Our mission here is to make sure there are no Invaders left and to find survivors, if any. The native language is Spanish, which Axel speaks. However, Mark is supposed to have earpieces that translate any language into our own."

Mark's expression showed that he almost had forgotten about those. Pulling a box out of his backpack with care, he opened the case and handed one to each of us. Once he'd finished showing us how they worked, we wondered what to do next. "I think we should split up into our groups for a little while," Ursula suggested.

Zita protested. "Split up? No way! We should stick together!"

Putting his hand on her shoulder, Harold, Ethan's third seat, agreed with Ursula. "It's okay. We'll be able to cover more ground that way."

*Whoa, he can speak,* I thought. *I didn't even notice he was with us the whole time!* Quickly ashamed, I mentally apologized for never really acknowledging Harold's existence.

When Zita didn't reply, Harold chuckled. "Besides, I don't want to stick to anyone! That would invade my personal space." He elbowed her, trying to get a laugh. The only response he got was a few eye rolls.

"No wonder you never speak," Jeremy muttered at Harold's attempt at a joke. "You don't have anything worth saying."

Yared smacked the back of the younger boy's head. "Sorry, Harold," he apologized for his second seat. "We're still trying to get to know everybody."

Taking off his helmet, Harold ruffled his blond hair and said, "I'm used to it. Nobody notices me." He put his helmet under his arm, walked over to Jeremy, and stood behind him. "I'm like a shadow," he whispered into the boy's ear, "silently stalking you."

Creeped out, Jeremy raised his shoulders, smacked Harold's tan face, and hid behind Yared.

Laughing, Mark brought us back the subject at hand. "All right, everyone, back to business. If we don't want to separate, then we'll compromise," he declared. "We'll split up into three groups instead of six. We will have Isle I and IV together, II and V, III and VI. Any objections?"

I was entirely fine with it; in fact, I couldn't agree more. He put the weaker groups, who were not used to fighting, with the ones made for combat; I, V, and VI. After it was decided, I gave the final instructions. "I've sent maps of the city to your bracelets and clipboards. Each of us will head in a different direction—*quietly*. Check every inch of rubble for signs of human life. In one hour, at seven o'clock, or nineteen-hundred hours, we'll meet in front of Guadalajara Cathedral. I marked it on the map. Mr. Nik said that places of worship were used as safe havens in ancient times. We can use it that way too."

In a tone of sadness, Ethan made everything more depressing: "It's been eight years since the Accident. How long can people survive with nothing?"

He was right, but we had to hope for the best. Twirling his pistol on his index finger, Mark made a good point: "We also have to remember that the Accident was just the *beginning* of the Invaders' plans. Why would they kill off everyone they wanted to rule over? I don't think their plan is to repopulate. I'm sure we'll come across people, friend and foe." He stopped twirling his gun, gripped it, and cocked it. "Now, enough chat; see you all later." With that, he and his team headed off.

Pondering that thought, the rest of us dispersed. To get a birds-eye view, Axel and I hovered overhead while Marlene, Donnie, and Ava jumped from rooftop to rooftop. Well, they would have if all the structures had had roofs. At times, we had to grab them and swing them onto the next vacant building.

"Anything yet?" Ava called up to us.

To make things easier, we used our scanners to search for thermal radiation. *Not a thing in sight,* I thought disappointed. "Nothing. Keep looking from your end," I yelled back.

Suddenly, Marlene stopped dead in her tracks. So unexpectedly that Donnie and Ava bumped into her back. Looking up at us, she motioned us to come down. We landed behind her and asked her what was wrong. She told us to scan the next building. I did as I was told, and my heart raced. I detected six life-signs. "We should go rescue them," I whispered.

Marlene just held up her hand, put her finger to her lips, and typed something on her bracelet. She sent a message to us all: "*Not friendly.*"

To prove it, she pointed to a man who could be seen through the window. He was wearing a black uniform with a gun slung around his shoulder. Another man came into view wearing the same outfit, but pointing the gun at something. I turned on the thermal scanner again and noticed he was aiming it at the other four people in the building. "There are hostages in there," I whispered.

"We have to help them!" Donnie said too loudly.

Suddenly, four shots rang out. The men looked out the window, saw us, and aimed their guns at us. Without thinking, I opened my left hand and pointed it in their direction, activating and firing my missile launcher, killing them both.

Shocked, everyone looked at me with terrified expressions. Ignoring the horrified feeling, I went into the house where they had been. Those monsters had just murdered a family: parents and their two teenage sons. I went over to the men I'd killed and raided their pockets, looking for any source of identification or clues. Turning one of the bodies over on its stomach, I found something I didn't like: they had brands on the back of their necks like us. Theirs, however, had letters as well as numbers that were separated in the center by a small circle logo. The logo was of two overlapping letters: *O* and *X*.

When the others finally came into the building, I flipped the body over so they wouldn't see the brand. Seeing the younger ones, I sighed and wished they had stayed outside. Thankfully, they were brave kids and were able to keep it together. Looking at the bodies, Donnie pressed his hands against his wooden bucket helmet and blamed himself, "Gosh, this is all my fault. Why did I have to go and say somethin'? I wanted to help but I ended up killin' 'em!"

"You did not," Marlene snapped. "It was them, not you."

We investigated a little while longer, until we came up with a hypothesis: the two Invaders must have lived with that family. When they ran out of supplies, they killed them.

Sooner than we thought, Axel and I got a message telling us it was time to meet the others. We took the bodies of the family outside and buried them in the small backyard of the apartment. Once we paid our respects, we headed to the cathedral.

The sun had just set when we arrived, and the stars were beginning to shine. As we stood outside, I marveled at the sight. The cathedral was the most beautiful building I have ever seen, even with most of it falling apart. The right steeple was still intact, but the left was destroyed. The entire front had holes in it, as if the Invaders catapulted rocks into it. The front door was ginormous and still locked.

*Not a problem*, I thought. Axel and I flew everyone in through the holes in the walls.

Going inside, we found its interior half-intact. The pews were turned over and scattered all over the place. The cracked ceiling was domed in, and parts were covered in what were once beautiful paintings. Straight ahead of us was what used to be an altar. It was cracked and perfectly covered the ground where it had once stood as if it had been deliberately placed there. The pillars behind it were crushed and collapsed. Stained glass windows were smashed in, leaving colorful bits and pieces scattered on the tile floor.

"This place must have been beautiful, and they *destroyed* it," Sami said coldly as she shined her flashlight on a beheaded statue.

Mark trudged through the debris, right up to where the altar was, and stared at it for good long while. Cecil finally went up to him and tapped him on the shoulder. Snapping out of it, Mark kept on walking.

We explored the entire floor for almost two hours. We found no signs of life anywhere. We stopped when we reached the back of the cathedral. "Didn't Mr. Nik say something about underground catacombs?" Ethan remembered as he picked up a piece of a broken statue.

"But where would we find them? This place is huge," Marlene stated.

"Uh, underground? Duh," Harold said, with his tongue out.

Zita elbowed him in the ribs. Chuckling, Harold patted her frizzy ginger head as if she were a pet. "Aww, somebody noticed me!"

After thinking for a moment, Mark looked like he had a revelation. Without saying anything, he ran out of the hall and back towards the chapel. When we found him, he was moving away bits of the altar slowly and carefully. "What are you doing?" Aaron questioned.

"Catacombs are located underground, right?" he said, pushing another piece away.

"That's what *I* said!" Harold yelled, frustrated.

Ignoring him, Aaron asked, "And that makes you want to play with rocks?"

Mark stopped for a moment and looked up at him. "Someone placed these pieces of the altar over a hole. There is *no way* they could have fallen like this on their own. Quick, help me move these—but be careful."

Aaron tried to assist, but he was too weak. Mark was much stronger than he looked. So Axel and I ran over to help. It was no sweat for us; we had it clear in no time. Removing the final piece, we revealed a dark hole underneath. Mark dropped a piece of rubble and counted two seconds before it hit the bottom. It wasn't too deep. He told Axel and me to carry him down. Flashlight in hand, Mark searched the new floor. After a few minutes, he called us all down. Once we were together, he had Axel do a thermal scan. "Nothing here that I can detect right now," Axel told us.

"Perfect, we'll rest here for the night," Mark replied.

After some protesting, we finally began to settle in. Sami and Becca found torches and torch holders on the walls. Lighting them all, we could see the room as a whole. It was small, with ruin everywhere, and smelled faintly of decay. Thankfully, no dead things were in sight. There were holes in the wall where bodies *should* have lain, but they were vacant.

We made room on the floor and sat down for dinner. With those smells in our noses, no one wanted to eat. Well, no one except Lucas. He couldn't have cared less.

We sat and told each other what we'd found while we were apart. Our group was the only one to find anything worth talking about, and I told them what I had done—though I kept the brands to myself. No one knew what to say. To be honest, I didn't feel guilty for killing the men in the black uniforms; in the moment, it felt like the right thing to do. Mark looked at me as if he wanted to say something, but I didn't want to talk about it anymore.

Thankfully, our conversation was interrupted when Ava whispered something in Marlene's ear. Smiling, Marlene said, "Me too." Slowly standing up, Marlene addressed the girls, "All right, ladies, Ava and I have to use the powder room. Sorry for the general announcement, boys, but I was wondering if any of the girls wanted to come too. We found what used to be the bathrooms earlier. We'll do our best with what we have."

We all began to laugh. *Thank goodness for Marlene,* I thought smiling. She always knew how to cheer people up.

"All right, ladies, you go up first. When you come back, the guys will go find a place," Ethan said, smiling.

"I hope it doesn't take too long," Sami said, stretching. "I might fall asleep while we're up there."

I flew the girls back up into the main church, and Marlene led us to what used to be the bathroom and was now basically a few holes in the ground. Quite disgusting, but we managed. Sami didn't dare fall asleep in there. Once we finished and returned, the boys left for their turn. While they were gone, we got settled for bed, and I started writing in here. As you can see, they were out quite a long time for me to write all of this, because they just got back now. That means it's time for bed, finally.

# THE ISLES

# CHAPTER 17

## Sami: VI

I am not so sure if I am cut out for these types of missions....
I am terrible under pressure. I figured that out when we found other
humans: good and bad, dead and alive.

This morning, Aaron shook me awake but told me to keep quiet.
He, Mark, and Cecil were waking up the others one by one. "What's
going on?" I whispered.

He tried to act confident, but I could tell that he was petrified. His
eyes shook with fear as he pointed up. Then I heard it: Shouts of angry
men and heavy footsteps echoed through the catacombs. Internally,
I began panicking. *They found us, this is it!* I thought in despair. I
desperately looked at Aaron for help, but he didn't know how to
comfort me.

After everyone was awake, Mark motioned us to follow him.
There was a crawlspace underneath one of the niches where a body
should've been. It was originally blocked by rocks and dirt, but,
judging from Mark's filthy appearance, it seemed he had been busy
clearing the way. Sticking a flashlight in his mouth, he led us through.

Becca, Lucas, and I insisted on going in last. Not because I was
afraid... well, that was part of it, but Becca and I could see quite well

in the dark. Lucas, on the other hand, had a harder time going in, so he let everyone go ahead of him. His wings were what gave him trouble. He still wore his cape over his navy combat uniform for protection, but it kept getting snagged on things. Thankfully, he made it through; Becca and I followed behind.

I felt bad for any of the team members who were claustrophobic. It was a tight squeeze. Becca's tail kept going in my mouth, which was very annoying. I could see fine except for the dirt getting in my eyes. *Lucas' goggles sound good right about now*, I thought jealously as I wiped my face.

From what I could see, there was writing on either side of the tunnel. It wasn't in English or Spanish, but looked similar to both. I was so curious; I hoped I would remember to ask about it later.

After about a century, we were out of the crawlspace and into an open room.

Thanks to our bad luck, Mark's flashlight died. We couldn't bring torches, and there were none on the other side. While the others frantically searched for their own lights, I decided to look around. There were three other pathways that could be explored: one in front and two to either side. "Let's go check it out," Becca whispered to me. Leaving the others behind, we ventured into the path straight ahead.

The corridor sloped downward, and we went further underground. Coming out of it, we found ourselves in a room with a high ceiling. Beautiful mosaics covered the walls, and the niches actually had bodies occupying them. Most of them were entirely decomposed, but some were still getting there.

Becca walked over to one of the bodies that used to be a little girl. She stood there for a little while, trying to read the epitaph underneath. Standing next to her, I noticed the depressed look on her face. Her yellow eyes brightened in the dark, revealing the tears that were soon to fall. She bit her lip, quickly wiped her eyes, and abruptly turned away. She continued down the next corridor without saying a word.

I hurried to catch up with her. When I finally did, I found her stopped in the middle of another room with three more pathways. I stood beside her and glanced from corridor to corridor, hoping to come up with an answer. Leaning over, she whispered, "Which way now?"

I was unsure and didn't know what to say. Thankfully, the others caught up to us before I was pressed to make a decision. They hadn't found a flashlight, but Alison's and Axel's armor gave off an interesting glow. The circles over their hearts, which were originally white, had changed to blue. That light branched out and outlined the parts of their armor that overlapped: the joints in their limbs, where their prosthetics and armor met, and around their wrists and ankles. It was just enough to see what was in front of us.

"Golly, this place is full of twists and turns, ain't it?" Donnie stated.

"How are we supposed to know which way leads where? We might as well bury each other now," Zita murmured hopelessly.

Leaning toward her, Harold whispered, "That was my line."

Without saying a word, Mark headed through the entry to the left. Confused, Cecil called out to him. "Where are you going? Are you sure that's the right way?"

Mark gave a confident response: "Absolutely."

We went down a few more paths before Mark began explaining. "Did anyone notice the Latin writing on the walls in the crawlspace?" He waited for a few people to admit they had before continuing. "Well, those were writings about the catacombs themselves. There was also a teeny tiny map at the very end of the crawlspace corridor. I memorized it."

"What does it lead to?" Alison questioned.

Mark looked back at her, smiled, and said, "The survivors."

*Survivors?* I doubted that when we entered another open room with more dead people and an old, locked door. The scary part was that some of the corpses looked and smelled way fresher than the others. The bodies of two grown men sat up against the wall on either side of the sturdy wooden door. They wore rags, and their cold, fragile hands clutched shotguns. A few more dead men lay around them, but their clothes seemed to be of a higher quality. "The Invaders know they're down here," Mark observed. "I hope they let us in… if there are any left." Judging by the expression on a few of our group members' faces, the better-dressed men were Invaders. Cautiously, Mark rapped on the wooden door. No response.

"This is pointless. Let's just bust it down!" Ursula demanded.

Ignoring her comment, Mark knocked once more, this time doing the "shave and a haircut" call-and-response; still nothing. Getting impatient, Ursula was about to charge the door when we heard the response. Suddenly, a small eye-slot opened toward the top of the door, and dark brown eyes peered out. Mark stared right back. The doorkeeper whispered something; even with my good hearing, I couldn't make it out. Without hesitation, Mark smiled and responded, "*Et cum spiritu tuo.*"

It wasn't Spanish, and my earpiece didn't translate it. None of us knew what it was, but the doorkeeper did. He chuckled and opened the door. He was a brown, thin, sickly-looking man with slick hair. His outfit was black, except for a white collar around his neck. In his grip he carried a torch, lighting up the room. He motioned us to quickly come inside. Not wanting the Invaders to find us, we obeyed. We followed him down the hall until we came to another door, which opened to another, then another, then another… so quite a few doors before we reached another room.

It was bigger than I expected and had seating like the church upstairs. Torches were lit on the walls, and at the back was another altar; this one was intact. We couldn't believe how many people were crammed into the stuffy underground room; hundreds, it looked like. The benches and aisles were fully occupied. Some people were sleeping, others keeping each other company, and the rest were on their knees mouthing words and tightly clutching what looked like beaded necklaces.

Axel began conversing with some of them and asked them many different questions. Mark spoke with the man in black, who was interested in who we were and where we came from. I had so many questions myself; but before I could ask anyone, I felt a tug on my tail. Turning around, I saw a small boy holding my tail to his chest as if it were a teddy bear. Looking over to Becca, I saw she had kids climbing all over her.

Once I turned around, I was tackled to the ground by children, being petted by many small hands. I was surprised by how gentle they were and how good it felt. I couldn't believe myself when I started purring. That had never happened before! I felt embarrassed until I heard Becca purring even louder than I was. Above me, I saw Lucas flying around some of the kids for fun. The adults weren't too happy about that, but they didn't stop him.

This went on for a little while before the children's parents pulled them off us and apologized. We told them not to worry about it; as long as it made the children happy, we didn't mind. I'm sure it had been a while since the mothers saw their children smile.

When Mark finished speaking, I went over to him and asked him a billion questions: "So where are we? How did you know the password? Who is that man?"

"Slow down, kitty," Mark interrupted, smiling. "I'll explain now." When everyone was in listening distance Mark began. "Everyone, this is Father Sandro, and he is pastor of this church."

*Is that his dad?* I thought to myself, confused. *Nah, they look nothing alike.*

"He and the surviving free people of Guadalajara have been hiding down here for longer than you've been at the Isles," he continued. "Their numbers have decreased as food became scarce. The men they send to scavenge rarely return. All they can do is pray, and we have answered their prayers. We must do whatever we can to get them all out safely."

The only one to object was Ursula. "How are we supposed to get them *all* out? And to where? Should we take them home or leave them here to die? How do we know that we won't get killed in the process?" She went on ranting and complaining; she sure was a pain.

Thankfully, Father Sandro answered Ursula before I could smack her: "The Invaders have a base here; I've seen it. If you can distract them, we can escape and hopefully find another home."

Ursula wasn't fond of that plan and complained some more. Mark tried to reason with her, but she wouldn't listen and got everyone riled up.

Interrupting the commotion, a little voice spoke up and made a suggestion. "Why don't we shut down the base, scatter the Invaders, and rebuild the walls of the church?" Jeremy asked. "This building is big and seems sturdy enough to protect you for a little while longer until they are all gone."

The man in black smiled and knelt on one knee in front of him. Putting his hand on Jeremy's shoulder, Father Sandro said some comforting words to him: "You have quite a lot of faith, son. That's an amazing, rare thing. Never lose it. You'll need it."

With that, he stood up and left to attend some of the other survivors while we discussed our options. After more bickering, we decided to go with Jeremy's plan and create a strategy for destroying the base and scattering the Invaders. Axel and Alison projected a scale hologram of the city of Guadalajara in the middle of our sitting circle. "Okay, time to get started," Mark said firmly. I was happy he knew what he was doing and was taking charge. Yet, I still wondered why he was acting so funny back at the Isles and how he knew all these things about the Mainland. Nevertheless, I kept quiet and let him explain.

"Father Sandro told me that the base is located at what used to be their soccer stadium, *Estadio Jalisco*." He pointed to a large spot on the map. "It's not too far from here, which is a good thing and a bad thing. Good for us because it takes less time to get there, bad for the people because the Invaders will be able to see us rebuilding the church. We must do it as quickly as possible and build from the inside out. What do you all think?"

Zita agreed wholeheartedly. "Sounds perfect," she said. "These folks barely have any strength. They wouldn't be able to handle the outside walls right now. Little by little is the best way to go in their present condition."

When everyone agreed, we went on to the bigger problem. "Now: how to infiltrate their fortress," Mark said grimly. "As you can see, it's big and probably well protected. The group that I accompanied yesterday got a quick look. What gave it away was that they've hung their flags all over the stadium. It's a red flag with an overlapping O and X in the center; not very creative, but not easy to forget."

As he described their flag, my eyes fell upon Alison, who rubbed the back of her neck, where her brand was hidden under her armor. What are you thinking about? I wondered curiously.

Interrupting my thoughts, Mark continued, "We only got a glimpse, but it looks like there's heavy automatic artillery everywhere. It fires at everything but the Invaders. We saw it shoot a pack of feral dogs while a couple of invaders were barely 20 feet away. That means they must each carry something that allows them to safely pass through the entrance. That's the first thing we need—besides weapons, of course. Next, we're going to need a way to get down to their control room without being noticed," he said, pointing to the field on the holographic stadium. "When we get there, we do a total shutdown and cause them to scatter. Now, I believe suggestions are in order."

With that, he shut up and awaited the others' input. We sat there in awkward silence for a few moments while everyone thought about it. "We could always split up," I suggested finally. "Some people act as a diversion while the others go in."

Mark processed that thought positively. "That's a really good idea. We'll need to split up into groups of equal strengths. But we can worry about that later."

"Axel and I can take the air and act as a separate distraction," Alison added.

Shaking his head, Aaron put in, "We need at least one of you to break down the doors for us. The other can stay in the air with Lucas and distract people."

Lucas didn't object and continued chewing on a piece of stale bread he'd found.

Mark smiled and concluded the discussion. "All right. I love our plans: short and sweet! So, overview: get sensors, create distraction, break into control room, download their information, destroy the computer, and get out as fast as we can."

Father Sandro seemed to be eavesdropping and half agreed with this plan but with a disappointed look on his face. He bent over and whispered into Mark's ear. Saying nothing, Mark nodded and Father

Sandro left. "Does everyone understand?" Mark asked finally. No questions were asked, and we began Stage One. A few of us were picked to retrieve whatever it was that the Invaders used to bypass the deadly defense system. First, we took in the bodies of the two Invaders that were outside the entrance. Alison and Axel scanned them, and found something strange embedded in the backs of their necks.

Taking a knife, Ethan cut a chip the size of a grain of rice out of one man's neck. "So, this is what they all have," Ethan marveled. "Not much to it."

Cecil began to panic when Ethan started poking it with his tweezers. "Wait, we shouldn't be playing with this in here! What if it's still active and tracking them? They could storm down here any moment!"

Ethan looked up at Mark, who wasn't worried. "I suspect it shuts down once their heart stops," Mark reassured us. "We'll get them going and try to make a replica. The three with the chips can pass through and get to the defense control room, which is usually located close to the border. They need to keep a human and artificial eye on the premises. Once they shut down the artillery, the rest can pass through."

Mark, Aaron, and Cecil sat with the chips for about two hours before they were able to figure out how they worked. They said they could activate and deactivate them, but replicating them was impossible with the tools they had. We needed others.

With a distressed tone, Marlene said she knew where we could get more. "The bodies of the Invaders we encountered yesterday are probably still in the apartment. We…we can go there."

The look on Alison's face seemed distant; I couldn't imagine what was going on inside her head, knowing she had killed those two men. To comfort her, Jeremy walked over and gave her a big hug. Tears fell down her cheeks as she held him close. *I didn't know Bionics could cry,* I thought.

Finally, we decided to send out a team to retrieve the chips. I was sent with Marlene, Axel, Aaron, Harold, and Ethan. Father Sandro saw us out, told us to be careful, and said he would be praying for us.

It took us a while to reach the surface, and the suspense was killing me. Terrible scenarios ran through my head as we made our way out of the catacombs. I let out a deep breath when no Invaders were up top to meet us. Cautiously, we snuck out into the dark of night, and Marlene led the way. Returning to the apartment Marlene's group had found yesterday as soon as possible, we found the slightly-ripe bodies. Ethan and Harold quickly got to work at removing the chips, which were located in the center of the *OX* symbol on their necks.

Then, we heard voices outside.

Looking carefully out the window of the second-floor apartment, I saw a group of men wearing all black and carrying guns and flashlights. They were conversing on the streets below, so I decided to listen. At first, they weren't saying anything important; then one of them said something that caused me to panic. "Well, if their bodies are up there, we might as well go get 'em. If we need more shelter, we don't want 'em stinkin' up the building."

Shaking, I told the others what was happening. Thankfully, they were cooler under pressure than I was. The Saviors quickly removed the chips, Aaron shut them down, and we started to head out the windows. However, my legs locked, and I stood there frozen. Aaron grabbed my hand, and Axel flew the two of us out the window and up to the rooftop.

After he put us down, Aaron kept holding my hand. Embarrassed, I abruptly pulled away. He gave me a dorky smile. *You're so weird,* I thought.

As soon as everyone was on the roof, Axel quickly flew back in, grabbed the two bodies, and threw them about two miles in the direction opposite from the church. I had no idea he was so strong! We all stared at him like he had twelve heads. He mouthed, "I will explain later," and we hopped across the rooftops and dashed back to the cathedral. I didn't dare look back.

Finally, we were safe and back in the catacombs. We found the others slowly reinforcing the walls of the underground chapel. The two Saviors found Mark and went over to him. "They're not potato chips, but they'll have to do," Harold joked, handing him the microchips.

"Perfect, this will help so much," Mark exclaimed as he took them.

An old man, resting from his work in a nearby pew, said something in Spanish: "I remember when we used those to track our pets. Now they use them in people. Have we fallen so far?"

Those words echoed in my head for a long time.

We told everyone that there were other Invaders looking for those men's bodies, but that we didn't stick around to find out what they really wanted. That gave us the push to finish the job as soon as possible. If they really were tracking those chips, we couldn't risk being with the survivors for much longer.

Father Sandro came over and suggested we get some rest before our mission tomorrow. He also asked if any of us would like to attend their Celebration the next morning; I *think* that's what he said, anyway. Mark seemed to know what he was referring to and excitedly accepted. The rest of us were unsure what they were talking about, so we stayed out of it.

After Father Sandro left, we were getting ready for bed when Axel explained to us why he threw they bodies so far away. "If they found them, they would have seen that people removed their chips, and they would become suspicious. If they did not find the bodies, they would believe it was a false reading and it may not arouse suspicion."

"Great idea, Axel," Mark commented, as he cleared the spot where he was going to sleep.

"The incision was so small," Ethan said, "are you sure they would've noticed it?"

Axel shrugged. "Better safe than sorry."

After that, everyone either went to bed or wrote in their record logs. When I first started writing, Mark came over to me and whispered, "I almost forgot. Sami, you asked me how I knew the password, right?"

Quickly, I nodded.

"It's an important call-and-response in these people's religion," he explained with a smile. "Father Sandro said '*Dominus vobiscum*' and the Latin response is '*Et cum spiritu tuo*'. The Invaders have a hatred for religions, especially this one, so they don't bother to learn anything about it. The majority of the population here is of the same religion or knows someone who practices it, so they know the response. That makes it easier to tell the good from the bad… to some degree, of course. So, don't forget the password in case we get separated."

*Thanks for clearing it up, but how did you know the response, then?* Keeping that thought to myself, I nodded, and he got up and went back to his place. *At least it's a start. He'll tell us soon.*

Letting more questions swirl in my head, I decided to get some sleep. Another day gone by without a single nap. I think I'm getting used to it, though.

I hope everything goes well tomorrow.

# THE ISLES

# CHAPTER 18

## Aaron: VI

I don't think anyone got a good night's rest before the mission today. Waking up, I felt like I was hit by a bus, and I looked like it too. I had bags under my eyes, and my hair was crazy spiky and untamable.

I wasn't the only one. Everyone's hair was matted, their faces dirty, and we all felt gross. Not to mention we were all filled with anxiety; except for Mark, surprisingly. He woke up about an hour before us and seemed chipper when he returned from wherever he went. In fact, he had such a smile on his face that words cannot describe it. Noticing our apprehension, Mark reassured us. "Guys, relax! I'm positive everything will work out, and it will be fine."

Ursula shook her head in denial. "How can you be so sure? Why do you have that stupid grin on your face?" She looked like she was about ready to punch his teeth out.

Mark smiled, dismissed her questions, and checked everyone's backpacks to make sure we all had the correct equipment. Without looking up from his checklist, he told us all to go "freshen up"…if that was even possible. Nevertheless, we left him to his checklist and prepared for the mission.

Getting ready the fastest, I headed back to Mark to clear things up. "Can I ask you a few things?"

"Sure, fire away," he replied nonchalantly as he wrote notes on his clipboard.

"Why are you so happy and excited this morning? Aren't you terrified?"

Stopping what he was doing, he looked right into my eyes and stated, "I am petrified, same as you all. But we have nothing to fear. You and I both know that we're doing what is right. That's one of the reasons I am happy. I know that if I die it will not be in vain."

*Wow, that was deep,* I thought, taken aback. After letting that sink in for a few moments, I asked him what his other reason was for being happy.

"Because," he said with a grin, "It's been a while since I have spoken and spent time with people who believe and stand for the same things I do. I actually got to go to Mass!"

Confused, I wanted to ask him so many more questions. I wanted to ask him about what he read in those books we stole and what had affected his attitude back at the Isles. Unfortunately, I had to wait. He gave me an answer before I could say anything. "I'll have to explain later, but here's my main point: Always seek the truth. We live in a world of lies and deceit. Once you know what is true, hold on to it; fight for it. Stand up for the truth, even if you're standing alone. Understand?"

I nodded slowly. I sat on the ground next to him and waited for the others. *What is the truth, Mark?* I wondered.

When everyone returned, we reviewed the plan and headed out. Anxiousness and fear rose inside of us as we got closer and closer to our destination. At last we reached the stadium. I wasn't mentally prepared to do this, but I had no choice. Standing in front of the enemies' ginormous headquarters, Mark gave instructions to the diversion team. "Okay, quick reminder of who's going where," he whispered. "Axel and Lucas, you two distract from the sky. Becca, Ursula, Harold, and Marlene are in charge of ground distraction. Zita, Jeremy, Donnie, and Ava are to stay put behind this rubble and keep watch in all directions."

Zita was relieved she was staying back, but the younger ones were disappointed. Rebuking them, Harold said, "I wish *I* could hide behind a boulder rather than act as bait. Then again, I really am the perfect distraction." He tried to flip his light hair dramatically, but it was too short.

"You try too hard," Jeremy muttered.

Mark smiled. "Anyway, so joining Cecil, Yared, Aaron, and me after we shut down the artillery will be Ethan, Sami, and Alison. Did I miss anyone?" No one spoke up, so the four of us went on our way, carrying the Invaders' reactivated microchips to shut down their weapons.

It was dawn, and the sun was starting to peer over their headquarters. Invader flags covered the stadium and flapped in the morning wind. There was a dirt path leading through the debris up to the front entrance, which was surmounted by towers with cannon-like weapons on top. To the left and right of us were large crates. Some intact and some destroyed. *They must've used those for cover when they took over the place.* I observed a skeleton lying against a crate riddled with bullet holes as we passed.

We were undetected by their artillery; the microchips worked. We approached the gate in the surrounding black barbed fence. When we were close enough, it opened automatically, and we were let in. Once inside the gate, we found the outside artillery control room. It was a security booth to the right of the main entrance. We snuck along and peeked in the windows. Inside, the so called "guard" was asleep. *How convenient,* I thought to myself. *Usually that only happens in movies or books.* Carefully, Mark went inside, crept up behind him, and injected him with a sedative.

"He was already sleeping," Yared joked.

Ignoring him, Mark cautiously removed the man's uniform, tied him up, gagged him, and hid him under the desk.

*That's gonna be embarrassing,* I thought, chuckling at the mostly-naked guard.

Mark handed Yared the uniform and commanded, "Put this on. If we're caught, you make it look like *you* caught us." While Yared was dressing himself, Mark typed away at the computer. Within seconds, he was granted access and the artillery shut down. "Okay, Cecil, send a message to the distraction team telling them to give us five minutes exactly before they begin making a mess of the place."

Without answering, Cecil quickly did as he was told. As we left the booth, I asked, "How were you able to get into the computer system so fast?"

Not even looking back at me, he responded, "I'm an expert computer hacker. Always have been; always will be." That didn't sound very good. I pushed the thought aside when the others caught up. Together, we headed into the enemy base.

The inside of the stadium was bigger than it looked. The ceiling was high, and it gave off the eerie feeling of a cold concrete cavern. It was poorly lit, and the air was damp. A large Invaders flag covered the front wall, and smaller ones hung over former information stands and booths. There were many pathways that led to other areas of the stadium.

Cautiously but quickly, we made our way through. We formed a single file line behind Mark, who kind of knew where he was going. He'd downloaded a map of the old stadium from the computer in the booth to his bracelet-thingy. "I'm not sure how many rooms they destroyed or built," he whispered after we took another wrong turn. "Sorry." We went back and continued. I frantically looked around to see if we were being watched, but there wasn't a soul in sight.

"It's like a ghost town in here," Yared observed as we passed another empty room.

Mark nodded. "Which is odd. With a base this big, you'd think it would be crawling with Invaders."

As he said that, we heard hell break loose outside: our five minutes were up. Axel and Lucas were making a surprising amount of racket up above, while the rest were attacking the sides of the stadium. It sounded like they were destroying whatever they could find. Their commotion and destruction attracted a lot of intention. Alarms went off in the building, the lights went red, and we heard the sounds of footsteps from all directions. We ducked into a dark hallway and waited for the people to pass.

The number of Invaders who passed frightened me; there were plenty of them here after all. Men and women alike, all dressed in black, rushed to the front gate to stop our friends. I was afraid for our distraction team; our enemies were equipped for battle. When they were all gone, Mark whispered, "That was it?"

Shocked, I looked at him and said, "What do you mean 'that was it'? There were probably a hundred people going out there!"

Not looking back, he replied, "There were less than that, which worries me. They *must* have more people than that here."

I kept my mouth shut after that, and we pressed on, more alert than before. Anytime someone heard a suspicious noise, we hid. It was a very intense game of hide-and-seek, but the goal was never to be found. There was one scary incident. We were almost to the field when we heard more footsteps—at the one time when I couldn't find a hiding spot. Before I could panic, Alison scooped me up, and we quietly hovered near the ceiling until three Invaders passed.

At last, we reached a guarded door to what used to be the field. Seeing us, the guards there raised their weapons. Before they could do anything, we shot them and hid their sleeping bodies. Yared was still upset that we were using tranquilizers instead of real bullets. "Now we have to worry about when they wake up," he mumbled as he adjusted the uncomfortable Invader uniform he was wearing. I kinda thought he had a point.

"Real guns are too loud; we need stealth," Mark informed us as he pushed a man's body out of the way. I wanted to suggest we remove the little microchips so the guys wouldn't make it past the main entrance the next time they left, but I didn't say anything. Hopping over the unconscious Invaders, Mark went to the door and granted us access into the control room. The doors opened wide, and we couldn't believe what was on the other side. It was the largest control room I have ever seen or probably ever will. It took up most of the soccer field! We hid behind some weapon racks that were close to the doors before looking around.

I poked my head out from behind a stand of machine guns and

marveled at what I saw. The bleachers had been replaced with desks and computers, and people sat at them, typing away. The stadium was originally open-roofed, but now was closed in by welded metal. In the center of the field was a gargantuan hologram. Directly below it was one large desk covered by a series of control consoles, which was protected by four glass walls but had no ceiling. There were more desks surrounding it, and these were clearly more important than the ones in the bleachers, which were much *much* smaller.

In the center of the blue hologram was a map of not just Guadalajara but all of Mexico. To the sides of it were security footage of what was going on outside. On one side, we saw Axel and Lucas flying frantically back and forth. Axel shot missiles at the enemies on the rooftop, killing a good number of them. Lucas swooped down, grabbed a handful of men, and threw them down to their deaths. I didn't think I could do that.

It took less than ten minutes to prove me wrong.

The other side was the ground footage. Becca dashed back and forth, confusing the guards. She would then pounce and attack until they were unconscious. Ursula jousted with a metal pole through lines of Invaders like nobody's business. Marlene and Harold turned one of the tower cannons on manually and fired rapidly and semi-randomly. Our friends put up a hard fight. Reinforcements had to be sent out more than once. *There are the rest of the people Mark was talking about,* I realized when I saw the images of hundreds more Invaders heading out to meet our friends. *I hope everyone will be okay.*

Saying nothing, Mark headed stealthily towards the main computer. I followed without hesitation. He sure could move fast; he crawled under vacant desks, silently shot workers and hid them, and kept going. He almost made it to the center of the field before he was finally caught, as he accidentally banged an unconscious Invader against a desk too loudly. "Intruders!" someone shouted. Another alarm went off. This time there were flashing blue lights along with the red ones, bathing the inner stadium with a purple glow.

The workers at the computers in the field area went after Mark, pulling out weapons of all kinds and preparing to attack. Their preparations were in vain: this time our friend got serious and used the pistol that had real bullets. He shot six dead and was cornered before Yared jumped out and helped. One by one, the rest of us came out and charged the Invaders surrounding him.

Stunned, the workers in the bleachers watched for a few moments as their comrades lower down were killed. Sami pounced from behind, Yared and Ethan charged head on, Alison attacked from above, and Cecil and I... well, we cowered for a few minutes. The sound of Mark being punched in the face and beaten made us change our minds. Mustering up our courage, Cecil and I jumped up and shot Mark's attackers in the back of their heads.

As their bodies fell to the ground, I began breathing heavily and looked at the pistol in my shaking hand. *I can't believe I did that,* I thought, disgusted with myself. Cecil, on the other hand, just looked at me and said, "Aaron, it had to be done." He ran over and made sure Mark was okay.

"I'm good," Mark confirmed as he wiped the blood from his mouth. "Surprised they didn't kill me right then and there." He then began running toward the main console. "Alison, fly me to the center controls!" he shouted. "Everyone else, make sure they don't get to us until our work is finished. Understood?"

Before we could yell back an answer, Alison scooped up Mark and flew him to the center of the stadium. Then, the Invaders in the bleachers came down to fight. First, they started shooting at Alison and Mark and then at us on the ground. Cecil, Sami, and I dove behind a desk where a dead man lay. "What should we do?" Cecil panicked.

"Calm down, we'll figure something out," Sami tried to reassure us, but there was no confidence in her voice.

Then, I got a crazy idea. "We need our own distraction team! Sami, you make sure no one hits Mark and Alison. Bring them to the ground. Cecil, you and I are going to do whatever it takes to get their attention off the guys at the main console. Ready?"

Neither of them objected, and we all ran out of our hiding places. Sami headed straight for the first gunman she saw and attacked. *Man, she is amazing,* I thought, impressed, as she pounced on another.

Snapping out of it, I ran to Cecil. The two of us ran around screaming like cavemen. We grabbed whatever could be used as a shield and protected ourselves. I had a metal scrap from a broken desk, and Cecil had a seat cushion. His wasn't very helpful, but if it made him feel better, why not.

Seeing what we were trying to do, the others joined in.

"This'll be fun," Yared said with a disturbing grin on his face, as if he loved combat more than anything. Gripping his pistol, he fired at every enemy he saw, getting a headshot every time. The Invaders were confused when they saw he was wearing a guard's uniform. At first glance, they thought he was on their side and didn't attack. It was too late for them to change their minds when Yared pulled the trigger. Surprisingly, Ethan was doing some serious damage with his knife; the short Savior was better at hand-to-hand combat than I expected. I guess he never even thought of reaching for his pistol.

The Invaders from the bleachers must not have been trained in combat; they fell left and right. What worried me was that it seemed like some didn't even care. Rather than fighting back or getting out of the way, they just stood there and waited for the attack. *What have they done to these people?* I thought as I knocked one of them on the head.

Out of the corner of my eye, I saw Mark and Alison finally make it to the console, but the workers quickly surrounded the cubicle. Since there was no top to it, people attempted to climb over; but Alison shot at them, knocking them backwards. The glass was bulletproof, thankfully, but they were doing whatever they could to make a dent in it. Nothing worked.

That's when a team came in with modified rifles and flamethrowers. Yeah, I know, what luck, right?

Trudging through puddles of blood, I attempted to take down one of the flamethrower men. I came from behind, so he didn't notice me until I tackled him to the ground. Throwing me off his back, he tried to stand. I didn't let him. I was much taller, so I put my arms around his neck and squeezed.

Struggling, the man flailed his feet and scratched at my arms. Finally, his heart stopped and I dropped the dead man to the floor.

Shocked at what I had done, I stood there staring at the body. "Watch out!" Sami shouted as she tackled me, saving me from a bad burn. "You can't freeze in the heat of battle," she scolded, hopping off of me.

Unsure of what to say, I sat there looking like an idiot, with my glasses falling off my nose. "I know, they're people too, but we have a job to do," she told me. "They're not innocent; it does not count as murder. Understand?"

I nodded, even though something told me that some of them *were* innocent.

Holding out her hand, Sami offered to help me up. *I pray nothing happens to you,* I thought as I looked into her green cat eyes. I don't know if I could live with myself if she got hurt. Once I regained my senses, I took her hand, got to my feet, and the two of us rushed back into combat. This went on for about ten minutes before we heard a robotic voice say something in Spanish that our earbuds translated: *"Memory wiped. Are you sure you want to destroy all evidence?"*

A few of the workers stopped mid-fight, trying to take in what they were hearing.

Then, the computer confirmed it: *"Evidence will be destroyed. Three-minute countdown starting: now."*

Most of the employees screamed, shouted, and ran desperately toward the exits. A few were so overtaken with rage that they attacked us with whatever force they had left. The team with the modified artillery went insane and set fires everywhere in an attempt to destroy everything—either to speed up the process or to prevent us from escaping.

"Time to go," Mark called when he and Alison caught up to us.

"How?" Ethan shouted back. "The exits have been destroyed!"

Mark yelled something to Alison. She nodded, hovered above the doors, and charged right through the wall. Man, she was strong. Within seconds, she came back and flew us through, two by two. Sami and I were last. Once we were on the ground we ran, in a desperate attempt to catch up with the others.

That was the longest and shortest three minutes of my entire life. Alison pulled me along in her left hand and Sami in her right. She held so tightly, I felt like I was losing circulation but didn't want her to let go. Looking over, I noticed she had tears streaming down her face. I wondered what was going through her head at that very moment. I wanted to ask, but it wasn't an appropriate time, since we were about to be consumed by a fiery explosion.

We were almost to the main exit when the first bombs detonated. The blasts started in the middle of the stadium, so we had a few seconds before we were burnt into crispy bacon. Alison turned on her rocket thrusters and rammed into everyone, pushing us all outdoors at once. She still held onto Sami and me, but I could feel my grip slipping. I was surprised by how far she pushed everyone. We crash-landed about twenty feet from where Zita, Jeremy, Donnie, and Ava were hiding and got behind debris piles, safe from the blast as it tore the stadium apart.

I hoped our distractors were okay.

We all fell to the ground; Alison still holding Sami's hand and mine as we lay there. I had an intense ringing in my ears, and I couldn't make sense of things, but that somehow seemed right. Struggling to sit up, I slid my hand out of the Bionic's and looked back at the stadium. It was engulfed in fire, and not much of it was left.

Turning away, I checked to see if our friends were all right. Cecil, Sami, and Ethan were unconscious; and the rest were awake. The others had arrived while I was dazed. All seventeen of us were back together and okay, with no major injuries. Not saying a word, all of us who were conscious jumped to our feet. Running as fast as lightning, we headed toward the cathedral, not once looking back. Alison, despite her exhaustion and armor malfunctioning, carried Sami, Axel carried Ethan, and Lucas carried Cecil. Finally, we made it to the cathedral and entered. Once the main doors were shut, we all collapsed to catch our breath.

Father Sandro and a few of the men were waiting in the main church for us. They had such horrified expressions on their faces; I wasn't sure if they were scared *for* us or *of* us because of what we had done. We were all covered with blood, but it wasn't ours. Sami's and Becca's fur was singed and some of our clothes had holes burned in them.

Shakily, Mark stood up and wobbled over to Father Sandro. As he reached him, he passed out. Father caught him and commanded the men to bring us all back down into the catacombs through another way. I was so happy we didn't have to go back through the crawlspace. Carrying Mark, they led us down through a new pathway they had created in our absence. When we were back in the catacombs, we carefully laid our unconscious friends on the ground. The rest of us sat down and had Zita and Harold attend to our wounds.

"'Become a Savior,' they said. 'It'll be fun,' they said," Harold complained as he stitched a gash in Ursula's leg. "I'd rather be a comedian."

"No offense," Zita replied as she bandaged Becca's arm, "but you would starve."

"I don't think this is the best time to be talking about this," Becca whispered when Zita was finished.

"Yeah, just shut up and stop the pain," Ursula commanded as Harold was finishing up.

"I'm trying, your majesty," Harold replied, finishing his last stitch.

Afterward, we sat in silence until, one by one, our friends regained consciousness. They were all right but had bad headaches. The last to wake was Mark. When he sat up and rubbed his face, we all became quiet. "Is everyone okay?" he mumbled slowly.

No one answered. We just stared at him and waited for answers. Coming over, Father Sandro finally asked why he had to destroy the entire base and kill all those people.

With his eyes fixed on the ground, ashamed to look Father in the face, Mark answered, "It had to be done. I hope you can forgive me. That base was not just the Invaders' base for Guadalajara, but for *all* of Mexico. They regroup there; and I realized that if it were destroyed, their survivors would disperse and be thrown into chaos."

*How do you know that?* I thought bitterly. He made so many assumptions with his ridiculous "theories" that I wasn't sure what was fact anymore.

Confused, Alison asked. "They're human beings; can't they fend for themselves?"

"They were human beings *once*," Mark replied in a depressed tone. "I downloaded every file that they had on that computer. I can show you what I mean." Pulling out his clipboard, he sent a bit of information to Axel, asking him to project it as a hologram. Obeying, Axel showed us a worker's file.

"This is a document of one of the Invaders who didn't join them voluntarily," Mark began to explain. "I wasn't able to examine it thoroughly, but from what I saw, I found out my theories were correct. It looks like the vast majority of them refused to join willingly."

Axel opened a checklist of requirements that the Invader had to fulfill. Some things that were checked off read, "Denied faith and family", "Adopted our way", "Does not think", and "Strange Voices." *Strange Voices?* I thought. *What does that mean?*

Continuing, Mark said, "That chip in the back of their necks puts information permanently into their brains. The chip tells them who they are and what their purpose in life is. When they knew the chip was effective, they checked off these things on the list."

"So, basically, we're going up against mindless zombies?" Jeremy concluded.

"Not entirely. Their minds work. But their will has been replaced with that of the Invaders."

"So, that *did* count as murder back there, didn't it?" I asked quietly.

A tsunami of guilt washed me, and as I watched people's faces fall, I was sure the others felt the same. Mark didn't say anything. That's when I became furious. "You were at the controls!" I screamed in his face. "You could have found a way to shut it down. We could have had an army of allies, and we murdered them all."

"Don't you think I *tried* to fix it?" Mark bellowed back. I sat there in shock as tears began to stream down his face. "I couldn't, and this is my fault. Their blood is on my hands; not yours. Understand? I have failed everyone, and I am so sorry. I saw no other way; I'm sorry." He pressed his palms into his eyes and put his elbows on his knees.

Father Sandro knelt down next to Mark and put his hand on his shoulder. He tried to encourage him in Spanish: "My son, this is not your fault. You tried to save them, but they were long gone. You all acted in defense; it was for a good reason. Wars exist, people die, and both sides believe they are doing the right thing. Maybe in a sense they are, but what really determines whether it is right or wrong is their cause. What are they fighting for? You children are fighting for freedom and justice; they are blindly fighting for power and the selfishness of their leaders."

Wiping away tears, Mark thanked the man in black. Smiling, Father stood up and addressed us all. "If anyone needs to clear their conscience, I am always ready to listen. Sometimes, a little guidance is all you need."

We thanked him, and he went away. We all sat there in awkward silence for a little while, until Jeremy fell asleep on Alison's lap and started snoring. Chuckling, Marlene said, "Smart kid. I think I'm going to do the same. Good night, everyone." With that, she lay down and snored away. One by one, everyone started to follow their example.

A few of us stayed up to write in our record logs. Before I started writing in mine, I asked Alison and Mark a question or two; Alison first. "Alison? Can I ask you something?"

Without looking up from her writing, she whispered, "Of course, what is it?"

I rubbed the brand on the back of my neck and whispered, "What were you thinking of as you were dragging Sami and me out the building? I noticed you were crying."

She froze in the middle of writing a sentence. Tears started welling up in her eyes.

"Oh, I'm sorry. I shouldn't have brought it up." Immediately, I felt stupid.

"No, it's all right," she sniffled. "While I was dragging you two through the flames, my mind flashed back to the day I pulled my twin siblings through the streets of my hometown during the Accident. Everything was on fire that day, too. I looked at your faces, and I saw theirs. I can't believe it's been eight years since they—" she broke off and began sobbing.

Something urged me to hug her. I wrapped my arms around her and held her close. Sami came over and joined in. Looking over, I noticed Mark with a giant grin on his face. Thankfully, he was in a better mood. I mouthed What? to him.

He shook his head and mouthed back, *Can't tell you. Trade secret.*

I rolled my eyes. *More secrets.*

When I was sure Alison was going to be all right, I plopped down next to Mark and started to ask him my main question. I didn't want to push my luck, because he seemed exhausted. "Why were you so moody back at our Isle? Like when you threw the knife into the bookshelf, then when you came back from the bathroom you were all chill?"

Taking a deep breath, he whispered to me, "Because I confirmed what really goes on within Saviors' walls."

"What do you mean?"

Looking around, making sure Ethan, Zita, and Harold were asleep, he said, "When I first came here, I wasn't alone. I arrived with my foster father. He stayed at Saviors so they could 'help' him, but it turns out they just wanted to see if he would be useful." He looked at the ground and whispered, "Knowing he was sick, they didn't see any need to keep him around, and so they killed him. They did that to most of the older folks who needed help. When I first found out, I needed more proof to confront someone about it. Now I've found what I needed—and more."

I couldn't believe my ears. They just killed people who were of no use to them? I thought, horrified.

"That's not all," he continued. "You know that whenever a baby is about to be born, they send the mother and child to Saviors so they can help things go smoothly? Well, if the baby shows any signs of problems they kill him or her, inside the womb or out, without telling the parents."

I was so speechless and horrified that I sat there staring. *They kill people?* I thought, disgusted. *They're supposed to be doctors. For crying out loud, their name is Saviors.*

Sighing, he went on, "Along with taking their manual, we stole their record book: 'The Saved'. Basically, it's a list of all the names that have ever been entered into their database, whether they murdered them or kept them alive."

Selfishly, I asked, "Was my name in there?"

"Of course. In fact, it was one of the very first ones because of your last name. A few others that are here and still living have the same last name as you. I'm pretty certain you're related to them."

At that my heart stopped. *They're alive?* I thought. *Who are they? Where are they?*

I asked Mark all these questions, but he declined to give me that information. He told me it would be too dangerous, because if I knew the answer and the Keepers found out, I might get myself and my family killed.

"Do you have family here?" I asked him before going to sleep.

"No, my family is on the Mainland," he replied, quickly brushing that aside. "I can't tell you any more just yet; it isn't safe. Sorry. Now get some sleep, you need it."

*Why is he not able to tell me? What does he mean it isn't safe?* I wondered.

All I know is I have a lot of questions, and he keeps a lot of secrets.

# THE ISLES

# Chapter 19

## Alison: VII

This morning I overslept. When I woke up, most of the survivors had cleared out and were up in the main church. Quickly, I put my armor on and made my way upwards. Rejoining them up top, I couldn't believe how happy the citizens looked. These were people who had *nothing*, yet they were still singing hymns of joy! Everyone was smiling as they started to rebuild the walls. *I thought Zita said they would regain their strength little by little?* I wondered as I watched a little old lady walk past me carrying a rock almost the size of her. Axel flew down and put her boulder in a higher part of the wall. "Why didn't you wake me up?" I complained to him.

Flying down, he smiled and joked, "Well, good morning to you too. Yes, I'm doing fine, thank you. And you?"

I punched his arm and helped him out. "You looked pretty banged up," he finally said after we placed a rock down together on a bed of mortar. "And some of your armor was damaged. The Isle III members fixed it for you. They touched mine up, too."

*I really have amazing friends,* I thought, smiling. They fixed my stuff and let me sleep.

After a few hours of nonstop work, we decided to take a break.

We'd made a lot of progress, but the walls weren't strong enough yet. As we sat down, Marlene's stomach let out a loud grumbling noise. "Sorry, I'm kinda hungry, and I don't have any food left. Does anyone have anything to spare?"

Looking in our backpacks, no one found much to munch on. Most of us had shared our food with the locals. "We can check the rubble at the Invaders' H.Q.," Jeremy suggested. "Maybe they have an underground bunker with supplies or something."

"The only problem is, we aren't sure if there will be people hiding in that bunker," Ethan reminded him.

Yared began to feel frustrated. "Well, what other choice do we have?"

Jumping up, Mark said, "None. Let's go."

Those of us who'd gone *into* the stadium yesterday were the ones to go search for food. All the rest stayed behind to help the locals and protect them if necessary… except for Lucas. He begged to join us because of his insatiable appetite. We still hadn't checked every building in Guadalajara; that would take a while. Enemies could've been lurking anywhere.

The moment we got to the stadium we began searching. Wreckage and ruin were the only things left to look at. The height of the walls had been reduced to a quarter of what they were, at most, and some parts had collapsed completely. Most of the barbed wire fence had been melted by the heat of the blast. We hoped there was something more hiding underneath all the debris. After a little while of searching aimlessly, Cecil remembered some helpful information. "Mark, didn't you download all the Invaders' information? Like their maps, plans, and stuff?"

Slapping his hand to his face, Mark responded, "Duh! Yeah, that would be useful. Sorry, guys, I haven't been thinking clearly." Pulling out his clipboard, he scrolled through for a bit until he found something. "We can check the remains of their kitchen; maybe some food survived."

"Yeah, maybe the fire grilled the chicken for us," Yared joked.

Making our way to what used to be the kitchen, I kept a sharp eye out for any signs of life. The only Invaders to be seen were dead ones. It was truly tragic: some were missing parts of their bodies, which scattered across the wreckage. Bloody handprints were pressed up against the walls, showing their failed attempts to get back on their feet and keep going. What made it even more tragic was that most of these men and women were just as much victims as the survivors in the church. *But who was their leader?* I wondered as I stepped over another body. *Why would they do this?*

"Here it was, everyone," Mark said when arrived at more rubble.

A refrigerator lay broken in pieces in one corner, and utensils were scattered all over the floor. Carts were knocked over, and the remains of the cooks lay underneath a fallen counter. Desperately, we began searching, but most of the food had been reduced to ash.

Feeling hopeless, Aaron asked, "Mark, are there any bunkers nearby?"

Checking his clipboard, he told us there were, but it wasn't close on foot. "It's a large bunker, enough to hold more than a hundred people. That means there must be a lot of food down there, but probably enemies as well."

We didn't care; we and the people at the cathedral needed food. Supposedly, the bunker was underneath the remains of the University of Guadalajara, which was an hour's walk away from the stadium. When we arrived, we were confronted with a field of rubble that had once been a well-respected institute of learning. Ripped banners, broken glass, and crushed columns littered the ground. "This place must've been amazing," Sami whispered, as she picked up a piece of the school's flag.

Flying upward, Lucas got an aerial view of what used to be the school. "It was bloody big, too," he called down. "If they made a bunker out of its basement, then there must be heaps of blokes hiding out down there."

Lucas descended, and Mark led us to the entrance: a manhole in the sidewalk. Pulling away the sewer cap, he went down first. Before going all the way in, he said that a few of us should stay up top in case things got out of hand. "This may be the only way in and out," he explained. "We need some people to keep watch up here and send us a message if something happens. Aaron, Sami, Yared, and Lucas will stay up top. Alison, Ethan, Cecil, and I will go in."

No one objected, but Aaron seemed a little worried. "What happens if you don't come up after a while, or we don't hear from you?"

"The map says it isn't that long a walk. Give us thirty minutes to get in and out. Message us, and if we don't respond, come get us. Got it?"

Everyone agreed, and we went in. It was definitely a sewer, and smelled so bad I lost my appetite. *More food for the others,* I thought, plugging my nose.

Mark led us down many different paths. As soon as we got out of one tunnel, he ducked us into another. We walked as quickly and as quietly as possible… well, they walked; I hovered instead. My armor made too much noise for walking. Finally, we reached a cleaner part of the sewer. Blocking our path was a large, circular metal door with a keypad right in the center of it.

"Perfect, just what we needed," Ethan mumbled.

"Hey, I'd expect that attitude from Yared or Ursula, not you," Mark whispered jokingly. Hooking up his clipboard to the panel, Mark worked on granting us access.

*How is he so good at this stuff?* I marveled silently. As far as I know, no one else on Isle III has been taught how to do things like that. Finally, there was a small beeping noise, and the door locks unlatched. We didn't burst through right away, since people would most likely be on the other side. Mark peeked through the crack, and then opened the doors wide and carefully walked inside. The only light in the room was a white projection on the wall in front of us. Doors on the left and right walls led to other rooms. There were people inside, but they didn't do anything when we entered. Hundreds of them sat in chairs, facing the white image. *What are they doing just sitting there?* I wondered, sneaking behind one of them. Looking to Mark for answers, I noticed a disgusted expression on his face. Suddenly, the projection image changed to static, and weird sounds and words filled the place.

# ALISON: VII

Abruptly turning away from the front of the room, Mark warned, "Whatever you do, do *not* look at the images." We all obeyed, despite our confusion. In a fierce tone he explained, "The Invaders are brainwashing these people. This isn't the first time I've seen it being done like this. Didn't you notice they're strapped to the chairs?"

Not looking at whatever the people were watching, Mark quickly shuffled sideways, and we followed him to the first door on the right wall. Thankfully, it was unlocked, and we quickly entered, not worrying about if there were people inside. With our bad luck, there were.

Alarmed, they all stood and reached for their guns, but Mark and I were too quick. We shot all seven of them before they could take their weapons from their holsters. Panting, Mark sank down to the floor and blocked the exit. Concerned, I asked if he was all right.

"Sort of," he replied, as if unsure. "We have to find a way to shut that down." He thought for a moment and went on, "My theory is that they brainwash them first and put the chip in their necks to reinforce it and track them. If we shut it down, maybe we can save them. I'm not sure how far into the process they are, but it couldn't hurt to try." Ending with that, he got back to his feet and searched the small room we were in. This, sadly, was not where the food was kept, but it was filled with computers.

"Do you think one of these could control the projector?" Ethan asked hopefully as he randomly poked a few keys on one of the keyboards. The computer made a sad beeping noise and the screen went black. "Oops," Ethan said, his shoulders shrugged.

"I'm sure it's fine," Mark said as he sat down at the computer next to it. Immediately, he typed away. "If one of these *does* control the projector, then we can definitely save them. We just need to send them a message that they can understand." He typed some more. After a few minutes, he slammed his fists on the desk in frustration. He abruptly stood up from the chair and sat at another computer.

He found what he was looking for on his fourth try. Of course, it was the computer that Ethan had turned off. "It was only on sleep, so nothing was disturbed," Mark told him as he went through the computer's files. "Yes! These are the controls for the projector," he beamed after he found something. "Oh, thank goodness, it tells us how far along they are into it. This is a new batch of people; there's still a chance."

We all gathered around him and watched over his shoulder. Entering a few commands, he shut down whatever was playing outside. I tried to hear if anyone would notice, but it was still dead silent. "Okay, brainwashing paused at 40%," Mark exclaimed happily.

"Forty percent? I thought you said they weren't too far in?" Ethan complained, grabbing his dark head of hair.

"They aren't. It's less than half," Mark argued. "Okay, time to send them a new message to play over and over and over again, until they snap out of it: a short and sweet message. Alison, you're going to be the one to say it."

The boys all turned around and looked at me, which made me uneasy. "No, I can't do it. I don't know what to say! What if I don't sound convincing enough?"

Smiling, Mark explained, "Your voice will be overdubbed by a robot translating it into Spanish, but we need your expressions to be convincing. I'm choosing you because you're a girl and you definitely give off that comforting, motherly vibe." Looking into my gray eyes, Mark said, "Do it for them."

The boys all stepped away from the computer. Taking a deep breath, I pressed Record and spoke as confidently as possible. "Citizens of Guadalajara, this is all a lie. Don't listen to them. Go back to who you were; don't let them change you. We need you to fight back! The world is in your hands." I finished the recording, and Mark came back and sent it out.

Patting my back, Mark complimented, "That was perfect; you convinced *me*." He walked over to the door. "Let's get some supplies and see what effect that has on them after a few minutes."

That plan had more complications than we thought. We left the room and found Invaders rushing around trying to figure out what was wrong with the image. When they saw us, they stopped what they were doing, grabbed their weapons, and attacked. We had no choice but to fight back. These *had* to be people who had volunteered. They were stronger than the ones back in the stadium. Also, the people strapped in the chairs and most of the ones who had died at the base looked like inhabitants of Mexico. These people looked like they were from all over the world.

It was an interesting fight. The enemies knew what they were doing and occasionally used the inhabitants as shields. Thankfully, we were smarter and more careful than they were. We were able to take them down and keep the inhabitants safe. During the fight, we received a message from our teammates on the surface: "*Are you all okay?*" While I was knocking out four men, I responded that we would be a little delayed but to stay up there and send another message in ten minutes.

Five minutes later, our attackers were on the floor, either wounded or dead. After we moved their bodies, a few people in the chairs began to scream; some in fear, others in confusion. The rest of the people were still staring at the screen. Running up to one of the screaming hostages, Mark asked what the problem was. The man just frantically asked questions, expecting an answer to them all at once. "Who are you, and what is your purpose in life?" Mark asked him before answering anything.

The man stopped panicking for a moment and stared at him, wondering why he had asked such a deep question. He replied: "My name is Miguel Rodriguez. My purpose in life is to help my family survive... speaking of which, where are they?!"

Mark smiled, unstrapped him, and instructed him to ask the same questions to the other shouting hostages, and keep that chain going. Quickly, he explained why. When Miguel understood, he went right to work.

Mark rejoined us, and we headed through a door on the left wall. Behind it, we found the jackpot: Crates of supplies were stacked everywhere. Food, bandages, water, you name it. While we were gathering the boxes, we received the next message from the team up top. We told them we were coming up but to give us ten minutes before they came down in a panic to retrieve us.

Once we all had two or more crates, we made our way back to the surface. Mark waved goodbye to Miguel and the others who were saved. They had convinced us that they could handle themselves if any other Invaders came to check on them.

Finally, we were all out of the sewer and headed back with the supplies. It was almost evening when we reached the cathedral, which was almost completely repaired on the outside. Axel was working on the collapsed steeple, and most of the locals were working on reinforcing the door and the walls around it. When they saw us with the crates, they all gave a loud cheer.

We rationed the food so that everyone got some, but there were still left overs. We'd taken up ten big crates with us. The boys each took two and needed help bringing theirs back, but I took four on my own. Not to brag or anything.

Before eating, Father Sandro gave us all a blessing, which was really nice. *I think I'm beginning to like the way they do things around here,* I thought. I would love to be happy when I have nothing, just like them. Looking around, I complimented my friends' work. "The place is coming along really nicely."

"I can't believe how much we got done in one day," Axel said, sounding satisfied.

"We worked our butts off with barely any breaks," Marlene reminded him.

"Well, no matter what it was, the point is that this cathedral is stronger now than it was before and will hopefully keep our friends safe when we leave," Zita concluded.

"That reminds me," Ethan chimed in, wiping crumbs off his face. "Has anyone even heard from the Keepers at all? I know I haven't."

No one else had either, not even Mark. "We really have been on our own, haven't we?" Ava asked timidly.

Pulling her close, Marlene comforted her. "We have each other, and that's all we need. This just proves that we don't need the Keepers. We can survive on our own, and we can help others survive as well."

She was right. We have had no assistance from them whatsoever. It makes me feel confident.

"Besides, the Keepers aren't the most trustworthy people anyway," Mark added.

At the sound of that, Jeremy began to get defensive. In fact, whenever someone said something that slighted the Keepers, he went crazy. "Well, how do we know *you're* trustworthy?" he accused, pointing his tiny finger. "You've taken control of us all, making plans and bossing us around! You haven't even graduated from Isle III yet, and you think you're in control of everything. If I didn't know any better, I'd say you're a spy for the Invaders."

Speechless, Mark just stared at him. "Why would you say something like that?"

Jeremy gritted his teeth. "The Keepers did everything they could to protect us and keep us safe. It's our job to defend them and respect them, even if it means our own deaths."

Mark rubbed the stubble on his face, and then held his chin in his palm, resting his elbow on his knee. Before saying anything, he stared at Jeremy. Without taking his hand from his face, Mark asked, "What did you do in class when you were just starting here?"

Taken aback by the question, Jeremy's reply sounded unsure. "Um, we read books from the Keepers' book list… I think."

"Is that when you were just starting, or in the middle?"

"In the middle, I think."

"Then what did you do when you first started?"

Jeremy's face had a mixed expression of frustration and confusion. "I don't know! Why don't I remember? I can't remember what happened last year or the years before." He thought for a moment, then became agitated. "Why do you care, anyway?"

Crossing his arms and leaning back against a stone, Mark rested his case. "There's the evidence right there. Think really hard, everyone. Do you remember anything of your life before you were part of the Isles?"

No one said anything.

Finally, I spoke up. "I remember the last day I was on the Mainland. I told some of you about that. But like I said before, I can't remember the names of my family members or even my last name."

"Exactly," Mark exclaimed, pointing at me. "And why is that? My theory is because if we knew who we were and what we believed in, most of us wouldn't agree with the Keepers' ways and what they say is right."

I couldn't believe what he was saying. *Could he be right?* I wondered. *Or is he really the enemy, like Jeremy said?* Yet everything he was saying made sense.

"So, how did they make us forget?" Ethan asked with concern.

Mark was afraid to look him in the eye when he gave him the answer. "When Aaron, Cecil, and I broke into the Saviors control room, I... sort of asked the boys to take books that Mr. Bamber didn't know about."

Ethan was baffled. "I don't understand why that would have anything to do with my question. Okay, we forgive you. Is that what you wanted to hear?"

Mark smiled and said, "Well, thank you for your forgiveness, but there's more. The three books we stole were titled *Blueprints*, *Doctor's Manual*, and *The Saved*. The first one, *Blueprints*, contains the layout of the entire Saviors' Isle, revealing hidden places that no student knows about. The *Doctor's Manual* is the rule book all the doctors at Saviors must follow. *The Saved* is the book where they document anyone they took off the Mainland.

"Whoever is 'rescued' from the Mainland has to complete a particular process before they're set free. If the patients don't forget certain information after the process is completed, they're considered a hazard—and immediately killed. If they do forget and pass the test, but are too old, they finish out the rest of their lives in the villages."

He looked at all our faces, one by one, and went on. "Haven't you noticed that all the people living in the towns around your facilities are over twenty? If they're healthy children, they enter the facilities to become puppets for the Keepers. If the children are 'defective' or unhealthy, they're killed as well. The Keepers think their actions are compassionate."

We all sat there in silence, taking in the painful truth he was throwing at us. No one was more shocked than the members of

Saviors. "All of our training ends with us murdering people the Keepers don't deem worthy?" Zita faltered, choking back tears.

"I'm sorry, but it's all in there. You can read it if you like. It's in my backpack, along with the other books. There's more I need to tell you all, but I'll have to save it for tomorrow." He made eye contact with each one of us and begged, "Promise me that you won't fall for the lies. I know some of you are wondering if Jeremy is right about me, but trust me: I'm on your side." Ending the conversation, Mark stood up and walked away, slumped over, with his hands in the pockets of his navy combat pants.

None of us said anything, and prepared to go to sleep right there. Nobody dared to ask about the books.

I definitely needed to document all of this today. I'm still having a hard time figuring out whether Mark is telling the truth or not. Is everything we lived for all for nothing?

Is it all a lie?

# THE ISLES

# CHAPTER 20

## Sami: VII

This morning, everyone was in a glum mood. What Mark told us yesterday got everyone thinking. I wish he would get it over with and tell us everything at once instead of keeping secrets.

When everyone was awake and ready, the commanders finally received messages from the Keepers. "They say it's time for us to come back," Mark began, once we were gathered around. "Now, I need to tell you all something important. When we get back, things might happen. The Keepers might have heard what we were talking about yesterday. Hopefully, only I'll be taken into custody. I've felt that they've been watching me the entire five years I've been here, waiting for me to say something they can hold against me."

*Only five years?* I thought, amazed. About the time I became a Mutant, he became a part of Isle III. It was all so weird.

Looking at our shocked faces, he said, "Yes, it's only been five years, but it's not safe to discuss why. The jet is coming to pick us up at ten o'clock tonight. Let's finish our work here before they arrive."

Throughout the day, we made a ton of progress. We continued to reinforce the walls and door of the church, found a little more food to store, and even acquired weapons just in case the survivors faced more trouble. During the late afternoon, a flood of new people came in searching for shelter. "It's the people the Invaders tried to brainwash!" Cecil exclaimed as they entered the church. They carried dozens of crates filled with supplies, weapons, and more. A man named Miguel Rodriguez went right up to Mark and gave him a hug. I've never seen someone who had been through hell act so cheerful. Miguel thanked Mark over and over again for his help and asked if there was anything that he could do.

Mark gave him the task of helping the survivors in the cathedral. He instructed Miguel to find more survivors, to assist them in rebuilding the beautiful city of Guadalajara, and to never lose faith in God and themselves, no matter what. Miguel accepted in a heartbeat and swore to do all he could until the day he died.

We finally got the last "brainwash survivor" settled in just before the jet came to pick us up, landing on what had once been the plaza in front of the church. We'd had people clearing it all day. Father Sandro gave us a goodbye blessing, and then we bid our friends farewell. We climbed into the jet and prepared to return to the Isles.

Before we took off, though, the pilot and co-pilot violently seized Mark before he could settle in, securing him with parachute cord and cuffing him. Throwing him into his seat, the pilot buckled him in tightly and slammed the protective bars down. We were perplexed as to why they made such an effort to keep him secure; it wasn't like he could go anywhere.

If the pilots had waited until we were closer to our destination, their plan might have worked.

We were airborne and getting up to speed when Mark made his move. Somehow, he slithered out of the tightly-wound cording. He was still in handcuffs, but that didn't slow him much. He slid a pocketknife-looking thing out of his sleeve and began messing with some buttons next to his seat. He was able to release the bars just a little and unlatch his seat belt; then he slid out and crouched next to Alison, asking her to cut the bar between his handcuffs using the jets in her hands. She was hesitant at first, but did it for him anyway, taking care not to burn him. Then he used a tiny stylus to pick the locks in each cuff, and removed the bracelets.

Unfortunately, the pilot and co-pilot heard the clatter of his cuffs and both jumped up to stop him. It was an unfair fight—not for Mark, but for his attackers. The pilot attacked first. With a knife in each hand, he dove for Mark's chest, but was dodged and thrown to the ground. Mark smacked him on the back of the head with the hilt of his own knife and put him to sleep. The other grabbed Mark from behind, trying to strangle him. Mark gripped the man's arms and threw him on top of his unconscious comrade; he struggled to his feet, but was knocked out from a punch to the face. I became very frightened. Mark had escaped from an impossible situation and had taken out two men as if it was nothing! The fighting style he used wasn't anything like what we were taught. *Who will he go after next?* I wondered.

Mark gagged and tied up his attackers, using the same cords they'd used on him. Before going into the cockpit, he held a little device up to their foreheads until it made a beeping noise. When he was finished, he headed to the front and released our safety bars. "You may now move freely about the cabin," he said over the loudspeaker. But we all remained in our seats, dumbfounded; we had no idea what to make of the whole situation. After fiddling with the autopilot for a few moments, Mark came back and began to apologize. "I know what you're all thinking, but you have to trust me on this. Please, this can save us all."

"What are you talking about? You just attacked those men and tied them up!" Aaron bellowed. "Who knows what they're going to do to us now?"

Sympathetically, Mark replied, "Aaron, please, you have to calm down. I don't have much time to talk. I've been interfering with the Bionics' video feed and your bracelet trackers ever since we landed on the Mainland. Unfortunately, I think they've overcome my interference. There's a chance they heard more than I originally thought."

Everyone was aggravated and began shouting. Jeremy was defending the Keepers, Aaron and Cecil were outraged that he was interfering with our communications, and the rest of us couldn't believe he'd done all these things in secret. I actually hissed at him when he tried to explain himself. I can't believe I did that now.

Moving towards Axel and Alison, he said, "Please, we don't have time. I know this is an insane request, but do you think I could tweak your Optic Transmitters just a little?"

They were so stunned that they didn't know how to reply. "Hold up," Axel started finally. "You want to go into our brains and mess around with our eyeballs? Are you nuts?"

Alison stared at Mark as if she was deciding whether she should blow his head off or to let Axel do it.

"Please," Mark begged. "I think it's time you had a little freedom. You don't understand; I know what they can do to you."

"What is that?" Alison questioned.

"Hold up your left hands," he told them. "You see that white circle around your ring finger with the line that runs all the way to your heart?"

"Yeah, it means I'm married to my armor," Axel said jokingly.

"I guess you could say that. Do you know why wedding rings go on that particular finger?"

"Because of the *vena amoris* vein that supposedly leads to the heart," Harold informed. In a comedic manner, he daintily held out his left hand as an example.

"Exactly," Mark stated. "What that actually is…" he paused. Rubbing the brand on the back of his neck, he did his best to look the Bionics in the eyes. "It's a kill switch," he said finally. "When activated, toxins are released into your veins to block your coronary artery, giving you a heart attack. It was confirmed in *The Doctor's Manual* under the requirements for Biomechatronic operations. There's an activation code under your files in *The Saved*."

Alison looked like she was going to scream, and Axel couldn't believe his ears. "No! That's not it at all," Axel denied. Thinking about it, he tried to make up an excuse. "The designer just thought it would look awesome!"

"Think about it! Have they ever told you what it's for?" Mark argued. "The Bionics are the most powerful people on all of the Isles.

They're strong enough to overcome the Keepers and every island if they want. Mr. Allaway and Mr. Nik don't have suits of armor, do they? So if you get any ideas, Mr. Allaway can get rid of you like that," he said, snapping his fingers.

Axel was trying to make up another explanation as tears slid down Alison's face. "If you let me help you," Mark said, "I can cut you off from the Keepers completely. No surgery required. I cut my clipboard off from them in the beginning. This morning, I did the same to my bracelet."

After some consideration, Alison and Axel both agreed to let Mark do it. Fearing their lives, a few other friends asked him to disconnect their devices as well. "I'm going to do everyone's," he explained, "but I can only do Axel and Alison right now. The rest of us will have to meet up in a safe place once we get back, if we get separated. I'll explain later."

Mark had Alison go first. She lay on her back on the floor with her hands close to her sides and her feet together. She grabbed Mark's shirt, pulled him close, and whispered something in his ear. He nodded and muttered something back. He took out his clipboard, a small silver device, and some wires with suction cups on them from his backpack. He connected the wires to the device, then the device to his clipboard. Four suction cups were placed across Alison's forehead, and two on her eyes. "Don't close your eyes," he instructed. "Stare right at them."

She began to shake, so I held her left hand. Aaron sat next to Mark on the other side and held her opposite hand. "Ready?" Mark asked. She nodded slowly, and he began the process. As I watched, I wondered what was going on. It took a few minutes before we could see anything happening. At first, she began to shake vigorously, and then she lay still and started drooling. That went on for almost 45 minutes. "What is going on?" Axel asked horrified, after she shook harder than the first dozen times.

"I know it looks bad, but remember, we're working with her brain," Mark replied, without pausing what he was doing.

"What are you doing to her brain?" Jeremy asked, frightened.

"I've already cut her off from the Keepers," Mark told him, "but now I'm doing what she asked."

"What did she ask? Because I probably don't want it," Axel demanded.

"She wants to remember," he replied. "Everything."

After a little while, Alison began to scream. "Remembering too much, too much!" Mark exclaimed. Frantically, he typed some commands on his clipboard and shut the whole thing down. Alison stopped shouting and began breathing heavily. Mark took away the suction cups and asked me to cradle her head. I stroked her forehead with my hand, and stared into her eyes, which seemed far away and distant. The black lines connected to her pupils were still there but something was different. The chain-looking mark had faded away.

Noticing this, Mark sighed in relief. "That's a good thing. Now, just hold her until she's calm."

Axel went through his entire operation in no time. His was much faster, because he didn't want to remember right now. He shook and drooled a little, but not as much as Alison. He recovered almost instantly. Sitting up when he was finished, Axel asked, "Are the chains in my eyes gone?" Mark nodded, and Axel stared at Alison and began to worry. "Will she be okay?"

"Yes," Mark said softly. "I wish she could have waited, but she seemed so sincere. I told her she can't tell anyone anything yet. I have another way of making everyone remember all at once. I just need time."

"Do you know something about her past that we don't?" I asked.

"Yes. I know things about all of you that you don't know," he replied. "I went through all your files, including everything documented since you arrived at the Isles."

*Why is he concealing all this from us?* I wondered, upset.

Before I could start an argument, Alison came to. She blinked a few times, looked straight up at me, and began sobbing. Quickly, she sat up and gave me a tight hug. "All this time…" she whispered raggedly.

While we took turns hugging her, Mark solemnly put his things away. "Alison, Axel, I need you both to put on these glasses," he said, handing them what looked like old-fashioned reading glasses with thick frames.

Putting them on, Axel asked, "What are these?"

"Optic Transmitters, so Mr. Allaway doesn't know I cut off your communication from him," Mark told him. "Those will let him know where you are, and you can receive messages from him, but you can't send any back. If you do, he can track your signal."

Confused, Ethan said, "Wait, why did they go through that whole process if you were going to give them those glasses?"

"Because now he can still think nothing has changed. They'll only wear them when we aren't with the Keepers. Just trust me."

Suddenly, something at the controls started making a beeping noise. "Oh no, I think a call is coming in," Mark said, sounding slightly worried. "I put the jet at normal speed so we would have seven hours, but now we only have two hours left. They must be wondering where we are." He jumped back into the cockpit and denied the call. "Strap yourselves in everyone; we have to go in at Mach 3. I'll have to put the pilots back where they belong. I used a miniature Memory Be Gone device to make them forget what happened. Also, I need one of you to tie me up like they did before."

Untying and ungagging the pilots, we quickly put them back into their seats. Yared and Ursula retied and cuffed Mark, and the rest of us sat down. Mark gave some last-minute instructions to his fellow Isle member. "Aaron, take good care of my backpack when they take me in, okay? Don't let them have it and don't take anything out, understood?"

Aaron promised and took the backpack.

Thankfully, the pilots became conscious in time to prepare the jet for landing. It didn't seem like they remembered Mark knocking them out at all. They just complained about the lumps on their heads and wondered what was for dinner tonight.

Thinking about that made my stomach rumble. *I hope they have leftovers for us.*

Finally, we landed, but our safety bars weren't released right away. When the back of the jet opened, a bunch of Seers rushed in with guns and surrounded Mark.

Mark smiled and jiggled his new handcuffs. They took him out of his seat, put him in one of the Seers cars, and drove him away. Once they were out of sight, our safety bars lifted.

Before we left, the pilot came out of the cockpit to apologize. "Sorry for that. We received an anonymous tip that Mark might be working for the Invaders and has been lying to you all this time. They're going to take him in for questioning. If he's innocent, then you'll see him again."

With that, we left him and headed for the cafeteria. While we were on our way, we got a message telling us to go straight to Stratum Zero's classroom and not to worry about food, because they would have some there. "Yay, food," Marlene said unenthusiastically.

When we entered, the Keepers applauded. They seemed quite satisfied with our work and wanted to throw a party. There was a variety of mouthwatering food and beverages on each counter, but we weren't really in the mood to eat. Noticing our attitudes, Mr. Nik addressed us all. "Please don't be upset about Mark. I am sure we're wrong about him. We just have to be sure, is all."

The Keepers sat down and chatted with us, asking us questions about our experience. We responded to them as best we could and never mentioned what Mark said to us the night before.

Soon, the clock struck the next hour, and Mr. Nik seemed to realize how tired we all were. "Oh my goodness, you are all five hours ahead of us! It must feel like five in the morning to you all," he said sympathetically. "We'll show you to your sleeping quarters. I hope you don't mind, but since the classes are back in session, you will all have to remain quiet and unseen. There is a community dormitory on the top floor where you can stay. Sleep late tomorrow, everyone."

Mr. Bamber then led us to our room. It had a beautiful view overlooking the ocean. The moon and stars reflected on the water, and the trees swayed gently in the wind. I wanted to enjoy the scenery, but I was too tired and upset. "If you need anything, there is a button on the wall to contact a staff member," the old man said, pointing to a round silver doorbell. Once he was sure we were settled, Mr. Bamber

# SAMI: VII

said goodnight and wheeled himself out of the room.

When he was gone, we decided on our sleeping arrangements. We girls slept in the beds against the right wall, and the boys were in the ones opposite against the glass. Despite my exhaustion, I couldn't get comfy in bed. Looking over, I saw Alison having the same problem as me. She still looked shaken-up from before.

Thankfully, she finally fell asleep just a few minutes ago. Honestly, I wanted to make sure she could sleep before I did. So now it's my turn. I really hope Mark is okay. I also hope he's actually on our side—but why should I question him anymore? He could have flown that plane anywhere, but he still took us back home. Why? He could have been free, but now he's stuck in confinement, wherever that is.

But I have a feeling we will see him soon.

# THE ISLES

# CHAPTER 21

## Aaron: VII

Nobody slept in this morning. In fact, we all woke up earlier than usual and immediately got dressed in the new clothes we were given. I have never been so happy to put on my Isle's blue polo shirt in my life. Those navy combat uniforms were so uncomfortable.

When I was done, I decided to check up on Alison. "Hey, how are you feeling?" I asked as I went over to see her. She sat on the edge of her bed, slumped over with her arms lying across her lap. She didn't hear me. I cleared my throat, which startled her. "Sorry," I apologized.

"No, no, I'm sorry. I was just thinking," she replied.

"Are you okay?"

"Yeah, I think so. It's just…." She seemed hesitant to finish. She looked up at me with tears in her eyes. "There is so much I want to say but shouldn't. I remember almost everything of my life before, but there are still bits and pieces that aren't there. Mark shut down the process before it was finished, I heard."

"Yeah, you heard correctly." Taking off my glasses, I cleaned them and said, "It was dangerous. Besides, Mark says he has another way of making *everyone* remember, but easier and less painfully."

She smiled as I put my glasses back on but didn't speak. The way she was staring at me kind of made me uncomfortable. That weird feeling I had when I first met her came back. *What is this?* I thought when I felt it.

"All right, who's ready?" Yared asked before I could say anything else. He headed for the door with Jeremy and Ursula close behind.

"To do what?" Ethan asked.

"Get Mark out and interrogate him ourselves," he replied with a smirk.

We finished getting dressed, grabbed our packs, and headed out.

"Classes will most likely be in session today, which is perfect," Yared said when we were in the elevator. "All the staff will be busy with the other students, and I'm sure the Isle Keepers are busy as well. But we have to be careful with our bracelets. Mark didn't disable them."

That reminded me. "Alison, Axel, do you want me to hold onto your glasses so they can't get a video of what we're up to? If they beep, you can check the messages."

They agreed and gave them to me. I placed them carefully in the front pocket of Mark's backpack. I was so tempted to open it and rummage through everything just because he told me not to, but I'd promised him I wouldn't. *But still...* I thought, staring at the tattered blue bag.

*Ding!* The elevator opened and we were on the cafeteria floor. Flinging the heavy backpack over my shoulders, I followed the others out.

Most of the students hadn't arrived yet. Only a few were there, studying. "We're early," Cecil whispered.

"We have to keep quiet," Marlene warned. "Everyone was told that the other Isle members left a while ago. We'll arouse suspicion."

We devised a plan that Cecil and I would get everyone's food, while the others hid in one of the vacant classrooms. I gave Ethan Mark's bag to hold and took his to fill with food. When we were ready, we split up. Cecil and I ducked into the kitchen and hid behind a counter. My heart was racing. *I feel like I'm in that first dinosaur movie,* I thought, as I heard a cook coming closer. Quickly, we stuffed our backpacks full of food when no one was looking. To be honest, that was more suspenseful than my time on the Mainland. Stuffing a few muffins in my mouth, I motioned to Cecil and we ran out. When we met up with the others, I looked like a chipmunk that was storing nuts in his cheeks for later.

"You should probably swallow all that before you choke and die," Sami said seriously.

*I can't tell if she's joking,* I thought as I gulped down my muffins. I mean, it was also hard to tell if she was smiling or not because of her fangs. *Which are awesome,* I thought as I stared at her.

Cecil elbowed me to stop gawking and help him hand out food. After we passed it out, I traded bags with Ethan and took Mark's back. We all ate as fast as we could, afraid that a teacher might walk in on us. We chose the classroom closest to Stratum Zero in case we needed a quick escape. That classroom was my homeroom when I was in Stratum Eight.

*I wish I could see Mrs. Pieper again,* I thought nostalgically as I looked around the room.

Be careful what you wish for, because you just might get it. She walked in and froze dead in her tracks. Her jaw dropped, and her coffee mug crashed to the floor. Her eyes jumped from face to face. Her expressions changed from terrified to shocked to just plain confused. Without thinking, Becca dashed behind her and shut the door. "What on Earth?!" Mrs. Pieper exclaimed.

Regaining my senses, I ran up to her and gave her a hug. "Wait, who are—" she pushed me away and stared at my face for a few minutes. "Aaron?"

"Yes, Mrs. Pieper," I said smiling. "How have you been?"

Her brown eyes welled up with tears, and she pulled me close, "I thought they did something terrible to you!"

I pulled away and put my hands on her shoulders. "Mrs. Pieper, we need your help."

She wasn't exactly paying attention. She kept commenting on how big and handsome I'd become. I already knew that, but... ya know. I towered over her now; I didn't realize how short she actually was. When she was done complimenting me, she snapped back into reality. "Oh, Aaron, you have to get out of here! They've taken Mark; they might take you too!"

We couldn't believe she knew that. On the inside I was freaking out, but I remained outwardly cool. Calmly, I asked, "How do you know that, Mrs. Pieper? Where have they taken him?"

She was afraid to meet my eyes. "I've been keeping an eye on him ever since I helped sneak him onto Isle III."

Behind me, my friends gasped. Mrs. Pieper kept her eyes to the ground and dared not to look up. A million questions swirled through my head, but I didn't want to upset her. Keeping it together, I chuckled and said, "I'm happy it was you who found us, then."

Taken aback by my response to the situation, she slowly replied, "I'm glad you're taking it so well." She took my hands and held them. "You have to hurry and get him out. Once he's safe, I can tell you more." Letting go, she went over to the whiteboard. She tapped it a few times and sent Mark's location to our bracelet mapping apps. She told us that Mark was hidden underneath the cafeteria in Isle III. Apparently, he was in the *actual* Nerve Center, where the Keepers met and Mr. Nik lived. Everything was run from that room. "It's the brain and heart of all the Isles," she said.

*Which is both creepy and nasty,* I thought.

"I'll cover for you as much as I can," she promised as she walked back over to me. "Go quickly. He's been in confinement long enough."

I thanked her, gave her another hug, and lead the others out. We snuck our way back to the cafeteria. When we got there, the other students were finishing up breakfast. We had to wait for them to clear out before we could do anything. We hid in the hall for twenty minutes until the bell rang.

Trying not to be seen as the other students went to their classes was the hard part for my friends. Lucas, Alison, and Axel hovered in the air over the passing students, while the others ducked into the bathrooms and the janitors' closet. Cecil and I, however, went against the crowd, telling whoever asked that we forgot something. They didn't see us much anyway; they were used to us roaming around.

Finally, everyone left, and we were alone in the cafeteria. Before we began searching for a way in, Marlene said she'd be right back. She ran to the kitchen and came back with food and a shiny silver pot. She handed out the snacks and gave her second seat the pot. "Here, Donnie, I think you should wear this instead," she said, munching on some cookies. "I think that wooden bucket is beginning to fall apart!"

"Golly, thanks, Top Banana!" he said gleefully. Quickly, he took off his broken bucket, ruffled his dirty-blond hair, and put his new "helmet" on. Not knowing what to do with the old one, he threw it behind him. It hit the nearest bookshelf and knocked some books out. "Oops," he said, embarrassed.

"Wait, that's it," Cecil exclaimed. "Look for books that have to do with lair, home, home improvement, or anything like that!"

He was a genius. Mr. Bamber's entrances were always operated by book levers, and the books always hinted at what they opened. *But what would Mr. Nik label his as?* I thought, as I ran over to a bookshelf. "We have to make sure we put everything back the way it was; otherwise the workers might get suspicious," I called as I carelessly threw books on the ground.

Everyone rushed to a shelf and frantically began searching. We were looking for a while before some of us began to lose hope. "We pulled out every book about living, evil lairs, and rooms," Ursula said frustrated.

"Why would he label it as 'evil'?" Ava thought aloud. "He doesn't know he's evil."

While Ava and Ursula were arguing about adjectives, the rest of us tried to think of what else it could've been. After a few moments, Alison said, "When I first got here, Mr. Nik said that he and the others *predicted* the Invaders would take over, and that history repeats itself. Maybe we should look for something on prediction or fiction books about the future."

"That might take forever, and we don't have forever," Lucas reminded as he flew above a shelf and sat at the top of it. "Also, looking through *all* the bloody futuristic books? Do you know how many there are?" He outstretched his arms and shook them slightly up and down. "Heaps!"

"He's right," Sami agreed. "We would be here forever."

Then, I remembered something. "Guys, I think I know the book! Cecil, you know the painting of Mr. Nik down by Classroom Twenty? The older members said it reminded them of something called 'Big Brother'. What book is that from? They told me the name, but I forget."

Snapping his fingers, he ran up the stairs to the sci-fi shelf and pulled out the book 1984 by George Orwell. "There's a blinking light in the back!" he yelled. "It seems like we need another book to open the door!"

"Well, what do you know," Alison said amazed. "I knew I hated that portrait of him for a reason."

"Okay, does anyone else know what the other could be?" I asked, interrupting Jeremy and Alison's dispute about the painting.

Unexpectedly, Jeremy gave a suggestion after failing to get the last word in their argument. "Communist Manifesto, by Friedrich Engels and Karl Marx. That is the first thing I read—well, that I can remember—when I came here."

"It was on Mr. Nik's reading list," Yared confirmed. "We had a bunch of different books to read from each Keeper, and that was one on his list. We had to take out important points of each book, memorize it, and practice it. No one was sure what any of them meant, exactly; we just did as we were told."

"We always do what we're told," Ursula stated as she crossed her thick arms.

Before another argument could start, I rushed over to the economics section. Quickly scanning it, I spotted a thin book that wasn't like the rest. It was the only one not covered in dust. "Come to Aaron," I said, pulling it out. I rubbed my hand over the old book and chuckled. "Of course it was this one."

Looking up at the empty space in the book shelf, I saw two buttons with LED lights in the back: one red, the other green. I reached my hand back and pressed the red one. As I took my hand out, it changed to green. Suddenly, I heard the sound of mechanical gears. "Aaron! Cecil! Over here!" Becca shouted from the middle of the cafeteria.

Coming back, I found that the floor tile with the number three on it had slid aside to reveal a spiral staircase. I was shocked. Sure, I knew there was a door *somewhere*, but I didn't expect it to be right under our noses. After we gawked for a few minutes, we snapped out of it and proceeded down cautiously. Axel led the way down the dark, winding staircase with his armor lights on. Alison went as the caboose, so no one would be left behind. I felt like I was getting sick going in circles down the stairs, but at last we reached the bottom.

We found ourselves stopped before a door with no handle. Axel waved his hand in front of it a few times to see if it was automatic, but nothing happened. I looked around and saw a small book slot on the right wall. Reaching past Axel, I put the books inside, and the metal door opened. We all shuffled our way inside the small hallway, only to find more closed doors. We had four choices: the first one on the left was 'Bed Chamber,' the second was 'Nerve Center,' the third was 'Inquiry,' and the last was 'Emergency Exit.'

"I like that one," Harold said, pointing to the fourth door.

Blinking a few times, Axel looked around and peered at the third door. "I'm getting thermal readings from the Inquiry room," he whispered. "I'm detecting eight bodies. One of them seems tied to something. One is hovering over him, and the other six are sitting around a table."

"It has to be them," Zita assumed.

"Oh no, one of them is coming this way!" Axel warned as he motioned us to get back. Without thinking, we all went through the Nerve Center door.

We closed the door behind us and couldn't believe what was inside. The place was enormous! Computers, shelves, lab counters, equipment, and any sort of science thing you could imagine lined the perimeter. On the walls were pictures of people, newspaper clippings, and written documents. Above the door we came in was a long portrait of the Keepers and Mr. Nik. In the center were seven computers surrounding one large blue hologram that looked just like the one inside the stadium at Guadalajara.

Ethan pointed to it and asked, "Anyone find that suspicious?"

"I find everything in here suspicious," Zita said, going through some old newspapers at one of the desks.

Walking over to one of their counters, I found some open blueprints. There was a watermark on all of them: Powell Enterprises. *None of the Keepers are named Powell,* I thought. Picking them up, I looked them over. They were advanced, complex blueprints for the defense technology the Isles used. When I was done reading them, something enticed me to take some. Unable to resist, I rolled a few up and shoved them in Mark's backpack. To cover my tracks, I took some blueprints that were in a bin next to the counter and placed them on the table as replacements.

"Guys, we should get out of here," Ursula said in a panicked tone as she picked up a bucket of bolts she'd accidentally knocked over. The Seers girl was nervous rather than impatient this time. She fiddled with her yellowish-gray hair and pressed Yared for them to leave. Denying her request, he pointed toward Alison, Axel, and Cecil, who were at the main computers.

"One minute," Alison told her. "We're almost finished copying all of their data onto Cecil's super-duper hard drive."

Without taking his eyes off the hologram screen, Cecil explained, "Mark's looking for something, and I bet this has what he's looking for. It's everything they have. I'm relieved it all fits onto my drive."

Losing his patience with Ursula pestering him, Yared yelled, "Well, hurry up! Is anyone watching the door?"

We weren't—and suddenly, Mr. Bamber came into the room. We all turned and stared at him, and he stared right back. It was an awkward moment. Donnie and Ava, who were supposed to be watching the entrance, slowly closed the door and locked it behind the Keeper. "What are you all doing?" Mr. Bamber cried as he wheeled himself towards us.

Before anyone could say anything, I went to him and said desperately, "Looking for Mark. Wally's men took him away, and we're here to find him!'"

"But how did you find this place?" he marveled.

"We used our brilliant minds and figured it out," I lied. "Mr. Nik had to live somewhere, right?"

Mr. Bamber stared at me, amazed. After a few minutes, he began to laugh. "Oh, my boy! You truly are incredible! I hope you haven't touched anything, though." He glanced around the room. Not seeing Cecil behind the hologram, the Keeper nodded and said, "Everything seems to be in order, thank you. I wouldn't want to put you all through what Mark had to last night. Walter goes too crazy… I feel bad for the boy. You really shouldn't be down here," he warned.

"But no one told us we couldn't come down here," I argued. "No one even knows this place exists."

Chuckling again, Mr. Bamber replied, "You're right. I will have to talk to Nik about that. As for your friend Mark, I can't tell you where he is, but I can put in a request for you to see him, if you'd like." With that, he asked Donnie and Ava to open the door for him, and went out. He beckoned us to leave before anyone else found us. *I really underappreciate Mr. Bamber and his obnoxious ties,* I thought, smiling as I followed him out. Thankfully, Cecil had just finished the download when we left.

"I will give you an answer in a little while," Mr. Bamber told us. "But for now, you have to go. Here is the exit. It goes right up to Stratum Zero's classroom. I'll be in touch. I will also ask Mr. Nik about whether it was wrong or not for you to come down here, okay?" He opened the exit door and led us to an elevator. Once we were all piled in and squished tight, he waved goodbye and the door shut.

It took an agonizing five minutes of being crammed in the elevator car before we were released into the classroom. Turning around, I watched as the elevator disappeared behind a bookshelf. "Huh, go figure," Cecil said.

"Well, that can't just be an exit. How else would Mr. Bamber get down there in his wheelchair?" Marlene pointed out as she sat down at one of the tables.

"We probably have a long time to figure that out, but we should go through their files for the time being," Axel suggested. "I found some pretty interesting things that we should check out. Cecil, can you look for the folder named 'Inquiry Footage,' and click on the file from last night?"

Cecil sat next to Marlene, pulled out his super-drive, and plugged it into a nearby laptop. There was a lot to go through, but he soon found it. Huddling around the computer, we watched as he clicked play. By the time we were ten seconds in, we were petrified. Mr. Bamber wasn't kidding when he said, "Walter goes too crazy." This is what we saw:

"Who do you work for?" Wally demanded.

Mark sat silently, tied to a chair at the head of a table in a dark, cold-looking room. His face was swollen and disfigured. His hair was a mess, and his shirt was torn.

"How did you get in here?" Wally yelled. "Ever since those books went missing from Saviors, ve have been vatching you." Wally bent over and stared our friend in the face. "Ve looked up your files, but found minimal information. Ve know everything about everyone else except you. Why is that?"

Mark looked up at him and said in a slurred voice, "I've only been here five years. You sent out a search party and came back with a few people. I was one of them, remember?"

"Oh, yes. I remember that. I don't remember rescuing *you*." Wally walked to the back of the room, put both of his hands on the table, and stared at Mark. After thinking for a few minutes, the Keeper took off his round glasses and chuckled. "Besides, I am pretty sure I already know who you *really* are."

They sat in silence for a few moments, until Wally got impatient. Stomping over to Mark, he punched him in the face, causing his chair to fall back, so that he hit his head on the concrete floor. Grabbing the chair, Wally abruptly pulled Mark back up. "I *will* find out why you are here, and it won't be the easy way anymore."

Cecil paused the footage. After a few moments of quiet, Cecil asked bleakly, "That was the *easy* way?"

The girls were tearing up, except for Ursula, who looked like she wanted to take the laptop and throw it at the wall. "Fast forward to when we were down there," she ordered, "when all the Keepers were with him." Cecil obeyed and went to today's interrogation:

Mark was still sitting at the chair, but looked much worse than before. I could barely recognize him. All the Keepers sat around the table, except Wally, who hovered over him.

"Don't make me repeat myself again," Wally said through gritted teeth. "Just tell Mr. Nik how you know what you know. This could just all be a misunderstanding. Ve could be wrong about you stealing the books and interfering with our communications." Bending over, he sneered, "But I know you are hiding something. Just tell us what ve vant to hear."

Trying to lift his head up to look at Mr. Nik, Mark said weakly, "What do I know that makes you angry? Is it that I have memories of my family?"

Shaking his head, Mr. Nik replied, "No son, that isn't it at all. We are just wondering why you think ill of us?" He tried to sound kind, but it ended up being horrifyingly creepy. His accent didn't help.

Mark scoffed, "You know, you could have asked my opinion without using the torture devices and the Nazi."

"How dare you!" Wally exclaimed and lifted his hand to slap Mark. Mr. Allaway jumped up, grabbed his arm, and gave him a stern look. Wally turned to his comrades and tried to defend himself. While no one was paying attention, Mark's head dropped and hung lifeless. We prayed he wasn't dead.

"Well, now, after your actions last night, Walter, I think the boy has the right to think of us however he wants to," Mr. Bamber scolded after Wally yelled a few times. "Nikita, if you don't mind, I have to use your bathroom." After the Headmaster agreed, my Keeper left the room.

Wally began to shout. "Nikita, I cannot take it anymore! You told me before, you are almost positive this is one of the kids ve have been after! Let's just kill the kid and get it over with!"

Abruptly, Mr. Mallory stood up and spoke in Mark's defense. "Hold yourself together, man! Didn't we start this corporation to bring peace and order back into the world?"

"He is right," Mr. Calvin said. "We cannot just go killing people for no reason."

"Ve already do so! What is the difference if ve kill one outside the emergency room?" Wally yelled but then clasped his hand over his mouth.

Dr. Damian Agro stood up now and tried to cover it up. "That is not true. We do not deliberately kill. We have lost lives, but none on purpose. In fact…"

Mr. Nik shushed him and pointed at Mark, who was snoring. "Didn't any of you notice that he fell asleep before Brian left?"

Mr. Allaway was the only one who said he noticed. "How long did you keep him up in that torture device last night?"

"All night, Cameron," Wally told the Scot, fixing his glasses. "To be honest, I fell asleep vhile he was in it."

"I don't think he heard your confession, so let's let him sleep," Mr. Allaway replied. "No harm done. We will see what he can tell us when he recovers a bit, but with what you did to the lad, one would think he would've cracked already if he were guilty."

The footage stopped by itself.

"That must have been when I unplugged the hard drive," Cecil said. "But it's enough proof for us, and hopefully for Mark."

"I think he has his own proof to go with ours," Yared said, pointing to Mark's cuffed hands underneath the table on the paused screen. "He was fiddling with his bracelet the whole time. I think he must have been recording it."

"Okay, but put this away quickly, before someone comes in and finds us," I advised.

When the drive was out of sight, we all sat down and thought of ways to get Mark out of Inquiry. We remained in Stratum Zero's classroom the entire day, leaving only to use the restroom and get food. The entire time we were in there, Mr. Bamber only visited twice. The first was to tell us that we would be able to see Mark first thing tomorrow morning. His excuse for us waiting until tomorrow was that Mark hadn't recovered from the time difference we'd experienced during our adventure. The second time he came in was in the evening, to tell us to go to bed. He told us that we ourselves weren't used to the time change either.

Doing as we were told, we went up to our dormitory.

If we aren't going to see Mark until tomorrow, we might as well get rested until then. Who knows what'll happen?

# THE ISLES

# CHAPTER 22

## Alison: VIII

I'm glad Mr. Bamber sent us to bed early, because I was drained. Not only was I still exhausted from the "operation" I had a few days ago, but I was also too overwhelmed by what was happening to Mark. As soon as we got back last night, it was lights-out for me. I was still out cold when Sami shook me awake this morning. "Wake up!" she shouted in my face for the tenth time. "Mr. Bamber sent a message to Aaron saying we'll meet with the Keepers after breakfast, but we have to eat before the other students."

Quickly, I jumped up. As fast as I could, I used the restroom, changed into my tank top and leggings, and put on my armor. We all rushed downstairs for breakfast. At that point, we didn't care if anyone saw us or not. Entering the cafeteria, we grabbed food and stuffed our faces until we were full. Well, Lucas was never full, so he filled his knapsack with bags of crackers and muffins. When he was done stealing food, we headed outside.

Mr. Bamber was waiting for us at the field. "Hello, everyone," he greeted. "Normally we would be meeting in Stratum Zero, but the other Overlords have a meeting today, so we have to go somewhere else." Behind him, we saw a large pickup truck approaching. It came to take us to the other Keepers. Pointing to it, Ursula said, "Sir, I don't think we're going to fit in that."

As if not hearing her, the old man told us to hop in. We all sat in the bed of the truck. It was a tight squeeze and uncomfortable, especially since Mr. Bamber sat in the back with us. Axel and I had to fly him in while Aaron folded his wheelchair and held onto it as we went on our way.

"This is ridiculous," Ursula muttered as her elbows dug into Ethan's and Yared's ribs.

The truck drove over every terrain in the training field, and it was miserable. We went through woods, over bumps, and across sand. Several times we were hit by twigs, splashed by muddy water, and had sand blown into our faces. Were they deliberately trying to make us miserable or did they just not care?

"Why is your Isle so *complicated*?" Yared asked as he tried to wipe the sand out of his eyes. Aaron and Cecil shrugged, and Mr. Bamber was asleep, so he couldn't answer.

I secretly wanted to search through the files and learn how they had created all these different terrains in one place. The one thing I hadn't noticed before was that there was a volcano on the island, just like on Isle I. *Was that here before the Keepers?* I wondered, as we drove away from it.

The painful drive took more than five hours; either they were wandering all over the place, or the island was bigger than I thought. We only stopped a few times to stretch and use nature's bathroom. I was overjoyed when we arrived at our destination: the southern shore of the island. Abruptly waking up, Mr. Bamber muttered something, looked around, and said, "Oh, we're here! That didn't take long." Ursula looked like she was going to strangle the old man but remained quiet and jumped out of the truck bed.

"I didn't realize how big our Isle was," Aaron marveled as he stretched.

"Oh, yes. In fact, this island used to be much, much bigger," Mr. Bamber said as we lowered him into his wheelchair.

"What happened?" Ava asked shyly.

# ALISON: VIII

Smiling, he looked at her and said, "That is a lesson for another day. Now it is almost lunch time. Let's hurry inside."

Mr. Bamber wheeled along the pebble path across the sand and up to a beach house. To the left and right of it, broken, ruined houses lined the shore. *What's so special about this one?* I wondered as we approached it and went inside.

The interior wasn't very big, but it felt cozy. Someone was keeping up with the cleaning, because the place was immaculate. The hallway walls were painted off-white, and the rough tile floor was beige. Soft music played from a radio in the kitchen to the left of us. To our right was a small family room with soft dark-brown couches and a matching coffee table. Its walls matched the rest of the house, but the floor had a fluffy beige carpet. Ahead of us was a staircase leading to a hidden second floor. Past the staircase was a door leading to another room.

"Come in, everyone. You must be hungry," a familiar voice called from the kitchen.

The kitchen was apparently the biggest room in the house; it fit everyone. The countertops were black marble, and Mr. Nik stood behind the island, preparing sandwiches. To his right were large windows, giving us a beautiful view of the ocean. Parallel to the windows was a long walnut dining table completely covered in food.

Mr. Nik kindly asked us to take a seat. There was a chair for each of us, and the two Keepers sat at the heads. I sat next to Sami, facing Aaron, who had his back to the window. Looking out it, I observed the ocean scenery. I noticed that some of the Isle Keepers were out there sitting in the sand, throwing rocks into the ocean and talking: I recognized Mr. Allaway, Mr. Mallory, Mr. Calvin, and Dr. Agro. I watched their movements, and wondered if they actually were remorseless killers. They seemed more like sentimental, misunderstood men.

Nevertheless, my mind was interrupted by Mr. Nik placing a gourmet sandwich in front of me. "I hope you like it! I made everything myself."

*He's too cheerful,* I thought. *There must be something wrong with the food.* I poked the sandwich with my fork to see if it would move, but nothing happened. I looked over and saw that Mr. Nik and Mr. Bamber were eating theirs. My friends began to eat slowly, so I did the same. Noticing our caution, Mr. Nik said, "Don't worry, nothing is poisoned. Why do you all think such ill things of us?"

We all stared at him, trying to act confused.

"Don't lie; I know you are all suspicious as to why we took your away your comrade," he said with his mouthful. "Now you are judging everything we do."

I let out a little sigh of relief. I thought he knew Mark had told us some things and was about to hold us all accountable for it. None of us said anything. We sat still and waited for someone to speak up. Finally, brave little Ava broke the silence. "We're scared."

Mr. Nik stopped mid-chew and looked at her. Swallowing his food, he obviously tried to think of something to say. "Why are you scared?" he finally asked her sympathetically.

"Because you told men with guns to take our friend away," she replied bluntly.

He wiped the crumbs from his mustache and sat back in his chair. "We had to, my dear. We have to make sure he isn't an Invader spy."

"But he isn't!" she cried, her eyes full of tears. "Please bring him back."

Apparently afraid of making the situation worse, he said, "If he gives us proof he isn't what we think he is, we will let him go. Until then, he remains with us for safety reasons. We can let you see him, though. Will that make you feel better?"

Wiping the tears from her face, she nodded.

"Good. But finish eating first," he said.

It was another hour before we could see Mark. We finished up lunch, used the restrooms, and then were finally taken to him. They led us down the hallway to the mysterious back room of the house. Going in, we found a few bookshelves and a desk. Mr. Nik went over and pulled one of the books off the shelf, revealing a hidden staircase going to a lower floor. *How predictable,* I thought. It was clever if you weren't used to it. Impatient, we carried Mr. Bamber and his wheelchair to the bottom rather than going to the elevator in the next room.

The basement was huge, dark, and spooky. Toward the back wall, we saw a lightbulb dangling over an operating table. Mark was strapped to it, and Wally was fast asleep in a chair in the corner. I gasped. *I remember this room,* I thought as I looked around. It was where they had operated on me eight years ago! Axel obviously had the same feeling of nostalgia. His jaw dropped, and he stared at the table.

Before our friends could ask us what was wrong, Mr. Nik flicked on the rest of the lights. "Walter, you know this dim light is bad for your eyesight."

Startled, Wally woke up and was shocked to see us. "Nikita! Why are the children here?"

"They are here to see Mark, that's why," Mr. Bamber told him forcefully. "I thought we agreed to leave him alone."

"Ve did, and I didn't touch him!" Wally bellowed in defense. "I strapped him here so he vouldn't escape if he woke up in the middle of the night, which he didn't. In fact he hasn't woken up at all. I thought he vas dead, but he is just probably still tired… or in a coma."

"Well, isn't that wonderful, a coma!" Mr. Nik exclaimed in frustration as we all walked over to them. He cursed a few times in Russian and then roared, "Unstrap him now, idiot!"

Wally obeyed, and Mark's arms fell limp off the sides of the table.

"If you don't mind, sir, I would like to examine him," Ethan asked politely.

Genuinely thrilled, Mr. Nik said, "Actually, I would love it if you did! You can show us what you can do; what you have learned!"

They turned the brighter lights off, and the Saviors went to work straightaway. Ethan first did a head-to-toe examination (with Mark's clothes still on, of course), and began asking Wally questions. "What did you inject him with as an act of torture?" he began.

"Lots of sleepy juice, probably," Lucas interjected, referring to anesthetic.

"There vere two different substances I used," the Keeper said, ignoring Lucas and handing Ethan the empty needles.

After slipping them into an analyzer in his medical kit, the Savior's Commander concluded, "One of these is apparently a modified form of batrachotoxin, a poison made from frogs that is known to cause paralysis."

"Wait—if that were the case, he would be dead already!" Zita cried, pausing in the middle of putting her curly red hair in a ponytail.

"Notice I said *modified*," he replied. "If I read this right, it was changed to act as a slow and painful process, which is good for us, because it gives us time. You see, he is becoming pale, and his veins are more visible." After analyzing the other needle, Ethan said, "This other one must also be modified. It's strychnine, but it's supposed to cause spasms as the muscles are contracted against their will."

"Oh, I injected that one first and he definitely had spasms; it vas quite amusing," Wally confessed with a smirk.

"You are a very sick man," Ethan said flatly. It clearly took a lot out of him to say that, so he hastily changed the subject. "Mr. Nik, these poisons were manipulated for a reason. What was that reason?"

"In case they were used improperly," he replied.

"Is there an antidote?" Ethan asked sharply.

"I think so," the Headmaster said, scratching his head, "but I don't know where."

I could tell Ethan was gritting his teeth in anger, even though he had his surgical mask on. Suddenly, Axel and Aaron ran back into the room with Dr. Damian Agro. I hadn't even noticed they had left. "Dr. Agro! Help us, please!" Zita cried in hysterics.

Quickly, the Keeper put on gloves and a mask and came to the table. "Ethan, there are chemicals labelled 'S.A.', 'B.A.', 'X', and 'Y' in that cabinet. Bring them here, along with a clean needle, test tubes, and such." Obeying, Ethan rushed over to the cabinet against the left wall. Turning to his other students, the doctor commanded, "Harold. Zita. Cut his shirt off."

Doing so, they revealed a pale-blue, muscular torso that seemed cold and lifeless. What was weird was that Mark had some sort of brand burned onto the right side of his chest: a small circle with three larger triangles around it, pointing to its center.

"It isn't too late," Dr. Agro said, relieved, ignoring Mark's brand.

"How?" Harold questioned.

"These substances are only supposed to inflict the pain that the pure poisons would, but without doing any serious harm to the rest of him," he explained, rubbing the sweat from his dark, bald head. "For example, there is one poison that gets into your bloodstream and begins to painfully dissolve your bones. We have reformulated that one so that the victim will feel the pain as if it is really happening, but their bones remain intact."

Trying to process this, Harold put it in his own simple terms. "So, it basically gets into your nervous system and sends signals to your brain, tricking it into thinking it's real poison? So it's sort of like a simulation?"

Nodding, the Nigerian Keeper replied, "Yes, pretty much. It is a form of torture."

"You think?" Zita snapped.

Shaking his head, Harold childishly scolded the keeper, "Dats not vewy nice."

Ethan ran back with the chemicals and other things. With hands as fast as lightning, Dr. Agro mixed them together. In no time at all, he created a bluish-green liquid and decanted it into the syringe. "Hold his arms and legs down," he ordered. "Ready?"

The Saviors members nodded, and their Keeper injected the antidote into Mark's neck, next to his brand number. He pulled the needle out, but nothing happened. Mark was still as limp as he was before. "Did it even do anything?" Ethan questioned.

Then, it kicked in. Mark's eyes opened, and he began screaming and thrashing like a madman. I jumped in and helped them hold him. "Strap him down! Strap him down!" Dr. Agro ordered.

It was a challenge, but we were able to do it after a few kicks and punches to the face from Mark. When he was secure, we all backed away and let him panic. This went on for almost three minutes. Finally, he stopped screaming, began panting, and looked all around the room.

He tried to open his mouth to speak, but couldn't breathe.

"Calm down, Mark," Dr. Agro warned. "Just let the antidote do its job."

Our friend became relaxed and slowed down his breathing. He turned his head to look at us. Laying his head back down, he smiled. "Hi…guys…" he croaked before he faltered. His face was bruised and swollen, and the veins on his head were still visible. Thankfully, they began to fade almost immediately.

Mr. Bamber wheeled himself over to the table. Shakily, he put his hand on Mark's arm and began to weep. "Nikita Patya," he said coldly, without looking back, "I am sick and tired of the way you do things around here. You *know* this is wrong. Why do you choose these methods?" Turning himself around, he looked Mr. Nik dead in the eye. "You are no better than the Invaders."

Shocked, Mr. Nik's mouth dropped open and no noise came out. Finally, he became cross. "You take that back," he growled.

"Before I do, let's take this outside. We don't want to say something in front of the children that we may regret."

"Agreed," the Headmaster said through gritted teeth. He turned around and stormed up the stairs. Mr. Bamber took a deep breath and looked at Mark, who smiled back at him. With tears in his eyes, the wrinkly old man patted his student's face and went to the elevator at the back of the room.

When they left, none of us spoke. The only thing to be heard was Dr. Agro and Wally quietly arguing in the corner, and Mark's heavy breathing.

"Yo, doc," Mark called as best as he could. "Can I get up now? I have to use the little boy's room, and I'm cold without my shirt."

Dr. Agro turned to him. "Yes, of course. You can move around if you are up to it. In fact, it would be best. You need to wake up your body a little. But not too much. You are still recovering."

Wally disagreed. "Whoa, hold up now. You cannot let him roam by himself! Ve haven't gotten anything out of him."

"He has gone through enough, Walter," the doctor said harshly. "*There is nothing to get.* We were only meant to be asking him questions, not torturing him to death. I don't care what you or Nikita say; I am letting him go."

He unlatched Mark and helped him get up. Our friend was so weak he had to use Axel and Aaron for support. The boys each took an arm and helped him up the stairs to the restroom. The rest of us went to the living room, leaving Dr. Agro and Wally alone.

Mark came back from the bathroom wearing fresh clothes, thankfully. I had felt so embarrassed staring at the brand on his attractive chest. He caught me looking a few times, and smiled when I turned away. Axel and Aaron helped him walk over and plopped him down on the couch. "Thanks, everyone," he said out of breath. "If you hadn't come along, I would have been done for."

"It's actually all thanks to Ava," Marlene told him. "If she hadn't asked Mr. Nik if we could see you, then we aren't sure what would have happened."

Little Ava smiled and ate a cookie she'd grabbed from the dining table. She offered one to Mark, but he rejected it politely, saying he was not a fan of sweets. Aaron went into the kitchen and came back with a fresh croissant, which Mark ate almost in one bite.

After consuming a few more croissants, Mark was finally regaining his strength. "That antidote really works fast. I mean sure, it's been an hour, but I thought it would take longer."

"I can't believe what they did to you," Sami said in a depressed tone.

He reassured her, "Don't worry about me, I can hold my own."

Wally came stomping down the hallway with Dr. Agro close behind. "I bet they already hightailed it out of here! Ve have been after this guy for years and now ve are letting him roam free? I mean, you can't trust that man. He is a dirty little—" he stopped midsentence when he saw Mark sitting on the couch with all of us in the living room.

Dr. Agro smirked. "You were saying, Walter?"

Without replying, the military man stormed out the door, pushing Mr. Calvin out of the way. The Assets Keeper did a double take, thought for a moment, shook his head, and came inside. "He gives

Germans a bad name," he muttered.

"Hello, little brother," Damian Agro greeted.

"Hi, Mr. Calvin!" Ava exclaimed.

"Hello, my dear Ava," he said, coming over to us. "How are my three favorite trainees doing?"

The Assets members all gave okay reports. "Look what Mr. Wally did to my friend," Ava said, pointing to Mark. She was trying to act half her age to get the Keepers to pity her and Mark. It seemed to work.

"I know," he said glumly. "It is awful, isn't it? But I have good news! I spoke to Mr. Nik, and he said Mark is free to go. If we have anymore suspicions, we will have to bring him in again. But I promise it will be less painful." Ava ran up and gave him a hug, followed by Donnie and Marlene. After Dr. Agro checked Mark over one last time, we went outside to get into the pickup truck. We watched as the two Keepers walked over to the beach where their comrades were.

I wished I could've heard what they were saying. It looked like Wally, Mr. Bamber, and Mr. Nik were still arguing, and the others were trying to reason with them. "Sami, can you hear their conversation?" I whispered. She nodded and said she would tell me later.

Once we were all piled in, we were driven back to the facility. The only good thing to come from the long trip was that Mark slept the whole time. Other than that, the ride was horrible. It was still cramped, boring, and I was in such suspense. I wanted Sami to tell me what the Keepers were talking about, but she wanted to wait until we were alone.

Thankfully, Ava and Donnie kept us entertained for the last bit of the ride. While Mark was sleeping, they kept rubbing the stubble that was growing on his chin.

"Cut it out," Marlene whispered, grabbing their hands.

"It feels funny," Donnie told her.

Rubbing her own face, Ava asked, "Am I going to grow that?"

Ethan was about to respond, but Ursula beat him. "When you're older." The boys all turned to look at her. She shrugged and rubbed her round chin. "You guys aren't the only ones to get facial hair, you know. We just don't get it as much."

We conversed about female facial hair for a little bit until finally we were back at the facility. Mark woke up and looked around. "Huh, we're back," he mumbled, looking up at the Research and Development building.

Next to the facility, you could see the sun beautifully setting over the waters. I would've liked to watch it, but we needed to get Mark inside. We helped him down and walked together to the building. Since dinner had ended, Aaron and Cecil went to the cafeteria to get everyone food while the rest of us went upstairs. The students were using the elevators, so we had to take the steps. It was difficult getting Mark up so many flights. He couldn't walk far without collapsing, so Axel carried him whenever he fell over. Mark obviously felt embarrassed by it.

We reached our room in time to watch the sun disappear below the horizon. Watching it, Mark smiled and whispered, "'Another day gone; a new one to come.'"

We were all ready for bed when Cecil and Aaron came back with backpacks full of food. They passed it all out, and we stuffed our faces. Lucas was given an entire backpack to himself. Graciously, he took it from Cecil, "Yes! Thanks heaps, man."

"I can't believe how much dragonflies eat," Cecil marveled, as Lucas shoved an entire bagel into his mouth.

"Not as much as a shrew," Mark commented.

Biting into a piece of steak with her sharp teeth, Becca put in, "I'm so glad Mr. Mallory didn't make one of us a shrew. Those guys need to eat more than Lucas."

Mark looked at the ground and mumbled, "That's because he already did."

Before Becca could say anything else, Harold decided to lighten the mood by attempting to crack a joke. He tried too hard, and that was comical in itself. We tried to have a good time despite everything that was going on. We told stories, laughed together, and really bonded. It was great.

When Harold finished telling another cheesy joke, Aaron stood up and grabbed something from under his bed. "Oh, before I forget," he said, with a mouth full of cupcake. He brought Mark his backpack, who accepted it with gratitude. Opening it, Mark slowly pulled out the blueprints. His eyes widened, and he seemed to be paralyzed again. Cautiously, he opened them and read them over. "Where... where did you get these?" he asked.

"Something told me to take them while we were in the Nerve Center," Aaron replied nonchalantly, then licked his fingers.

Mark's smile faded. Looking like a deer in headlights, he asked, "How did you get into the Nerve Center? And when?"

With his pinky finger still in his mouth, Aaron slowly replied, "When we tried to rescue you. You were in the room next door."

"I was that close?" Mark said quietly at first, and then much louder the second time. "I was *that close*?!" He groaned in frustration and put his head in his hands.

Cecil went over and sat on the edge of Mark's bed. "Guess what we got?" he whispered.

Mark looked up as Cecil pulled the super-drive from his backpack. "Is that what I think it is?" he asked, staring at the drive. Cecil nodded.

Mark looked at the drive and began quietly laughing. He then threw his head back and laughed harder. He jumped up from his bed and began celebrating like a sugar-high toddler. "I cannot believe it!" he exclaimed with his hands on his hair. "You guys are absolutely incredible. After five years of trying and trying, I was never able to get down there. You all did it without even thinking about it."

I couldn't help but laugh as I watched him dance around. *I've never seen someone so happy*, I thought. I wanted to ask him what the blueprints were, but didn't want to ruin the moment. He took the drive from Cecil and gave him a big hug. "Yes, yes, yes!" he sang.

"What is it?" Aaron asked, confused.

"Finally, after five years," he paused and looked up at his friend. "I can go home," he whispered. He laughed again and threw his arms out. "We all can. We can put an end to this nightmare!"

"Hold up," Yared stood up from his bed and held his hand up.

# ALISON: VIII

"Run that by me again. 'Home'? 'Nightmare'? What are you talking about?"

"Oh, it takes too long to explain," Mark replied ecstatically. After he calmed down, his tone changed drastically. "And it's not safe to explain here," he said solemnly, "but I can show you some things." Pulling out his clipboard, he attached the drive and went through some files. When he found what he was looking for, he asked Axel to project it as a hologram.

"I can't show you everything here," he explained, "but I can show you things to convince you once and for all that this place is truly a nightmare."

He showed us the footage of… my operation eight years ago. "Is that…?" Sami gasped as Axel projected a still shot of ten-year-old me all mangled and laying on a table.

"Yes. This is Alison's surgery," he said. "We all know they saved her life and replaced her limbs, but what we don't know is what they did to her brain. If any of you are sensitive to gory images, I suggest you look away."

I watched in horror as they operated on me. It was an aerial view from a camera in the light fixture, apparently. Dr. Agro and Mr. Allaway were carefully attaching the robotic parts to the right side of my body. My burnt skin was peeled away and melded together with this new technology. Blood covered my body and dripped onto the floor.

The most gruesome part was learning where the scar on my forehead came from. They performed a kind of open-skull surgery. The incision was over an inch wide and went across my whole forehead, leaving my pink, fleshy brain exposed.

"How else did you think they did it?" Mark asked quietly.

"Why are they doing that?" Ava asked, as she watched from behind Marlene.

…er things, they're implanting microchips in her brain …ntrol her new body parts," Mark explained. "Also, so …do basically whatever they want with her."

…n it off. I don't want to see anymore!" I cried finally.

"Not yet. There's something I need to show you."

Mark skipped to the end of the video, when the two Keepers were about to close up my head. "How do we make her forget?" Mr. Allaway asked.

"We have a separate, surgery-free process for that," Dr. Agro informed him, "but since we operated on her brain so extensively, I do not think she will remember anything too important."

"All right, but is there a way to reverse the process if necessary?"

"Of course. Memories are never forgotten, they are just hidden away."

With that, they finished their operation. Mark turned off the video and pulled up a scanned, handwritten document.

"And here are Mr. Nik's instructions for the operation," Mark told us. "In this part here, he wrote about the patient's memory:

*Each person must become as vulnerable and confused as little children if this is going to succeed. If past the age of five, wipe their memory and give them nothing but their first name. Even the last name can be a trigger word for remembering their past. Their ignorance is our advantage. The less they know, the more we can teach them and the easier it is for them to be disciplined. It is like a great leader once said: "He alone, who owns the youth, gains the future."*

Petrified and hysterical, the little ones began to cry. They were only ten years old, but they still understood what it all that meant. Mark had Axel turn off the projection, and he put his clipboard away. "Don't tell anyone what you've seen, understood?" When everyone promised, he said, "Thank you. Now: time for some rest. Who knows what's going to happen tomorrow?"

I was so shocked about everything that I haven't been able to sleep. I needed to think about all of it, I guess. But now, I believe I'm done thinking—thankfully.

# CHAPTER 23

## Sami: VIII

Once again, we had another sleepless night, which is bad for a cat. Everyone sleeps less and less as the days go on. I guess there's too much to think about, now that we are learning the truth. Mr. Bamber and Mr. Nik's conversation yesterday swirled through my head. *Was it true?* I thought, as soon as I got up. It had to be; it came right from the horse's mouth. I wanted to tell Alison about it, but I needed an opportunity.

Mark got up before everyone, as usual, and was going through the blueprints and Cecil's super-drive. He was already dressed and cleaned up. He'd even shaved that stubble that was growing in. Noticing his stubble gone, Donnie complained, "Awe, that fuzzy stuff on your face ain't there."

Laughing, Mark replied, "I heard you were having fun with it while I was sleeping." When Donnie nodded, Mark looked at the boy nostalgically and replied, "I'm glad it kept you busy. You and Ava remind me so much of... some other little kids I know." Quickly changing the subject, he looked back down at his clipboard and kept typing.

To be honest, I wondered what he would look like with a beard.

He was already pretty good-looking; I wondered if having a beard would add to it.

Uh, ignore that comment.

Sitting up, Ethan rubbed his eyes. "How long have you been up, Mark?"

"A few hours," he said, not looking up from his clipboard.

"Dude, you really should still be sleeping," Aaron said mid-yawn. He was still in his bed, like a few of the others. When he sat up, he had terrible bed-head. I mean Aaron's hair was naturally spiky, but that was ridiculous.

Mark noticed it too, so he laughed and said, "Man, you should go look in the mirror and try to comb that rat's nest."

Aaron smiled, got out of bed, put his taped glasses on, and sluggishly headed towards the bathroom. "I wanna know more about those blueprints when I get back," he called.

"So, what's on the agenda today?" Marlene asked as she stretched.

"I have a feeling I'll be seeing the Isle Keepers again today," Mark told her. "I sent a message out last night on a frequency that they don't presently know about. If they find traces of it, they'll be all over me."

Ursula rolled her head back and groaned. "Why would they care about some dumb frequency? Why would they be tracking them anyway?"

"Because they have trust issues," Mark explained. "If someone really were a spy for the Invaders, that person would need to communicate with his base on the Mainland. If the Keepers find that communication, they can intercept it and track down the one who sent it."

"I mean, it makes *sense*, but it's just annoying," she replied agitated.

Thinking for a moment, Donnie finally said what we were all thinking. "Well, are ya?"

Mark looked at him with surprise. "Am I what?"

"Are you a spy for the Invaders?"

# SAMI: VIII

We all stared at Mark, who became uncomfortable. I mean, who wouldn't feel weird? People he thought were trustworthy friends were doubting him. "No, I am *not*. I only sent a message to some friends of mine on the Mainland," he said with a smile. Just like that, we trusted him again. I felt like we were bipolar in our feelings towards him. Even though he was all "Secrets. Secrets. Lies. Lies. Tell you later," we still remained on his side.

Realizing what he said, Jeremy exclaimed, "You have friends on the Mainland that aren't dead?!"

"As far as I know, they're all alive," Mark said hopefully. "But I can't explain anymore—not here, anyway."

*He always says he'll explain later, and he never does,* I thought, upset. *What is he waiting for?*

Then, Aaron came back from the bathroom with his hair less spiky. "What did I miss?"

"Nothing, don't worry," Cecil said.

After Aaron told us about his experience trying to tame his hair, Mark remembered something he had to do. "Oh! Give me your bracelets and clipboards," he exclaimed. "I can disable the trackers now." Without hesitation, everyone handed their equipment over.

"You know, they still never gave us an official name for these bracelets," Yared complained when he gave his to Mark. "Can't we just name them ourselves?"

"Of course, we just never had time," Axel, said trying to fix his own hair. His white curls wouldn't stay down. "Let's do it now, though. Any ideas?" Everyone tried to think of something clever, but we got zip. A few ideas were thrown out there, but not everyone agreed on them. Mark was working on the last clipboard when Jeremy thought of something. "Why not BoMF?"

"Bomf?" Yared questioned.

"Yeah, an acronym: Bracelet of Many Functions," he explained. "It's simple, short, and sweet. Just our style, right, Mark?"

Mark looked up and smiled. "Exactly. I think that's a good name." No one else could come up with anything better, so we all agreed. Naming things was harder than we thought; no wonder it took the Keepers so long.

"All right, that's the last one," Mark said finishing up. He handed us all back our BoMFs. Everyone was grateful, feeling much safer now that they couldn't track us.

"So... now what?" I asked after brushing my teeth.

Suddenly, there was a noise like a dying whale. Aaron clutched his stomach and suggested, "We could go get breakfast?"

Packing up, we all headed downstairs, only to be disappointed. We had missed breakfast *and* lunch; we were up there longer than we thought. Everyone was already back at class, and the kitchen staff was on break. "Where is everyone? I am bloody starving!" Lucas exclaimed, even though he'd eaten his leftover muffins back in the bedroom.

"They don't know we're here, remember?" Mark reminded him weakly as Axel put him down. He'd collapsed on the way there again. "The only ones who do are the Keepers and some staff members. Let's keep it that way. You'll survive until dinner. Be grateful that you have a meal to look forward to. A lot of the people on the Mainland don't have that much."

Embarrassed, Lucas kept quiet.

"There you all are," a familiar nasal voice called out behind us. Turning around, we saw Mr. Bamber wheeling himself towards us. "Mark, how are you feeling?" he asked, concerned.

"Better than yesterday, sir, thank you," he told his Keeper.

"Oh, good! You definitely gave me a scare, my boy," he said relieved. "Wally got a good scolding for his actions, don't you worry."

*I think he deserves more than a scolding,* I thought harshly.

"But as for Mr. Nik," Mr. Bamber looked around the room to make sure no one was listening and continued in a lower tone, "I tried to convince him to let you go, but he wants you back into custody until you make a confession. What's worse is, he has Mrs. Pieper with him for questioning." Taken aback, Mark asked Mr. Bamber to run that by him again. "You heard me. He has Mrs. Pieper," he repeated. "The janitor was cleaning the hallways when he heard her say something that made him suspicious. So, he went straight to Mr. Nik and told him what she said."

"Which was what?" Mark asked.

"He heard her say to someone that she helped you 'sneak into' here."

Mark's face became almost as pale as it had been from the poison yesterday.

Putting his hand on Mark's arm, Mr. Bamber said, "Mr. Nik wants you back now, or else she will be punished in your place." The old man shakily took a deep breath. "I don't understand what they are talking about, Mark. You came back with the rescue team! I was there. I saw you. I remember you! What is happening?" Mr. Bamber's voice sounded so desperate, but Mark couldn't say anything to comfort him.

To be honest, I had a feeling in my gut that this man had no clue what was going on. If anyone would listen to our reasoning, it would be him. *If we can tell him what we know, maybe he will be with us,* I thought. Alison told us that he had also watched his family die when the Invaders came.

"Take me to her," Mark said at last.

"First, I want the truth, son," Mr. Bamber ordered.

Mark sighed, looked him in the eye, and... told him. "Yes, I came back with the rescue team. I was documented as too old to join any of the Isles, but I didn't want to live alone in the village at Saviors. Mrs. Pieper helped me out. She got me into Stratum 15 on Isle III. Not only that, but she helped me to slip in undetected so I wouldn't have to have my mind wiped. She believed it would be easier for me to blend in if I kept my memory and all the knowledge in it."

Mr. Bamber stared at him and thought for a little while.

Aaron then spoke up, "So that's how you were able to pass the Commencement Tests with such flying colors in less than a year. You must have learned all that already back on the Mainland."

Mark nodded.

After a few minutes of processing, Mr. Bamber asked, "Then just how old are you? The children in Stratum Twenty are around twenty-one, twenty-two years old."

"I'm actually twenty-five," Mark confessed.

Everyone was shocked. To be honest, I felt really awkward, and my face turned red. Even though there's nothing wrong with thinking guys ten years older than you are attractive, I still felt weird. I hope no one noticed me blushing....

Mr. Bamber was also surprised. After a moment, he started laughing and clapping. "My boy, you are a grown man. No wonder Yuki had to sneak you in. Honestly, I am so happy she did. I have always felt like you were a son to me. The gears in your head are always turning." He grabbed Mark's arms and shook them gently. "Makes me so proud. Well, now that I know the truth, we can go to Mr. Nik and tell him to release Mrs. Pieper."

As they started on their way, Mr. Bamber called to the rest of us while we were standing there awkwardly. "You all can come too, if you'd like. In fact, I would prefer it."

We followed Mr. Bamber back down to the Nerve Center. Mark marveled at just the sight of the door. He probably couldn't believe how close he was now. Mr. Bamber took us into the room labelled 'Inquiry,' where Mrs. Pieper and some of the Keepers were waiting.

At the sight of Mark, Mrs. Pieper stood up from her chair and rushed over to give him a hug. "Oh, are you all right? What did they do to you?!" she cried, her eyes filled with tears.

Wally took one look at us and complained, "Why did you let them *all* come down? They aren't supposed to know this place exists, Brian."

"They found it on their own yesterday, so it doesn't matter. Besides, this room is big enough," Mr. Bamber replied boldly.

Once we were all piled in and standing against the walls, Mr. Bamber began to explain to Mr. Nik what he had learned. "Yuki's actions were harmless. She and this boy, actually young man, are innocent. Yuki helped Mark become a part of Isle III because he was afraid to live his life alone on Isle II. The only reason why he knows so much is because he didn't go through the Process. Yuki believed it would be easier for him to fit in that way." He spoke of the 'Process' like we didn't know that they had wiped our memories.

Mr. Nik took all of this into consideration, but of course Wally immediately had something to say. "There is more to it!" the Seers Keeper argued. "Can't you see the look in his eyes, that that isn't the whole truth? It's a revenge story. Maybe he thinks ve are the bad guys and killed a friend of his…or maybe he thinks ve are all insane and means to put an end to everything ve have done." Wally went rambling on for a while with mindless excuses. Some of them might even have been true.

"Enough, Walter," Mr. Nik said finally. "I believe his story. However, I know there is more to it."

He motioned Mark to sit down who obeyed. "Mark, now that you have all your friends here," the Headmaster began, "I want you to explain some things: why you stole those books from Isle II, those assumptions you made about us while you were back at Guadalajara, and why, while you were on the plane coming back, someone was interfering with our communications. The pilots can't recall anything that happened. Why is that?"

Mark was trapped. We all wanted to know the truth but were afraid he would say the wrong things. He kept telling us confusing bits and pieces, after all, and sometimes changed his reasons and story! He was like a writer who didn't remember what he said in previous chapters and just kept going, hoping the stories would all coincide in the end.

Mark took a deep breath and replied, "They tied me up on the plane—the Seers who took me into custody can tell you that—so I have no idea about the interference or the pilots' memories. My assumptions were made by observation and reasoning. I know you were watching us the entire time, and each assumption I made was after a suspicious point came up. If you remember, we were discussing memories, which led to my theory of why you erase minds."

Mr. Nik thought about all of this for a while and then said, "You still didn't explain why you stole those books. Mr. Bamber instructed you to steal *two* files, yet you stole much more than that."

Mark paused.

"You see? Hesitation!" Wally yelled. "Why can't ve just use that lie detector the Isle III kids have been working on?"

"Because it is not ready yet," Mr. Bamber argued. "And if the person tells a lie, it hurts them. We don't need more of that."

Before Mr. Nik could repeat the question, Mr. Allaway came bursting through the door. "Come quick! We have an *actual* emergency."

The Keepers rushed into the Nerve Center, and we followed. We watched as they hurried to their designated computers clustered around the hologram. An alarm was triggered, and the lights were flashing red. Security footage was playing from each Isle, but we saw nothing suspicious. "Should I sound the alarm in the facilities, Nikita?" Mr. Allaway asked.

"No, we don't need a panic," he replied. "We need to know what we are up against."

Mark seemed to be off the hook for now, at least until this was resolved.

"How long have they been here?" Mr. Calvin asked as he pressed a few buttons.

"We are uncertain. For all we know, they could have been here for two weeks," his brother said. "Our first suspicions of their presence were when the three books were stolen from our control room. We thought Mark and the boys did it when they broke in there, but we *did* have other suspects. Walter was so convinced that it was Mark that we didn't consider these others. Now I am thinking the boy is innocent."

Wally apparently couldn't believe his ears. "Are you kidding me? The boy is caught red-handed!" Going over to Mr. Nik, he tried to keep his voice down, but he was bad at whispering. "We know who he really is. I mean, sure, ve searched his room and read his record log and didn't find any proof, but I am telling you. He did this. He became a thief like his deadbeat brother."

*They searched his stuff and read his log?* I thought, horrified. I guessed we really didn't have anything to ourselves. And we knew he actually stole the books. *Why are the Keepers suddenly thinking otherwise?*

Mark didn't seem surprised that they'd gone through his stuff. However, you could see anger in his eyes when Wally called him a thief and his brother a deadbeat.

Mr. Nik looked back to the monitor, slammed his fists on his desk, turned around, and addressed Mark. "You say you are innocent, then? Well, let us prove that. Capture the intruders and bring back those missing books. Then we will never suspect you again. Agreed?" He held out his hand.

 Mark shook it and said, "Agreed. When should I start?"

"'You' plural," he replied pointing to all of us. "They are going with you for multiple reasons: to help you, to make sure you do not escape, and also, I think of it as another challenge. As you can see, I like things like that. You will head out tomorrow. Go have dinner and get some sleep; I want you all up before the crack of dawn."

With that, he dismissed us and had Mrs. Pieper and Mr. Bamber escort us back upstairs. The rest of the students were in the middle of dinner, so we had to exit through the Stratum Zero classroom. "Yuki, I'm sorry you got entangled in this spider's web," Mr. Bamber apologized when we were in the classroom.

"No, don't worry about it. I did something I wasn't supposed to, and I knew I would get caught in the end. But at least they know the truth." She winked at Mark when Mr. Bamber wasn't paying attention. Okay, now I was definitely sure that there was more to the story than that.

"Mark, I need to speak to you alone," Mr. Bamber said before he left.

"Of course, sir," Mark replied. "Guys, go back to the dorm. I'll meet you there for dinner."

We went upstairs and waited for Mark. While we sat in silence, Mrs. Pieper brought us a large cart of food. We thanked her repeatedly, grabbed our fill, and ate at our beds. She stayed with us and ate her dinner next to Ava. We tried to have light, happy conversation, but nothing fixed our moods. Out of the blue, Ava asked Mrs. Pieper, "Are we going to die?"

Mrs. Pieper scooped her up onto her lap and told her, "No, my dear, it will be okay. I promise."

"Are you and Mark going to die?"

She hesitated before answering. "I don't think so. I told Mr. Bamber the real truth. He will protect us. I promise."

"What *is* the real truth, Mrs. Pieper?" Aaron pleaded. "We only know bits and pieces, and sometimes they don't make sense!"

Before she could answer, Mark came back with Mr. Bamber right behind him. They both had serious expressions on their faces. Mrs. Pieper placed Ava on the bed and stood up to meet them. "Brian! What are you—"

Mr. Bamber held up his hand to silence her. He smiled and said, "I will do whatever it takes, Yuki. I was so blinded by revenge that I did not see what was happening right in front of my eyes. Mark told me everything. I will prepare my students tonight, and I need your help. We are finishing this while we still can."

Without saying anything, she nodded and prepared to go with him to do whatever they had to. She gave us some instructions before she left. "Pack your bags, prepare your weapons, and get your rest. I have a feeling there's no easy way out. We're going to end this before it's too late." With that, they left.

We sat in an uncomfortable silence. I was petrified. Jeremy, who was more scared than I was, asked shakily, "M-Mark? What is she talking about?"

He was packing his things when he replied, "I promise, Jeremy, I'll explain it all tomorrow. I know you're all going to say I keep saying that, but I promise. When we find the intruder, we'll explain it all."

He said "we." Who is "we"? I wondered.

After we packed our bags, loaded our weapons, and charged our BoMFs, we went to bed. Before sleeping, I went over to Alison. I *had* to tell her what I'd heard Mr. Bamber and Mr. Nik saying yesterday. "Alison?" I whispered.

Lying under the covers, she opened her eyes and looked at me. "Yes?"

"Yesterday, the conversation I heard," I looked to see if Mark was listening before going on. He was too engrossed in his clipboard to pay attention. I went on, "Mr. Nik said that Wally is almost positive that they *knew* Mark before, and that his name isn't really Mark. They also said that he did some bad stuff."

The Bionic's eyes widened. "What kind of stuff?"

I shook my head. "We left before I could find that out. What do you think?"

"I don't know what to think," she sighed. "Despite what they say or what he may have done, we have to trust him. It's our only option."

Ending the conversation, I crawled back into bed. The lights were off, but it wasn't a problem for me to record today in my log. The only trouble I had was, I kept nodding off. *Curse these cat instincts*, I thought as I pulled my whiskers to try and stay awake. As quickly as possible, I wrote everything down.

Looking over right now, I see Mark is still sitting in the dark, working on his clipboard. I have a terrible and eerie feeling that when this is all over, nothing will ever be the same.

# THE ISLES

# CHAPTER 24

## Aaron: VIII

We were up, dressed in our navy combat uniforms, and out into the fields before the sun came up. Mr. Nik, Wally, and Mr. Bamber were waiting there for us.

"We aren't sure where the intruders are or how many of them there are," Mr. Nik told Mark. "The last place we thought we saw them was Isle II, Saviors. You should check there first. Dr. Agro is waiting for you at the runway. He will take you to the Isle, and then you are on your own."

"Do we have a time constraint?" Mark asked before we departed.

The Headmaster furrowed his brow and gritted his teeth. "Just don't take forever," he growled.

We made our way to the runway and found Dr. Agro waiting by a jet. We entered and settled in. "Buckle up everyone, we are going to go quite fast," the Keeper instructed as we were taking off. "And if you need any assistance, you can trust me; I am a doctor."

I still marveled at how fast the jets could go; we Overlords really did a good job. We arrived in about a half-hour, forty minutes tops. When we got off the plane, the sun was just starting to come over the horizon. We were at an airport far from the village. "I wish the best of luck to you all," Dr. Agro said before he left us.

"Is there any specific place you think they could be?" Mark asked quickly.

"The last time we thought we detected them was inside our facility," Dr. Agro explained, "then they escaped to the outskirts of the island. I would check from the outside going in if I were you. Oh, and we are letting you use one of our helicopters: Knight #2. It is one of our largest, used for rescue missions, so don't damage it."

Mark thanked him, and the doctor took his leave. Once the Keeper was out of sight, Cecil said, "You already know where they are, don't you?"

Mark smiled and replied, "Of course! Now let's get moving."

We followed the Saviors members to where the helicopters were stored. Dr. Agro wasn't kidding when he said the one he was lending us was big. It was a long, gray, military-style helicopter, with a red number 2 painted on each side. The inside looked as big as the outside, and was able to hold about fifty passengers. "Nice and roomy," Marlene complimented as she buckled herself in.

"This is the same copter they took me here in," Mark marveled as he went to the cockpit. He brushed his fingertips over the buttons and seemed to be experiencing nostalgia. Snapping himself out of it he called to me. "Hey, Aaron, I need you to be my co-pilot!"

Ecstatic, I ran into the cockpit and sat down next to him. One glance and I was bewildered. Sure, I was trained to fly aircraft, but this had way too many buttons. Mark knew what he was doing right away, though, and prepared to take us into the air. "Have you flown one of these before?" I asked before he put his headset on.

"A few times, before I was taken here," he replied. He called to the others as we were taking off. "I hope you're buckled in, everyone! I haven't flown one of these in years, so it might be a bit bumpy!" Hearing this, everyone braced themselves.

When we were in the air, though, I didn't know what he was talking about. He flew just fine. Where he was taking us was my main concern. We didn't seem to be heading inland, so I figured we were taking Dr. Agro's advice and starting on the outskirts. We were about to land when I noticed that there was another island next to Saviors, one I hadn't known about before. "Mark, do you see that?!"

"Of course I do," he chuckled. "That's where our guests are waiting for us!"

*Wait, guests? Over there?* I thought. *Why are we landing on the edge of Isle II?*

I waited until we were out of the helicopter to ask him. "Why didn't we fly over there if that's where they're waiting for us?"

Cecil heard me asking this and immediately became confused. "Wait, who is waiting for us where?"

Mark just pulled some supplies from the helicopter and began walking to the shore. "Hey! You didn't answer my question!" I yelled.

Without looking back, he held up his hand and motioned us to follow him. He led us to a dock with a large, rusty old speedboat that apparently hadn't been used since the dinosaur age. Mark hopped in and attempted to start it. I questioned his motives: "You want us to get there in *that*?"

Cecil was still confused, and was now getting agitated because we were ignoring him. "Get where?!"

When the boat started, Mark came back and began explaining: "We're heading to The Forbidden Island, where our intruders are located. The helicopter draws too much attention, and I'm sure it's being tracked. This boat has probably been forgotten about and is less likely to be seen."

Curious, Sami asked, "Why is it called The Forbidden Island?"

"You'll find out when you get there," he replied, smiling.

We had to wait even longer for answers. It took us twenty minutes to reach the beaches of The Forbidden Island. It was truly beautiful at dawn and seemed entirely untouched by humanity. "Okay, they shouldn't be too far," Mark said when we docked. "There's an old village a little way inland from here; I think that's where they said they would be."

As we walked, you'd think we would have come across some signs that people used to live here, but there were no roads, no houses, no power lines, nothing. Not even ruins. Just nature… nature everywhere. Finally, we walked out of the woods and into a village that was still inhabited by people. Live people! At first I thought this was one of Mr. Nik's ideas of prison. But that wasn't right, because these people were happy. Children played, parents went about their work, and everyone was smiling. I noticed all the people had similarities in appearance: their tan skin complexion, almond eye shape, and black hair color. *Were they born here?* I thought as I looked around.

As we passed through, the natives were shocked to see us and became afraid. Most of them ran back into their huts, except for one man, who stomped towards us. He was about four inches taller than Mark, who was about 6' 3", stocky and wearing only a brown wraparound skirt. The big guy walked right up to Mark and began speaking in a tongue we didn't recognize.

"Um… sorry, but do you speak English?" Mark asked politely.

"Yes," the man said coldly. "Now, who are you and what are you doing here?"

"We come in peace," Mark told him, with his hands out as if offering him an invisible gift. "We came here looking for some friends. They probably explained why we've come; are they nearby?"

The man tried to keep a straight face, but let out a hearty laugh. He grabbed Mark and gave him a bear hug… which looked more like he was trying to snap him in half. "Yes, yes, we have been waiting for you." Dropping our friend, he said, "Come, follow me."

While we were on our way to the man's house, the inhabitants started coming back outside. Their way of life seemed so simple and peaceful. They had no electricity, no vehicles, no high technology whatsoever. Our host was telling everyone that we meant no harm, that we were friends. Most of them look relieved, but some still acted cautious, especially when they saw the Mutants and Bionics. I mean, I can't blame them. Seeing human cats and cyborgs walking around in a place like that must have been terrifying. Thankfully, Lucas wore his goggles and cape, so no one saw that he was a freaky bug.

Finally, we reached the man's hut at the edge of the village, close to the beach. Before entering, the big guy slapped his hand to his face.

"Oh, silly me! I almost forgot," he turned to us and introduced himself. "My name is Kapono Iokua, and I am the chief of this village."

"Pleased to meet you. I'm Mark, and these are my friends." One by one, we quickly said our names.

"The pleasure is all mine," Kapono said when we finished. "Come now, your friend has been waiting."

*"Friend" singular?* I wondered, confused. *I thought Mark said there were many of them.*

Following him into the hut, we found a figure dressed all in black, sitting at a wooden counter, with their back towards us and their head down. "It's been a long time," a young woman's voice said. Then, she turned around on her tall stool.

She had dark-brown, short curly hair that was pulled back by a cloth headband. Her skin looked soft and frail, and she had a few freckles on each cheek. She had a solid, athletic stature and wore a uniform of all black, from her fingerless gloves to her boots. Her jacket, adorned with patches on each arm and a name tag over her heart, was rolled up to her elbows and unzipped, revealing her white undershirt and a dog tag with the letter H on it. Her cargo pants were tucked into her high combat boots.

*Her uniform looks like ours, except it's black,* I observed as I looked her up and down. *Hers seems heavier and warmer, though. I don't know how she's surviving this heat.*

"Hey, beautiful. Sorry, I've been busy," Mark finally responded after she turned around.

She hopped down from her chair, crossed her arms, marched right up to Mark, and looked up at his face. Her ocean-colored eyes watched him closely. *Man, is she short,* I thought as Mark looked down at her caringly.

Before he could say anything, she began crying, and flung her arms around his neck. Mark stood up and held her close to him, with her legs dangling in the air. "We thought you were dead," she whispered mid-sob as she rubbed the brand number on the back of his neck.

"Now why would I die on the job, huh? I told you I would be

gone a while, didn't I?" he replied, getting teary-eyed himself.

The girls around me began bawling, even Ursula, which was a shock. We guys didn't get too emotional, but it was definitely a touching scene.

After a few minutes, he put her down and began to compliment her. "You have definitely blossomed into a beautiful woman," he said, wiping the tears from her eyes. He looked her up and down and noticed the dog tag hanging from her neck. He took it, shook his head, chuckled, and rubbed it between his forefinger and thumb. Putting it back down, he turned his attention back to his friend. "Hey, did you get taller?" he asked jokingly as he patted her head.

She punched him in the arm... quite hard. "I've been the same height since you met me all those years ago."

"Oh, this is wonderful," Kapono exclaimed. "Why don't we all sit down, and I will bring some beverages." He took us into a little sitting room that had two bamboo couches and a small coffee table. Half of us had to sit on the floor; the rest got the sofas. Mark and his friend sat on couches opposite each other.

"Now, I think some introductions are in order," Mark said once everyone was settled.

"Yes, why don't I go first," the young lady suggested. "I'm Shannon Hollinger, a member of operation Resist Rescue Protect Retake, or RRPR for short, and a good friend of your buddy Mark."

"Just friends?!" Marlene cried, sounding very disappointed.

Everyone couldn't help but laugh. "Yes—sorry, Marlene. We have a good brother-sister bond," Mark explained, grinning.

Shannon smiled and corrected him. "It's good most of the time." Continuing, she said, "The idea of our operation is pretty much explained in its name. Ever since the Mainland was taken over, our job has been to work undercover in an attempt to reclaim it and save as many lives as possible. We thought we were making good progress until we realized another operation was at work. They would interfere with our rescue missions and take people before we could get to them. A few times, we've caught members of their organization breaking into our bases and stealing our blueprints and things like that.

"We also gathered intel that this particular organization was building an army to stop the Invaders, but not for the good of humanity—only for their own good. Our source said that two of the leaders originally worked for the Invaders, but left because they didn't like the way the Invaders did things and decided to take over the world 'properly'."

"What? No, you're *lying*!" Jeremy yelled in defense. "If anything, Mr. Nik and Wally were training us to go against the Invaders and save the world!"

Mark put his hand on the boy's shoulder and told him, "She isn't lying, Jeremy. I'm sorry. I found the proof of it all. That was why I came to the Isles in the first place."

Finally, the truth was out.

"Sorry I haven't been completely honest with you all, but I had no choice," he explained. "Years ago, Nikita Patya heard of our organization and wanted to know what we were up to and if we would be on the same page. He started by sending out spies. We captured a few he sent and interrogated them. We had no difficulty getting them to talk; they told us everything... well, almost. They couldn't remember details about who they worked for or even about themselves. That aroused our suspicion.

"Then they started 'Phase Two,' I guess we can call it. They began kidnapping some of the people we rescued and told them that they were being rescued from us. They also stole a lot of our equipment and blueprints. Aaron most graciously took three back for me without realizing it. What really put it over the top was when one of the spies died spontaneously when we caught him, a little while after their Phase Two was put into play. Our scientists looked him over and found traces of an electronic tracker, like the Invaders had, in the back of his neck—one that released a fatal, fast-acting poison if triggered. They must have known we were getting information too easily, so they made sure there were no loose ends."

Taking a deep breath, Mark explained where he fit into all of it. "Five years ago, we set up a mission for one of us to go undercover and confirm whether what we had learned was true or not. We were hoping that maybe, just maybe, this organization could become an ally, that everything was just a misunderstanding. We didn't want to storm the place before we knew for sure. We were going to vote on who should go, but I volunteered to our leader in private. He tried to talk me out of it, but failed. He said I wasn't cut out for that kind of work." Taking a shaky breath, Mark looked at the ground and went on, "To be honest, I always felt useless and unimportant back home. I felt hated and untrusted because of my past. I thought maybe if I could do this, I… would feel like I was finally doing my part, and people would look past my old life.

"I waited until everyone was asleep before I departed. I left a message for everyone to wake up to and went out to wait for Wally and his 'rescue team.' No one knew they would come that night except me. I did a little research of my own. I found out that that night would be his last spent 'rescuing' on that continent, so no one could come after me without causing a ruckus.

"However, Shannon heard me moving around and found me leaving. I didn't tell her exactly where I was going, but told her I'd be gone a little while. She thought I was just clearing my head after the big fight my brother and I got into that night…. What an awful fight it was, and a terrible way to say goodbye. Shannon had no idea I had volunteered for the mission, so she went back to bed expecting to see me the next day. But Wally and his team came before dawn and took me and a few others, including my foster father, away.

"We were all taken to Isle II to be examined and have our memories erased. The first person I met there was Mrs. Pieper. She was visiting her husband, who was sick but slowly recovering. I bumped into her in the hallway and began talking to her for a bit. She told me she was going to visit him, and I asked if I could join her. She didn't refuse."

Mark's eyes welled up with tears as he went on, "When we got to his room, we discovered that he was dead. We caught the nurse, who was trying to make a quick escape. The woman was sobbing hysterically. Apologizing to Mrs. Pieper, she handed her something and bolted. The nurse had given Mrs. Pieper the empty syringe she'd used to inject a poison into her husband, killing him painlessly.

"There was also a note: a list of patients. Some of their names were crossed off, and Mr. Pieper was one of them. The nurse went around killing patients who were ill or badly injured. Recently, I learned that the same had happened to my foster father, who I thought was living on Isle II. Anyway, I clutched that list tightly and decided right then and there that the Isles were evil and the Keepers needed to be stopped. I trusted Mrs. Pieper with my reason for coming here, and she agreed to help me no matter the cost. I think you all know the rest from there," Mark concluded.

Everyone sat in silence. Even Kapono stood in the doorway quietly. "What monsters," the chief said at last. "First, they kidnap and murder my Hawaiian brethren, then they destroy these beautiful islands to build their cold, evil facilities, and now this." He clicked his tongue. "What has our world come to?"

"'Hawaiian brethren'?" Ava asked softly.

"Yes, my dear. Hawaii is the name of these eight—well, seven now—islands that you all call the Isles," he explained kindly. "Your Headmaster has control over only six of them. He sank the smallest island, Kahoolawe, while testing explosive artillery. A long time ago, that island was used for military training and even as a bombing range. They even nicknamed it 'The Target Isle'. But those men exercised extreme caution and did not go as far as he did.

"Since this island is the second smallest," he continued, "they did not think it useful, so they did not bother with it. They also thought that it was still quarantined after the Invaders bombed all these islands. Thankfully, this island, Niihau, was never fatally attacked. We have lived here in secret ever since. Even before the time of the Invaders, our island was always secret and never influenced by the outside world. As you can see, we have no electricity or technology of any kind. We live here to maintain the Hawaiian culture, so we can pass it on to other generations."

"Not to be nosy, but how do you know all this?" Yared asked.

The chief smiled and said, "The RRPR members are not the only ones who have a man on the inside. How do you think the Keeper of Isle II was so easily swayed from thinking that Mark stole those books?"

There was so much to take in that my head hurt; I hoped no one asked more questions. Looking around, I saw that half of my friends had confused or angry expressions, while the rest were crying and depressed. "Well, now we know why you couldn't tell us the truth before," Sami said to Mark, wiping tears from her beautiful green cat eyes.

"If you were all crying like this while they were watching, that would be enough to kill us all," Harold said jokingly, trying to lighten the mood. It worked for a split second, which was better than nothing.

Changing the subject, Mark asked in a depressed tone, "Shannon, where are the others? Did they come with you?"

She chuckled nervously. "Well…they didn't exactly know I left to come here."

Mark's eyes widened, his jaw dropped, and his cup almost slipped from his hand. "W-what?"

Suddenly, Chief Kapono began laughing for no reason. His laugh was so hearty and funny that we all joined him and couldn't stop. Despite the inappropriate timing, we all needed it. "Why are we laughing?" Lucas asked, gasping for air. Shannon shrugged and took deep breaths to calm down.

"Excuse me for laughing at a bad time," Chief Kapono apologized. "The expression on your face, Mark, was absolutely priceless." He began fanning his face with his hands. "I will be right back," he said, walking out of the room.

After the chief left, Shannon began to explain herself. "One person was supposed to come alone first anyway. It was originally going to be your brother, but he took a bad hit when our headquarters was infiltrated two months ago. Not only were he and a few others injured, but we also had to relocate… so that took time, and we still aren't finished."

Mark's face paled, and he began to panic. "Will he be all right? How are you all holding up?"

"Calm down, he's much better now," she informed. "They

broke a few of his ribs, but he's healed up. As for the rest of us, we're hanging in there. We like our new location much better. It's safer. So anyways, he healed in time to answer your first call, but the doctors wanted him to come later, so I volunteered. Of course, your brother wouldn't allow it, and the others agreed with him, as usual. They even made me co-commander of the building team, just to keep me away from here until it was time. However, you sent out the second signal sooner than we expected. The others weren't prepared for it, but I was. I left the director an apology note and headed out without anyone's knowledge."

Mark hardly knew what to make of all that. After a few moments, he started scolding her. "Why did you do that? What about your condition? They were right—you shouldn't have come here alone, it's too dangerous!"

Defensive, she leaned forward and replied boldly, "I can handle myself, and you know that. I came here because I worked with Myles in the control room, and we were the ones who knew the most about this place. He was the only one who supported me in volunteering! You've all seen me protect myself and others, even after my injury. So why are you treating me like this?!"

Mark abruptly stood up and shouted, "Because if anything happened to you, we wouldn't know what to do with ourselves!"

Shannon was completely taken aback by his response, and slumped back onto the couch.

Sighing, Mark plopped back down and said softly, "You're my best friend, Shannon, and you brought my family back together after we were separated for so long. Not only that, you gave us hope, showed us our real purpose in life, and so much more. I think I can speak for everyone when I say that I owe my *life* to you and your family."

Shannon bit her lip. "I think we should discuss this later," she suggested. "It's getting late, and you all should rest."

Mark nodded. "I think we'll finish introductions tomorrow, then. Shannon and I took up so much time I don't want you all sitting here for eternity."

# THE ISLES

With that, we all got up and stretched. We had been sitting there for a long time, and the sun was beginning to set. Chief Kapono came back from wherever he was and told us that we could stay the night with him, but there wasn't exactly enough room in the house for everyone.

Mark suggested that those who couldn't fit inside could sleep outside, under the stars. No one objected; in fact, everyone slept outside that night, either because the view was so beautiful or because they felt guilty. For me, it was a mixture of both.

I'm not complaining at all, though, because this view truly is amazing. I wish I could take pictures with this record log, because I've never seen anything like it. Chief Kapono's backyard overlooks the ocean, which reflects the purple and blue starry night sky.

Man, what a day today has been. Right now, some of the other kids are writing in their logs, like me, and the rest are sleeping. I can see Mark and Shannon sitting at the edge of the beach by a palm tree, watching the shooting stars and talking. I really want to know their whole story, but I guess I can only handle one thing at a time.

Today's one thing was learning the ugly truth about our lives.

# Chapter 25

## Alison: IX

We woke up this morning to the sound of beautiful music. Going into the kitchen, we found Chief Kapono, Mark, and Shannon sitting around the counter, singing and playing instruments. Chief Kapono was singing and strumming a tiny guitar called a ukulele. Mark was lightly rapping on the table, keeping the beat, and Shannon sang harmony with the chief. The three of them were wearing fresh new clothes: Chief had a red nature-patterned skirt on today, Mark wore a green floral polo and khaki shorts, and Shannon was dressed in a beautiful black ankle length dress with white Hawaiian flowers.

"Good morning, everyone," the chief greeted, still playing. "What do you think of our trio? I taught your friends here a traditional Hawaiian song, complete with lyrics. They have lovely voices and rhythm. I am actually very impressed."

They both thanked him. "It's been awhile since I've heard music and played along to it," Mark confessed. "I'm surprised I can still keep time."

"Oh, Mark, always so modest!" Shannon said, poking his chest. "You could never forget how to drum, even if they wiped your memory."

Mark chuckled. "Well, I guess I can thank you. That's a lot coming from the most talented girl in existence."

She smiled.

Standing behind Mark and Shannon, Marlene waved her arms around, frustrated. Her expression seemed to say, "They're just friends?!"

The chief noticed Marlene's irritation and laughed. Not explaining the situation to the clueless Mark and Shannon, he put his ukulele on the counter and complimented them both. "The two of you are quite talented."

"No, don't stop!" Ava cried. "I want to hear more!"

Grinning, the chief said, "You will hear plenty of it later; we are having a festival this evening. You will be able to see and hear our entire culture in one night. Don't worry, your friends here said it was safe to stay one more evening."

Mark nodded. "The Keepers asked for an update, so I sent out a message telling them that we haven't found anything yet and are still searching. They don't expect us to come back anytime soon anyway."

Hearing that, everyone cheered. Honestly, I was relieved. We deserved a vacation day.

"Now, who's hungry?" the Chief asked, clapping his large hands together.

Since we were going to rest for the day, I left before breakfast to take my armor off and put on my gray T-shirt and shorts instead of the tight tank top and leggings. Going outside, I stood on the sand and let my organic and Bionic body breathe in the salt air. It felt nice to feel somewhat normal again.

When food was ready, Axel called me in and I ran in to join them. I must say, breakfast was delicious. There were so many exotic foods, I wished I could try them all. Chief said there would be more at the festival, and I couldn't wait. That was the first meal we had together where we didn't talk about depressing or tear-jerking topics—at least until the end.

"Okay, everyone," Mark said as he finished up his haupia pudding. "Now that we're all here and safe, I think it's time that I tell you what you've all been waiting for."

Everyone became tense as he pulled a book from his backpack: *The Saved.* Turning to his friend, he said, "Shannon, this counts as their introductions, so pay attention."

She laughed and told him to get on with it. "The suspense is killing *all* of us."

Mark continued, "I'm thinking that if you all know your last names, and who you were, then maybe it will trigger some memories like Mr. Nik wrote in his instructions. 'There is power in a name,' a good doctor once said."

"A doctor? Doctor who?" Ava asked curiously.

"Precisely," was Mark's simple reply. "Now: we're going to start from the back and work our way forward. I've already found you all and have them tabbed." Flipping through the pages, Mark went to the last tab. "First is Ursula Zimmerman, age seventeen, born in Germany."

Everyone turned to look at her. After seeming to have zoned out for a few minutes, Miss Zimmerman's eyes widened, and she gasped. She took some deep breaths, and her eyes began to well up with tears. "Are you remembering?" Mark asked softly.

She began to nod and started smiling. "I can see their faces. I can hear their voices," she told us, choking up. "It's as if something inside me has been unlocked." Looking around, she remembered, "My hometown in Germany was beautiful. My family, my friends...."

"There's more in here, but I'll let you all look at it later," Mark said happily. "Now I'll go through them a little faster, so you all can fight over the book sooner:

"Lucas White, age fifteen, born in Australia; Harold Spears, age fifteen, America; Ethan Shaw, age nineteen, America; Zita Raneri, age sixteen, Italy; Axel Ramirez, age eighteen, Argentina; Yared Prinz, age eighteen, America; Donald McArthur, age ten, America; Becca Irwin, age fifteen, Canada; Cecil Grant, age sixteen, America; Ava Conner, age nine, England; Marlene Best, age seventeen, America."

"I am the *best*!" Marlene shouted jestingly as tears fell down her face. "I had a family and a foster father." As she said *foster father*, her face lit up. "No. Way," she gasped, but explained nothing else.

Everyone experienced their flood of memories differently. Some were sobbing, others laughing and dancing excitedly. They began to tell each other what they remembered and what their lives were like. No one could believe how they had forgotten so many memories.

Interrupting the excitement, Mark said, "Wait, I'm not done! There is one more surname."

The others who were left seemed confused, but I knew. Looking up at me, Mark smiled and read the names, "Alison Alexus, Sami Alexus, Aaron Alexus Junior, and Jeremy Alexus. All of them from America, and one big, happy family."

We all looked at one another and stood there for a few moments. They couldn't believe what they were hearing. Sami and Jeremy began sobbing, and Aaron stood there astounded.

"I can't believe all this time I thought my siblings were dead. Turns out they were always with me," I said, smiling. Sami and Jeremy ran to my arms and Aaron group-hugged us from behind. I held them close and never wanted to let go again.

Now the room was filled with amazed, crying people, including Chief Kapono. Everyone joined in on our group hug. When we let go, Aaron turned around and yelled at Mark. "Why didn't you tell me *they* were my siblings?! I mean, you told me they were alive, but I could barely sleep at night because I wondered where they were."

Mark laughed. "That would have ruined the surprise. Alison knew, though. As the oldest, it was her right."

"Yeah, now I can really boss you guys around," I told them jokingly.

With a grin, Mark placed the book on the counter. "Now you guys can go through it, but be careful. We're going to need this to help the others."

Ursula snatched the book and sat down in the living room. The rest of my friends huddled around her, and they looked at it together. While they were reading, my siblings, Mark, Shannon, the chief, and I stood around the kitchen counter. "So how does it feel to be reunited?" Shannon asked.

"Like something I cannot describe," Sami told her, wiping tears from her cat eyes. "I'm just happy you told us now. If you'd waited any longer, I think my own brother might have begun to like me," she joked.

"Oh, please no," Aaron said, putting his hands on his face. "Wiping all memories from my mind now." He groaned.

I couldn't help but smile. I had noticed that. *That would have been awkward,* I thought.

Mark laughed and said, "That's the trade secret I mouthed to you back on the Mainland. You were *totally* about to fall for your sister."

Aaron moaned and smacked himself. "Gross. Gross. Stop. Stop," he repeated.

Interrupting the conversation, which went over his head, Jeremy asked, "What happened to our parents? Are they here too?"

Shaking his head, Mark said softly, "They didn't make it. The book says that the Keepers found two dead adults shielding three small children. It was a miracle. Looking around, they found Alison about hundred feet away, limbs hanging off and all. She had with her a backpack containing photographs, nametags, your father's wallet, and other things. They confirmed the identities of all of you and took you with them."

I tried to hold back my tears. *They died protecting us,* I thought, *and we barely remember them.*

Trying to make the mood lighter, Aaron stopped hitting himself and pointed something out. "Wait, I just realized something. Alison, you said you had twin siblings? Does that mean Sami and I are twins?"

Everyone began to laugh. "No, seriously. I don't see it," Aaron said, looking Sami up and down.

Punching his arm, Sami replied, "Because I don't look the same as I did when we were born, stupid."

"That's probably why you found her attractive," I teased. "She looks the most like you."

"Hey!" Aaron protested. He then thought about it. "Well, probably."

"Ah, the first sibling quarrel," Mark said sighing. "I remember when I met my siblings for the first time—we began arguing almost immediately. First time I met my brother, we were fighting over Shannon's wallet."

"Wait, when you first met them?" I questioned. "And why her wallet?"

"That's another long story we'll save for another time," he replied. He had a lot of stories to tell.

Smiling, Shannon remembered that day. "That was an interesting encounter. You know, you've lost your city accent and lingo."

Mark shrugged. "It comes out sometimes, sweetheart. Besides, it's because of you I have a better vocabulary and am always coming up with 'theories'."

"Wait, so the whole 'theories' thing isn't yours?" Aaron asked, confused.

"Not entirely," Mark confessed. "She's the detective, not me. I just picked up a few deduction tips and tricks."

Looking at Shannon, Aaron said, "I guess we have you to thank for him being confusing."

"Naw, he was already confusing when we first met," she told him.

From the other room, Marlene shouted, "Why are you two just friends?!"

Shannon giggled, but Mark kept his eyes to the ground. *What's going on between you two?* I wondered.

After that, we stood around chatting for about another hour or so until the other members were done looking through the book. "What about you, Mark? What's your last name?" Aaron asked when the others came back into the kitchen.

Grinning, he replied, "Hodgins. My full name is Mark Timothy Hodgins. I hope to introduce you to the rest of my family once our job is done here."

"Do you really believe you can win?" Ava asked hopefully.

"I know we will," Shannon said with confidence.

"Well, before you do any winning," the chief interrupted, "you will all take part in our festival tonight!"

Everyone let out a loud cheer. We were all excited to attend the festival. Donnie, Ava, and Jeremy danced around and tried to sing the Hawaiian song that we heard earlier. They got the melody okay, but needed to work on the words a bit.

"Thank you so much for allowing us to stay with you, chief," Mark said gratefully when the kids calmed down. "Sadly, we'll have to leave sooner than I had hoped. We're leaving tomorrow morning while it's still dark. When this is all over, may we come back and visit?"

With a hearty laugh, he said, "Of course you may! In fact, I already spoke to Shannon about that." Looking at her for answers, Mark only got a shrug. *Another secret*, I thought, disappointed.

After that, we spent the rest of the day helping with festival preparations. The event was to take place on the beach behind the chief's house. The girls decorated the place with flowers and prepared the food. The boys did all the heavy lifting by setting up the stage, torches, tables, and making the statue of the ancient king they were celebrating look presentable. Not many of us girls knew how to cook, let alone prepare Hawaiian dishes. I had more fun doing it than I expected. Together, we made food to feed over one hundred people, plus Lucas and his crazy appetite.

When we were just about finished, Marlene accidentally flung some food at Ursula while she struggled to stir a sticky dessert. Instead of apologizing, Marlene snorted and laughed.

Smirking, Ursula wiped the mess off her face, grabbed a bowl of rotten fruit, and warned, "You never want to challenge a Seer in a fight." She chucked fruit at Marlene.

A food fight ensued. We ducked behind the counters and prepared for battle. Whatever leftovers we could find we used as ammunition and fired away. The Hawaiian women who were teaching us laughed at the spectacle and decided to join in. At one point, Ursula aimed for Marlene, who ducked right as Mark was walking in. His head was decorated in red tomato.

*Perfect timing,* I thought, chuckling. His face was priceless. He stood there in shock as the fruit dripped down his face. It was stuck in his hair and covered his green shirt. None of us could contain our laughter. Shannon was laughing so hard she collapsed. Smirking, Mark took the remaining fruit from his hair, grabbed some more that was nearby, and began throwing them at his friend while she was still on the ground. To back her up, we did a "girls versus boy" round. We chased him around the counters and picked up whatever scraps were hanging off us or on the floor. Ava grabbed his legs to slow him down. Shannon was about to tackle him, but he grabbed her and threw her over his shoulders like a sack of potatoes. Holding her and having Ava on his feet, he continued to throw food at the rest of us.

"To victory!" Marlene cried as she led us into the final stretch of the battle. We all threw at the same time. Ava let go, and Shannon got free and helped us out. When we had him cornered, we chucked what we had left. Pretending he was hit, he dramatically grabbed his chest and sank to the ground and played dead.

Sitting on his lap, Ava poked his chest. "Ha! We beat you."

Laughing, he said, "Stop! That tickles."

The ten-year-old grinned mischievously and continued to tickle him. She didn't stop until he was on the ground in stiches, begging for mercy. Giving in, she jumped off him, and he stood up. Looking around at our mess, we realized it was time to clean up. While we picked up the scraps, Marlene said, "Despite this mess, it was totally worth it."

"Totally," Ursula replied, grinning.

Finally, the sun was setting on the ocean waters, and it was time for the celebration. As the sun disappeared, Shannon said, "Another day gone; a new one to come."

Aaron smirked. "Did you steal that quote from Mark or did he take it from you?"

Shannon looked at her friend, who just shrugged. "You say good stuff, beautiful," Mark replied.

The time came for the party, which they called a luau, to begin. The Hawaiian women wore beautiful strapless floral maxi skirts like Shannon. The female dancers wore grass skirts with orange tank tops, accessorized with grass bracelets and anklets, and a flower necklace and crown. The men all wore grass skirts and no tops. Thankfully, they didn't give our guy friends those outfits. We were, however, given flower necklaces and crowns called leis.

It's hard to describe in detail everything that happened tonight. There was so much going on it was amazing. It was definitely one of the best nights of my life. Their music was incredible; they had dozens of musicians, and the dancers really added emphasis to the melodies with their rhythm and grace. At times, the audience would dance along with the people on the stage. Despite the fact that we had no idea what we were doing, we joined in.

The most popular dance was called Hula. Halfway through the song, the chief pulled Mark on stage and told the dancers to teach him in front of everyone, to help the audience. At first, Mark's movements were too harsh and he had trouble keeping up. Eventually, he got the hang of it, but it was still comical nonetheless, especially since he was forced to wear a grass skirt over his khakis. When he was finished, Mark told them that one day, he had to show them something called "break dancing".

Hopping off the stage, Mark walked over to Shannon, "What do you think? Should I keep the skirt?" He twirled in it.

Not even looking at the skirt, she raised one eyebrow and shook her head. Mark laughed, took it off, and gave it to Ava. "Yes!" she exclaimed as she pulled it over her head. It was way too big for her. She had to hold it in place and it dragged in the sand. Not caring, she danced around with Donnie and Jeremy.

One of my favorite dances was the fire dancing. Men came out onto the bamboo stage carrying flaming torches. They were able do a choreographed dance, and not get burned. They were twirling them and throwing them up into the air, catching them, and doing all sorts of crazy stunts. The main fire dancer had the "brilliant" idea of throwing his flaming staff to Axel halfway through the performance. My friend almost didn't catch it. When he had a good grip on it, Axel decided to show off. He flew up into the night sky and added a special flair to their performance. The natives were amazed—not just at the light show, but at seeing Axel *fly*. They couldn't believe their eyes. When he landed, everyone cheered and clapped.

Throughout the night, people would come around and offer us food. It was scrumptious; I never tasted anything like it. They had cooked most of the hot food over an open pit; the rest we had prepared earlier. I tasted one of everything and felt like I was going to explode by the end of the evening.

The luau went on late into the night. But when it finally did end, they had one more song to sing. There were only three people singing the final song: Chief Kapono Iokua, Mark, and Shannon. Mark sat on the floor with a small drum on his lap, and the chief and Shannon played ukuleles and sang. The three of them sounded amazing. The feeling that the Hawaiian music stirred in me was like none other. It was mellow, lifting, and melodious; it made me happy.

They got the loudest applause when they finished. To close, the chief gave a speech. Thankfully, Mark had updated our earpieces so they could translate Hawaiian:

*"My brethren,"* he began, *"tonight this festival in celebration of Kamehameha Day has, I believe, been one of the best celebrations we have had."*

The audience clapped and shouted in agreement.

*"And not only that,"* he continued, *"I could not be happier to share this night with our new friends. They are living proof that there is still hope for the land outside of Niihau and the rest of the Hawaiian Islands. Tonight, before we sleep, let us pray that our new friends have the best of luck with their mission and succeed in taking back our islands!"*

We were given loud applause and pats on the back, after which we spent some time chatting with the locals and sharing stories. Finally, it was time to pack it all up. After everything was cleaned and everyone cleared out, we all prepared for bed.

Mark, Shannon, and the chief were inside talking while the rest of us got ready. We slept outside once again, as it was another beautiful night. The starry night sky reflected off the ocean shore, the palm trees swayed in the warm gentle breeze, and everything was peaceful. I wished on a few shooting stars, hoping that all would be well.

I really don't want to leave, because once we do, trouble will only follow.

# THE ISLES

# CHAPTER 26
## Sami: IX

This morning, we woke up before the sun did. Mark told us to quickly pack our things and to say our goodbyes to the chief. We all grabbed our stuff and waited at Kapono's house.

"Chief Kapono Iokua," Mark began. "It has truly been a blessing and a pleasure to have met you. I'm hoping that when we meet again, the world will be different."

That small but profound goodbye was enough to cause the chief to cry. He gave our friend a bear hug. This time we thought he was actually going to snap him in half, because Mark's back cracked a few times. Afterward, Shannon personally thanked the chief and kissed him on the cheek. We all said our goodbyes and headed on our way. Jealous, Mark complained as we were heading to shore, "Oh sure, kiss him but not me."

She chuckled. Marlene was behind them, flailing her arms in frustration again. "Why are they just friends?!" she whispered angrily.

While we were riding back to Saviors in the speedboat, Mark relayed the plan to us. "We spoke with Mr. Bamber and Mrs. Pieper before you got up," he began. "The plan is this: we bring Shannon in as our prisoner, and they take her into custody."

"Whoa, whoa, hold up," Cecil interrupted. "Why do you want to do that? Aren't we trying to *avoid* that?"

"Don't worry, bro, she can handle it," Mark told him. "Besides, it won't be long. She sent out a distress signal to RRPR headquarters. Once they see it was her, they'll be here in a heartbeat. They'll help us take over."

I couldn't believe my ears. "We're taking over the Nerve Center?" I asked, with my jaw dropped.

"We have to," Shannon said boldly. "But we won't be alone. Mr. Bamber has a plan of his own."

We got back to Isle II and piled into the helicopter, which was right where we left it. Yared and Ursula put Shannon in chains and gagged her, though they didn't like it one bit. "Everyone buckle up!" Mark called from the cockpit. "We're headed to the center of Isle II. I'll send a message to Dr. Agro letting him know we're on our way."

When we landed, we found the doctor waiting for us at the helipad. We exited the helicopter and brought him our "prisoner". He did not look pleased when he saw her; in fact, he was more disappointed. "*This* is our threat?" he complained. "This child broke into my facility, kept herself hidden, stole my books, and caused so much trouble?" Bending over to meet her at eye level, he studied her.

She stared right back with her blue eyes and didn't flinch.

"I do not believe it," he said scoffing. "There is something more going on here, little girl, is there not?" he asked, removing her gag. She refused to answer. "Can you at least tell me your name?" he said with a slightly kinder tone.

Finally, she spoke. "I will refrain from giving you my name, but I will inform you that I am *no child*."

Standing up straight, he began chuckling. "Oh, my dear, you think you are so tough. How old are you? Fourteen? Sixteen maybe?"

"I am twenty-three," she replied, smirking.

The smile disappeared from the Keeper's face. Feeling awkward, he immediately put the gag back on her. After that, he said nothing, but commanded that we all followed him to the jet to take off for Isle III.

Every hair on my mutant cat body stood up as we approached

our destination. Anxiety and fear took over me like a parasite. *Don't show fear; they sense fear*, I repeated to myself, worrying I would ruin the whole plan. Thankfully, my sister was sitting next to me. Noticing how I was feeling, she began to pat my hand. The look in her eyes told me everything was going to be okay. I trusted her.

Finally, we landed. Shannon was the last one to get off the plane... well, she was dragged off by the Seers, actually. I hated how we had to act ruthless towards her, but there was no other way. We had to play the part. I thought it was convincing, but Wally and Mr. Nik had their doubts. "Are you sure this is the only intruder?" Wally asked, sounding suspicious.

"Absolutely positive," Mark replied without hesitation.

"She doesn't seem so bad. How can such a pretty little thing cause so much damage?" Wally questioned as he stroked her freckled face.

Abruptly, Shannon pulled her head away. I bet she would have bitten his finger off if she wasn't wearing a gag.

"Do not aggravate her, Walter," Dr. Agro cautioned. "I think she is much tougher than she looks... She is most definitely older than she looks."

Slightly confused, Wally looked at his Nigerian colleague with an odd expression on his face and stepped away from the prisoner.

"We will take her with us and discuss what to do with the other Keepers," Mr. Nik chimed in. Addressing us, he said, "You will remain under watch. Mr. Bamber has offered to keep an eye on you all in Stratum Zero's classroom." As he turned to walk away, he looked at us out of the corner of his eye and gave us a final warning: "If any of you try to pull anything, you will wish you had never been born."

With that, he and Wally took Shannon away, leaving Dr. Agro with us. "Yeah, that's not creepy at all," Harold mumbled.

We headed to the cafeteria and waited in Stratum Zero for Mr. Bamber to show up. He was supposed to be guarding us, but he was doing a terrible job. We all sat there in an awkward silence. Mark had a distressed look on his face and didn't seem to be breathing well. "Mark, you good?" Aaron asked with concern.

He shook his head. "I'm worried for her. She says she can handle it, but still..."

"She seems pretty tough. I may not know her like you do, but I'm positive she will make it through," Aaron told him.

He smiled. "You're probably right, thanks. Besides, I have to remember she's had plenty of training, even before we were with RRPR. I just hope she has her mask."

Before I could ask about that last part, Mr. Bamber wheeled into the classroom with Mrs. Pieper right behind. "How are you all feeling?" he asked with concern.

Everyone felt okay, but not the good kind of okay. Mr. Bamber grinned and nodded. "That's fine; I wasn't expecting you to be feeling good. If you were, I would be quite concerned." Taking a deep breath, his tone become serious, "Are you ready to finish this?"

That was when he relayed his plan to us. As he was explaining the steps, it got so quiet you could hear a pin drop. We were all in shock. None of us wanted to go through with it, but we had no choice. It had to be done. While he was explaining, Mrs. Pieper piled the weapons she had smuggled in onto the counter: guns, knives, spears, weird machinery from the labs, and whatever else she could find. Aaron and Cecil began tinkering with a few of the items while the rest of us took our pick. They had ideas for some new weaponry. Once they were done and we were armed, we headed out.

I'll explain the plan as it happens, because it all hasn't been carried out yet.

Step One was to overthrow the electronic portion of the Isles. We needed to shut everything down: computers, lights, the chips in our brands, everything. Some of the machines that the Isle III students were working on had their own power supplies, which was good and bad. Hopefully, the students would be on our side and use them against our enemy and not us.

"Cutting off the power to all the Isles is going to take a lot more effort than you think," Mr. Bamber whispered, as we snuck into the empty cafeteria. "Not only do we have to shut it down from the Nerve Center downstairs, but there are four other stations that we need to take control of to override the entire system."

"Why did you have to make it so complicated?" Yared complained.

Looking at him, Mr. Bamber said flatly, "In case some idiots ever tried to override the entire system."

Yared made a face that seemed to say, *Obviously*.

"Okay, I'll head downstairs with whoever wants to accompany me," Mr. Bamber said as he pulled the books from the shelves to open the door. "But Yuki, Mark, Aaron, and Cecil will have to lead the way to the other computers. They know this facility the best. Split up accordingly. I will give you instructions on what to do once you get there."

Telling him we understood, we began to depart. I headed out with Aaron and Donnie. "The secretary works on one of the main computers," Aaron explained. "To be honest, I had no idea we had a secretary until just now. This will be interesting."

"So that means you don't know where it is?" I grumbled as we walked.

"Of course I do," he defended. "It's a tall, long desk in the waiting room that leads to where I took my Commencement Test. There wasn't a secretary sitting there last I saw it, so let's hope she isn't there now."

He took us up to the top floor and across a glass sky bridge with a beautiful view. The sun was beginning to set beyond the waters. It was such a shame that the Keepers had wicked intentions, because the Isles were such a stunning place to live. I hoped that we could fix everything and restore the islands to their natural beauty.

As we entered the room, Aaron cursed under his breath. There were a man and a woman sitting at the desk towards the back of the room. We tried to peek in and not be seen, but we failed. "May we help you?" the woman called when she saw us.

We had no choice but to approach her. "Um, hi," Aaron said nervously. "Is this the secretary's desk?"

"Yes it is, young man," she said with a smile. "How may we be of assistance?"

Aaron was obviously trying to think of something, but couldn't put anything to words. Then, Donnie spoke up. "Why's this desk on the top floor where no one can find it?" Standing on his tiptoes, he peered over the desk at the woman.

"Excuse me?" she asked confused.

The boy put his arms on the desk, leaned over, and let his legs dangle. "We been wandering around for hours looking for help, and we ain't found nobody."

Not sure what to say, the woman looked to her male colleague for assistance. "Well, usually we don't have visitors, as two of you obviously are," the man said, staring at me.

"Well, I think y'all should make it more convenient," Donnie continued to complain. He rambled on about the inconveniences of having a secretary's desk where no one could find it.

It didn't take long before the workers were annoyed. "Listen, kid," the woman snapped, "if you don't have any business here, just go back to whoever you're supposed to be with!"

Out of protest, Donnie stomped over to one of the chairs and stood up on it. Then he began hopping from table to chair to table while yelling and taunting the secretaries. "Stop that!" the man yelled as he stood up and marched over to Donnie. He tried to grab him, but the boy quickly jumped away. He tried a few more times but wasn't fast enough.

"Lisa, can you help me?" he shouted. The woman rushed to his aid, and together they tried and failed. While that was going on, Aaron snuck behind the desk and began typing away.

Lisa saw him. "Hey! What are you doing?" she bellowed.

Before she could get to him, Donnie did something which will forever surprise me: He tackled her and bit her on the neck. Her coworker attempted to come to her rescue, but Donnie threw his head back and smacked the man in the face with his pot-helmet, knocking him unconscious. Then, he threw his head forward and whacked the woman unconscious. He jumped off her back before she collapsed on her face.

Aaron and I stared at him. Fixing the pot on his head, Donnie reminded, "We learn defense moves in Assets too, ya know. Now get goin'."

Snapping back into reality, Aaron got back to work. After about fifteen minutes, he called the others on his BoMF. "I'm ready here. Anyone else?" One by one they responded that they were ready.

"Okay. On the count of three, launch it," Mr. Bamber said from the device. "Ready? One, two, three!"

Aaron clicked enter, and the lights went out.

"Perfect. Now: time to get Shannon back," I heard Mark say over Aaron's BoMF.

I took out a flashlight, and we made our way down the stairs. The plan was to head straight for the kitchen, but we had to take a few detours. Apparently the secretaries regained conscious after we left and sent out a distress signal, so we had a few guards on our tail. We tried to lose them, but they cornered us on the stairs. Thankfully, they made a mistake: It was dark and we were the only ones with a flashlight. I gave it to Aaron and told him to shut it off at my signal. Slowly, I got down on all fours, gave him the signal, and pounced.

I showed them very little mercy. I ripped the weapons from their hands, clawed off their helmets, and tackled them all to the ground. Their blood stained the floor as they lay there unconscious. I did my best not to kill them, but a couple fell down a few flights of steps. Without saying a thing, I grabbed as many of their guns as I could carry and pulled Aaron and Donnie down the stairs.

"What did you do?" Aaron demanded as I lugged them into the kitchen. I didn't have time to answer. We were the last ones to make it, but we weren't the only ones to have a hard time. Some of our friends were covered in bruises, and others in blood which wasn't their own. I handed out weapons to those who didn't have any.

"So now what?" Ursula asked, panting.

"We go get Shannon. The Keepers left her alone downstairs, so we have an opening," Mrs. Pieper explained.

"Ursula, you're coming with Alison, Lucas, Harold, Marlene, and me to get her back," Mark said, reloading his pistol. "The rest of you, meet us outside. There's an exit downstairs that leads to the field;

we'll go out that way."

Understanding, we parted ways. We went to the field and waited for what seemed like forever; it was torture. Every second felt as if we waited for death itself. Any noise we heard, we pointed a weapon at. Usually, it was the wind or ruckus from the alarmed people inside. Becca and I didn't sense anything dangerous until Mark and the others came out.

Harold and Marlene ran out first, their guns cocked. "I'm ready, I'm ready, I'm ready," Harold repeated in an irritating voice as they ran.

"Cut it out!" Marlene snapped.

Mark followed behind them, carrying Shannon, who was unconscious. The expression on his face told me that we had a problem. Ursula, Alison, and Lucas were defending them from the rear; guards in Seers uniforms were chasing and shooting them. "We have to get to the jet!" Mr. Bamber cried.

Axel scooped the Keeper up, took to the air, and led the way once the others were caught up. The jet Mr. Bamber was talking about was his own private plane at the far end of the training fields. Thankfully, when we cut the electricity, the fields went back to what they originally were: an enormous meadow. It turned out that all the various terrains had been tactile holograms controlled by a master computer. With the power down, they were gone.

I remained in the back of the column with my sister and held off as many of the Seers as I could. We shot them down, knocked them over, collapsed the ground before them, but nothing worked. The guards kept coming, though there was no sign of the Keepers—that is, until we got closer to Mr. Bamber's jet. The other six were blocking our escape with an army of Seers behind them; no students, though, thank goodness. I didn't want them to turn against us before we could talk.

"Brian Bamber!" Mr. Nik roared. His brow was furrowed, and his dark eyes meant business. He was dressed in a navy combat uniform instead of his usual shirt and tie.

Still in Axel's arms, Mr. Bamber looked down at the Headmaster below him and begged, "Nikita, listen to me. You know what you are doing is wrong." Axel brought Mr. Bamber back down and sat him in his chair. "You all do! You know that it doesn't make you any better than the Invaders!"

The other Keepers tried to ignore him, but they all knew he was right—and I felt like most of them were afraid to do anything about it. Wally pulled out his gun and pointed it at Mr. Bamber. After cursing at him in German, he said, "You had better start talking if you vish to see tomorrow."

Before Mr. Bamber could say anything in his defense, a bomb went off in the building in front of us, where the plane was. Wally's men were caught in the blast, and it blew the rest of us off our feet. Almost everyone was knocked unconscious.

The few of us who were in the back were still awake, but shaken up. There was an intense ringing in my ears, and I struggled to my feet. Before I collapsed again, I saw a bunch of people in dark combat suits and scarves around their mouths attacking Mr. Nik's men. Then, they came over to us and carried us back to wherever they'd come from. I passed out in the arms of the man who was carrying me.

Right now, I don't know where I am. I woke up a few hours ago in a bed. Around me, the people who had saved us were bandaging our wounds. None of them have showed me their faces yet. They asked if I need anything, but I turned them down. Not wanting to disturb them, I just began to write down everything that happened.

One of them just told me to get some rest, so I think I will listen now.

I hope I wake up tomorrow.

# THE ISLES

# Chapter 27

## Aaron: IX

All I remember from last night was that something blew up, and I woke up on a huge ship. Apparently, we were on the RRPR's main battleship. I keep wondering how the Keepers haven't found it yet.

This morning we were awoken by a very high-pitched female voice on the loudspeaker system. "Rise and shine, everyone! Big continental breakfast waiting in the dining hall."

Sitting up, I found myself in a cozy bed in a room with all my male friends minus Mark. *The girls must have gotten a separate cabin,* I thought, as I put my glasses on. I was lucky they were still intact. I looked around. "Guys, are you okay?"

"I think we're good," Yared reassured me as he jumped down from the bunk above me. Everyone seemed to be all right. We were a little banged up, but our wounds were wrapped in bandages. Did they do that? I wondered as I rubbed the medical tape on my forearm.

"Hey, this bathroom is huge," Donnie called from a large white room to the left of me. Poking his wet head out of the doorway, he said, "And the lightin' is real bright! There's more than one lightbulb!"

"You know our lives are sad when we get excited about lightbulbs," Harold commented as he walked out of the bathroom past half-naked, wet Donnie. He was wearing fresh new clothes that he'd found somewhere. Looking down at his black T-shirt and bottoms, he said, "Eh, black isn't my color. That's more for the creepy Mutants."

"Get stuffed," Lucas snapped while flying upside down above him. "You *know* I could knock you out before you could blink."

While they were arguing, the rest of us freshened up and changed. When we were ready, we headed to the dining hall. Going out into the hallway, we looked both ways down the long corridor and were immediately stumped. "Okay, which way?" Ethan asked, scratching his tan temple.

Yared shrugged and pushed Cecil and I forward. "Figure it out, geeks."

"Overlords," I corrected.

Yared rolled his dark eyes. "Whatever. Just get us to where the food is."

Having no other choice, Cecil and I led the way. We had no idea where we were going. We got lost about five times. We would have been wandering forever if we hadn't bumped into the lady who made the announcement. We ran into her as she exited the control room; that's how lost we were.

"What are you all doing here?" she asked, surprised when she saw us. She was a ridiculously tall, thin young woman in a black combat uniform like Shannon's. Peeking out of her unzipped jacket was a silver dog tag with a beautiful H etched into it. *Also like Shannon's*, I thought when I noticed it. Her long brown hair was wavy and the bangs were cut straight across; it was so perfect it seemed unreal. Surprisingly, she was wearing makeup.

*That's determination*, I thought. We were at war, and she still made sure she looked her best. She seemed very familiar, but I couldn't put my finger on it at the time.

Looking up at her, Yared interrupted my staring by apologizing. "Sorry, we're just looking for the food."

"Don't worry, boys, I'll lead you there," she said, smiling. "You're probably starving and feeling a bit confused, right?"

We all nodded. "We'll clear it up when all of your friends are awake," she said.

We followed her through many more hallways until we were above deck. Looking toward the horizon, we could see the Isles and two other battleships about the same size as the one we were on. I'd never seen, let alone been on, a ship so ginormous. They were large enough to hold helicopters and small planes, not to mention all the crew and cargo.

*No wonder we couldn't find the dining hall,* I thought as we walked across the deck. There was a door at the front end of the ship leading below. Going down into a large, low-ceilinged room, we found hundreds of people eating breakfast. I wasn't expecting so many. White tables and benches were set up all over; it looked like your classic cafeteria, with gray floors and walls; nothing compared to the beautiful library at Isle III. The only nice touch to the boring eating area were the large portraits of higher-ranking staff members and powered-down flat screen TVs on each wall. Some of the faces in the paintings looked familiar, but I was afraid to go and look at one up close.

"Here we are, fellas," our guide said at last. "Come grab some grub. You can sit by me."

After we filled our trays, we found the announcer lady sitting with our female friends. They waved at us from the other side of the hall. "How are you boys feeling?" Marlene asked as we sat down.

"I think we're all good," Donnie said, stuffing a whole pancake into his mouth.

Smiling, the boy's commander tapped the pot on his head and replied, "Good, because we need you."

"I'm glad you're all alive," our new friend said. "Sorry about that crazy stuff last night. I'm relieved you weren't too close to the blast." She was about to eat her fruit when she realized she'd forgotten to introduce herself. "Oh, my name is Aymie, by the way."

"Hi, Aymie," was our simultaneous reply.

Giggling, she said, "Hi all! So, I met all the ladies here, now how about you gentlemen?" One by one we went through our names and told her a bit about ourselves. She kept asking us questions about who we were and avoided any questions we had about RRPR. I guessed she wasn't allowed to tell us certain things just yet.

*Maybe that's why Mark keeps so many secrets*, I thought as Aymie dodged another question.

We ate and chatted for about an hour until Aymie stood up and bid us farewell. "It was a pleasure meeting you all," she said, picking up her empty coffee mug, "but unfortunately I have to run. I have to do a few things, but I will meet you later in the Director's conference room. Someone will be waiting for you on deck."

After we left, we decided we should head out as well. As we got up to leave, Ava asked, "Where are Mark, Shannon, Mr. Bamber, and Mrs. Pieper? Does anybody know?"

To be honest, I'd forgotten. I felt so stupid and guilty. *How could I forget one of my best friends?*

Going up to the deck, I was thankful when we found that Mark and the others were the ones waiting for us. They looked terrible. Shannon was in a wheelchair, and both her arms were wrapped in bandages from wrist to elbow. Her legs and face were covered in small cuts and bruises. Poor Mr. Bamber seemed pale and lifeless as he struggled to breathe through the oxygen tubes that ran up his nose. Thankfully, Mrs. Pieper and Mark were less banged-up, but still looked shaken. "Sorry we couldn't meet you this morning," Mark apologized. "We wanted to stay with Shannon and Mr. Bamber in the infirmary."

"Don't apologize, we would have done the same," Cecil told him.

Mark led us to the opposite end of the ship and back below decks, but closer to where the cabins were. We went past the control room and then to an even lower level, until we reached a large, locked metal door. It wouldn't open without swiping an identification card and a retinal and finger scan. To no one's surprise, Mark had clearance, and the door swung open.

It was a dim room, and in the center was a wooden table with twelve swivel chairs: one at each head, and five on each side. The space was big and the red rug made it feel cozy. Covering the walls were framed newspaper articles, photographs, and drawings. Behind the chair at the head of the table was a large map with different colored pins in it.

I looked around at the information on the walls. Many clippings were related to Mr. Nik and whatever information they had about him, the Keepers, and the Isles. *They must have known about Mr. Nik longer than they say*, I thought as I examined the back wall. Unfortunately, all the articles were too tragic to read. I was walking away when one caught my eye.

Going over to the corner, I bent over and examined the tiny newspaper column. In bold letters, the title read, "*Mysterious Terrorists Strike Again.*" The location of this attack was a small town in Washington State, U.S.A. called Leavenworth. There were two pictures wrapped by the text. The first was of a family with the mayor, standing in front of odd-looking buildings. The second was of the same buildings, destroyed by fire, with dead bodies in the streets.

Something about those photographs seemed all too familiar, and then I read the caption of the first picture: "*Mayor Charleston with his military friend Mr. Aaron Alexus and his wife (Mrs. Bridget Hertz Alexus) and children in front of Hertz German Chocolate Shoppe.*"

I gasped. I couldn't fathom what I was seeing. The faces looked all too familiar: the father had blond hair like Jeremy and me and wore glasses. The mother was beautiful and had the same heart-shaped face as my sisters. "Alison, Sami, Jeremy! Come look at this," I immediately called to my siblings.

Rushing over, they marveled at the small newspaper clipping. They couldn't believe it either. We'd found a picture of our family. "Is that me?" Jeremy asked, pointing to the baby in the woman's arms.

"I think so," Sami whispered, running hairy fingers over the photograph.

"Look at us, we were so cute. What happened?" Alison said jokingly, trying not to cry.

Our admiration was interrupted by the sound of the door opening. Quickly, we stood up and turned to face our host. Walking in was a slightly wrinkled man with white hair. He stood straight and tall and had the mannerisms and look of a military officer.

"Please, everyone, sit down," he said kindly, motioning to the seats. There were almost enough when we added a few folding chairs. Mark and Mrs. Pieper stood in the back corner, hidden from view with Shannon and Mr. Bamber. Once we were seated, the man introduced himself. "Hello, boys and girls, my name is Director Stanley Wyght, and I oversee this operation: Resist, Rescue, Protect, Retake. I'm also the founder of Wyght's Home for Young People. I apologize for our abrupt arrival, but there was no other way to get you out of that situation last night."

Walking to the seat in front of the wall map, Director Wyght sat down, rested his forearms on the table, and continued. "Many of you may not know this, but the Invaders have been around far longer than you believe. They were around before I met Nikita Patya and Walter Jarvis, which was a little less than thirty years ago.

"When I was in the military, I was sent to a Middle Eastern country to do fieldwork. While I was there, we captured an enemy base that was unlike any other we'd found. Instead of murdering people or using them as hostages, this new threat would capture them and run experiments on them. We thought of it as one man's crazy scheme, at first, but later we found another base doing the same thing.

"After doing a little more research and investigation, we discovered their true intentions. Their first objective was to control the minds of ordinary citizens, forcing them to do their bidding— which was to create the world anew. The Invaders started out as a sort of cult; their own religion, you may say. They are officially known as the Order of Xenophon and have been around for centuries. More recently, they have made themselves widely known. They are made up of many different ethnic groups, but are united with one objective: to create the world in their image. To do that, they have to take total control of everything."

The director took a deep breath and made eye contact with us. "As for your Keepers, they were a part of that vision until about fifteen or so years ago. Patya and Jarvis opened their eyes to what was going on, but what they decided to do about it was no better than what they were doing when their eyes were still shut. They wanted to overthrow the Invaders and complete the job with *themselves* at the head." He paused for a moment. "That is where you came in. They needed an army, but where could they find one if the Invaders took over most of the world?

"The answer was simple. The Invaders usually only took adults whose brains had stopped growing and developing, whereas Patya chose children who still had their whole lives ahead of them. Not only was it easier to make a child obey him, but they had time to grow and become stronger in mind and body."

Director Wyght sighed, scratched his face, and went on, "I know you've probably heard most of that already, but now you're hearing it from a man who has seen these men for what they are. I met the two of them while I was overseas, and we became good friends. They visited me and the children several times at my home." He thought for a moment and chuckled, "Actually, I'd bet my life that your lifestyle on the Isles is almost exactly what I teach at my place, but that's not important." Standing up and stepping out from behind the table, Director Wyght went over to the door. "So, allow me to bring in my highest-ranking officers: my Royals. You've already met a few, but I think some formal introductions are in order."

"Ooh, royalty," Ava marveled. I think she was expecting princesses.

The first one to enter was a very tall man, about as tall as Chief Kapono Iokua, but extremely muscular; definitely not a princess. He had light skin and dark hair with bright red highlights that was styled into a small Mohawk. Oddly enough, his arm hair was darker than his head hair. If that weren't peculiar enough, he had violet eyes. Yes, violet eyes. He and his comrades wore the same uniform as Aymie and Shannon, but his jacket was tied around his waist.

"Hi," he began. "I think we'll make our introductions quick; we have a lot to do. So anyway, my name is Nicolas Eerkens, but you can call me Nic with a C; not to be confused with your Nik with a K. I'm 26 years old, Co-Director of RRPR, and the Veteran Royal Combatant." Standing off to the side, Nicolas made room for the next member.

He was a pale-looking fellow with layered hair black as night that fell to the middle of his neck. His thick bangs crossed between his sharp, reddish-brown eyes. He was a few inches shorter than Nicolas, but had a strong build. "Sonny Wilcox, age 25, Royal Combatant," he said in a low, raspy voice with his arms crossed in front of him. "I still don't know why we have to say our ages," he mumbled.

Hearing him, Director Wyght said, "It adds trust if they know you're all close in age. No more comments." The director waved in the proceeding officer, a thinner man a few inches shorter than Sonny. He had white hair and timid light blue eyes. His skin was pale like Sonny's, and looked very soft.

"Blake Bain, age 24, Royal Umbrella," he announced.

*What are these "Royal" things, and why an umbrella?* I wondered. *Why is his hair white? Is he part Bionic, like Alison and Axel?*

"Myles Powell, age 19, Royal Veteran Drone," said the next one, with a grin on his face, interrupting my thoughts. He looked a little like me, but shorter. He had eyes almost as blue as mine and light hair; his wasn't spikey and he didn't have glasses, though. Powell was the name on the blueprints, I thought. Unconsciously, I stared right at him while I was trying to figure out if he knew the owner. Realizing I was looking at him, he made eye contact with me, smiled, and said, "I guess you're Aaron?"

Taken aback, I slowly replied, "Yes. How did you know that?"

"Mark told me that you recovered a few of my missing blueprints, so I wanted to thank you!" he said, reaching out for a handshake. After we shook, he continued, "Those designs I made when I was very young, so they're of sentimental value…," he drifted off for a moment and went on, "not to mention they're also important to our organization. I cannot thank you enough."

Confused, I nodded. *He made them when he was younger? How much younger?* Those blueprints had complex designs. Surely someone had to be almost Mr. Bamber's age to create something like that.

# AARON: IX

Myles wanted to talk more, but was stopped when the next member came in to introduce herself. "Johanna Watterson, age 23, Royal Veteran Umbrella." She was an inch shorter than Myles and had dark blonde hair that was pulled back in a bun. Her sea-green eyes scanned the room, as if desperately looking for someone. When she saw Mark and Shannon hiding in the corner, she let out a sigh of relief. Before she could say anything, she heard the last members approaching and made way for them.

Walking in were Aymie and a young man. The man behind her had features very similar to Mark's: same height, same face shape, same hair color. However, he was stronger and his hair was thicker, layered, and wispy. His striking eyes were the color of emeralds. Around his neck was a leather cord. Hanging from it was a key with a Celtic knot design and four small silver rings on either side. I thought it was cool.

Before introducing themselves, Mark stepped out of the corner and approached them. When they saw him, they froze. Slowly, Mark stepped closer. For a few minutes, they all stared at each other, as if what they saw wasn't real. After coming to terms that it was real, they all started sobbing. Finally, the man flung his arms around Mark and pulled him close. "I'm sorry. I am so sorry," I heard him say.

After he pulled away, Aymie ran up and began punching Mark in the chest with the sides of her fists. "Why did you do this to us?!" she cried as she clutched his shirt and collapsed against him.

Mark grabbed her before she sank to the floor. It took a few minutes before they and the other officers pulled it together. The only one who wasn't fazed was the guy with dark hair, Sonny. I'm sure he must have felt some emotion. After all, five years had gone by since Mark left without saying goodbye or telling anyone.

Calming down and wiping the tears from his eyes, Mark apologized to us. "Sorry about that, everyone, but allow me to introduce you to my family: Shane and Aymie Hodgins. We're triplets, believe it or not, so we're all twenty-five, if you really need to know our ages."

*Well, that makes sense,* I thought as my eyes looked back and forth at the three siblings. They had the same skin tone, eye shape, and hair color. Also, the three of them were tall; the boys were two inches taller than me, and Aymie wasn't too far behind.

"Hello again, everyone," Aymie said as she wiped the running mascara off her face.

Shane gave us a big toothy smile and waved, trying to hide the fact that he was crying. Turning to Mark, the brother reached in his pocket and pulled out a dog tag identical to the ones Shannon and Aymie were wearing. "You left this behind," Shane said, holding it up.

Mark took it and put it on. "It would have ruined the whole operation," he reminded. He looked up and noticed the key and rings around Shane's neck. "I see you traded yours in," he said, poking it.

Shane chuckled. "Tell you later." He almost started crying again and gave his brother another hug. "We missed you, man."

And the sobbing started up again. When they finally pulled themselves together, Shannon spoke up from the corner of the room. "I'm going to interrupt the bawling, if you don't mind. Is it my turn to re-introduce myself?"

Shane's face lit up at the sound of her voice. The others behind him just began to smirk. "Told you she was alive," Myles said teasingly, slapping his back. "It was only a few days. Geez, you worry too much!"

Shannon slowly wheeled herself out of the corner to where Mark and the others were standing. Without asking any questions, Shane snatched her out of her chair and held her so they were eye level. With one hand, he pulled her face close and sweetly kissed her. When he pulled away, he pressed his forehead against hers and began crying again.

Mark was happy for them, but he was slightly jealous. "Sure, kiss him and not me," Mark muttered under his breath.

Not hearing him, Marlene interjected, "Oh… that's why she and Mark are just friends." She sounded disappointed. Her remark caused the room to fill with laughter. Even the emotionless guy smirked! That was an improvement. Shannon was laughing so hard, she almost fell out of Shane's arms. With a grin, Shane carefully put her back in her wheelchair and stood behind it.

"All right, everyone, let's settle down," Director Wyght said smiling. "Hopefully, we'll have some time for fun later. Right now, time to talk business. So, Mr. Brian Bamber, I hear you have a plan."

Struggling to speak, Mr. Bamber weakly replied, "Yes, we do. Step One was a success, and Step Two was completed thanks to you. This may not be the safe house I was thinking of, but it works."

"I'm glad we could be of some assistance, but I'm so sorry you're in this condition," Wyght said sympathetically. "If it is uncomfortable, please refrain from speaking. I don't wish you to hurt yourself more."

"Thank you, sir, it is much appreciated," the Keeper said graciously. "I can have my colleague here explain Step Three, which requires your help."

Mrs. Pieper came out from behind Mr. Bamber's wheelchair and began to explain. "Our first two steps were: shut down the electronics and to get to a safe house before the ensuing panic. I believe we completed those as best we could. Step Three is a little trickier, because now we're dealing with the children.

"Each child is branded on the back of their neck when they enter a facility. Inside that brand is a microchip that is used only when necessary. Thankfully, Mr. Bamber was its creator. He knows how to disable them for good. They are currently deactivated in the kids who are with us. However, we still need to disable them in the other children, all at once. If we don't do that, then all hope is lost.

"Part Two of Step Three is to broadcast a video of the recent footage of Nikita and Walter revealing their true goals. Shannon went through a lot of pain to get this footage, but now we will show everyone what vicious beasts they really are. If the children are not convinced by that, there's plenty more that we can give them. We're planning for each of our Isle commanders here to say a few words about all this to their fellow Isle members." With that, she exhaled and walked back to Mr. Bamber.

"Thank you," Director Wyght said kindly, after taking some notes. "I believe that's enough for today. We have a lot of work to do."

# THE ISLES

Standing up straight and blowing a small silver whistle, Director Wyght got his officers' attention. Each immediately stood up straight with their hands behind their backs and heads forward. Even Shannon sat as proper as she could in her wheelchair.

Calling everyone by their last names, he began to give orders in military fashion. "Eerkens, S. Hodgins, and Wilcox; You will prepare the teams for attack. I have a feeling this won't end well. Bain, M. Hodgins, and Powell; You will assist Bamber's team in making the videos and send them out to the six islands' faculties immediately. A. Hodgins and Watterson; You two will attend to Hollinger's and Bamber's injuries."

Addressing Shannon in a softer tone, he said, "I need you back in the field. When the paralytic drug wears off and some of your bruises heal, do you think you can handle it?"

Without making eye contact, she replied sternly, "Yes, sir."

"Good," he replied, satisfied. "Dismissed!"

We exited the room and followed our group to the gigantic control room. There were monitors of all shapes and sizes covering the walls. The computers' colorful, blinking LEDs gave the room a crimson tint. Typing away at the desks were soldiers so engrossed in their work they didn't bother to turn their attention to the seventeen strangers shuffling in behind them.

"All right, let's begin recording in order, according to Isle," Myles said looking at Mark's clipboard, "So, Miss Alison is up first!"

This took us the entire day to do— and it was a long day. What was cool and terrifying at the same time was that I got to be the representative for Isle III, since the people of the Isles viewed Mark as a traitor. Thankfully, there were plenty of things to look at and explore to pass the time. Rather than sightseeing, I got to know Myles and Blake a bit better. Myles didn't have much time to chat, although he wished he could talk to Cecil and me for hours about the stuff we had created at the Research and Development Isle.

"So, why are you an Umbrella?" I asked Blake while Ethan was recording his video with Myles. "And why a Royal one? What does that mean?"

# AARON: IX

Fiddling with a large still camera, the young white-haired man replied, "It's just the name of one of our Branches. 'Umbrella' is the title of those of who do random, generic stuff; like cooking, cleaning, and so on. Royal just means I did something worth noticing."

"So, you're kind of like our Assets?"

Blake shook his hand, then shrugged. "Eh, kind of. We have our own Farming branch. If you split Assets in half, we would be the non-farming part."

Sort of understanding, I nodded in agreement. We talked a little more, and I found out some interesting things. Myles is a child prodigy, and Blake has white hair because he has a weird disease thing; I forget what it's called. Also, Nic and Shane were junior Olympians as kids. Shane did well in his division, but Nic not so much. I wanted to ask more questions, but Blake avoided many of them, like Aymie did this morning.

"It's not that we can't tell you," he explained as I recorded today's events in my log, "it's more like it will take away from what's really important." He held up his camera and showed me pictures he had taken of us while we were recording our videos. "Besides, I tell stories better in photographs than words."

Myles then called Blake to assist him with camera trouble. Blake looked at me with his light blue eyes and said, "Good talking with you, Aaron. Now, you keep on writing. Add words to my photos." Getting up, he went to assist his little blond friend.

Finally, I've finished writing in here, and Sami's video is completed. Time to send them out! I hope it works as planned....

# THE ISLES

# CHAPTER 28

## Alison: X

I wanted to remain on the ship for a few more days, but our plan commands otherwise, so we leave in the morning. Tomorrow's move has left me restless, so I decided to stay up and write about today.

Breakfast this morning was, well, dreary. Hardly anyone spoke, and most of us barely ate. Except Lucas, of course. I think he was so nervous he ate twice what he normally eats, which is a lot for a dragonfly-human-thing. Breaking the silence, Ava asked, "Are Mark and his friends going to join us?"

"Maybe later," Marlene replied, rubbing the girl's head. "I'm sure they're busy fixing up Mr. Bamber and working on his chip-deactivating doodad."

"Golly, I sure hope he and Shannon are gonna be okay," Donnie said, concerned. Before anyone could reassure him, though, a bell went off, and we followed all the soldiers up on deck. Up top, we found Shane, whom we mistook for Mark…again.

"Don't worry about it, everyone," he said smiling. "It happens all the time. It used to be easier to tell us apart before he got a 'normal' haircut." He made a motion from the top of his head to the left side of his face, hinting at his brother's old hairstyle.

# THE ISLES

I was positive he was often mistaken for Mark because the similarities are uncanny. What confused me was, even though they're triplets, Shane appears stronger and… well, more *attractive* than his brother. Don't get me wrong, Mark is good-looking and fit, but Shane is even more so. His muscles can be seen easily through his black combat uniform. His green eyes are beautiful, and his smile perfect.

Ahem. Anyway, enough about that.

"So: at the moment, Mark, Myles, and Blake are with Mr. Bamber and Mrs. Pieper working on the deactivating device," Shane continued, rubbing his layered hair. "Right now, we need your help training our soldiers for the day."

"Why do you need *our* help?" Yared asked, crossing his arms. "Your guys are pretty tough already, if I do say so myself."

Smirking, Shane replied, "I know. The reason is because they've never fought 'children' before. It's going to be hard for them to beat up kids if they don't know what they're up against. We need to make sure they understand that whoever refuses to join us after those messages we sent are undoubtedly hostile, and there's no way to change their minds." Taking a deep breath, Shane chuckled and motioned to the Mutants and Bionics. "Besides, some of you are enhanced, and we aren't totally sure what you can do. You have to give us some insight if we're going to win this together."

Backing down, Yared simply nodded. It was a lot for us to take in, especially the realization we had to fight our friends. Everything we thought we knew had to come crumbling down. After telling him we would help, Shane replied, "Thank you. In the field, we'll try to reduce the damage and spare as many lives as we can. Okay?" He clapped his hands together. "All right, let's get started."

I thought we needed to go to a different part of the ship to fight, but all the soldiers came marching out right in front of us. Leading them was two of the men we met last night: Nicolas Eerkens and Sonny Wilcox. When the fighters were in place, they stood at attention and waited for instructions.

"Listen up, maggots!" Nicolas bellowed to the soldiers. "We have the rest of today to train for this unforeseen battle! Do *not* fail me."

"Sir, yes sir!" was their response.

Then, the training began.

The way we did it was, we would go up three at a time and do a one-on-one fight with Nicolas, Sonny, or Shane, demonstrating each technique and ability we possessed. They would then explain it to the soldiers in military terms. Lastly, the soldiers would practice the moves with each other and decide how to defend themselves against them.

First up, were the members from Assets and Saviors. They didn't have as much hand-to-hand combat training as the rest of us. What they did have, however, was good technique with anything that could be used as a weapon. Marlene explained that the Assets members would most likely have gardening tools or household items on hand, while the Saviors would have sharp surgical equipment. She then demonstrated her remarkable skill with the beloved sheep shears, which she kept clipped to her belt. She *almost* cut Nicolas, who is a master of martial arts, marksmanship, and any other violent art. Not only that, but the guy is strong—like, inhumanly strong. His strength matches that of a big Seers member crossed with a mutant gorilla (a definite possibility on the Isles), which scared me. Apparently, he could lift things six times his size and not break a sweat. I'm not over-exaggerating; I don't think the guy is fully human.

After the Saviors and Assets members finished showing off their tools and moves, they came back to sit down while the soldiers were practicing. Trying to catch his breath, Donnie said, "Gee, these guys are tough! I think we'll be fine."

Lying on his back, Ethan panted, "Let's just hope we don't get this tired during the *actual* fight."

Marlene flipped her sheep shears in the air, caught them, and clipped them back on their belt. "I think we'll be fine," she echoed Donnie. "That was fun, though." She turned around and pointed to Nicolas. "We have to do that again sometime."

The big guy laughed. Next, he motioned for the Research and Development members to head over. Standing up, Aaron and Cecil pulled out their advanced weaponry. "You better watch out for this bad boy," Aaron warned as he approached them. "This is a custom-made gun that doubles as a Taser for non-lethal situations, and a neurotoxin injector otherwise." He held it in the air and shook it between his thumb and first finger. "That comes in handy when people wear bulletproof armor. It fires a dart at high speeds, but when it makes contact, there are microscopic tentacles that find a way into your skin and release the poison."

Not fazed, Sonny scoffed. "I've seen worse. So, who's next for show-and-tell?"

Chuckling nervously, Cecil pulled out a palm-sized, metal cylinder. Before Sonny could ridicule it, Cecil pointed his weapon towards him and pressed the button. The dark-haired officer dodged the blue fireball, which exploded when it made contact with the wall behind him.

*Please don't make us clean that up,* I prayed.

"This little tube fires a mixture of combustible elements that are compacted into a marble-sized sphere," Cecil explained proudly. "When it makes contact with any surface, it reacts, and blows up to whatever radius I set it to. Aaron and I made these weapons while we were waiting to get Shannon out of custody."

Sonny didn't respond but grinned as if to say, *Not bad, kid.*

The two boys fired at the soldiers for practice. Thankfully, the RRPR guys were good when it came to spontaneous attacks. There were a few who were sedated or burned a bit, but nothing major, thank goodness. Before Aaron and Cecil sat down, they addressed the soldiers and told them to keep in mind that the other members of Isle III might have even worse weaponry.

After the fighters understood, they sat down—and Seers was next. I sort of felt bad for Yared, Ursula, and Jeremy; compared to these guys, our friends knew nothing about fighting. They were put to shame in everything that they tried against Nicolas, Sonny, and Shane, who dodged and retaliated whatever our friends threw at them. Several times our comrades were knocked from their feet; that really crushed the pride that Seers member uphold so dearly.

# ALISON: X

Thankfully, their spirits were lifted a little when Nicolas stated that their skills were far above average. "Relax, guys, you're some of the best young fighters I've seen," he complimented. "You also went up against three Royals, whose entire lives have been spent in fighting and training. Well, Sonny and I. Shane's new to our group."

Pressing his thumb to his forehead, Shane wiggled his fingers and stuck out his tongue. After his childish tease, he reminded, "I'm still faster, have better balance, and am more flexible and agile than all of you."

"Yeah, well, not all of us were so lucky as to wear tight suits, do flips and tricks for peanuts, and live with clowns like you did," Nicolas snickered, rubbing his red-highlighted Mohawk.

To prove his point, Shane did a backflip, walked on his hands, and flipped himself back upright. "Do it again!" Ava exclaimed, clapping.

Shane bowed. "Anything for a fan! But first, let's keep going."

Next was the Mutants' turn. Shane offered right away to go up against Becca. "I want to see how fast you really are," he taunted. Apparently, along with doing flips and tricks, Shane could sprint at an impressive speed. For a normal human, he was the best of the best; I heard a rumor that he had a shorter running time than the Olympics world-record holder. Becca went up to him and waited for Nicolas to give the word. As soon as they said go, she dashed about the ship as fast as she could, obviously trying to show off. After making a few laps to confuse Shane, she fought him as hard and as fast as she could.

It was the fastest fight I'd ever seen, and it ended in a tie. Becca's reflexes were quicker, but he was stronger than she was. She was a fast runner, but needed to work on adding that speed to her combat skills. He would block her attacks and get right back up whenever she knocked him down. Becca hit Shane more, but her hits weren't as effective. In contrast, whenever Shane hit her, she was out of sorts for a few moments. If he wanted to, Shane could have easily finished her off. After about thirty seconds of blur, they attacked at the same time, collided, and flew backwards, landing on their backs. Jumping up unscathed, Shane laughed, went to Becca, and helped her up.

"You're pretty good, kiddo," he complimented. "That Carl guy wasn't kidding."

I was so confused. *How does he know Mr. Mallory?*

Becca was just as perplexed as I was but said nothing. Putting her furry hands on her knees, she bent over and tried to catch her breath. "How did…my attacks…not…you know?"

He smiled. "You're so fast with your feet that you forgot to add that speed to your attacks," he explained. "Use that momentum to knock people down like we did to each other."

*Called it,* I thought proudly.

Understanding, she nodded and went back in line. She plopped down beside me. She was panting so hard I thought she was going to pass out. Her dark hair was a huge frizzy mess and sweat dripped down her chestnut skin and cheetah fur. *How did an ordinary human tire out a Mutant and not even seem the least bit worn out?* I wondered.

Witnessing that spectacle, my sister was scared out of her skin… fur. She was afraid to face Sonny, so she tried to make up an excuse if she performed poorly. "I think I do better in the dark," she told him quietly.

"Well, that makes two of us," he retorted. "Let's just get this over with. Show me what you can do."

With that, she pounced. Sonny was good, but not as fast as Shane. He was barely scratched and retaliated quickly. Sami ended up on her back more than once. For some reason, she kept getting distracted. Every time she went to attack from behind, she couldn't help but stare at his neck, as if he had something sticking out of it. While her guard was down, Sonny would attack, and she would stagger backwards. The way Sonny was fighting seemed all too familiar; our styles were similar. I thought he was copying us very well, but he seemed to know our methods even better than we did.

The fight was over within minutes, ending with Sami on the ground again. Crossing his pale arms, Sonny said, "You've been holding back. I won't ask you to fight again, but give it all you've got next time. It could be your last fight if you don't."

# ALISON: X

Understanding, Sami thanked him and came back to us to make room for Lucas and Nicolas. While she was walking to her place, she looked back at him several times. She sat down with a confused and horrified look on her face.

Lucas and Nicolas' match began before I had a chance to talk to her. Their fight went on for a solid five minutes: Lucas didn't give the guy a chance to breathe. He flew circles around him, picked him up and dropped him from the air, and always tried to go for the kill. Apparently, dragonflies never backed down when attacking prey and showed no mercy to a fallen foe. This instinct was raging in Lucas. Thankfully, our friend was able to resist the urge somewhat.

Despite all this, no matter what Lucas did, Nicolas was able to counter it and stay on his feet. I can't even begin to describe how he fought; it was incredible. Nicolas finished the fight with barely a scratch, which baffled our bug friend. "Wait a second," Lucas said from the ground, trying to catch his breath. "I've knocked you on your bum I don't know how many times, and you still get up and come at me." Fluttering his wings for a few moments, he tried to get airborne, but was too exhausted. "I can barely move, and you're standing there like it was no big deal!"

Overconfident, Nicolas shrugged and told him to sit down. When the soldiers finished practicing, it was Axel's and my turn. Nicolas requested that we do a three-against-two fight. "Oh, and make sure you give it everything you've got," he reminded. "We need to be ready."

*Are you sure about that?* I wondered as we went up. *I don't think they understand what we can do.*

Looking at us, Shane asked jokingly, "Hey, does Mr. Nik shout a bunch of random words in Russian to make you both comply?" He began shouting things in what he thought was Russian.

Sonny cringed. "You killed it. You mercilessly killed it."

Denying it, Shane said, "I think I said 'freight car' pretty well."

Impatient, Nicolas interrupted their bickering, and our battle began.

Axel made the first move; a terrible one, but a move. He tried tackling Shane, who quickly dodged and threw him against the wall.

Recovering, Axel fired missiles back. While Shane was distracted with them, his comrades came after me.

The rest was a blur. Sorry for the lack of detail, but I don't remember what happened. I only recall that it was intense, I was full of adrenaline, and my armor was wearing down. These guys put up one heck of a fight and did it without weapons. We gave our all, and they still kept coming. It was *insane*. We dropped them from the air, kicked them across the ship, and did enough damage to break every bone in their bodies, but nothing was enough to stop them.

The part of the fight I remember the clearest was how we stopped. We were all on the brink of fainting but wanted to give it one more shot. Supporting each other, Axel and I stood shoulder to shoulder while our three opponents staggered to their feet and raised their guard. We were about fire a blast of light when our armor shut down, and Axel and I collapsed.

"Well, I'm glad that works. Now to test the chips," said a familiar nasal voice from behind us.

Suddenly, our armor turned back on, and we were back on our feet. Turning around, we found Mr. Bamber holding a small device with Mrs. Pieper pushing him through the crowd. I was happy to see that he had regained a little color, but unfortunately, he still had the oxygen tubes. "Mr. Bamber, I'm glad to see you're all right," Cecil sighed in relief.

"Well, I'm alive, and that's all that matters," he replied smiling. "I was just testing one of our defensive weapons. Thankfully, it works without causing any damage. When all of you finish up out here, please meet us in the control room. We have some things to discuss."

I couldn't have been happier that he ended our fight. Axel and I sat down while the three RRPR Royals taught their soldiers tricks and moves to use if they encountered Bionics. They were a little out of breath but had no problem demonstrating.

"I don't think these guys are fully human," Axel whispered as he wiped the sweat from under his curly white hair.

I shook my head. "They *have* to be human. Just really good at what they do."

# ALISON: X

We were too tired to argue, so we quietly watched. Getting to the final minutes of practice, Shannon emerged from below decks. She was out of her wheelchair and her arms were free of bandages, revealing horrifying wounds. Noticing her cuts, Sonny smirked and said, "When those turn to scars, we'll match." He turned his arms face up to show her, then put them back at his sides.

*How could I not have noticed that?* I wondered when I saw his scars.

"Then they were worth it," Shannon said with a smile, interrupting my staring. "Am I too late to practice with you all?"

"You're just in the nick of time. We have a few moments left," Nicolas told her, wiping the sweat from his face. "What would you like to practice?"

"You can give me a quick overview of each of their techniques," she told him. She looked around at our bumps and bruises and changed her mind. "Maybe I should wait. You all seem too exhausted."

Nicolas insisted. "I'll fight you," he offered, "using a little taste of each of their techniques. However, you have to wear your mask, and I'll go easy on you since you're still recovering. No arguing." Behind him, Shane made a face of disapproval, but didn't object. Sonny crossed his arms, ready to watch the show.

Nodding, Shannon pulled out a small black triangle and put it over her nose and mouth. It clicked and expanded outward, reaching her ears. She groaned, rolled her neck, and looked back at Nic. After a moment, glowing lines appeared: three vertical lines over her mouth, and two horizontal ones going from the center up to each ear. "Ready," she growled in a voice not her own.

"That's badass," Yared complimented.

She laughed in her normal voice, but before she could say anything, Nicolas attacked. Shannon is a way better fighter than I expected. Her height and size are very misleading. Despite the surprise, she was able to avoid his punch. She attacked mostly with her hands and could counter almost every move. Nicolas said he was going "easy" on her, but it didn't appear that way. They went all out.

Finally, Shannon knocked Nicolas to the ground with a side-kick, and the fight ended. "Well, I don't think I'll need to explain anything more to you," he said, still lying down. Going over to him, she helped him up, and he complimented her, "Awesome job as usual, but less boxing and more *not* boxing. Use your entire body."

"Sorry," she replied, panting. Taking off the mask, she reminded him, "You know it's my preferred method."

Raising his hand, Cecil said, "Excuse me? What is that thing you have for your face? Why did your voice change before?"

"It helps me breathe," Shannon replied as it collapsed to its smaller state. "Mark mentioned back on the Forbidden Isle that I had gotten injured. I won't give you details, but it helps me to fight without passing out." She pointed to the center of the tiny machine. "It also has a special microphone inside that makes my voice sound like whatever I want it to." Putting it back on, she pressed a button. After it beeped, she proved her point. In Cecil's voice, she explained, "I can copy speech patterns and tones."

Cecil's eyes got wide. "That's cool and creepy at the same time."

Leaning toward him, Yared whispered, "It's badass."

"Anyway," Nic said, interrupting, "let's have everyone get back to where they need to be."

After Sonny gave the order, the soldiers left, and we rejoined Mr. Bamber and Mark in the control room, where our video transmissions were playing repeatedly across all the monitors. "Everyone please listen to me, there isn't much time to waste," Yared's transmission begged. "Nikita Patya and the other Keepers are not what they have pretended to be." Each video had the same message, but each Isle member put it into their own words, making it more personal.

Another transmission looped a video of Shannon's interrogation. She had had a hidden microphone and camera on her person as she was taken into custody. We hoped that the footage of what they had done to her would be our ticket to getting some of the Isles people on our side. They were almost as brutal with her as they were with Mark.

It was a first-person video. It showed her arms strapped palm-up to a chair, and you could see Wally and Mr. Nik clearly. They kept asking questions about how long she had been on the Isles, if she was working with Mark, did she really steal the books, and things like that. For every answer she gave, they made a slit in her arm or punched her if it wasn't what they wanted to hear. At one point, you could see drops of blood blocking part of the camera's view.

"I think we're getting to people," Mark said, looking up at one of the monitors. "I've been checking security footage from each Isle, and there's already a rebellion starting inside each facility. Right now, I can't determine how many of the residents and students will be on our side, but I'm praying there are more than I suspect." Coming over to us, he continued, "Well, let's not worry about that until later. The main thing is carrying out Step Three: taking over."

*This is the part I dread most,* I thought, holding my breath.

"I have a disturbing feeling that not all of us will live see the outcome of these events," Mark said, looking at the floor. "So tonight, I want you all to enjoy yourselves together, like it's the last time you'll see each other. If there's something you need to say to someone, say it tonight." Taking a deep breath, he looked up and made eye contact with each of us. "I could never repay any of you for what you're doing with us now, and I wish you didn't have to go through with this. Whatever happens out there, just remember this: never lose hope. My prayer is that we'll all walk out of this alive and can save many people. If dying in this fight is our fate, though, then so be it. I believe in every single one of you, and I am grateful to have known you all. Thank you for everything."

He ended that tear-jerking speech and went back to his work. I couldn't wrap my brain around what he'd said, and frankly, I still can't and don't want to.

We left him, went to their lounge room, and spent the rest of the evening together. We sat down on leather couches that made a U-shape around a long wooden coffee table, and faced a powered down television. Almost everyone fit; a few of us sat on the red-carpeted floors with our backs against the couches. On the wooden walls were images of photos that Blake had taken. They were all newer, because all the members looked the same as they did now, and Mark wasn't in any of them.

*Poor guy,* I thought as I looked around. *He missed out on five years of his family's life.*

At first, it was hard for us to have fun. We started telling stories and making up fantasies about how things will be when the Keepers are no longer in control, but it was more depressing than enjoyable. We then moved the conversation to the subject of all the Keeper's accents, and how they all spoke English quite clearly despite them. Unfortunately, we just started arguing over which Keeper had the best accent.

Thankfully, Shannon, Johanna, and Aymie came to join us, interrupting our disagreement.

Our first laugh was when Aymie showed up without any hair. She had been wearing a wig the whole time! The only thing on her head was a bright pink bandana. No wonder her hair looked so nice, I thought as she came in.

"What happened?!" Ava cried when she saw her. "Are you okay?"

We felt bad, but couldn't help but laugh. Aymie had a good sense of humor and played along. "I accidentally put hair remover in my tea this morning." Sitting down, she looked Ava in the face and asked, "Do I scare you now?"

Giggling, the little girl said, "Never. You are just as beautiful!"

Aymie smiled and hugged her close, and that's when things perked up. Those girls knew how to have fun, and they made the most of the time we had. They kept our topics happy and made us all feel good. The greatest thing was Johanna's sarcasm. I think Harold was falling in love with the officer and her humor. He tried too hard to impress her with his awful pickup lines.

When the rest of the guys came, that's when things got crazy. They made up hilarious games, told the funniest stories, and made sure nobody was thinking about what was to come. Even Sonny was enjoying himself. For someone of his personality, that was rare… although, when Sonny came in, Sami watched him like a hawk, as if he were an intruder. *What's wrong now?* I wondered.

Thankfully, being part-cat, she was easily distracted. She stopped staring and went back to enjoying herself.

My favorite part of the night was when Shane whipped out a guitar covered in stickers from different places. After tuning up, he played and sang some songs for us. I could listen to him sing and watch him play all day. Everything about him was mesmerizing. After a few solos, Mark found some drumsticks and began to keep a beat on the coffee table, while the three girls sang harmony. Ava got up a few times and danced to the rhythm. It took her a few tries, but she eventually got a few of us to join her.

"Just like old times," Shane said, laughing as he ended another song.

"Sure is," Mark replied, twirling a drumstick between his fingers. "Looks like *Left Lane Only* is back."

Curious, Ava asked, "What were the old times like? Why is music so much fun?"

Unfortunately, before they could answer, everyone was called to bed. "That will be a story for another time," Mark apologized.

With tears in her eyes, Ava cried, "But what if we don't get another time?"

The room was silent. Going over to the little girl, Marlene took her by the hand and made her a promise. "There *will* be another time," she said softly. "Whether it be here or in a life to come, that time will be waiting for us."

Sniffling, Ava replied, "Will you always be with me?"

Marlene rubbed the girl's dark, fluffy hair. "Of course! Nothing could separate us, kid. Not even the worst possible thing you could imagine."

I prayed that was true.

There was a second reminder over the loudspeaker. This time, we decided to listen to it. However, it took us forever to say our good nights; we didn't want to separate. Sometimes, just thinking about the future is enough to break you down again.

To comfort us, Shannon sang one final song. It was an old lullaby in a language called Gaelic that her parents sang to her. As she sang, I felt my eyelids getting heavy and my nerves settling down. During the final verse, almost all the other RRPR members joined in. It was beautiful.

When it ended, we all took a deep breath and went to our cabins.

While the other girls were in bed, I went over to Sami and asked her what had happened during the fights, and why she found that one officer so suspicious. "You kept staring at Sonny's neck like it had knives sticking out of it," I whispered. "You kept losing focus."

Her luminous cat eyes shone in the dark. There was fear in them. She tried to say something, but nothing came out. Instead, she took her claw, etched a symbol into the side of the wooden bunk, and left. Ignoring the fact that that was vandalism, I turned the blue lights in my Bionic hand on and took a closer look at her drawing. I gasped and clasped my hand over my mouth. It was an overlapping *O* and *X*, like what we'd found on the neck of the Invaders.

I turned my lights off and sluggishly walked back to my bunk. I sat on the bed and wrote everything down.

Right now, I'm still thinking about the fact that Sonny has the symbol of the Order of Xenophon branded into the back of his neck. Sonny *can't* be one of them. Why would he be fighting against them? With this in mind, I'm going to try to fall asleep thinking happy thoughts.

I'm praying tomorrow won't be as horrible as I imagine.

# Chapter 29

## Sami: X

Today was the beginning of the rebellion.

Early this morning, before the sun came out, we met in the dining hall. The cooks had prepared a bountiful breakfast. Everyone ate in silence. I wasn't hungry; not only was I worried about today, I also couldn't shake that feeling that Sonny might be an Invader. *Will he betray us?* I worried.

Interrupting my distressed thoughts, Becca waved her hairy cheetah hand in front of my face. "Sami! Stop daydreaming and eat something," she instructed quietly. "You need your strength."

I nodded and forced down some food. As I practically inhaled a sausage, I looked over to see Lucas going up for fourths. I chuckled. *He's getting ready.*

When Lucas came back, Mr. Bamber broke the awkward silence. He told us that he had set off the chip deactivation device last night and had gotten back a positive reading. "I am hoping for at least one-third of the entire Isles population to be on our side," he explained. "Not only will we have the enhanced children, but many of the staff and other inhabitants will undoubtedly join us."

He was the only person to speak during the entire meal. When it was over, the dreaded moment arrived: It was time to depart. The first step was to head for our designated posts on the borders of each island. The worst part was that they were separating us. I didn't want us to leave each other.

"Here are the leading units going to each island," Director Wyght explained. "Everyone must report back to the outskirts of Isle III tonight with their allied forces. Going to Isle I: Alison, Harold, Donnie, and Bain; Isle II: Ethan, Axel, Ava, and Powell; Isle III: Aaron, Lucas, M. Hodgins, Mr. Bamber, Mrs. Pieper, and myself; Isle IV: Marlene, Cecil, Ursula, and A. Hodgins; Isle V: Yared, Becca, Eerkens, and Watterson; Isle VI: Sami, Jeremy, Zita, Wilcox, and S. Hodgins. Additional troops will be following your orders. Do not engage if at all possible; we need as many people as we can get for the real battle on Isle III."

With that, we said our long goodbyes and went our separate ways. As I was walking away, I overheard Mark's friend, Blake, say something troubling: "Aymie, it happened again. This dream was too real."

"No, Blake, not another," she cried. "How bad was it?"

There was an awkward silence. "Not all of them are going to make it," he said solemnly.

I couldn't believe my ears. I was about to rush over to them and ask what he meant when Sonny nudged me onto the boat we rode to shore.

We arrived at Isle VI at first light. Going onto the beach, I was happy to have my little brother with me, but was still worried about my other siblings—not to mention I couldn't stop thinking about Blake and his dream. "Hey, cat-woman," Shane called to me, noticing my distress. "Don't worry; everyone is going to be fine. From what I can tell, you can all take care of yourselves, and we have your backs." Giving me a wink, he dashed ahead.

Finally, we reached the back of the facility, which was billowing smoke; the rebellion had already started.

"Time to let them know we're here," Sonny said, taking out a flare gun. Every soldier behind us did the same, and they fired simultaneously. Within seconds, we had a stampede of Mutants headed for us. We prepared to engage, but thankfully, they were on our side. The first one to approach us was my old friend, Alex the Aye-Aye. "Nice to see you again, Sami," he greeted me, wiping the blood from his mouth. "We all saw your transmission, and a few of us started to revolt immediately. The rest were too afraid. We kept getting weird threatening messages in our heads that played over and over again." Big eyes to the ground, he went on, "Then Wally began to publicly torture a few of those who went against them. That *really* scared us."

Then, he looked up and smiled. "When the strange voices in our heads stopped, we could think straight again, and for the first time we felt... free. That's when we stepped up." He motioned to the group behind him. "There are still many who stand with the Keepers, due to loyalty and fear, but we're doing our best to detain them now. Those still with Mr. Mallory are some staff and younger Rank members who are full-on Mutant like us. They were practically raised believing in the Keepers, so whatever we have to do, let's do it fast."

As he finished, we heard gunshots, screaming, and the sound of another stampede. Shane and Sonny shouted orders for all the Mutants to head for the shore. Without hesitation, we did as they asked. "We have allies in the water, too," Alex explained as we ran. "Zeke is leading the other water-breathing Mutants. We released him and a few others into the ocean; hopefully none of those against us got out."

Reaching the shore, I saw a familiar face swimming amongst the waves. "What took you so long?" Zeke shouted. "They've been trying to destroy your boats! Come back and defend them."

We all plunged into the water, except for Shane, who seemed a bit skeptical. Sonny called for one of our flying feathered Mutant friends to fly him aboard.

*What's his problem?* I replied as I shook the water out of my fur. *Maybe he's part cat like me; I hate water.*

Finally, everyone was aboard, preparing cannons, guns, nets, and any sort of weapon we could find. "Zeke, lead the others ahead!" I shouted into the waters below. "Head for Isle III. We'll meet you there." Obeying, he quickly swam ahead with an entire army of sea

Mutants behind him.

Then, things got bloody.

It started with the enemy sea Mutants. We began by shooting missiles into the water and blowing up the hostiles below us. We were tossed back and forth until the bombing ceased. I dared not to look into the ocean, but out of the corner of my eye I noticed the once clear blue waters turning red with blood. Then came attacks from the flying Mutants above us. Our winged allies took care of them from the air, and we fought off the ones who landed on deck. I was approached by a Mutant sparrow a few years younger than me. "Kella, please don't do this," I begged as she came closer.

"It's too late," she screeched back. Her head was bleeding and her arms had lost many feathers. "You betrayed us, Sami. We were supposed to trust you. You were going to lead us." With that, she lunged.

A bird trying to take down a cat wasn't the best idea. I hated every minute of fighting her, but had no other choice. She grabbed, but I scratched her until she bled and let go. Flying up into the air, she dived down and knocked me over. While she was pecking my head with her beak-like lips, I struggled to my feet. Growling, I threw my arms behind me, dug my nails into her flesh, and threw her over my shoulder. Full of adrenaline, I pounced on her and began punching her in the face.

I saw nothing but blood as I beat Kella to death.

When she stopped squirming, I rolled off her and began sobbing.

After my allies shot down a few that never landed and scared off the rest, our enemies beat a hasty retreat. The only ones left on the ship were us and the dead. Rushing over to me, Jeremy shouted my name. "Sami! Sami! What's wrong?" He took one look at the dead sparrow and turned away. His eyes welled up with tears, and he couldn't look back.

Then Sonny came over. He glanced at the one I'd killed, and back at me. I didn't dare look up at him. Unexpectedly, he squatted down and put his hand on my shoulder. "This isn't your fault. None of this is."

Without lifting my head, I replied mid-sob, "She said... she knew I was supposed to lead them. She said I betrayed them!"

The man shook his head, put his first finger under my chin, and lifted my face. The look in his red eyes was like nothing I ever saw before. Whatever was in them told a story that I couldn't understand. "You betrayed no one," he replied as kindly as his raspy voice would allow. "I know where you are; I know the feeling. You did what you had to." He smiled and wiped the tears from my eyes.

I thanked him and stood up. Taking Jeremy's hand, I brought my brother over to Zita to get bandaged up. Behind me, I overheard Shane say to Sonny. "Your mom would be proud."

We went over to Zita and waited for our turn; she and a few RRPR members were attending to everyone's wounds. We were all bruised and shaken up. It was a grisly feeling watching people you grew up with be killed... and it was worse having to kill them.

I burst into tears and started bawling.

It was about mid-afternoon by the time it was all over, and it took us the rest of the day to recuperate. Jeremy was so deeply in shock that he didn't move until we reached the shores of Isle III. *Please don't think bad of me,* I prayed as I rocked him back and forth in my arms.

We docked and headed across to where the others had made camp beyond the beach. There were dozens of green tents set up, and the ground was covered in large metal crates, weapon racks, and mini-tanks. Approaching it, I was relieved to see that all our friends were still alive, and I saw many more familiar faces. When we entered the main tent, Jeremy ran to Alison and Aaron and hugged them.

"How were your fights?" I asked my other siblings.

Aaron grinned and tapped the sides of his glasses. One of the lenses had cracked. "If I didn't have bad eyesight, I would have no eyes." His smile faded, and he sighed. "So, other than almost having my eyes shot out, probably no better than yours."

Alison smiled and rubbed Jeremy's head. "We're alive, and that's all that needs to be said."

Clutching her half-robotic body tightly, Jeremy whispered, "Are we going to die?"

Alison took a deep breath. "I don't know, Jeremy," she replied honestly.

"Well, I won't let *any* of us die," he replied, determined. "I'll do whatever it takes to keep everyone safe, even Mark." Tears fell from his eyes. "I'm sorry if I was mean to him or anyone. I… I don't know why I loved the Keepers."

"They were the only 'family' you ever had," Alison explained. "Now you have us, and no one can change that."

Jeremy looked up at her with his bright blue eyes and nodded.

Before another word could be said, we were called outside to eat. We all sat around the camp and did our best to keep our spirits up. It was nice to speak with our old friends again. They asked me so many questions about what happened, what the Mainland was like, who RRPR were, and so on. I answered as best as I could without making everything more depressing.

I finished my food quickly and told my comrades I would be right back. I headed out to find one of the Royal officers. The first one I came across was Johanna, who was sitting with the Saviors. Harold kept trying to crack jokes to make her laugh, but her sarcastic remarks were too quick. Timidly, I went over and cleared my throat. "Excuse me, Johanna?"

Turning around, she looked at me with a mouthful and said, "Yes?" She swallowed. "What's up?"

I was nervous and started playing with my tail. "Can I ask you something?"

Noticing my behavior, she jumped off the crate she was sitting on and pulled me aside. "Of course; you can tell me anything," she said softly.

I took a deep breath. "Before we left, I overheard Blake say that he had a dream and that…" I paused. "He said not all of us would make it."

Johanna shook her head. "Curse Blake and his dreams." She sighed. "Blake is said to have a special gift—to be able to see things before they happen. It's called precognition. However, sometimes he's wrong. The future is not set in stone."

"What if he isn't wrong this time?" I cried, not believing her.

Bending over, she put her hands on my shoulders. Her green eyes looked directly into mine, and she said, "Whether he is right or wrong should *not* change the way you act today. Don't worry so much about the future that you ruin the time you have now. Understand?"

Sniffling, I rubbed my black cat nose and replied, "Yes. Thank you."

She stood upright. "You are welcome. If you ever need to talk about *anything*, even personal stuff, do not be afraid to come to me. I'm a trained listener and the best secret-keeper ever." She winked. "I didn't earn the title Dr. Johanna Watterson for nothing." With that, she tapped my arm and went back to the Saviors.

Breathing deeply, I returned to the group I had left.

I remained with my fellow Mutants until the sun set, and the Isle commanders, along with their second and third seats, were called to the main tent. Going inside, we found the same set-up as the Director's conference room back on the ship, but not as nice. The table and chairs were plastic, and the maps were tattered and ripped.

We all sat down, and Director Wyght began, "Unfortunately, we lost a lot of brave and valuable allies today." Honoring those who didn't make it off the islands, he said, "They will never be forgotten and have not died in vain. I have arranged a meeting for tomorrow with the Keepers, to see if there is any way to reduce the damage. If they do not surrender," he took a deep breath, "then we go to war. We have posts around the island with our allies waiting for our command to act. No doubt the Keepers have the same." He looked longingly at our faces as if an old memory had flashed through his head. Shaking it away, he dismissed us. "Go get some rest and thank God that we lived to see another day."

Ending with that, we all left to our tents. This time, they put all seventeen of us in one long tent instead of separated like on the ship. Instead of sleeping, we sat in silence together. No one said anything, but it was a comforting feeling just being with each other once again. After some time, we began writing in our record logs.

Not too long ago, Shane came in and called Marlene outside.

Curious, I began eavesdropping.

"Are you serious?" I heard Marlene say. "You knew her?"

"Yes," Shane replied softly. "She was my superior officer. I took her place after—" his voice broke. Clearing his throat, he said, "She wanted you to have this."

There was a silence. Marlene quietly wept. "Oh, my sister. Why do I remember so little?"

"It's okay," he comforted. "She never forgot you, and frankly, neither did I. I promised I would find you and give this to you. I'm happy I fulfilled my promise."

She sniffled. "Thank you, Shane."

Marlene came back inside, rubbing her eyes with her fluffy pajama sleeve. I didn't want it to look like I heard her, so I went back to writing.

Marlene is asleep now and has something clutched tightly in her hands. I can't help but wonder what it is. As they say, cats are curious. However, now it's my turn to sleep. Questions can wait 'til daylight.

# CHAPTER 30

## Aaron: X

We woke up this morning to the sound of an obnoxious trumpet blast. Quickly, everyone was on their feet and packed in the blink of an eye. The higher-ranking officers and the original seventeen Isle members met with Director Wyght, Mr. Bamber, and Mrs. Pieper in the director's tent.

"I am taking Mr. Bamber, M. Hodgins, S. Hodgins, and the six Isle Commanders with me to the meeting," the director began. "According to what Mr. Bamber tells me, we may have a good chance of putting off the fight until tomorrow, and we may attain more allies. We are going to meet in the main field outside of the facility. Anyone opposed to my plan or any interjections?"

"Permission to interject, director," said Sonny.

"Permission granted, Wilcox."

"I want to go with you and see the Keepers face to face," Sonny told him. His red eyes glistened beneath his dark bangs. "It's about time I gave them a piece of my mind."

Smirking, the older fellow agreed without hesitation.

Out of the corner of my eye, I saw my twin sister looking worried. Her cat eyes shook nervously, and she played with her tail. *What's up with Sami?* I wondered. I thought Sonny was cool; emotionless, but cool. *Maybe she's still recovering from her fight with him the other day.*

When the meeting concluded, we went out and prepared until midday. Noon rolled around and it was time to meet. Thankfully, the power was still out and the fake terrains were down. Taking a truck across the long field, we found the remaining Keepers waiting alone, right behind the Research and Development facility. Within a hundred feet, we parked the truck, hopped out, and went to meet them. They looked like they'd been through hell. We let Director Wyght approach first and stayed behind him.

Seeing him, Mr. Nik's eyes got wider, and he chuckled. "After all these years, I never thought I would see you again, Wyght."

The director looked at Mr. Nik and Wally. They were both covered in bruises, their clothing tattered and torn. Blood oozed from a cut on Mr. Nik's chin and went down his neck and over his scar. One of the lenses in Wally's glasses was missing, and his nose had a bandage across it. "Patya and Jarvis. You've looked better," was his rejoinder.

"Speak for yourself," snapped Wally as he observed Director Wyght's own contusions.

"So, this is how you repay an old friend? Have you come to attack us some more?" Mr. Nik asked sternly. Suddenly, his eyes fell on the two Hodgins brothers. He looked closely at them, scoffed, and said. "So, *Mark* was the Hodgins with us. Walter was wrong; *we* had the thieving deadbeat."

Mark's face became red with anger, but he kept his cool.

Mr. Nik looked at Shane and went on, "I could've sworn it was this cocky brother. I think the haircut fooled me." Looking around, he asked, "Where's your sister?" When they didn't respond, the Russian grit his teeth and pointed at Mark. "I thought I finally had at least *one* of you. I thought I had gotten a slice of my revenge. Turns out I underestimated you all."

Interrupting him, Director Wyght answered the question, "First, we only sent out messages. Your slaves did the rest. Now: I want you to surrender. Think of how many lives and resources we can save if you do. If you and the others come quietly, this can all be over today."

Mr. Nik laughed. "Are you *joking*? After a lifetime of endless terror, you're asking me to give up everything, when I finally got so close? Why do you even want to shut us down? Isn't 'the enemy of my enemy my friend'?"

Softly, Director Wyght replied, "My 'friend' would never do the things you do. You are a disgrace to humanity. You know what you're doing makes you no better than the Order of Xenophon, and your actions are no better than any other crimes committed by the worst of criminals. The ends do not justify the means." Turning to the other Keepers, he tried to change their minds. "Don't you realize what you're doing? You're murdering human beings, manipulating children, and using them for your own selfish ends. What has Patya promised you? A share of the world? Your own continent to rule?"

Mr. Bamber chimed in as best as he could with his condition. "He is right, you know. Cameron, you devoted your life to technology and helping the disabled. Carl, you are a brilliant scientist and biologist, but dangerous genetic mutations is no way to go about improving humanity. Damian, you are one of the greatest minds in the medical field. You rescued so many lives in the first war against the Invaders. So why did you join the worst of them after that experience? You have been *murdering* people; no matter if they are born or unborn. There is no way to sugarcoat it. Lastly, Calvin the agriculturist, who rescued thousands from famine, is ready to throw away everything— just like his brother." The wrinkly old man sighed. "As for me, I made the terrible mistake of joining to avenge the death of my family against the Invaders. In the process, I became one of them. I regret my mistake wholeheartedly, and I am going to fix it."

That speech apparently struck a nerve. The Keepers stood in silence, reflecting on his words. A few minutes went by before Mr. Calvin, who was missing his awful wig, began sobbing hysterically.

"*Warmduscher*," Wally insulted under his breath. Turning to his colleagues, Mr. Nik asked the Keepers to give their final decision.

"I stand with Brian and Marlene," Mr. Calvin vowed as he

looked at Marlene kindly.

Before any of the other Keepers could state their choices, Wally pulled out his pistol and shot Mr. Calvin in the chest. Mr. Calvin staggered backwards, his mouth filled with blood. Struggling to speak, his final words were an apology to Marlene. "My… child. Forgive me, I—" Then, Mr. Calvin collapsed and went still.

Screaming, Marlene rushed to her Keeper's side. "Mr. Calvin!" she screamed in his face as she tugged on his overalls. "Don't leave me! I finally remembered you!" She put her palms on his bloody chest and sobbed. "You did so much for me…"

Determined to stop her from spilling any secrets, Wally aimed his gun at her. Shane ran behind him, screaming, "Stop!" and bear-hugged him so tight he couldn't move his arms. Sonny dashed up and kept Mr. Nik from assisting his companion.

What happened next was quite unexpected.

Looking at the young man, Mr. Nik's eyes widened. He dropped the gun he'd pulled and stared at Sonny. "Erik?" he whispered.

"That is *not* my name, you sadistic monster!" He began screaming in Mr. Nik's face, spit flying, calling him many horrible but deserved names, and not just in English. He swore in Russian, German, and other languages I couldn't even recognize. The words I did understand I don't dare to repeat. Everyone stopped and stared.

After Sonny's multilingual rant, Mr. Nik was unfazed; he just kept gawking. "I thought they killed you when they took you away… after your mother died." Turning to Mark, he gritted his teeth and shouted, "You took my son from me!"

"You took most of these kids' whole families from them," Mark said coldly. "How does karma feel? It doesn't even come close to what you've done to all of us."

"Listen closely, *Nikita*," Sonny bellowed. "First of all, I *ran away* after you raised me in captivity. Second, my mother was married and pregnant with me when you kidnapped her and took her as a concubine. So no matter what you think or what she told you, I am not your son. If I were, I would be so ashamed I would *kill myself.*"

Behind me, I heard Sami let out a deep breath.

# AARON: X

It's like I said; unexpected. If I live after all this, I want to hear *his* story too.

Everyone was silent and still. The first one to speak was Wally. "I vatched you die," he said in shock, still trapped in Shane's arms. Peering closely at his neck, he stuttered, "Y-y-you… have Erik's brand… but how?" Sonny turned around and stared at the Keeper. Amazed, Wally whispered, "You have her eyes."

Saying nothing, Sonny turned back. I leaned over to try and get a glimpse of what Wally was talking about. Then, I saw it: an O and an X. *No way,* I thought, *an Invader.*

When Sonny got back in line, Shane let Wally go and stood next to his friend. "So: back to our demands, Nik," Sonny continued. "Will you surrender?"

Snapping out of it, Mr. Nik became his menacing self again. "Never, Erik. I will give you the rest of the day to prepare." With that, the Keepers left us, taking away Mr. Calvin's body.

"No!" Marlene cried as she started to chase after them. Yared ran up and held her back. "Let go! Please, Yared." She began hitting his face and chest.

"I'm sorry," he whispered as he threw her over his shoulder.

She beat her fists against his back and screamed. "Calvin!" she cried again and again, until she was too exhausted. She finally let her arms dangle and just wept.

We returned to camp with heavy hearts and prepared for the day ahead. When Marlene saw Donnie and Ava, she became hysterical and held them in her arms. She didn't have to say anything. They understood and cried with her.

We dared not speak with the others about Sonny and Mr. Nik's incident. We didn't need anyone doubting our new friends. Plus, Mr. Calvin's death was tragic enough. Crossing her arms, Ursula looked at the Assets sobbing on the ground and said, "Wally really gives us Germans a bad name."

Harold scoffed. "Yeah. He and Mr. Nik really stereotype the German and Russian people, don't they? It's awful."

Zita shook her head. "It doesn't matter where you come from or what your ancestors have done. It's what you do that determines what people think of you."

"You're both starting to talk like Mark and Shannon," Ethan teased. "Don't start getting confusing on me, you two." Smiling, the Savior's second and third seats promised they wouldn't.

When Marlene, Donnie, and Ava calmed down, we were all called to assist with the preparations. Throughout the day, I spent time with Myles and the tech guys of RRPR. Together we silently worked on their cannons, guns, radios, and so on. Myles kept asking me all sorts of questions about how I knew so much, what my favorite studying methods were, and so on. I was happy he was talkative. It kept my mind off everything.

Then, Shane took Myles aside for a minute. "Hey, buddy, can I talk to you real quick?"

Nodding, the Royal Drone excused himself and joined his friend.

While I was working, I overheard Myles's conversation with Shane and Shannon. I didn't mean to eavesdrop, but I had to get some things that were near the mini-tank they were talking behind. "You sure that'll work?" Shane asked. "If it does, we can end this with fewer casualties."

"I have my doubts, but what choice do we have?" Myles told him. "These kids shouldn't have to go onto the battlefield like this. It isn't fair. We need help."

Teasing, Shannon reminded him, "You talk like you're the oldest one here. You're the same age as several of them, Myles."

"Anyway," he continued, "my point is that we're ridiculously outnumbered. We lost many of our allies just trying to get them here, let alone when we blew up the other facilities."

There was an awkward silence amongst them.

"All I know is that we can't do this without the approval of the Director," Shannon said finally. "We already initiated Step One without telling him; we should at least let him know what's going on. Step Two should be a last resort. We don't need to lose any more lives than necessary."

Neither of them questioned her statement; they just agreed.

# AARON: X

That conversation played in the back of my mind almost the entire day. The concern must have shown on my face, because Cecil asked if I was all right later that evening. "Some of the RRPR members are planning something," I whispered. "I don't know what it is."

Cecil shrugged. "We have to trust them. We may not understand now, but give us time."

"We trusted the Keepers," I pointed out. "Look where that got us! Cecil, you and I have worked our entire lives to build up these islands and create things no one could've imagined before. We weren't slaves; we had lives ahead of us with the Research and Development Isle. Now we're killing our own friends and tearing it all down! Is that what we're supposed to do?"

Taking a deep breath, my best friend scratched his head of honey-blond hair and replied, "We may have accomplished great things, but what was the point? What was our *purpose*? We were blind to the truth. They abused and used us. They did to us whatever they wanted and called it a 'challenge.' Not everyone survived those challenges unhurt. We were never free, Aaron. Face it: we were slaves to the devil."

His words hit me *hard*. I shut up and thought about it. I didn't want to believe it, but he was right. Our entire lives have been a lie. Almost everything the Keepers told us was a lie. Whatever we had accomplished at Ilse III was meaningless now. I felt hollow, but knew I had to start again from here to make my life meaningful. After a few moments, I apologized. "I'm sorry, man. With everything that's happening, I can't think straight."

He chuckled. "It's all good. Now, let's go meet the others and enjoy this final night together."

His voice made me realize that not all of us would be here tomorrow, and for a long moment, I forgot how to breathe. I felt like someone had punched me in the solar plexus.

After a brief hesitation, during which he just looked at me with a sad, lopsided look on his face, we headed into our big tent and met the others. We all sat up for a while and talked. We told each other *everything*, deepest secrets and all. If we didn't survive tomorrow, we wanted to make sure that our names and memories wouldn't be forgotten. I know that Alex and Alison were recording it all. I won't write down everything we revealed, but I will mention something about the last story that was shared: Marlene's.

"Last night, Shane called me outside the tent," she explained. "He told me that my big sister had lived with him and the others. He said that we looked so much alike." Tears streaked down her face. "She was his superior in their Agricola branch. She was a farmer like me." Reaching under her pillow, she pulled out an old pocket watch. "This is the best heirloom in the Best family," she explained smiling. She opened it and showed us what was inside: a ticking watch and a photo of the Best family. Mr. and Mrs. Best stood behind two girls. The older one looked about twelve, and she held a beautiful baby.

"What happened to your family?" Ava asked, quietly.

Wiping her eyes, Marlene explained, "My parents were taken by the Invaders. My sister took care of me until Director Wyght found her and took her in. They wanted to take me, too, but Mr. Nik's men got me first." She laughed. "Mr. Calvin took me in and raised me as his own daughter." Her eyes became distant, and she began to cry again. "When I was older, he begged Mr. Nik not to take away my memories, but it was no use. They wiped me clean, and I forgot everything. He had to treat me like a regular Asset member. When I finally remembered our times together... Wally shot him."

The room was silent. "I'm so sorry, Marlene," Ursula said compassionately. "I promise that we will avenge your parents, your family, and Mr. Calvin tomorrow. I will do whatever it takes, even if it means my own death."

"Please don't die, Ursula... but thank you for saying that." Marlene put her pocket watch back under her pillow. "I think it's time to sleep. Good night. I love you all." With that, she closed her eyes and fell almost instantly into an exhausted asleep.

That was the first time I'd heard anyone say they loved me in all the years I'd been on the Isles. I never understood the concept of love, or what it really meant. Yet to hear the words "I love you" gave me the courage and strength to continue. I think the rest of us felt the same way. One by one, my friends told each other "I love you" and went to sleep.

After I told them I loved them, I didn't head to bed. Instead, I snuck outside to the shore to clear my head. My siblings followed me, and we said the longest good night. I began to sob in Alison's arms as I whispered how much I loved them over and over. The four of us cried together until we had no tears left. Finally, they went back inside and tried to sleep.

I stayed outside for a little while longer. I watched the moon reflect off the clear waters. The sand felt good beneath my bare feet, and the salt wind brushed against my face and through my spiky hair.

"Mind if I join you?" a voice behind me said.

Startled, I jumped and turned around. It was Mark. "Hey," I replied, taking off my broken glasses and wiping the tears from my eyes. "I couldn't sleep."

Coming over, he said, "Me neither." He took a deep breath and shoved his hands in his pajama pockets. "For five years, I was undercover living with you all. I can't help but feel like I've become one of you, ya know?"

I chuckled. "Yeah, welcome to the Satan's Pawn club."

He smiled. "Well, we're no longer pawns. We're free." He longingly looked out to the ocean and said, "Isn't the world amazing? It's ruined, and its people are falling apart. Yet, despite our brokenness, we're still fighting to make it better. If there are still a few people willing to find the truth, the rest will follow."

"That was pretty deep, man," I replied.

Laughing, he replied, "I can't take all the credit. Shannon told me something like that when I was your age. She helped me realize that we *do* have meaning to our broken lives. No matter the outcome, everything happens for a reason."

Mark's blue eyes looked into mine, and he said, "Thank you, Aaron. Five years ago, I never thought I would amount to anything, that I could only be a burden. I went undercover because I figured everyone would be fine without me if I never came back. I hit rock bottom. What was the point? I didn't care if I survived or not." He took a shaky breath. "Shannon would always remind me how important I was, but I never understood until I met you. A little kid who kept wetting his pants," he said chuckling. Remembering that day we met, he grinned and went on, "The way you looked up to me was like nothing anyone had ever done before. I realized then and there that what Shannon told me was true. I looked at your little face and thought, 'This is why I'm here. If I can save an amazing child like this, then it's all worth it.' You saved me from myself, Aaron. Thank you."

I was touched. "Of course," I replied, smiling, trying not to cry. "I'm happy you entered my life. To be honest, I don't know who I would be without you after all these years."

Mark smiled and patted my shoulder. After that, we both quietly watched the waves until we were too tired to stand. I gave him a manly hug goodnight, and we went our separate ways.

I don't know if I'll be alive after tomorrow. I don't know if I'll lose some or all of the family I finally found, and the one I already had in Mark and the rest of the Seventeen. That's what I've come to think of us as.

I needed to write everything down. If I don't make it tomorrow, I want this record log to not only be a memory of me, but also of the incredible people that I love.

The only things I am grateful to the Keepers for are my friends and this record log.

I pray we all make it. But if someone has to fall, let it be me. Only me.

# Chapter 31

## Alison: XI

Exactly a month ago, we began writing in these record logs. Today is the day that ended it all. Everything we knew, everything we thought we loved and everything we *did* love, was destroyed in a single day.

This is my last entry. I'm only writing this so those of you in the future know what happened that day. I can't ask any of the other "Seventeen," as Aaron called us, to do it. We can't even call ourselves that anymore. The other survivors are facing pain and loss as crushing as mine.

I have to be the strong one.

We woke up before sunrise, feeling anxious and uneasy as we prepared for battle. It took all our energy to change into our new black combat uniforms. No one wanted to eat, pack, or do anything. We were scared to the point that we could barely move. Soon, we Seventeen were practically dragged into the Director's tent, where he gave a final rundown of what was to come. Supposedly.

"Here's how we're hoping to play it," he began, pointing at an island map on the table. "First, we send in our regular soldiers and then you and your comrades. The other Isle members are spread around the perimeter of the island with our other forces. The water Mutants will remain around the boats to protect our wounded and cargo."

I was afraid he was going to ask us to leave each other again. "Please let us fight together!" I begged without thinking.

Kind and compassionate, the older man replied, "I'm not asking you to split up and join them; they understand that you're needed here to face Nik and the others. I'm asking you to each send out a quick audio transmission, giving them some words of hope. I want them to feel you are with them even though you are miles apart. Can you do that for me?"

We all agreed, and the meeting ended. We followed Shannon and Mark to the tech tent. One by one, we quickly recorded our messages. They were short and to the point. I felt like they needed to be longer, but Shannon thought otherwise. "Not everything has to be big and showy to be affective," Shannon told us as she sent the messages. "The smallest, simplest thing can touch the hearts of so many individuals."

Mark agreed. "Your friends trust you and know you care. That's enough to keep them going."

When that was finished, we met up with the others and lined up at the front of the camp, waiting in suspense until it was time to go. Nervous, I shook in my armor. Hearing the irritating clanking, Axel came over and grabbed my metal hand, which made me blush. To be honest, I had only ever thought of Axel as a friend. It never crossed my mind that maybe, just maybe, he might have had deeper feelings for me.

"It will be all right," he whispered into my ear. "We will be fine."

"It's not us I'm worried about," I replied as I looked at the others. "We have armor and enhancements. They don't. How will *they* survive?" At the thought of some of them not being there, I began to have trouble breathing. My lungs wouldn't fill with air, and I felt like I was suffocating.

"Shhh, calm down, it's all right," Axel comforted as he helped steady my breathing. "We will protect them. That's what we're here for."

"And if we fail?" I asked, doubtful, looking into his gray eyes.

Staring back, he sighed. "We do what they would've wanted: we keep fighting. We won't let them die in vain."

He let go of my hand and hugged me, pulling me close and rubbing my white hair. I wrapped my arms around his armor and leaned the side of my face against his chest. "Okay," was my only reply.

Finally, it was time. The trumpets blasted and the Royal officers shouted. Axel and I let go of each other and went to line up with everyone. Looking back, I saw Mr. Bamber and Mrs. Pieper wave us off. I could see the tears in their eyes as they bid their distant farewells. We had no time to say a proper goodbye; we were immediately called to march.

We led from the front. We led our soldiers into battle.

As we walked, I replayed our strategy in my head. Mr. Nik and the Keepers were hiding in the back of their lines, closest to the facility, behind a horde of children and young adults. They would never dare lead from the front for fear of being shot in the back. Our plan was to get there and defeat the problem at the source. Shannon believed that if we took away the head, the body would collapse.

We found ourselves walking off the beach and into a rainforest. *The Keepers got the power working again,* I thought, upset, as we waded through. We crossed a third holographic terrain before we were blocked off. The first line of resistance was the middle-aged men and women who lived in the cities and towns on the Isles, a majority of whom were war veterans. They were led by a Seers staff member who had to be almost sixty years old.

Nicolas and Shannon tried to reason with them. "You don't have to do this," Shannon begged, taking off her mask. "You have to know they're using you."

No one responded. Growing agitated, Nicolas did his best to remain calm. "You came here heroes. Don't die villains. We don't want to fight you."

"Fight or die," the leader stated flatly. With that, he led them into a charge.

Not wanting us to lose our strength yet, Director Wyght's soldiers took care of them. Their skill was breathtaking, especially the highest officers'. Nicolas had the strength of a gorilla—literally. He grabbed large boulders off the rocky terrain and chucked them at the lines of fighters, crushing several at a time. He almost never used his firearm. Shane raced past our opponents, literally leaped over them, and took them down quickly. Sonny gripped pistols in each hand and fired one at a time, never missing a shot.

Shannon put her mask back on and stood with Mark. They stayed close to us and fended off any who drew near. Not too far behind us, Myles, Blake, Aymie, and Johanna drove mini-tanks, firing only when necessary.

It was a slaughter. All the Isles militia members were dead or dying within minutes, and we suffered no casualties at all. "This was too easy," Shane remarked as he ran back to us.

"If it's too easy, there's much worse to come," Sonny muttered, putting his guns back in their holsters.

"Aren't you a ray of sunshine," Yared said, clutching his modified AK-47.

Chuckling, Shane said, "That *is* his name, right? Sunny."

Sonny glowered at him and motioned us to keep moving.

As we proceeded, we encountered more and more enemies. They began to grow larger in number but lesser in age, and none would even consider surrendering. They had been brainwashed too well. The closer we got to the Keepers, the younger his soldiers were. It was a clever yet disgusting move on Mr. Nik's part, absolutely typical of him.

It wasn't until we reached the adolescents that we Isle members had to engage.

The first line of teens we met were mostly Assets and Saviors— Not many Mutants or Seers, and absolutely *no* Bionics, which worried me. I feared what awaited us farther in.

As usual, Nicolas and Shannon tried to reason with the enemy. Usually, the others heard them out at least, but these teenagers wanted nothing to do with us. Before our friends even opened their mouths, we were attacked.

# ALISON: XI

Immediately, I rushed into action. Axel and I were able to take out at least five at a time with brute force. We flew into them, threw them, and attacked them head on. I only knocked them out; I didn't have the heart to kill them…yet. With us helping, that fight was over in no time. We walked over our wounded enemies, leaving them crippled but alive. Thanks to us kids, the RRPR troops suffered no serious injuries in that battle.

"I don't like this," Ava cried as she stepped over one of her unconscious friends. She couldn't help but look down at her fallen Assets comrades.

Donnie went over and lifted her head up, making her face forward. "It's all right, Ava," he comforted her as they walked together. "It was their choice. And they *had* a choice. We'll get through it. I won't let nothin' happen to you."

The little girl smiled. "No, I won't let anything happen to *you.*"

Coming over to her friends, Marlene put her arms around them. "Hey, I'm Top Banana! If anyone is going to protect anybody, it's gonna be me."

We walked for a while longer and had almost reached the main field when we heard gunshots in front of us. Cursing under his breath, Mark told us to drop. "Seers students and staff members," he shouted as we took cover.

Looking closely, Shannon yelled, "They're heavily armed."

"That won't stop us," Shane reminded us, as he grabbed her and climbed up a tree to hide. Hanging upside down from a branch like a bat, Shane tried to count the number of islanders approaching. "There are hundreds, and they have artillery," he called down.

As he was speaking, a shell struck the tree next to them, smashing it to splinters. "Nyah nyah, missed us," Shane teased.

"No time for your ridiculous childish nonsense," Sonny scolded. "We need a plan."

With no time to think of one, I decided to just act, and the others followed. Axel, Nicolas, and I went to take out their heavy artillery while the rest took on the foot soldiers. We destroyed the weapons with no problem. Three missiles each from Axel's and my armor did the trick.

Everything was going according to "plan" until one of us fell.

In the middle of fighting, I heard a sudden shriek from behind me. Turning, I saw Ursula lying on the ground, surrounded by her fellow Seers. Without hesitating, I shot each of her attackers dead, one mini missile per skull. I flew to her side to find that one of her leg bones had cracked in half and was sticking out of her skin. Blood was gushing from the wound, staining the ground around her.

*I can amputate it and bandage it,* I thought, hopeful. "It's going to be okay!" I told her as I prepared to cut off part of her leg.

Grabbing my arm, she stopped me. She turned over and revealed the head of an electric spear lodged in her neck. Her dark eyes filled with fear as she faded away. She mouthed the words, "Thank you," and stopped breathing.

Carefully, I closed the eyelids of my lifeless friend.

I couldn't believe it. Ursula was gone. *I failed,* I thought, distressed. *I failed her.* Then, Axel's words came rushing back. I looked back at her face, brushed her light hair off her cheeks, and made her a promise. "You will not die in vain."

Now we were Sixteen.

Enraged and full of adrenaline, I looked at the sky and screamed as loudly as I could. Taken aback, several of the soldiers on both sides stopped to look at me. I stood, whipped myself around, and charged the enemy lines. At that moment, my sanity was gone. I rushed into my enemies, throwing them into trees. I burned them with to ash with the flames from my boot thrusters, shot them with missiles, and did whatever I had to. In the moment, I felt nothing.

Then, the fight was over, all the enemy dead and several lives lost on our side. Still numb, I ignored everyone around me and kept pressing forward.

We soon met the second-to-last line of resistance: mostly Research and Development members with new weapons. As soon as we were in their sights, they attacked. They fought with anything from fire swords to flame-throwers.

I ducked behind a boulder and took shelter next to Harold, the

Savior with the cheesy jokes. He put out a fire in his blond locks and whispered, "Stop, drop, and roll, Harold. Try that next time." Peeking over the rock, he saw that Ethan and Zita were cornered. He took a deep breath, then turned to me and chuckled. "Even if I don't die by fire, put that on my tombstone. I know I won't be remembered for who I was, so make sure that they remember me for my sense of humor." Before I could respond, he leaped out of cover and rushed toward his companions.

"Harold, wait," I cried, but it was too late. He launched himself into the middle of the groups of enemy soldiers to keep them from shooting Ethan and Zita. He didn't die by fire. While he was on the ground, Harold was kicked and beaten to death in less than a minute by the angry monsters he'd tried to stop. Furious, Zita made a final attempt to rescue her friend and rushed in among them. Grabbing her by her red hair, an older Research and Development member dragged her away with his comrades following close behind.

Ethan tried to save her. As he was running towards her, a grenade was thrown. Screaming, I flew in and snatched Ethan off the ground before it went off. I wasn't fast enough to save Zita.

The grenade landed directly in front of Zita and the men who grabbed her. Seeing it, they tried to scramble, but it was too late; it detonated. The blast threw them off their feet and the fragmentation tore them all to pieces. No one survived.

Now, a third friend was lost. Now, we were Fourteen.

As Ethan and I hovered above the horrific scene, he clutched my forearms and began sobbing. "I couldn't save them. I couldn't save them," he repeated.

With no time to mourn, Ethan and I landed, and we pushed on. Finally, we reached the last line of the Keepers' defenses. Protecting the facility was a sea of Isle members, none of them no older than twenty. Of course not. The Keepers were cowards. Most of their child soldiers were the Spliced and the other Seers. Mr. Nik and the Keepers huddled beside artillery and tanks operated by faithful Research and Development members. I recognized so many faces it made me sick.

Confused, I wondered, *Where are the Bionics?* I prayed they weren't hiding, ready to ambush us.

We didn't engage at first. Even with our blood pumping and our emotions bouncing off the walls, we didn't dare attack. In fact, we begged them to surrender. One boy tried, but one of his "friends" shot him in the back. Nobody else tried after that.

Then, they forced our hand by throwing grenades at us. Ducking for cover, we decided it was our turn to retaliate. It devolved into chaos: Shots were fired, people were screaming, and blood was everywhere you turned. I emptied my missile racks into the tightest clusters of the enemy I could find, as Axel killed the artillery. We fought with everything we had and tried to make it to the back of the lines to finish off Mr. Nik once and for all.

I'm not going to begin to describe all the bloodshed and horror that went on, but before I get to the end, I will tell you how honorable the deaths of my other friends were.

Cecil and Aaron fought back-to-back through it all. They fired at enemies with their handmade weapons and took out great numbers of them. They were beginning to feel confident, until a grenade knocked them off their feet. Cecil was thrown one way, Aaron another. Trying to get up, my brother found himself under the gun of a merciless Seer.

Before the trigger could be pulled, Cecil struggled to his feet and tackled Aaron's attacker. Bringing him to the ground, Cecil showed no mercy. Even with a gun pointed to his chest, Cecil plunged a dagger into the member's heart. The Seer's mouth filled up with blood.

Using the last of his strength, the enemy pulled the trigger and took Cecil's life as his own drained away.

Thirteen.

Screaming, Aaron ran to his best friend's side and grabbed his body before it fell. He clutched Cecil close and rocked back and forth, begging his friend to come back. But there was nothing he could do. Placing him gently on the ground, Aaron screamed incoherently as he grabbed his friend's weapon and went to avenge him.

Not far away, Donnie, Ava, and Marlene worked as one brave trio, taking down whoever stood in their way. Marlene promised them that she would protect them no matter what—and she did. Her arms were cut to ribbons, and she was losing blood, but it didn't matter. She took hits for her younger friends. Every time they seemed worried, she smiled and made jokes.

What ended it was nothing to laugh about. A grenade was thrown right where they were fighting. Marlene knew what to do, and she did not hesitate: she pushed her two friends out of the way and threw herself on top of the grenade as it detonated.

It was a horrible way to die. It was the most heroic thing I've ever seen.

Twelve.

After witnessing this horrific event, Donnie and Ava didn't know what to make of anything. Shocked, they just sat there amid the fighting and sobbed. Finally, Ava stood up, grabbed Marlene's shears, and leaped into the fray. "For Marlene!" she cried.

Donnie threw the metal pot off his head, jumped up, and stood side-by-side with her. "For Marlene!" he repeated. Together they fought for their Top Banana and everything she stood for. But too quickly, they began to be overpowered, slowly losing their strength. Donnie was thrown away from Ava by a near-miss grenade blast and almost collapsed.

"Donnie!" she shrieked as she rushed to help him. She was almost there when she was shot from behind by a smirking young Seer whom I shot an instant too late. Staggering forward, Ava came face to face with her friend. "I'm going to see Marlene," she whispered as tears rolled down her face. "She promised."

She closed her dark eyes and fell at Donnie's feet.

Eleven.

Screaming like a banshee, Donnie scooped up his friend and held her body in his arms while he bawled like a baby. He sat there with her on his lap the rest of the fight. No one, on either side, dared to go near them.

Behind him, Becca *almost* made it through to the Keepers when she was attacked by a kid Spliced with hyena DNA. Laughing eerily, the hyena Mutant said, "It looks like most of your friends are dead. Why not give up?"

Growling, Becca attacked him. She brought him to the ground and scratched up his face. Being stronger, the hyena threw her off and fought her in circles. The two of them went at each other until neither of them could stand. They had maimed each other with scratch marks, bites, cuts, and bruises. The hyena struggled to his feet and cackled. "I'm… not ready to go."

"Well, I am," Becca wheezed. Blood stained her cheetah fur, and her frizzy brown hair was caked in dirt. "I've made my life meaningful. You will leave knowing you *didn't*." She pounced and bit into his neck. When he stopped squirming, Becca staggered to her feet and looked around for Sami and Lucas. Finding them, she smiled at them one last time before she collapsed from her injuries—and never stood up again.

Ten.

Her best friends saw her fall and began to scream. They rushed to where she lay. Sami fell to her knees, and Lucas flew above the body frantically, shouting and begging Becca to wake up. She never did.

Losing so many allies crushed our spirits. Our friends were gone, our numbers were diminishing, and nothing seemed to be working.

Then came a glimmer of hope. Charging in from the left was Chief Kapono Iokua and his Niihau brethren. From the right came hundreds more fighters, led by Mr. Allaway and Dr. Agro. "They got our transmissions!" I heard Shannon cry out.

I made eye contact with Mr. Allaway as he led the rest of the Bionics to our side. Looking at me, he smiled and nodded, giving me encouragement.

"Thank you," I whispered, and we all went out to fight again.

That's when things began to turn around. I wasn't about to let my friends die in vain, and I was *not* going to lose any more. I fought side by side with Axel and my other Bionic buddies. Together, we dealt a great deal of damage to the enemy. We fought for hours on end that day, with no sign of a truce, and no quarter offered. Our tanks mowed down enemy soldiers, the ground fighters showed no mercy, and we Bionics attacked from above.

Realizing they were losing, the Keepers scuttled back like the bugs they were. They ordered their R&D fighters to turn every single advanced weapon they had on us and fire all at once. We weren't going to let that happen. Axel and I dove down into the machines full force and destroyed them all—along with their operators.

Finally, our main unit pushed its way through the fight and reached the place where the Keepers were cowering. The men I had once feared and respected were hiding behind the strongest soldiers and best artillery they had. Always the best for them.

We dropped into fighting stances and prepared to engage them. Those Seers who were left fought harder than we were capable of. Soon, we were all bleeding from head to toe, but still pressed on. We began to tire out, and Mr. Nik's pawns kept coming. Hope was fading. One final howitzer was aimed towards us. Before it fired, though, we heard a loud beeping and *KAWHOOOM!* the cannon exploded, shredding those nearest it and knocking the rest of us off our feet, in various stages of disrepair. Somehow, Shannon had blown up the last and largest of the Keepers' cannons. It didn't injure anyone on our side, but I can't say the same for our opponents. Unfortunately, the Keepers survived. Mr. Mallory and Mr. Nik were barely scathed. Wally, however, had shielded Mr. Nik, and lost part of an arm.

Struggling, we all tried to get up. Shane and Sonny were on their feet first. While Shane quickly helped the others up, Sonny picked up his pistol and went for Mr. Nik. "Nikita Patya!" he bellowed, aiming his pistol. When the Headmaster stood and looked at him, Sonny shouted, "You are hereby sentenced to death for crimes against humanity." He shot Mr. Nik in the side. "That's for these children." He fired again. "That's for my companions and me." He pulled the trigger a third time, striking the Headmaster in the center of the chest. "That is for my mother!"

Mr. Nik staggered backwards and fell to his knees. Spitting out blood, he laughed. He threw his head back and laughed harder. "No! It can't end like this," he screamed. He tilted his head and looked at Mark, who was helping my youngest brother stand up. Gritting his bleeding teeth, he remarked, "If I go, I am taking a Hodgins with me." Channeling his adrenaline, he yanked a small pistol out of an ankle holster and fired at Mark's torso.

Shockingly, he missed.

He missed because Jeremy, my towheaded little brother whom I had known only for a few days, jumped in front of Mark. The bullet struck dead in the center of our beautiful, loyal little boy's forehead. He died instantly, eyes wide open, and flopped to the ground.

Nine.

I'm sorry. I can't even see to write. I'll finish this when I can... No, keep it together, Alison. You can finish now. You will finish now.

When Jeremy fell, Mark wailed, "No!" and crumpled to his knees, cradling in his arms the small body of the boy who saved him. His hands were shaking as he caressed my brother's face. "No, no, no, Jeremy, no," he repeated hysterically. He put his head on my brother's chest and sobbed.

Mr. Nik was taken aback. He'd never *disliked* Jeremy; he had always been a faithful Seer. Turning the blame around, he cursed Mark, "You did this! You took everything from me," the Headmaster cried, blood spurting from his mouth, "My accomplishments, my dreams, and my son. Finally, the world could have been fixed, and you wanted to watch it burn. You Hodginses have always had a knack for ruining my life, and the lives of others!"

Turning towards me, the hateful Russian stared at me and said with whatever breath he had left, "I don't know whether to thank or hate you. Your father spared my life all those years ago." Shakily, he rubbed his hand over the scar on his neck. "I saved you and your siblings to thank him. Your successful operation started it all. But if I had never saved you, none of this destruction would have happened." Weakly, he lifted his finger and pointed towards me. "Never forget this: you Alexuses are just as bad as the Hodginses! You are responsible for this devastation. Because of your family and theirs, the chances of the world starting anew are lost!"

I told him, my voice as flat, cold, and deep as glacial ice, "How dare you! You just murdered a ten-year-old boy. You just murdered my *brother*. We trusted you with our lives and you betrayed us all. You, *Mr. Nik*, are a despicable, violent coward who has done nothing but evil for decades while pretending to yourself that the end justified the means. How dare you blame my family or Mark's for your betrayal of humanity?" Then, I slapped him hard across the face with the good right hand he had grafted onto me.

He spun around, crashed to the ground, and breathed no more.

Watching his friend die, Wally fell to his knees. "Nikita," he whispered longingly, somehow ignoring the searing pain of his missing limb. He and Mr. Nik had been partners for more than thirty years, and now it was over. While the Keeper had his guard down, Nicolas struck a final blow to the back of his head. Wally collapsed, dead before he hit the ground.

One Keeper remained: Mr. Mallory. Surrounded, the weakling raised his hands over his head and surrendered. At our demand, he sent a message to the rest of the Keepers' soldiers, and the fighting ceased. It was over. It was all over. Mr. Mallory was lucky I had already exhausted my missile supply. It took Axel and half a dozen other Bionics to hold me back, to keep me from strangling Mr. Mallory with my bare hands.

The battle ended with the sun setting over the bloodstained field. Bodies lay strewn across every terrain. I flew over the island, witnessing the carnage. "Why did it have to happen this way?" I whispered, tears in my eyes. I couldn't bear it. The adrenaline was gone, and I had nothing left but regret. I couldn't believe what they had done... I couldn't believe what *I* had done.

Axel hovered next to me and held my hand. "It's over, *bella*," he said. "The Isles can be rebuilt; remade. They can truly become a safe haven for survivors."

Not knowing what to say, I cried. I sobbed so hard I couldn't focus on staying airborne. Axel grabbed me and brought me back down to the others, where Sami and Aaron came over and held me close.

Just when we'd barely gotten him back, our brother was gone. Together, we wept.

Behind us, Shane and Aymie tried to comfort Mark. "I can't believe it," I heard Mark say dully. "Why did he do it? Why?"

Pulling him close, Shane said, "Because he loved you. Like we all do."

The sun had set and the moon was high in the sky when everyone finally decided to head back to the ships. The surviving Isle commanders and their second and third seats, the nine of us, got together with the RRPR Royals and other high officers in the lounge of the battleship. Mr. Bamber and Mrs. Pieper were with Director Wyght back on Isle III, in control of clean-up.

We sat in the room and stared at each other. There was no singing like last time, no jokes. Everything was quiet until Nicolas finally said, "We took the enemy survivors into custody, including Mallory. We officially have Cameron Allaway and Damian Agro on our side. Also, as we speak, our finest soldiers are searching for the remains of your eight friends. They deserve a hero's burial. We are determined to give them one."

Sniffling, Yared asked, "What about the others?"

Eyes to the ground, Nicolas replied, "I'm sorry. Our fighters are burning their bodies as we speak."

Sami put her head into her furry hands and cried once again. Lucas rubbed her back while Aaron put his hand on her knee. "There's no other choice," Lucas whispered.

"So much death," Donnie muttered, as he stared at Marlene's bloody sheep shears. He'd put her watch in the pocket next to his heart—where, he said he felt it ticking against his chest. He pulled the metal pot Marlene gave him over his watery eyes. "Gosh, Marlene. Ava."

Silence took over the room again. We thought over the day. With everyone still around, I took out my record log and began writing.

I was in the middle of writing about the battle when Sonny peeked over and noticed my recordings. He chuckled. "Did Nikita tell you to do that?"

I couldn't bear the sound of his name. Not wanting to be rude, I replied, "Yes."

"Figures," he retorted. "It was probably me who gave him the idea."

"Please, may I ask you all something?" Aaron interrupted, looking around at the older members. "Why does he hate you Hodginses so much? What did you do? Sonny, how are you that monster's son?"

Shane shook his head; his layered hair bounced back and forth. "We can't explain that now. This isn't the time or place."

Before Aaron could get agitated, Mark held up his hand. His eyes were puffy, and his cheeks were stained with tears. "Please, Aaron," he begged. "It really is a story for another time. Please. I can't handle it right now." So, Aaron backed off and kept his mouth shut. Mark took Jeremy's death harder than anyone, even us, his siblings. He obviously felt guilty for it and everything else that happened. "If I never had come here…" he muttered to himself over and over.

Occasionally, Shannon heard him and would slap his hand. After slapping him a few times, she realized he wasn't fazed. She turned to Shane and looked at him. Understanding what she was saying, Shane hesitantly nodded. She turned back to Mark and put her hand under his chin. "This is *not* your fault," she whispered. She leaned toward him and gently kissed his cheek.

It was an innocent kiss between friends, and it was enough to lift his spirits. Mark turned bright red and felt his cheek. He looked at Shannon, then at his brother, and back.

"That was a one-time thing, Mark," Shane told him with a grin.

Mark was still stunned. His reaction was enough to make us all smile. Shannon laughed and said, "Just like your brother."

"Eh, I was more embarrassed," Shane replied as he took her hand. Since that one time when they reunited, Shane hadn't kissed her again. I'd overheard him asking to give her another kiss, but she denied him, saying that they had made a deal and would stick to it.

*I would love to know what that's about*, I thought, curious. Their relationship was such a mystery.

When the redness in Mark's face had faded, Ethan grinned and said, "The others would have loved to see that. Marlene would have freaked out."

Agreeing, Lucas said, "She would've said something like, 'Wait,

I thought they were just friends? Aren't they just friends?'"

Sami giggled. "Yes, but probably not in an Australian accent."

That's when things began to turn around. Instead of reflecting on how our friends weren't with us, we focused on the lives they had lived. We remembered the best of times we had together. It made everything worthwhile. We relived Harold's cheesy jokes, Ursula's impatient attitude, Zita's caring nature, Cecil's intelligence, Ava's adorableness, Becca's kindness, Marlene's bravery, and Jeremy's sacrifice.

Finally, the exhaustion kicked in, and we decided to head to bed. The days ahead would be busy, and we needed our strength back. We rose and bid the officers goodnight.

As we were heading out, Yared turned around and addressed Mark. "Yo, when you tell us that 'story for another time,' you had better clear up what's going on between you three." He pointed to him, Shannon, and Shane. "All I know is, it's complicated, and you guys are really confusing us."

Laughing, Mark promised, and we all went our separate ways.

"I never thought that *you* would be curious about romance," Ethan teased.

Yared shrugged. "I prefer conspiracy. Looks like they got that too."

We finished discussing the confusing relationship, and the eight of us went back to our sleeping quarters. I hated how we had to be separated from the boys again, but we were back on the ship, and that was protocol. I sat on my bunk looking around at the four empty beds. Holding back tears, I finished writing.

To be honest, I didn't think I could live with myself after today, but now I understand how selfish it would be if I didn't. My friends and my little brother died protecting us and ensuring a better future for us. They would never want us to cower and hide. If we did, what would their deaths mean?

I am promising my fallen friends something right now. No matter what happens, no matter what the situation, I will never take my life or the life of anyone I care about for granted. No matter what.

# Epilogue

## Alison, Sami, and Aaron

It's been almost three months since the battle, and things are slowly getting better. We have been rebuilding and renewing the Hawaiian Islands, those that still exist. Chief Kapono Iokua has been declared the new "Headmaster" of the Isles and now oversees it all. When we first met the chief, he and Shannon made a promise. Chief Kapono swore that, once the islands were restored, RRPR could build safe havens and another base here. That promise was kept.

Together, the Hawaiians, the surviving Isle residents, and RRPR personnel have been busy restoring the islands. The facilities have been rebuilt and improved, and each island has kept its original roles and inhabitants. However, their rules have changed for the better.

On Isle VI, the *GEHTA*, Genetically Enhanced Human Testing Area, was shut down. There will be no more Splicing. However, they are going to continue to research the possibility of using animal genes in medicines. The villages have been upgraded and happily inhabited. Also, we've created water passageways throughout the facility and town for the aquatic Mutants to travel through. Now, the people of the villages and *all* the Mutants can connect and become one community. Those who are helping lead Isle VI are Alex the Aye-Aye, Zeke the

Shark, and a few others working under them. They're in charge of helping the rest of the Mutants adapt to their new selves and assist those who are in recovery. When they're ready, the water Mutants have a unique job to do. Zeke is training them to help him protect the waters around the Isles whenever they need to.

Next, Isle V: Seers. The Seers are still as tough as ever, but their attitudes have changed. They've *wanted* to help and aren't so smug and prideful about it. They are now an organized protection force that keeps order and justice among and on the islands. At the moment, their leader is an older Seers member, but Yared will take his place when it's time.

The fourth island, Assets, is flourishing, producing almost twice as much as they were before. With the regulations gone, we now have a surplus of food, clothing, and everyday items. The people living in the villages have begun to assist the Assets members in their daily duties, making the processes go faster and more efficiently. Not forgetting the old Assets Keeper, we rebuilt their beautiful domed facility and renamed it Calvin Center.

We'll save Isle III for later.

After the horrific battle, Saviors was extraordinarily busy. They saved many lives on the spot and many more still since. Every day, it seems, they have newly-trained doctors to assist them with all the wounded. Their hospital facility has been expanded and restored to house all the patients.

Isle I, Biomechatronics Testing, never suffered any damage. Apparently, Mr. Allaway connected with RRPR long before the battle began, and they had been coordinating ever since. Turns out he was *always* on our side, right from the moment they did the first Bionic surgery. However, he could never find a way to cross Mr. Nik without getting anyone hurt. When we finally gave him an opportunity, he seized it. Since no restoration was needed to that facility, those of Isle I went to work with Saviors to give the wounded prosthetics when needed. Their prosthetics, however, are not weaponized like the Bionics'. That could get out of hand.

The remaining Keepers are continuing to lead the Isles under the chief. Mr. Allaway will still lead Isle I and make new Bionic equipment and advanced technology with Mr. Bamber, who is enjoying his final years in this life.

Dr. Agro had a change of heart when Wally shot his brother. He said he saw their entire lives together flash before his eyes. He remembered when they were starving children in Nigeria, when they were taken by the Invaders, when they escaped, when they saved people, and finally when they became *worse* than the Invaders by working with Mr. Nik and Wally. Dr. Agro regretted everything he did after that, from refusing to offer villagers care to murdering children unborn and born. He has devoted his life to attempting to fix what he had undone—not only for the people he killed and his own conscience's sake, but for his brother, who valued human and plant life more than anything.

Mr. Mallory did not have a touching conversion story. He spent a month and a half in captivity. Whenever Nicolas, Shane, and Mark went to see him, he would repeat this to Mark over and over: "I kept my promise. I never forgot you, and I welcomed you." Finally, when we were halfway done with rebuilding, the three RRPR Royals got the scientist to confess and help them. Mr. Mallory ended his animal experimentation and has now devoted his life to assisting Alex and Zeke in their new jobs and is helping Assets with raising livestock.

Finally, we'll tell you about the changes to Isle III.

The Department of Research and Development has been restored, and they continue to build technology, weapons, simple appliances, and more for the Isles and RRPR. The fields of Isle III are now memorials and cemeteries that will be forever honored and never forgotten. Nine large stone memorials stand in a circle behind the facility. Etched into them are portraits and epitaphs of the beloved leaders who fell in the revolution: Calvin Agro, Ursula Zimmerman, Harold Spears, Zita Raneri, Cecil Grant, Marlene Best, Ava Conner, Becca Irwin, and Jeremy Alexus.

Looking upon our friends' faces, so beautifully carved in the stones, we couldn't help but cry once more. The pain of them not being with us is unbearable. Mark is still suffering terribly. He sits in front of our brother's grave every so often, leans his forehead against it, and sobs. Multiple times, his siblings, with difficulty, have had to drag him away to keep him from thinking about it.

Despite the sadness, we try to remember the happiness and love they brought us. We also can't help but smile whenever we read Harold's epitaph. It was his final request, and we fulfilled it. It reads: "Stop, drop, and roll, Harold. Try that next time." Despite what he thought, we will never forget him for who he was.

Every time we think about our fallen comrades, we take deep breaths and understand what they would want us to do. They would want us to move on, protect others, and tell their stories.

As for the three of us, we have agreed to never stop fighting. The Invaders are still at large, and they must be destroyed at any cost. We've unofficially joined RRPR in their cause and are working with the nine Royals. When we're ready, we will each take our oaths and officially join their group.

Currently, we're preparing to head to the Mainland to finish building the main RRPR base that was destroyed. Director Wyght and Mrs. Pieper are going to remain behind with the Chief and Keepers for now, while we go with their highest-ranking officers and a handful of troops. They told us that we would see them again once the base is done and that area is cleared. Thankfully, Axel, Donnie, Ethan, Yared, and Lucas are going to assist us in rebuilding. After all we've been through, we wouldn't want to be separated. Hopefully, when the base is finished they will join RRPR, just like we intend to.

Our plan is to leave for the Mainland tomorrow, but it's a long journey. Most of the fast, high-tech equipment was destroyed in the battle, so we have to take it slow. Shane hates that idea with a passion and is doing his best to deal with it. Occasionally, we get a complaint from him, but only when Shannon and Johanna aren't around.

The good news is that we were promised we would hear Mark's and his siblings' life stories on the way there. We will finally hear the "tale for another time" Mark was always talking about. He says that we will be shocked when we hear about their past. Frankly, despite whatever the past held for them, we are intrigued to learn more of the truth.

We also want to hear Sonny's story, too, and why Mr. Nik thought he was his son named "Erik". He told us that he isn't comfortable sharing that information yet, and that his tale is not a happy one. Respecting his privacy, we decided to leave it at that and wait until he was ready.

The three of us agree that we are going to record their stories in a separate log. They told us they never had a chance to write anything down, so we're going to do it for them. Shannon says that these stories, our life stories, are of great value and should never be forgotten. Every day she reminds us that one ordinary person and their story is enough to change the course of history. "Your story means something," she tells us, "so write it!"

So. tomorrow begins a new journey and a new day. Whatever that day holds, it's sure to be one mystery after another.

## THE END OF BOOK 1 OF
## THE TERRA TESTIMONIES

# THE ISLES

# DON'T MISS

## BOOK 2

# THE MAINLAND

# THE ISLES

# HEADMASTER'S NOTES

## Mr. Nik

### Entry 2971:

Today, we have made great progress towards our long term goal. The Challenges were a success, and we now have personally taken Seventeen Isle Members under our wing. They may never understand this, but I am very proud of them. Watching them grow all these years has been inspiring. With them at our side, nothing can stop us.

Today's entry is not like one my normal recordings. Rather, it will be a section of notes. My colleagues have complained saying that it is difficult to keep track of all 17 Isle Members! I understand there are many, but it is a necessity. Together they are strong.

At the Keepers' request, I have organized a brief list of the Isle Commanders and their second and third seats. I have also added information about the Keepers and myself, for consistency. (Although, when writing my own description I will try to keep it humble.)

Tomorrow, they depart for the Mainland. Frankly, I am not sure what they are going to expect. All I know is that we have to move quickly. The next wave is coming. We need to be prepared.

# THE ISLES
## Headmaster's Notes

**HEADMASTER**: Nikita Patya

The leader of all the Isles. He comes off as intimidating because of his dark eyes and ugly scar across his neck. Even though he misses Russia, he has made a home for himself and his colleagues on the Isles. He is well organized, loves challenges, and has a remarkable black mustache.

## ISLE I - Biomechatronics Testing

**ISLAND COLOR**: Gray

**KEEPER**: Cameron Allaway

A brilliant Scottish Inventor with a crooked nose and a knack for enhanced prosthetics. He would do anything to save a life. (Who said red-heads have no souls?) He is patient, understanding, and is always there for his Bionics.

**COMMANDER**: Alison

The first successful test subject of Isle I and a beautiful young woman with short white hair and gray eyes. After getting her entire right half of her body replaced with prosthetics, Alison has grown in skill and intelligence and has gained my trust. However, recently Cameron has told me that he has noticed some doubts in her. No matter. She will understand it all one day.

**SECOND-IN-COMMAND**: Axel

We rescued this curly haired Bionic from Argentina not too long after saving Alison. Both of his legs are machine, but that doesn't stop him. He does as he is told and strives to do his best each time. Like all the Bionics, he has gray eyes, pale skin, and a scar going across his forehead from the surgery. Not hard to identify a Bionic in a crowd, that is for sure.

# MR. NIK
## ISLE II - Saviors

### ISLAND COLOR: Red

### KEEPER: Dr. Damian Agro

One of the most skilled men in the medical field. Even after saving thousands from death in Nigeria, Dr. Agro is determined to continue to save those who are worthy of life. He is strict and serious but not the type of man to shout. He keeps his temper and veils all other emotions.

### COMMANDER: Ethan

A short Savior with olive skin and dark hair. With Ethan, you cannot measure his maturity just by looking at his size. He is very passionate about his work in medicine and cares deeply for his companions.

### SECOND-IN-COMMAND: Zita

Originally the Isle II Representative with Ethan but now serves under him. She is very caring and only wishes to help. She has frizzy red hair, a freckled face, and kind green eyes and always greets her patients with a smile.

### THIRD-IN-COMMAND: Harold

Harold is a skilled Savior without trying. Even though he tells terrible jokes all day when he should be studying, he still manages to pass his exams with flying colors. However, he never brags about his grades. He claims that his only skills are being comedic and good looking. He has a tall stature, sandy blond hair, and tan skin; so, I'll let you be the judge of that last part.

# THE ISLES
## ISLE III - Research and Development

### ISLAND COLOR: Royal Blue

### KEEPER: Brian Bamber

A wheel-chair ridden inventor and engineer with a love for obnoxiously bright ties. This white-haired old man never ceases to make me laugh. Whether it's his nasal voice or the way he designs his entrances, Mr. Bamber is truly one of a kind.

### COMMANDER: Mark

This one I have trouble describing. Frankly, no one knows too much about him. Brian claims he came back with Wally's last rescue team in America, but Wally thinks otherwise. All I know is that he is Overlord 1. His appearance is pale skin, dark hair, blue eyes, and a fit build. One thing I do know for sure is that he has been saying some odd things. I believe this one needs to be on close watch.

### SECOND-IN-COMMAND: Aaron

Aaron was the youngest one to pass the Commencement Tests. This six-foot, blond, spiky haired Overlord has a bright future ahead of him at R&D! He is brilliant, reliable, and knows how to be a good friend. He is the only one of the Seventeen to wear glasses, and unfortunately, he has had a record of enuresis. Poor kid

### THIRD-IN-COMMAND: Cecil

Another brilliant young mind. Cecil is a quick thinker and not afraid to ask questions. He looks up to his Overlord companions and would do anything for them. He is a few inches shorter than Aaron, has honey colored hair, and green eyes.

# MR. NIK
# ISLE IV - Assets

### ISLAND COLOR: Green

### KEEPER: Calvin Agro

Younger brother of Dr. Damian Agro and a remarkable agriculturist who had rescued many from famine in his homeland. He and his brother are similar in appearance: smooth black skin and dark eyes. The distinct differences are that Calvin is shorter, rotund, and wears a brown wig on his bald head. I never understood why. He is kind, nurturing, although a bit naïve.

### COMMANDER: Marlene

A hardworking Asset who is greatly favored by her Keeper and many younger members. She cares deeply for those she is put in charge of and does her best to make sure they're all happy. She has light brown hair and blue eyes. Even though she is an Asset, she has great fighting skills with her preferred weapon: sheep shears.

### SECOND-IN-COMMAND: Donald (aka Donnie)

Donald is a little Asset with a big heart. He would do anything for his best friends. He has dirty blond hair and gray eyes. He is usually covered in dirt from working in the fields. The easiest way to identify him is by the bucket he wears as a helmet.

### THIRD-IN-COMMAND: Ava

The youngest of the Seventeen. She is an adorable little girl with dark eyes, caramel colored skin, and bushy hair that is usually tied up into pig tails. She truly loves all of her friends and her Keeper and strives to do her best every day.

# THE ISLES
## ISLE V - Seers

### ISLAND COLOR: Navy

### KEEPER: Walter "Wally" Jarvis
A German military general with a strong stature and tough
nature; he is also my closest companion. He has crew cut, dark blond
hair and gray eyes. Despite his strict and serious background, he
enjoys making jokes and having a good time. He is almost never seen
without his round glasses....then again, he can't see without them.

### COMMANDER: Yared
Yared has an unquenchable thirst for combat. Whenever there
is a chance to fight, he is there. He is a strongly built young man with
dark skin, brown shaved hair, and chestnut eyes. He is not afraid to
speak his mind and will never back away from a challenge.

### SECOND-IN-COMMAND: Jeremy
Another young member with big responsibilities. This blond,
blue-eyed boy is faithful to his Keeper and me. He always speaks up
in our defense and doesn't give up easily. He knows his place and his
duties and fulfills them with excellence.

### THIRD-IN-COMMAND: Ursula
A solid, coltish young lady with a bad attitude. She is impatient,
obstinate, and will argue on anything. She has flaxen hair and
intimidating gray eyes. She is impressive in the field of combat; no one
should dare go near her.

# MR. NIK
# ISLE VI - Genetic Testing

### ISLAND COLOR: Black

### KEEPER: Carl Mallory
A brilliant scientist and biologist with a love for animals… especially human ones. He is passionate about his work and firmly believes he will better humankind with his experiments. He has long dirty blond hair, green eyes, and an unpleasant aroma. (We don't like to talk about that last part.)

### COMMANDER: Sami
A Mutant, black housecat. She has luminous green eyes that work well in the dark, sharp nails as claws, and black fur all over her. She has a timid nature and gets tired very easily, but that doesn't mean she is a slacker. She works hard and is always there for her companions.

### SECOND-IN-COMMAND: Becca
A yellow eyed, dark skinned, golden furred Cheetah Mutant with a kind heart. Despite her deadly bite and unmatchable speed, Becca never wants to hurt anyone. She hates when a friend is upset and will do anything to comfort them.

### THIRD-IN-COMMAND: Lucas
An Australian Mutant dragonfly with an insatiable appetite. His large compound eyes and membranous wings make him difficult to look at. However, when he wears his cape and goggles, he only appears to be a sandy blond haired boy with an interesting fashion sense. Nonetheless, Lucas is a good friend, a great student, and an invaluable ally.

# THE ISLES

# ABOUT THE AUTHOR
## Sara Francis

Ever since she could remember, Sara Francis was always a story teller. At first, she told them through music as a song writer. In her early teenage years, Sara Francis felt called to tell stories through work as a writer and media communicator for an online magazine. From there, everything fell into place.

Now, Sara Francis has a BS in Media Communications, is the author of several books, and is a speaker. Throughout it all, there is always a story she is trying to convey. Whether she tells them through her writings, art, or music, her stories always have a deep, truth filled meaning behind them. Every word she writes, everything she designs, every song she performs means something more and connects with the world we live in today. Through her work, she hopes to inspire people and encourage them to seek what is true.

Sara Francis is determined to light a torch in the darkness with the desire that people will do the same and make the world bright again.

# THE ISLES

# More Information

» Visit Sara Francis' site for her other books, updates, services, study guides, and more: **www.sara-francis.com**

» Want to read more? Visit Sara Francis' blog for writing advice, author interviews, and short stories of the characters in The Terra Testimonies: **www.sara-francis.com/blog**

» Follow Sara Francis on social media:
  » Facebook:@sarafrancisauthor
  » Twitter: @sfrancis_author
  » Instagram: @sarafrancis_author
  » Visit the author's site to subscribe to her YouTube channel!

» Any questions or would like to book Sara Francis for an event or workshop? Contact us at **info@sara-francis.com**

*Author Request:* If you enjoyed the book, please be sure to tell your friends, share on social media, or leave a review on Amazon, Lulu, Goodreads, or any book review site!

CPSIA information can be obtained
at www.ICGtesting.com
Printed in the USA
JSHW020315110622
26817JS00001B/20

9 780998 993300